Praise for #1 Internationally Bestselling Author
KARIN SLAUGHTER

"KARIN SLAUGHTER IS ONE OF THE BEST CRIME NOVELISTS IN AMERICA."
—*The Washington Post*

"[Karin Slaughter writes] crime fiction at its finest." —Michael Connelly, *New York Times* bestselling author

"One of the hottest names in thriller writing." —*OK!* magazine

UNDONE

"Complex, sad, twisted and delicately plausible all at once, and what is otherwise a finely wrought procedural deepens into something more . . . her pacing is impeccable, the final mayhem exquisitely honed." —*Houston Chronicle*

"Electrifying . . . Slaughter ups the emotional ante with every twist and turn in this disturbing thriller." —*Publishers Weekly* (starred review)

"A case as complicated and sophisticated as crime fiction gets . . . *Undone* is one of her best. . . . Perfect midsummer mystery reading." —*The Globe and Mail*

"This is a fast-paced read with a complex plot that contains enough twists to keep even the most veteran mystery reader guessing the identity of the culprit until the very end. Highly recommended as a high-octane summer read." —*Library Journal* (starred review)

"Slaughter has always been a talented writer, but in recent years her work has just gotten better and better. . . . Razor-sharp suspense and emotional depth."
—The Daily Beast

"Slaughter creates a story every bit as addictive as an HBO series (we can only hope!). . . . It's a heart-pounding race to the finish that reveals as much about the hunters as the hunted."
—*The Atlanta Journal-Constitution*

"A compelling look at how two flawed people work to overcome their shortcomings and combat pure evil."
—*People*

"A complicated spider web of secrets and tangles."
—*Los Angeles Times*

FRACTURED

"Slaughter continues to be angry, fiercely focused and one of the most talented young crime novelists."
—*The Washington Post*

BEYOND REACH

"The ending is such a surprise it left me momentarily speechless. . . . Slaughter's novels are as gripping as anything from Kathy Reichs or the early Patricia Cornwell, and when she gets into the intricacies of relationships she hits the ball right out of the park. Additionally, there's enough gruesome medical detail to make genre junkies line up for the next installment." —*BookPage*

"Slaughter delivers a shocking, unforgettable twist that is devastating. . . . Storytelling at its enjoyable, unsettling best." — *The Atlanta Journal-Constitution*

"[Slaughter's] plotting is twisted and flawless. If you have followed the series like I have, when you finish the last page your jaw will drop. I guarantee it."
—*Tulsa World*

TRIPTYCH

"Delivers the breathless tension that's a hallmark of Slaughter's work . . . The ending contains enough slam-bang action to keep you pinned to your seat."
—*San Francisco Chronicle*

"Slaughter's gift for building multilayered tension while deconstructing damaged personalities gives this thriller a nerve-wracking finish." —*USA Today*

"Karin Slaughter writes with a razor. . . . Slaughter is better than Cornwell can ever hope to be. *Triptych* elevates her to the top of my list of favorite crime writers." —Cleveland *Plain Dealer*

"[Slaughter] has produced one of 2006's most remarkable achievements. . . . This is easily the best thing Slaughter has written, a novel of power and substance that is shocking and painful at times, but also gripping and resonant. *Triptych* launches a major new phase in her career, and it's a delight to behold."
—*The Philadelphia Inquirer*

"A compelling, bleak tale about the intertwined fates of three men . . . The plotting and characterization are gripping and clever as always—with a couple of big twists in there for good measure."
—*Romantic Times*

"It is next to impossible to put the book down. . . . Masterfully constructed fiction."
—*Winston-Salem Journal*

FAITHLESS

"Smart . . . [a] muscular thriller."
—*Entertainment Weekly*

"[Slaughter's] best yet . . . Her novels smolder with reality. . . . She writes with confidence and precision as well as passion." —*The Washington Post*

"The people in *Faithless* are so real and so well developed that the reader can't help but feel empathy for them, and thus we are drawn even deeper into the ingenious plot." —*Chicago Sun-Times*

KARIN SLAUGHTER

UNDONE

A NOVEL

A DELL BOOK
NEW YORK

2010 Dell Mass Market Edition

Published in the United States by Dell,
an imprint of The Random House Publishing Group,
a division of Random House, Inc., New York.

DELL is a registered trademark of Random House, Inc.,
and the colophon is a trademark of Random House, Inc.

Originally published in hardcover in the United States
by Delacorte Press, an imprint of The Random House Publishing Group,
a division of Random House, Inc., in 2009.

This book contains an excerpt from the forthcoming book *Broken* by
Karin Slaughter. This excerpt has been set for this edition only and
may not reflect the final content of the forthcoming edition.

978-0-440-24445-5

Cover design: Carlos Beltran

Printed in the United States of America

www.bantamdell.com

2 4 6 8 9 7 5 3 1

To my readers . . .
thank you for trusting me.

UNDONE

PROLOGUE

THEY HAD BEEN MARRIED FORTY YEARS TO THE DAY and Judith still felt like she didn't know everything about her husband. Forty years of cooking Henry's dinner, forty years of ironing his shirts, forty years of sleeping in his bed, and he was still a mystery. Maybe that was why she kept doing all these things for him with little or no complaint. There was a lot to be said for a man who, after forty years, still managed to hold your attention.

Judith rolled down the car window, letting in some of the cool spring air. Downtown Atlanta was only thirty minutes away, but out here in Conyers, you could still find areas of undeveloped land, even some small farms. It was a quiet place, and Atlanta was just far enough away so that she could appreciate the peace. Still, Judith sighed as she caught a quick glimpse of the city's skyscrapers on the distant horizon, thinking, *Home.*

She was surprised at the thought, that Atlanta was now a place she considered her home. Her life until recently had been suburban, even rural. She preferred the open spaces to the concrete sidewalks of the city, even while she admitted that it was nice living in so central a location that you could walk to the corner store or a little café if the mood struck you.

Days would pass without her even having to get into

a car—the type of life she would have never dreamed of ten years ago. She could tell Henry felt the same. His shoulders bunched up around his ears with tight resolve as he navigated the Buick down a narrow country road. After decades of driving just about every highway and interstate in the country, he instinctively knew all the back routes, the doglegs and shortcuts.

Judith trusted him to get them home safely. She sat back in her seat, staring out the window, blurring her eyes so that the trees bordering the road seemed more like a thick forest. She made the trip to Conyers at least once a week, and every time she felt like she saw something new—a small house she'd never noticed, a bridge she'd bumped over many times but never paid attention to. Life was like that. You didn't realize what was passing you by until you slowed down a little bit to get a better look.

They'd just come from an anniversary party in their honor, thrown together by their son. Well, more likely thrown together by Tom's wife, who managed his life like an executive assistant, housekeeper, babysitter, cook and—presumably—concubine all rolled up into one. Tom had been a joyful surprise, his birth an event doctors had said would never come about. Judith had loved every part of him on first sight, accepted him as a gift that she would cherish with every bone in her body. She had done everything for him, and now that Tom was in his thirties, he still seemed to need an awful lot of taking care of. Perhaps Judith had been too conventional a wife, too subservient a mother, so that her son had grown into the sort of man who needed—expected—a wife to do everything for him.

Judith certainly had not enslaved herself to Henry.

They had married in 1969, a time when women could actually have interests other than cooking the perfect pot roast and discovering the best method to get stains out of the carpet. From the start, Judith had been determined to make her life as interesting as possible. She'd been a room mother at Tom's school. She'd volunteered at the local homeless shelter and helped start a recycling group in the neighborhood. When Tom was older, Judith took a job doing light bookkeeping for a local business and joined a running team through the church to train for marathons. This active lifestyle stood in stark contrast to that of Judith's own mother, a woman who toward the end of her life was so ravaged from raising nine children, so drained from the constant physical demands of being a farmer's wife, that some days she was too depressed to even speak.

Though, Judith had to admit, she had herself been a somewhat typical woman in those early years. Embarrassingly, she was one of those girls who had gone to college specifically to find a husband. She had grown up near Scranton, Pennsylvania, in a town so small it didn't merit a dot on the map. The only men available to her were farmers, and they were hardly interested in Judith. Judith could not blame them. The mirror told no lies. She was a bit too plump, a bit too bucktoothed, and a bit too much of everything else, to be the sort of woman Scranton men took for a wife. And then there was her father, a stern disciplinarian whom no sane man would seek out for a father-in-law, at least not in exchange for a bucktoothed, pear-shaped girl who had no natural talent for farming.

The truth was that Judith had always been the odd one in the family, the one who didn't quite fit in. She read too much. She hated farmwork. Even as a young girl, she was not drawn to animals and did not want to be responsible for their care and feeding. None of her sisters and brothers had been sent away for higher education. There were two brothers who had dropped out of ninth grade, and an older sister who had married rather quickly and given birth to her first child seven months later. Not that anyone bothered to do the math. Enveloped in a constant state of denial, her mother had remarked to her dying day that her first grandchild had always been big-boned, even as an infant. Thankfully, Judith's father had seen the writing on the wall so far as his middle girl was concerned. There would be no marriage of convenience with any of the local boys, not least of all because none of them found her remotely convenient. Bible college, he decided, was not just Judith's last—but her only—chance.

At the age of six, Judith had been struck in the eye by a flying piece of debris as she chased after the tractor. From that moment on, she'd always worn glasses. People assumed she was cerebral because of the glasses, when in fact the opposite was true. Yes, she loved to read, but her tastes ran more toward trashy dime novel than literary. Still, the egghead label had stuck. What was it they used to say? "Men don't make passes at women who wear glasses." So, it was surprising—no, more like shocking—when on Judith's first day of college in her first class, the teaching assistant had winked at her.

She had thought something was in his eye, but there was no mistaking Henry Coldfield's intentions when, after class, he had pulled her aside and asked her if she'd like to go down to the drugstore and have a soda with him. The wink, apparently, was the beginning and end of his gregariousness. Henry was a very shy man in person; strange, considering he later became the top salesman for a liquor distribution company—a job he passionately despised even three years past retirement.

Judith supposed Henry's ability to blend had come from being the son of an Army colonel, moving around the country so often, never staying at one base more than a few years at a time. There was no passionate love at first sight—that came later. Initially, Judith had simply been attracted to the fact that Henry was attracted to her. It was a novelty for the pear from Scranton, but Judith had always been at the opposite spectrum of Marx's philosophy—Groucho, not Karl: She was more than willing to join any club that would have her as a member.

Henry was a club unto himself. He was neither handsome nor ugly; forward nor reticent. With his neatly parted hair and flat accent, *average* would be the best way to describe him, which Judith later did in a letter to her older sister. Rosa's response had been something along the lines of, "Well, I suppose that's the best you can hope for." In her defense, Rosa was pregnant at the time with her third child while her second was still in diapers, but still, Judith had never forgiven her sister for the slight— not against herself, but against Henry. If Rosa failed to notice how special Henry was, it was because Judith was a poor writer; Henry too nuanced a man for mere words on a page. Perhaps it was all for the best. Rosa's sour observation had given Judith a reason to break from her family and embrace this winkingly introverted, mercurial stranger.

Henry's gregarious shyness was only the first of

many dichotomies Judith had observed in her husband over the years. He was terrified of heights, but had earned his amateur pilot's license as a teenager. He sold alcohol but never imbibed. He was a homebody, but he spent most of his adult life traveling through the Northwest, then the Midwest, as promotions moved them around the country much like the Army had done when Henry was a child. His life, it seemed, was all about making himself do things he did not want to do. And yet, he often told Judith that her company was the one thing that he truly enjoyed.

Forty years, and so many surprises.

Sadly, Judith doubted her son held any such surprises for his spouse. While Tom was growing up, Henry was on the road three weeks out of every four, and his parenting came in spurts that didn't necessarily highlight his more compassionate side. Subsequently, Tom became everything his father had shown him during those growing years: strict, unbending, driven.

There was something else to it as well. Judith didn't know if it was because Henry saw his sales job as a duty to his family rather than his passion, or because he hated being away from home so much, but it seemed that every interaction he had with their son held an underlying tension: *Don't make the same mistakes I've made. Don't get trapped in a job you despise. Don't compromise your beliefs to put food on the table.* The only positive thing he recommended to the boy was marrying a good woman. If only he had been more specific. If only he hadn't been so hard.

Why was it that men were such exacting parents to their male children? Judith guessed they wanted their sons to succeed in places they had not. In those early days, when Judith was first pregnant, the thought of a daughter had spread a rapid warmth through her body, followed by a searing cold. A young girl like Judith, out there in the world, defying her mother, defying the world. It gave her an understanding of Henry's desire that Tom do better, be better, have everything that he wanted and more.

Tom had certainly succeeded at his job, though his mouse of a wife was a disappointment. Every time Judith came face-to-face with her daughter-in-law, she itched to tell the woman to stand up straight, speak up and, for the love of God, grow a backbone. One of the volunteers at the church had said the other week that men married their mothers. Judith hadn't argued with the woman, but she'd defy anyone to find a lick of similarity she shared with her son's wife. Except for the desire to spend time with her grandchildren, Judith could never see her daughter-in-law again and be perfectly happy.

The grandchildren were the sole reason they had moved to Atlanta, after all. She and Henry had uprooted their retirement life in Arizona and moved almost two thousand miles to this hot city with its smog alerts and gang killings just so they could be close to two of the most spoiled and ungrateful little things this side of the Appalachia.

Judith glanced at Henry as he tapped his fingers on the steering wheel, humming tunelessly as he drove. They never talked about their grandchildren except in glowing terms, possibly because a fit of honesty might reveal that they didn't much like them——and then where would they be? Their lives turned upside down for two small children who were on gluten-free diets, strictly regimented nap-times and tightly scheduled playdates, but only with "like-minded children who shared the same goals."

So far as Judith could see, the only goal her grandchildren had was to be the center of attention. She imagined you couldn't sneeze without finding a like-minded, self-centered child, but according to her daughter-in-law, it was an almost impossible task. Wasn't that the whole point of youth, to be self-centered? And wasn't it the job of the parent to drill that out of you? Certainly, it was clear to all involved that it wasn't the job of the grandparents.

When little Mark had spilled his unpasteurized juice on Henry's slacks and Lilly had eaten so many of the Hershey's Kisses she'd found in Judith's purse that she'd reminded Judith of a homeless woman at the shelter last month who was tweaking so badly on methamphetamines that she'd wet herself, Henry and Judith had merely smiled—chuckled, even—as if these were merely wonderful little quirks that the children would soon grow out of.

Soon was not coming soon enough, however, and now that they'd reached the ages of seven and nine, Judith was starting to lose faith that one day, her grandchildren would turn into polite and loving young adults who did not feel the urge to constantly interrupt adult conversation and run around the house screaming at such high decibels that animals two counties over started howling. Judith's only consolation was that Tom took them to church every Sunday. She of course wanted her grandchildren exposed to a life in Christ, but more importantly, she wanted them to learn the lessons taught in Sunday School. *Honor thy mother and father. Do unto*

*others as you would have them do unto you. Don't think you're
going to waste your life, drop out of school and move in with
Grandma and Grandpa any time soon.*

"Hey!" Henry barked as a car in the oncoming lane
shot past them so close that the Buick actually shook on
its tires. "Kids," he grumbled, gripping the wheel
tightly in his hands.

The closer he got to seventy, the more Henry seemed
to embrace the role of cranky old man. Sometimes, this
was endearing. Other times, Judith wondered how long
it would be before he started shaking his fist in the air,
blaming all the ills of the world on "kids." The age of
these kids seemed to range anywhere from four to forty,
and his irritation ticked up exponentially when he
caught them doing something that he used to do himself, but now could no longer enjoy. Judith dreaded the
day they took away his pilot's license, something that
might come sooner rather than later, considering that
his last checkup at the cardiologist had shown some irregularities. It was one of the reasons they had decided
to retire to Arizona, where there was no snow to shovel
or lawn to maintain.

She said, "Looks like rain."

Henry craned up his neck to see the clouds.

"Good night to start my book."

His lips curled up in a smile. Henry had given her a
thick historical romance for their anniversary. Judith
had given him a new cooler to take to the golf course.

She squinted her eyes at the road ahead, deciding she
should have her vision checked again. She was not so far
from seventy herself, and her eyes seemed to be getting
worse every year. Dusk was a particularly bad time for
her, and her vision tended to blur on objects that were at

a distance. So it was that she blinked several times before she was sure of what she was seeing, and only opened her mouth to warn Henry when the animal was right in front of them.

"Jude!" Henry yelled, one arm shooting out in front of Judith's chest as he wrenched the steering wheel to the left, trying to avoid the poor creature. Judith thought, oddly, about how the movies were right. Everything slowed down, time inching by so that each second seemed to take an eternity. She felt Henry's strong arm bolt across her breasts, the seatbelt biting into her hip bones. Her head jerked, slamming into the door as the car swerved. The windshield cracked as the animal bounced against the glass, then hit the roof of the car, then the trunk. It wasn't until the car shuddered to a stop, spinning a full 180 degrees on the road, that the sounds caught up with Judith: the *crack, thunk, thunk,* all overlaid with a high-pitched screaming that she realized was coming from her own mouth. She must have been in shock, because Henry had to yell at her several times, "Judith! Judith!" before she stopped screaming.

Henry's hand was tight on her arm, sending pain up her shoulder. She rubbed the back of his hand, saying, "I'm all right. I'm all right." Her glasses were askew, her vision off-kilter. She put her fingers to the side of her head, feeling a sticky wetness. When she took away her hand, she saw blood.

"It must've been a deer or . . ." Henry put his hand to his mouth, stopping his words. He looked calm but for the telltale up and down of his chest as he tried to catch his breath. The air bag had deployed. A fine, white powder covered his face.

Her breath caught as she looked ahead. Blood had spattered the windshield like a sudden, violent rain.

Henry pushed open the door but did not get out. Judith took off her glasses to wipe her eyes. The lenses were both broken, the bottom part of her bifocal on the right side missing. She saw that the glasses were shaking, and realized that the tremor came from her own hands. Henry got out of the car, and she made herself put on her glasses and follow him.

The creature was on the road, legs moving. Judith's head ached where it had smacked into the door. Blood was in her eyes. That was the only explanation she had for the fact that the animal—surely a deer—appeared to have the shapely white legs of a woman.

"Oh, dear God," Henry whispered. "It's—Judith—it's—"

Judith heard a car behind her. Wheels screeched against asphalt. Doors opened and closed. Two men joined them on the road, one running toward the animal.

He screamed, "Call 9-1-1!" kneeling down beside the body. Judith stepped closer, then closer yet. The legs moved again—the perfect legs of a woman. She was completely nude. Bruises blackened her inner thighs—dark bruises. Old bruises. Dried blood caked around her legs. A burgundy film seemed to cover her torso, a rip at her side showing white bone. Judith glanced at her face. The nose was askew. The eyes were swollen, lips chapped and split. Blood matted the woman's dark hair and pooled around her head as if in a halo.

Judith stepped closer, unable to stop herself—suddenly a voyeur, after a lifetime of politely looking away. Glass crunched beneath her feet, and the woman's eyes shot open in panic. She stared somewhere past Judith, a dull lifelessness to her gaze. Just as suddenly, her eyelids fluttered closed, but Judith could not suppress the shudder that went through her body. It was as if someone had walked over her grave.

"Dear Lord," Henry mumbled, almost in prayer. Judith turned to find her husband gripping his hand to his chest. His knuckles were white. He stared at the woman, looking as if he might be ill. "How did this happen?" he whispered, horror twisting his face. "How in God's name did this happen?"

DAY ONE

CHAPTER ONE

SARA LINTON LEANED BACK IN HER CHAIR, MUMBLING a soft "Yes, Mama" into her cell phone. She wondered briefly if there would ever come a point in time when this felt normal again, when a phone call with her mother brought her happiness the way it used to instead of feeling like it was dragging a piece of her heart out of her chest.

"Baby," Cathy soothed. "It's all right. You're taking care of yourself, and that's all Daddy and I need to know."

Sara felt tears sting her eyes. This would hardly be the first time she had cried in the doctors' lounge at Grady Hospital, but she was sick of crying—sick of feeling, really. Wasn't that the reason that, two years ago, she had left her family, left her life, in rural Georgia, and moved to Atlanta—so that she would no longer have the constant reminder of what had come before?

"Promise me you'll try to go to church next week."

Sara mumbled something that might sound like a promise. Her mother was no fool, and they both knew that the possibility of Sara ending up on a pew this Easter Sunday was highly unlikely, but Cathy didn't press.

Sara looked at the stack of charts in front of her. She was at the end of her shift and needed to call in her dictation. "Mama, I'm sorry, but I need to go."

Cathy exacted a promise of another phone call next week, then rang off. Sara kept her cell phone in her hand for a few minutes, looking at the faded numbers, her thumb tracing the seven and five, dialing out a familiar number but not sending through the call. She dropped the phone into her pocket and felt the letter brush against the back of her hand.

The Letter. She thought of it as its own entity.

Sara normally checked her mail after work so she didn't have to drag it around with her, but one morning, for some unknown reason, she had checked her mail as she was heading out. A cold sweat had come over her as she recognized the return address on the plain white envelope. She had tucked the unopened envelope into the pocket of her lab coat as she left for work, thinking she would read it at lunch. Lunch had come and gone, and the letter had remained unopened, traveling back home, then out to work again the next day. Months passed, and the letter went everywhere with Sara, sometimes in her coat, sometimes in her purse to the grocery store or on errands. It became a talisman, and often, she would reach her hand in her pocket and touch it, just to remind herself that it was there.

Over time, the corners of the sealed envelope had become dog-eared and the Grant County postmark had started to fade. Every day pushed Sara further away from opening it and discovering what the woman who had killed her husband could possibly have to say.

"Dr. Linton?" Mary Schroder, one of the nurses, knocked on the door. She spoke in the practiced code of the ER. "We've got a P-O-P-T-A female, thirty-three, weak and thready."

Sara glanced at the charts, then her watch. A thirty-three-year-old woman who had passed out prior to admission was a puzzle that would take time to solve. It was almost seven o'clock. Sara's shift was over in ten minutes. "Can Krakauer take her?"

"Krakauer *did* take her," Mary countered. "He ordered a CMP, then went to get coffee with the new bimbo." She was obviously perturbed by this, and added, "The patient's a cop."

Mary was married to a cop; hardly shocking considering she had worked in the emergency room at Grady Hospital for almost twenty years. Even without that, it was understood at every hospital in the world that anyone in law enforcement got the best and quickest treatment. Apparently, Otto Krakauer hadn't gotten the memo.

Sara relented. "How long did she lose consciousness?"

"She says about a minute." Mary shook her head, because patients were hardly the most honest reporters when it came to their health. "She doesn't look right."

That last part was what got Sara out of her chair. Grady was the only Level One trauma center in the region, as well as one of the few remaining public hospitals in Georgia. The nurses at Grady saw car wrecks, shootings, stabbings, overdoses and any number of crimes against humanity on an almost daily basis. They had a practiced eye for spotting serious problems. And, of course, cops usually didn't admit themselves to the hospital unless they were at death's door.

Sara skimmed the woman's chart as she walked through the emergency department. Otto Krakauer hadn't done more than take a medical history and order the usual bloodwork, which told Sara there was no obvious diagnosis. Faith Mitchell was an otherwise healthy thirty-three-year-old woman with no previous conditions and no recent trauma. Her test results would hopefully give them a better idea about what was going on.

Sara mumbled an apology as she bumped into a gurney in the hallway. As usual, the rooms were overflowing and patients were stacked in the halls, some in beds, some sitting in wheelchairs, all looking more miserable than they probably had when they'd first arrived for treatment. Most of them had probably come here right after work because they couldn't afford to miss a day's wages. They saw Sara's white coat and called to her, but she ignored them as she read through the chart.

Mary said, "I'll catch up with you. She's in three," before letting herself get pulled away by an elderly woman on a stretcher.

Sara knocked on the open door of exam room 3— privacy: another perk afforded cops. A petite blonde woman was sitting on the edge of the bed, fully dressed and clearly irritated. Mary was good at her job, but a blind person could see that Faith Mitchell was unwell. She was as pale as the sheet on the bed; even from a distance, her skin looked clammy.

Her husband did not seem to be helping matters as he paced the room. He was an attractive man, well over six feet, with sandy blond hair cut close to his head. A jagged scar ran down the side of his face, probably from a childhood accident where his jaw slid across the asphalt under his bicycle or along the hard-packed dirt to home plate. He was thin and lean, probably a runner, and his three-piece suit showed the broad chest and shoulders of someone who spent a lot of time in the gym.

He stopped pacing, his gaze going from Sara to his wife and back again. "Where's the other doctor?"

"He got called away on an emergency." She walked to the sink and washed her hands, saying, "I'm Dr. Linton. Can you catch me up to speed here? What happened?"

"She passed out," the man said, nervously twisting his wedding ring around his finger. He seemed to realize he was coming off as a bit frantic, and moderated his tone. "She's never passed out before."

Faith Mitchell seemed aggravated by his concern. "I'm fine," she insisted, then told Sara, "It's the same thing I said to the other doctor. I feel like I've been coming down with a cold. That's all."

Sara pressed her fingers to Faith's wrist, checking her pulse. "How are you feeling now?"

She glanced at her husband. "Annoyed."

Sara smiled, shining her penlight into Faith's eyes, checking her throat, running through the usual physical exam and finding nothing alarming. She agreed with Krakauer's initial evaluation: Faith was probably a little dehydrated. Her heart sounded good, though, and it didn't seem like she'd suffered from a seizure. "Did you hit your head when you fell?"

She started to answer, but the man interjected, "It was in the parking lot. Her head hit the pavement."

Sara asked the woman, "Any other problems?"

Faith answered, "Just a few headaches." She seemed to be holding something back, even as she revealed, "I haven't really eaten today. I was feeling a little sick to my stomach this morning. And yesterday morning."

Sara opened one of the drawers for a neuro-hammer

to check reflexes, only to find nothing there. "Have you had any recent weight loss or gain?"

Faith said "No" just as her husband said "Yes."

The man looked contrite, but tried, "I think it looks good on you."

Faith took a deep breath and let it out slowly. Sara studied the man again, thinking he was probably an accountant or lawyer. His head was turned toward his wife, and Sara noticed another, lighter scar lining his upper lip—obviously not a surgical incision. The skin had been sewn together crookedly, so that the scar running vertically between his lip and nose was slightly uneven. He had probably boxed in college, or maybe just been hit in the head one too many times, because he obviously didn't seem to know that the only way out of a hole was to stop digging. "Faith, I think the extra weight looks great on you. You could stand to gain—"

She shut him up with a look.

"All right." Sara flipped open the chart, writing down some orders. "We'll need to do an X-ray of your skull and I'd like to do a few more tests. Don't worry, we can use the blood samples from earlier, so there won't be any more needles for now." She scribbled a notation and checked some boxes before looking up at Faith. "I promise we'll rush this as much as we can, but you can see we've got a pretty full house today. X-ray's backed up at least an hour. I'll do what I can to push it through, but you might want to get a book or magazine while you wait."

Faith didn't respond, but something in her demeanor changed. She glanced at her husband, then back at Sara. "Do you need me to sign that?" She indicated the chart.

There was nothing to sign, but Sara handed her the

chart anyway. Faith wrote something on the bottom of the page and gave it back. Sara read the words *I'm pregnant*.

Sara nodded as she crossed through the X-ray order. Obviously, Faith hadn't yet told her husband, but there was a different set of questions Sara needed to ask now, and she couldn't do so without giving away the news. "When's the last time you had a pap smear?"

Faith seemed to understand. "Last year."

"Let's take care of that while you're here." Sara told the man, "You can wait outside."

"Oh." He seemed surprised, even as he nodded. "All right." He told his wife, "I'll be in the waiting room if you need me."

"Okay." Faith watched him leave, her shoulders visibly slumping in relief as the door closed. She asked Sara, "Do you mind if I lie down?"

"Of course not." Sara helped her get comfortable on the bed, thinking Faith looked younger than her thirty-three years. She still had the bearing of a cop, though—that no-nonsense, don't-bullshit-me squareness to her shoulders. Her lawyer husband seemed like an odd match, but Sara had seen stranger combinations.

She asked the woman, "How far along are you?"

"About nine weeks."

Sara put this in her notes as she asked, "Is that a guess or have you seen a doctor?"

"I took an over-the-counter test." She changed that. "Actually, I took three over-the-counter tests. I'm never late."

Sara added a pregnancy test to the orders. "What about this weight gain?"

"Ten pounds," Faith admitted. "I've kind of gone a little crazy with the eating since I found out."

In Sara's experience, ten pounds usually meant fifteen. "Do you have any other children?"

"One—Jeremy—eighteen."

Sara made the notation in the chart, mumbling, "Lucky you. Heading into the terrible twos."

"More like terrible twenties. My son is eighteen years old."

Sara did a double take, flipping back through Faith's history.

"Let me do the math for you," Faith offered. "I got pregnant when I was fourteen. I had Jeremy when I was fifteen."

Not much surprised Sara anymore, but Faith Mitchell had managed to do it. "Were there any complications with your first pregnancy?"

"Other than being fodder for a Lifetime movie?" She shook her head. "No problems at all."

"Okay," Sara answered, putting down the chart, giving Faith her full attention. "Let's talk about what happened tonight."

"I was walking to the car, I felt a little dizzy, and the next thing I know, Will's driving me here."

"Dizzy like the room spinning or dizzy as in light-headed?"

She thought about the question before replying. "Light-headed."

"Any flashes of light or unusual tastes in your mouth?"

"No."

"Will's your husband?"

She actually guffawed. "God, no." She choked on an incredulous laugh. "Will's my partner—Will Trent."

"Is Detective Trent here so I can talk to him?"

"Special Agent. You already did. He just left."

Sara was sure she was missing something. "The man who was just in here is a cop?"

She laughed. "It's the suit. You're not the first person to think he's an undertaker."

"I thought lawyer," Sara admitted, thinking she had never met anyone who looked less like a police officer in her life.

"I'll have to tell him you thought he was a lawyer. He'll be pleased you took him for an educated man."

For the first time, Sara noticed the woman was not wearing a wedding ring. "So, the father is . . ."

"In and out of the picture." Faith didn't seem embarrassed by the information, though Sara supposed that there wasn't much that could embarrass you after having a child at fifteen. "I'd prefer Will didn't know," Faith said. "He's very—" She stopped mid-sentence. She closed her eyes, pressed her lips together. A sheen of sweat had broken out on her forehead.

Sara pressed her fingers to Faith's wrist again. "What's happening here?"

Faith clenched her jaw, not answering.

Sara had been vomited on enough to know the warning signs. She went to the sink to wet a paper towel, telling Faith, "Take a deep breath and let it out slowly."

Faith did as she was told, her lips trembling.

"Have you been irritable lately?"

Despite her condition, Faith tried for levity. "More than usual?" She put her hand to her stomach, suddenly serious. "Yes. Nervous. Annoyed." She swallowed. "I get a buzzing in my head, like there are bees in my brain."

Sara pressed the cold paper towel to the woman's forehead. "Any nausea?"

"In the mornings," Faith managed. "I thought it was morning sickness, but . . ."

"What about the headaches?"

"They're pretty bad, mostly in the afternoon."

"Have you been unusually thirsty? Urinating a lot?"

"Yes. No. I don't know." She managed to open her eyes, asking, "So, what is it—the flu or brain cancer or what?"

Sara sat on the edge of the bed and took the woman's hand.

"Oh, God, is it that bad?" Before Sara could answer, she said, "Doctors and cops only sit down when it's bad news."

Sara wondered how she had missed this revelation. In all her years with Jeffrey Tolliver, she'd thought she had figured out every one of his tics, but this one had passed her by. She told Faith, "I was married to a cop for fifteen years. I never noticed, but you're right—my husband always sat down when there was bad news."

"I've been a cop for fifteen years," Faith responded. "Did he cheat on you or turn into an alcoholic?"

Sara felt a lump in her throat. "He was killed three and a half years ago."

"Oh, no," Faith gasped, putting her hand to her chest. "I'm so sorry."

"It's all right," Sara answered, wondering why she'd even told the woman such a personal detail. Her life over the last few years had been dedicated to not talking about Jeffrey, and here she was sharing him with a stranger. She tried to ease the tension by adding, "You're right. He cheated on me, too." At least he had the first time Sara married him.

"I'm so sorry," Faith repeated. "Was he on duty?"

Sara didn't want to answer her. She felt nauseated and overwhelmed, probably a lot like Faith had felt before she'd passed out in the parking lot.

Faith picked up on this. "You don't have to—"

"Thanks."

"I hope they got the bastard."

Sara put her hand into her pocket, her fingers wrapping around the edge of the letter. That was the question everyone wanted answered: *Did they get him? Did they catch the bastard who killed your husband?* As if it mattered. As if the disposition of Jeffrey's killer would somehow alleviate the pain of his death.

Mercifully, Mary came into the room. "Sorry," the nurse apologized. "The old lady's kids just dropped her here. I had to call social services." She handed Sara a piece of paper. "CMP's back."

Sara frowned as she read the numbers on the metabolic profile. "Do you have your monitor?"

Mary reached into her pocket and handed over her blood glucose monitor.

Sara swabbed some alcohol on the tip of Faith's finger. The CMP was incredibly accurate, but Grady was a large hospital and it wasn't unheard-of for the lab to get samples mixed up. "When was the last time you had a meal?" she asked Faith.

"We were in court all day." Faith hissed "Shit" as the lancet pierced her finger, then continued, "Around noon, I ate part of a sticky bun Will got out of the vending machine."

Sara tried again. "The last *real* meal."

"Around eight o'clock last night."

Sara guessed from the guilty look on Faith's face that it had probably come out of a takeout bag. "Did you have coffee this morning?"

"Maybe half a cup. The smell was a bit too much."

"Cream and sugar?"

"Black. I usually eat a good breakfast—yogurt, fruit. Right after my run." Faith asked, "Is something wrong with my blood sugar?"

"We'll see," Sara told her, squeezing some blood onto the test strip. Mary raised an eyebrow, as if to ask if Sara wanted to place a wager on the number. Sara shook her head: *no bet*. Mary persisted, using her fingers to indicate one-five-zero.

"I thought the test came later," Faith said, sounding unsure of herself. "When they make you drink the sugary stuff."

"Have you ever had any problems with your blood sugar? Is there a history in your family?"

"No. None."

The monitor beeped and the number 152 flashed on the screen.

Mary gave a low whistle, impressed by her own guess. Sara had once asked the woman why she didn't go to medical school, only to be told that nurses were the ones who practiced the real medicine.

Sara told Faith, "You have diabetes."

Faith's mouth worked before she managed a faint, "What?"

"My guess is that you've been pre-diabetic for a while. Your cholesterol and triglycerides are extremely elevated. Your blood pressure is a little high. The pregnancy and the rapid weight gain—ten pounds is a lot for nine weeks—plus your bad eating habits, pushed you over the edge."

"My first pregnancy was fine."

"You're older now." Sara gave her some tissue to press against her finger so the bleeding would stop. "I want you to follow up with your regular doctor first thing in the morning. We need to make sure there's not something else going on here. Meanwhile, you have to keep your blood sugar under control. If you don't, passing out in the parking lot will be the least of your worries."

"Maybe it's just—I haven't been eating right, and—"

Sara cut her off mid-denial. "Anything over one-forty is a positive diagnosis for diabetes. Your number has actually inched up since the first blood test was taken."

Faith took her time absorbing this. "Will it last?"

The question was one for an endocrinologist to answer. "You'll need to talk to your doctor and have him run some more tests," Sara advised, though, if she had to make an educated guess, she would say that Faith was in a precarious situation. Except for the pregnancy, she would be presenting as a full-blown diabetic.

Sara glanced at her watch. "I would admit you tonight for observation, but by the time we processed you and found you a room, your doctor's office would be open, and something tells me you wouldn't stay here anyway." She had spent enough time around police officers to know that Faith would bolt the minute she got the chance.

She continued, "You have to promise me that you'll call your doctor first thing—and I mean that, first thing.

We'll get a nurse educator in here to teach you how to test your blood and how and when to inject yourself, but you've got to follow up with him immediately."

"I have to give myself shots?" Faith's voice went up in alarm.

"Oral meds aren't approved for use in pregnant women. This is why you need to talk to your doctor. There's a lot of trial and error here. Your weight and hormone levels will change as the pregnancy progresses. Your doctor's going to be your best friend for the next eight months, at least."

Faith seemed embarrassed. "I don't have a regular doctor."

Sara took out her prescription pad and wrote down the name of a woman she'd interned with years ago. "Delia Wallace works out of Emory. She has a dual specialty in gynecology and endocrinology. I'll call her tonight so her office knows to work you in."

Faith still seemed unconvinced. "How can I suddenly have this? I know I've put on weight, but I'm not fat."

"You don't have to be fat," Sara told her. "You're older now. The baby affects your hormones, your ability to produce insulin. You haven't been eating well. The stars lined up and it triggered you."

"It's Will's fault," Faith mumbled. "He eats like a twelve-year-old. Doughnuts, pizza, hamburgers. He can't go into a gas station without buying nachos and a hot dog."

Sara sat down on the edge of the bed again. "Faith, this isn't the end of the world. You're in good shape. You've got great insurance. You can manage this."

"What if I . . ." She blanched, breaking eye contact with Sara. "What if I wasn't pregnant?"

"We're not talking about gestational diabetes here. This is full-blown, type two. A termination won't suddenly make the problem go away," Sara answered. "Look, this is probably something you've been building up to for a while. Being pregnant brought it on faster. It will make things more complicated in the beginning, but not impossible."

"I just . . ." She didn't seem capable of finishing a sentence.

Sara patted her hand, standing. "Dr. Wallace is an excellent diagnostician. I know for a fact that she takes the city insurance plan."

"State," Faith corrected. "I'm with the GBI."

Sara assumed the Georgia Bureau of Investigation's plan was similar, but she didn't quibble. Faith was obviously having difficulty absorbing the news, and Sara had not exactly eased her into it. You couldn't unring a bell, though. Sara patted her arm. "Mary will give you an injection. You'll be feeling better in no time." She started to leave. "I mean it about calling Dr. Wallace," she added firmly. "I want you on the phone with her office first thing in the morning, and you need to be eating more than sticky buns. Low-carb, low-fat, regular healthy meals and snacks, okay?"

Faith nodded, still dumbstruck, and Sara left the room feeling like an absolute heel. Her bedside manner had certainly deteriorated over the years, but this represented a new low. Wasn't that anonymity why she had come to Grady in the first place? But for a handful of homeless men and some prostitutes, she seldom saw a patient more than once. That had been the real pull for

Sara—the absolute detachment. She wasn't at a stage in her life where she wanted to make connections with people. Every new chart was an opportunity to start all over. If Sara was lucky—and if Faith Mitchell was careful—they would probably never see each other again.

Instead of going back into the doctors' lounge to finish her charts, Sara walked past the nurses' station, through the double doors, into the overfilled waiting room and finally found herself outside. There were a couple of respiratory therapists by the exit smoking cigarettes, so Sara kept walking toward the back of the building. Guilt about Faith Mitchell still hung heavy on her shoulders, and she looked up Delia Wallace's number in her cell phone before she forgot to follow up. The service took her message about Faith, and Sara felt slightly better as she ended the call.

She had run into Delia Wallace a couple of months ago, when the woman had come in to see one of her wealthy patients who had been airlifted to Grady after a bad car accident. Delia and Sara had been the only women in the top five percent of their graduating class at Emory University Medical School. At the time, it was an unwritten rule that there were two options for female doctors: gynecology or pediatrics. Delia had chosen the first, Sara the latter. They would both turn forty next year. Delia seemed to have everything. Sara felt like she had nothing.

Most doctors—Sara included—were arrogant to one degree or another, but Delia had always been an avid self-promoter. While they drank their coffees in the doctors' lounge, Delia quickly offered the highlights of her life: a thriving practice with two offices, a stockbroker husband and three overachieving kids. She'd shown Sara pictures of them all, this perfect family of hers who looked as if they had walked out of a Ralph Lauren advertisement.

Sara hadn't told Delia about her own life after medical school, that she had gone back to Grant County, her home, to tend to children in rural areas. She didn't tell Delia about Jeffrey or why she moved back to Atlanta or why she was working at Grady when she could open her own practice and have some semblance of a normal life. Sara had just shrugged, saying, "I ended up back here," and Delia had looked at her with both disappointment and vindication, both emotions conjured by the fact that Sara had been ahead of Delia their entire time at Emory.

Sara tucked her hands into her pockets, pulling her thin coat closed to fight the chill. She felt the letter against the back of her hand as she walked past the loading dock. She had volunteered to cover an extra shift that morning, working straight through for nearly sixteen hours so that she could have all of tomorrow off. Exhaustion hit her just as the night air did, and she stood with her hands fisted in her pockets, relishing the relatively clean air in her lungs. She caught the scent of rain under the smell of car exhaust and whatever was coming off the Dumpster. Maybe she would sleep tonight. She always slept better when it rained.

She looked down at the cars on the interstate. Rush hour was at its tail end—men and women going home to their families, their lives. Sara was standing at what was called the Grady Curve, an arc in the highway that traffic reporters used as a landmark when reporting trouble on the downtown connector. All the taillights were bright red tonight as a tow truck pulled a stalled SUV from the left-hand shoulder. Police cruisers blocked the scene, blue lights spinning, casting their eerie light into the darkness. They reminded her of the night Jeffrey had died—the police swarming, the state taking over, the scene combed through by dozens of men in their white suits and booties.

"Sara?"

She turned around. Mary stood with the door open, waving her back into the building. "Hurry!"

Sara jogged toward the door, Mary calling out stats as she got closer. "Single car MVA with pedestrian on foot. Krakauer took the driver and passenger, possible MI on the driver. You've got the woman who was hit by the car. Open frac on right arm and leg, L-O-C at the scene. Possible sexual assault and torture. Bystander happened to be an EMT. He did what he could, but it's bad."

Sara was sure she'd misunderstood. "She was raped and hit by a car?"

Mary didn't explain. Her hand was like a vise on Sara's arm as they jogged down the hallway. The door was open to the emergency triage room. Sara saw the gurney, three medics surrounding the patient. Everyone in the room was a man, including Will Trent, who was leaning over the woman, trying to question her.

"Can you tell me your name?" he asked.

Sara stopped short at the foot of the bed, Mary's hand still on her arm. The patient was lying curled on her side in a fetal position. Surgical tape held her tightly to the frame of the stretcher, pneumatic splints binding her right arm and leg. She was awake, her teeth chattering, murmuring unintelligibly. A folded jacket was under her head, a cervical collar keeping her neck in line. The side of her face was caked in dirt and blood; electrical tape hung from her cheek, sticking to her dark hair. Her mouth was open, lips cut and bleeding. The sheet they had covered her with was pulled down and the side of her breast gaped open in a wound so deep that bright yellow fat was showing.

"Ma'am?" Will asked. "Are you aware of your condition?"

"Move away," Sara ordered, pushing him back harder than she intended. He flailed, momentarily losing his balance. Sara did not care. She had seen the small digital recorder he had in his hand and did not like what he was doing.

Sara put on a pair of gloves as she knelt down, telling the woman, "I'm Dr. Linton. You're at Grady Hospital. We're going to take care of you."

"Help . . . help . . . help . . . ," the woman chanted, her body shivering so hard the metal gurney rattled. Her eyes stared blankly ahead, unfocused. She was painfully thin, her skin flaky and dry. "Help . . ."

Sara stroked back her hair as gently as she could. "We've got a lot of people here and we're all going to help you. You just hang on for me, okay? You're safe now." Sara stood, lightly resting her hand on the woman's shoulder to let her know she was not alone. Two more nurses were in the room, awaiting orders. "Somebody give me the rundown."

She had directed her request toward the uniformed emergency medical techs, but the man across from her started talking, delivering in rapid staccato the woman's vitals and the triage performed en route. He was dressed in street clothes that were covered in blood. Probably the bystander who had given aid at the scene. "Penetrating wound between eleventh and twelfth ribs. Open fractures right arm and leg. Blunt force trauma to the head. She was unconscious when we arrived, but she gained consciousness when I started working on her. We couldn't get her flat on her back," he explained, his voice filling with panic. "She kept screaming. We had to get her in the bus, so we just strapped her down. I don't know what's wrong with . . . I don't know what—"

He gulped back a sob. His anguish was contagious. The air felt charged with adrenaline; understandably so, considering the state of the victim. Sara felt a moment of panic herself, unable to take in the damage inflicted on the body, the multiple wounds, the obvious signs of torture. More than one person in the room had tears in their eyes.

Sara made her voice as calm as possible, trying to bring the hysteria down to a manageable level. She dismissed the EMTs and the bystander by saying, "Thank you, gentlemen. You did everything you could just to get her here. Let's clear the room now so that we have space to keep helping her." She told Mary, "Start an IV and prep a central line just in case." She told another nurse, "Get portable X-ray in here, call CT and get the surgical on-call." And said to another, "Blood gas, tox screen, CMP, CBC and a coag panel."

Carefully, Sara pressed the stethoscope to the woman's back, trying not to concentrate on the burn marks and crisscrossed slices in the flesh. She listened to the woman's lungs, feeling the sharp outline of ribs against her fingers. Breath sounds were equal, but not as strong as Sara would've liked, probably because of the massive amount of morphine they had given her in the ambulance. Panic often blurred the line between helping and hindering.

Sara knelt down again. The woman's eyes were still

open, her teeth still chattering. Sara told her, "If you have any trouble breathing, let me know, and I'll help you immediately. All right? Can you do that?" There was no response, but Sara kept talking to her anyway, announcing every step of the way what she was doing and why. "I'm checking your airway to make sure you can keep breathing," she said, gently pressing into the jaw. The woman's teeth were reddish pink, indicating blood in her mouth, but Sara guessed that was from biting her tongue. Deep scratches marked her face, as if someone had clawed her. Sara thought she might have to intubate her, paralyze her, but this might be the last opportunity the woman had to speak.

That was why Will Trent would not leave. He had been asking the victim about her condition in order to set up the framework for a dying declaration. The victim would have to know she was dying before her last words could be admitted in court as anything other than hearsay. Even now, Trent kept his back to the wall, listening to every word being spoken in the room, bearing witness in case he was needed to testify.

Sara asked, "Ma'am? Can you tell me your name?" Sara paused as the woman's mouth moved, but no words came out. "Just a first name, all right? Let's start with something easy."

"Ah . . . ah . . ."

"Anne?"

"Nah . . . nah . . ."

"Anna?"

The woman closed her eyes, gave a slight nod. Her breath had turned more shallow from the effort.

Sara tried, "How about a last name?"

The woman did not respond.

"All right, Anna. That's fine. Just stay with me." Sara glanced at Will Trent. He nodded his thanks. She returned to the patient, checking her pupils, pressing her fingers into the skull to check for fractures. "You've got some blood in your ears, Anna. You took a hard knock to your head." Sara took a wet swab and brushed it across the woman's face to remove some of the dried blood. "I know you're still in there, Anna. Just hang on for me."

With care, Sara traced her fingers down the neck and shoulder, feeling the clavicle move. She continued down gently, checking the shoulders front and back, then the vertebrae. The woman was painfully undernourished, the bones starkly outlined, her skeleton on display. There were tears in the skin, as if barbs or hooks had been imbedded under the flesh, then ripped out. Superficial cuts sliced their way up and down the body, and the long incision on the breast already smelled septic; she had been like this for days.

Mary said, "IV's in, saline wide open."

Sara asked Will Trent, "See the doctors' directory by the phone?" He nodded. "Page Phil Sanderson. Tell him we need him down here immediately."

He hesitated. "I'll go find him."

Mary supplied, "It's faster to page him. Extension 392." She taped a loop from the IV to the back of the woman's hand, asking Sara, "You want more morphine on board?"

"Let's figure out what's going on with her first." Sara tried to examine the woman's torso, not wanting to move the body until she knew exactly what she was dealing with. There was a gaping hole in her left side between the eleventh and twelfth ribs, which would explain why the woman had screamed when they tried to straighten her out. The stretching and grinding of torn muscle and cartilage would have been excruciating.

The EMT had put a compression pack on her right leg and arm along with two pneumatic splints to keep the limbs stabilized. Sara lifted the sterile dressing on the leg, seeing bright bone. The pelvis felt unstable beneath her hands. These were recent wounds. The car must have hit Anna from the right side, folding her in two.

Sara took a pair of scissors out of her pocket and cut through the tape that kept the woman immobile on the gurney, explaining, "Anna, I'm going to roll you onto your back." She braced the woman's neck and shoulders while Mary took care of the pelvis and legs. "We'll keep your legs bent, but we need to——"

"No-no-no!" the woman pleaded. "Please don't! Please don't!" They kept moving and her mouth opened wide, her screams sending a chill up Sara's spine. She had never heard anything more horrific in her life. "No!" the woman yelled, her voice catching. "No! Please! *Noooo!*"

She started to violently convulse. Instantly, Sara leaned over the stretcher, pinning Anna's body to the table so she wouldn't fall onto the floor. She could hear the woman grunt with each convulsion, as every movement brought a knife of pain to her side. "Five milligrams of Ativan," she ordered, hoping to control the seizures. "Stay with me, Anna," she urged the woman. "Just stay with me."

Sara's words did not matter. The woman had lost consciousness, either from the seizure or the pain. Long after the drug should have taken effect, the muscles still spasmed through the body, legs jerking, head shaking.

"Portable's here," Mary announced, motioning the X-ray technician into the room. She told Sara, "I'll check on Sanderson and the OR."

The X-ray technician put his hand to his chest. "Macon."

"Sara," she returned. "I'll help."

He handed her the extra lead apron, then went about preparing the machine. Sara kept her hand on Anna's forehead, stroking back her dark hair. The woman's muscles were still twitching when Sara and Macon managed to roll her onto her back, legs bent to help control the pain. Sara noticed that Will Trent was still in the room and told him, "You need to clear out while we do this."

Sara helped Macon take the X-rays, both of them moving as fast as they could. She prayed that the patient would not wake up and start screaming again. She could still hear the sound of Anna's screams, almost like an animal caught in a trap. The noise alone would set up the belief that the woman knew she was going to die. You did not scream like that unless you had given up all hope on life.

Macon helped Sara turn the woman back on her side, then went off to develop the films. Sara took off her gloves and knelt beside the gurney again. She touched her hand to Anna's face, stroking her cheek. "I'm sorry I pushed you," she said—not to Anna, but to Will Trent. She turned to find him standing at the foot of the bed, staring down at the woman's legs, the soles of her feet. His jaw was clenched, but she didn't know if that was from anger or horror or both.

He said, "We've both got jobs to do."

"Still."

Gently, he reached down and stroked the sole of Anna's right foot, probably thinking there was nowhere else to touch her that wouldn't cause pain. Sara was surprised by the gesture. It seemed almost tender.

"Sara?" Phil Sanderson was in the doorway, his surgical scrubs neatly clean and pressed.

She stood up, lightly resting her fingertips on Anna's shoulder as she told Phil, "We've got two open fractures and a crushed pelvis. There's a deep incision on the right breast and a penetrating wound on the left side. I'm not sure about the neurologic; her pupils are nonresponsive, but she was talking, making sense."

Phil walked over to the body and started his examination. He didn't comment on the state of the victim, the obvious abuse. His focus was on the things he could fix: the open fractures, the shattered pelvis. "You didn't intubate her?"

"Airways are clear."

Phil obviously disagreed with her decision, but then, orthopedic surgeons didn't generally care whether or not their patients could speak. "How's the heart?"

"Strong. BP is good. She's stable." Phil's surgical team came in to prep the body for transfer. Mary returned with the X-rays and handed them to Sara.

Phil pointed out, "Just putting her under could kill her."

Sara snapped the films into the lightbox. "I don't think she'd be here if she wasn't a fighter."

"The breast is septic. It looks like—"

"I know," Sara interrupted, putting on her glasses so she could read the X-rays.

"This wound in her side is pretty clean." He stopped his team for a moment and leaned down, checking the long tear in her skin. "Was she dragged by the car? Did something metal slice her open?"

Will Trent answered, "As far as I know, she was hit straight-on. She was standing in the roadway."

Phil asked, "Was there anything around that might have made this wound? It's pretty clean."

Will hesitated, probably wondering if the man realized what the woman had been through before the car had struck her. "The area was pretty wooded, mostly rural. I haven't talked to the witnesses yet. The driver had some chest complaints at the scene."

Sara turned her attention to the X-ray of the torso. Either something was wrong or she was more exhausted than she'd realized. She counted the ribs, not quite trusting what she was seeing.

Will seemed to sense her confusion. "What is it?"

"Her eleventh rib," Sara told him. "It's been removed."

Will asked, "Removed how?"

"Not surgically."

Phil barked, "Don't be ridiculous." He strode over, leaning close to the film. "It's probably . . ." He put up the second film of the chest, the anterior-posterior, then the lateral. He leaned closer, narrowing his eyes as if that would help. "The damn thing can't just drop out of the body. Where is it?"

"Look." Sara traced her finger along the jagged shadow where cartilage had once held bone. "It's not missing," she said. "It was taken."

CHAPTER TWO

WILL DROVE TO THE SCENE OF THE CAR ACCIDENT IN Faith Mitchell's Mini, his shoulders slumped, the top of his head pressed tightly against the roof of the car. He hadn't wanted to waste any time trying to get the seat adjusted—not when he had taken Faith to the hospital and especially not now that he was driving to the scene of one of the most horrific crimes he'd ever seen. The car was holding its own on the back roads as he traveled down Route 316 at well over the posted speed limit. The Mini's wide wheelbase hugged every curve, but Will backed off the gas as he got farther away from the city. The trees thickened, the road narrowed, and he was suddenly in an area where it was not uncommon for a deer or possum to wander onto the road.

He was thinking about the woman—the torn skin, the blood, the wounds on her body. From the moment he'd seen the medics wheeling her down the hospital corridor, Will had known that the injuries had been wrought by someone with a very sick mind. The woman had been tortured. Someone had spent time with her—someone well practiced in the art of pain.

The woman hadn't just appeared on the road out of thin air. The bottoms of her feet were freshly cut, still bleeding from a walk through the woods. A pine needle was embedded in the meaty flesh of her arch, dirt darkening her soles. She had been kept somewhere, then somehow managed to walk to her escape. She must have been held in a location close to the road, and Will was going to find the location if it took him the rest of his life.

Will realized that he had been using "she," when the victim had a name. Anna, close to Angie, the name of Will's wife. Like Angie, the woman had dark hair, dark eyes. Her skin tone was olive and she had a mole on the back of her calf just down from her knee, the same as Angie. Will wondered if this was something olive-skinned women tended to have, a mole on the back of their leg. Maybe this was some kind of marker that came in the genetic kit along with dark hair and eyes. He bet that doctor would know.

He remembered Sara Linton's words as she examined the torn skin, the fingernail scratches around the gaping hole in the victim's side. "She must have been awake when the rib was removed."

Will shuddered at the thought. He had seen the work of many sadists over his law enforcement career, but nothing as sick as this.

His cell phone rang, and Will struggled to get his hand into his pocket without knocking the steering wheel and sending the Mini into the ditch by the road. Carefully, he opened the phone. The plastic clamshell had been cracked apart months ago, but he'd managed to put the pieces back together with superglue, duct tape and five strips of twine that acted as a hinge. Still, he had to be careful or the whole thing would fall apart in his hand.

"Will Trent."

"It's Lola, baby."

He felt his brow furrow. Her voice had the phlegmy rasp of a two-pack-a-day smoker. "Who?"

"You're Angie's brother, right?"

"Husband," he corrected. "Who is this?"

"This is Lola. I'm one'a her girls."

Angie was freelancing for several private detective firms now, but she had been a vice cop for over a decade. Will occasionally got calls from some of the women she had walked the streets with. They all wanted help, and they all ended up right back in jail, where they used the pay phone to call him. "What do you want?"

"You don't gotta be all abrupt on me, baby."

"Listen, I haven't talked to Angie in eight months." Coincidentally, their relationship had become unhinged around the same time as the phone. "I can't help you."

"I'm innocent." Lola laughed at the joke, then coughed, then coughed some more. "I got picked up with an unknown white substance I was just holding for a friend."

These girls knew the law better than most cops, and they were especially careful on the pay phone in the jail.

"Get a lawyer," Will advised, speeding up to pass a car in front of him. Lightning cracked the sky, illuminating the road. "I can't help you."

"I got information to exchange."

"Then tell that to your lawyer." His phone beeped, and he recognized his boss's number. "I have to go." He clicked over before the woman could say anything else. "Will Trent."

Amanda Wagner inhaled, and Will braced himself for a barrage of words. "What the hell are you doing leaving your partner at the hospital and going on some fool's errand for a case that we have no jurisdiction over and haven't been invited to attend—in a county, I might add, where we don't exactly have a good relationship?"

"We'll get asked to help," he assured her.

"Your woman's intuition is not impressing me tonight, Will."

"The longer we let the locals play this out, the colder the trail is going to get. This isn't our abductor's first time, Amanda. This wasn't an exhibition game."

"Rockdale has this covered," she said, referring to the county that had police jurisdiction over the area where the car accident had occurred. "They know what they're doing."

"Are they stopping cars and looking for stolen vehicles?"

"They're not completely stupid."

"Yes, they are," he insisted. "This wasn't a dump job. She was held in the area and she managed to escape."

Amanda was silent for a moment, probably clearing the smoke coming out of her ears. Overhead, a flash of lightning slashed the sky, and the ensuing thunder made it hard for Will to hear what Amanda finally said.

"What?" he asked.

She curtly repeated, "What's the status of the victim?"

Will didn't think about Anna. Instead, he recalled the look in Sara Linton's eyes when they rolled the patient up to surgery. "It doesn't look good for her."

Amanda gave another, heavier sigh. "Run it down for me."

Will gave her the highlights, the way the woman had looked, the torture. "She must have walked out of the woods. There's got to be a house somewhere, a shack or something. She didn't look like she'd been out in the elements. Somebody kept her for a while, starved her, raped her, abused her."

"You think some hillbilly snatched her?"

"I think she was kidnapped," he replied. "She had a good haircut, her teeth were bleached white. No track marks. No signs of neglect. There were two small plastic surgery scars on her back, probably from lipo."

"So, not a homeless woman and not a prostitute."

"Her wrists and ankles were bleeding from being bound. Some of the wounds on her body were healing, others were fresh. She was thin—too thin. This took place over more than a few days—maybe a week, two weeks, tops."

Amanda cursed under her breath. The red tape was getting pretty thick. The Georgia Bureau of Investigation was to the state what the Federal Bureau of Investigation was to the country. The GBI coordinated with local law enforcement when crimes crossed over county lines, keeping the focus on the case rather than territorial disputes. The state had eight crime labs as well as hundreds of crime-scene techs and special agents on duty, all ready to serve whoever asked for help. The catch was that the request for help had to be formally made. There were ways to make sure it came, but favors had to be played, and for reasons not discussed in polite company, Amanda had lost her heat in Rockdale County a few months ago during a case involving an unstable father who had abducted and murdered his own children.

Will tried again. "Amanda—"

"Let me make some calls."

"Can the first one be to Barry Fielding?" he asked, referring to the canine expert for the GBI. "I'm not even sure the locals know what they're dealing with. They haven't seen the victim or talked to the witnesses. Their detective wasn't even at the hospital when I left." She didn't respond, so he prodded some more. "Barry lives in Rockdale County."

A heavier sigh than the first two came down the line. Finally, she said, "All right. Just try not to piss off anyone more than usual. Report back to me when you've got something to move on." Amanda ended the call.

Will closed the cell phone and tucked it into his jacket pocket just as the rumble of thunder filled the air. Lightning lit up the sky again, and he slowed the Mini, his knees pressing into the plastic dashboard. His plan had been to drive straight up Route 316 until he found the accident site, then beg his way onto the scene. Stupidly, he had not anticipated a roadblock. Two Rockdale County police cruisers were parked nose to nose, closing both lanes, and two beefy uniformed officers stood in front of each. About fifty feet ahead, giant xenon work lights illuminated a Buick with a crumpled front end. Crime-scene techs were all over, doing the painstaking work of collecting every piece of dirt, rock and glass so they could take it back to the lab for analysis.

One of the cops came up to the Mini. Will looked around for the button to roll down the window, forgetting that it was on the center console. By the time he got the window down, the other cop had joined his partner. Both of them were smiling. Will realized he must look comical in the tiny car, but there was nothing to be done about it now. When Faith had passed out in the parking lot of the courthouse, Will's only thought was that her car was closer than his and it would be faster using the Mini to take her to the hospital.

The second cop said, "Circus is thataway." He pointed his thumb back toward Atlanta.

Will knew better than to attempt to pull out his wallet from his back pocket while he was still in the car. He pushed open the door and clumsily exited the vehicle. They all looked heavenward as a clap of thunder shook the air.

"Special Agent Will Trent," he told the cops, showing them his identification.

Both men looked wary. One of them walked away, talking into the radio mike on his shoulder, probably checking with his boss. Sometimes local cops were glad to see the GBI on their turf. Sometimes they wanted to shoot them.

The man in front of him asked, "What's with the monkey suit, city boy? You just come from a funeral?"

Will ignored the jab. "I was at the hospital when the victim was brought in."

"We've got several victims," he answered, obviously determined to make this hard.

"The woman," Will clarified. "The one who was walking on the road and was hit by the Buick that was being driven by an elderly couple. We think her name is Anna."

The second cop was back. "I'm going to have to ask you to get back in your car, sir. According to my boss, you don't have jurisdiction here."

"Can I talk to your boss?"

"He figured you'd say that." The man had a nasty smile on his face. "Said to give him a call in the morning, say around ten, ten-thirty."

Will looked past their cruisers to the crime scene. "Can I get his name?"

The cop took his time, making a show of taking out his pad, finding his pen, putting pen to paper, printing the letters. With extreme care, he tore off the page and handed it to Will.

Will stared at the scrawl over the numbers. "Is this English?"

"Fierro, numbnuts. It's Italian." The man glanced at the paper, offering a defensive "I wrote it clear."

Will folded the note and put it in his vest pocket. "Thank you."

He wasn't stupid enough to think the cops would politely return to their posts while he got back into the Mini. Will was in no hurry now. He leaned down and found the pump handle to lower the driver's seat, then pushed it back as far as it would go. He angled himself into the car and gave the cops a salute as he did a three-point turn and drove away.

Route 316 hadn't always been a back road. Before I-20 came along, 316 had been a main artery connecting Rockdale County and Atlanta. Today, most travelers preferred the interstate, but there were still people who used it for shortcuts and other nefarious pursuits. Back in the late nineties, Will had been involved in a sting operation to stop prostitutes from bringing johns out here. Even then, the road was not well traveled. That two cars managed to be here tonight at the same time as the woman was wildly coincidental. That she had at that point managed to walk onto the road into the path of one of them was even more fantastical.

Unless Anna had been waiting for them. Maybe she had stepped out in front of the Buick on purpose. Will had learned a long time ago that escape was sometimes easier than survival.

He kept the Mini at a slow crawl as he looked for a side road to turn down. He had gone about a quarter of a mile before he found it. The pavement was choppy, the low-riding car feeling each and every bump. An occasional streak of lightning lit the woods for him. There were no houses that Will could see from the road, no run-down shacks or old barns. No lean-tos sheltering old stills. He kept going, using the bright lights at the crime scene as his guide so that when he stopped, he found himself parallel to the action. Will pulled up the emergency brake and allowed himself a smile. The accident site was about two hundred yards away, the lights and activity making it look like a football field in the middle of the forest.

Will took the small emergency flashlight out of the glove box and got out of the car. The air was changing fast, the temperature dropping. On the news this morning, the weatherman had predicted partly cloudy, but Will was thinking they were in for a deluge.

He made his way on foot through the thick forest, carefully scanning the ground as he walked, searching for anything that was out of place. Anna could have come through here, or she could have been on the other side of the road. The point was that the crime scene should not just be confined to the street. They should be out in the forest, searching within at least a mile radius. The job would not be easy. The forest was dense, low-lying limbs and bushes blocking forward progress, fallen trees and sinkholes making the nighttime terrain ever more dangerous. Will tried to get his bearings, wond ing which direction would lead him to I-20, whe more residential areas were, but gave up after the compass in his head started spinning toward nowhere.

The grade shifted, sloping downward, and though it was still far away, Will could hear the usual sounds of a crime scene—the electric hum of the generator, the buzz from the stadium lights, the pop of camera flashes, the grumblings of cops and crime-scene techs occasionally punctuated by surprised laughter.

Overhead, the clouds parted, sending down a sliver of moonlight that cast the ground in shadow. Out of the corner of his eye, he saw a patch of leaves that looked disturbed. He crouched down, the weak beam of the light not helping him much. The leaves were darker here, but he couldn't tell if that was from blood or precipitation. Will could definitely tell that something had lain in the spot. The question was, had that something been an animal or had it been a woman?

He tried to get his bearings again. He was about halfway between Faith's car and the crumpled Buick on the road. The clouds moved again, and he was back in darkness. The flashlight in his hand chose this moment to give up the ghost, the bulb going yellowish brown, then black. Will slapped the plastic case against his palm, trying to get some more juice out of the batteries.

Suddenly, the bright beam of a Maglite illuminated everything within a five-foot radius.

"You must be Agent Trent," a man said. Will put up his hand to keep his retinas from burning. The man took his time lowering the flashlight to Will's chest. In the _____ of the crime-scene lights, he appeared to be _____ odiment of a Macy's Day parade balloon— _____ e top, tapering to almost a point at the _____ man's tiny little pinhead floated above his shoulders, the flesh of his thick neck spilling up over his shirt collar.

Considering his girth, the man was light on his feet. Will hadn't heard him making his way through the forest. "Detective Fierro?" Will guessed.

He flashed the light into his own face so Will could see him. "Call me Asshole, because that's what you're gonna be thinking about me the whole lonely way back to Atlanta."

Will was still crouched down. He glanced toward the crime scene. "Why not let me have a peek first?"

The light was back in Will's eyes. Fierro said, "Persistent little fucker, aren't you?"

"You think she was dropped here, but she wasn't."

"You're a mind reader?"

"You've got an APB for all suspicious cars in the area and you've got your crime-scene guys going over that Buick with a sieve."

"The APB is a code 10-38, which you'd know if you were a real cop, and the closest house to here is an old geezer in a wheelchair about two miles up." Fierro said this with a disdain that was more than familiar to Will. "I'm not gonna have this conversation with you, pal. Leave my scene."

"I saw what was done to her," Will pressed. "She wasn't put in a car and dropped. She was bleeding from everywhere. Whoever did this is smart. He wouldn't put her in a car. He wouldn't risk the trace evidence. He sure as hell wouldn't leave her alive."

"Two options." Fierro held up his pudgy fingers and counted them off for Will. "Leave on your own two feet or leave on your back."

Will stood up, straightening his shoulders so that he

was standing at his full six-three. Pointedly, he looked down at Fierro. "Let's try to work this out. I'm here to help."

"I don't need your help, Gomez. Now I suggest you turn around, get back in your little girl car and go gentle into that good night. You wanna know what happens here? Read a newspaper."

"I think you mean Lurch," Will corrected. "Gomez was the father."

Fierro's brow wrinkled.

"Look, the victim—Anna—probably lay down here." Will pointed to the depression in the leaves. "She heard the cars coming, and she walked onto the road to get help." Fierro didn't stop him, so he continued, "I've got a canine unit on the way. The trail is still fresh now, but it'll be gone with the rain." As if on cue, lightning flashed, followed closely by a clap of thunder.

Fierro stepped closer. "You're not hearing me, *Gomez*." He thrust the butt of his flashlight into Will's chest, physically pushing him away from the crime scene. He kept doing this as he spoke, punctuating each word with a sharp jab. "Get your fucking *GBI*, three-piece fucking *undertaker* ass back in your little red toy car and get the *fuck* off my—"

Will's heel struck something solid. Both men heard it, and both men stopped.

Fierro opened his mouth, but Will indicated he should keep quiet, slowly kneeling down to the ground. Will used his hands to brush away some leaves and found the outline of a large square of plywood. Two big rocks framed the corner, marking the spot.

There was a faint sound in the air, almost a crackling. Will knelt down farther and the noise turned into a few muffled words. Fierro heard it, too. He drew his gun, keeping the flashlight alongside the muzzle so he could see what he was going to shoot. Suddenly, the detective no longer appeared to mind Will's presence; instead, he seemed to be encouraging Will to be the one pulling back the sheet of plywood and putting his face in the line of fire.

When Will looked up at him, Fierro shrugged, as if to say, "You wanted on the case."

Will had been in court all day. His gun was at home in the drawer by his bed. Fierro either had a large goiter on his ankle or he was carrying a backup piece. The man didn't offer the gun and Will didn't ask for it. He would need both hands if he was going to pull back the plywood and get out of the way in a timely manner. Will sucked in his breath as he moved the rocks, then dug his fingers carefully into the soft ground, getting a good grip on the edge of the board. It was standard size, roughly four-by-eight, and half an inch thick. The wood felt wet under his fingers, which meant that it would be even heavier.

Will glanced back at Fierro to make sure he was ready, then, in one swift motion, pried back the sheet of plywood. Dirt and debris scattered as Will quickly backed away.

"What is it?" Fierro's voice was a hoarse whisper. "Do you see anything?"

Will craned his neck to see what he had uncovered. The hole was deep and crudely dug, a thirty-by-thirty-inch square opening going straight down into the earth. Will kept at a low crouch as he made his way toward the hole. Aware that he was again offering his head as a target, he quickly glanced inside, trying to see what they were dealing with. He couldn't see to the bottom. What he did discover was a ladder resting a few feet down from the top, a homemade deal with the rungs nailed crookedly to a pair of rotting two-by-fours.

Lightning cracked in the sky, showing the tableau in full glory. It was like a cartoon: the ladder to hell.

"Give me the light," he whispered to Fierro. The detective was more than accommodating now, slapping the Maglite into Will's reaching hand. Will looked back at the man. Fierro had taken a wide stance, his gun still pointed at the opening in the ground, fear widening his eyes.

Will shone down the light. The cavern seemed to be L-shaped, going straight about five feet, then turning into what seemed to be the main area of the cave. Pieces of wood jutted out where the roof was shored up. There were supplies at the base of the ladder. Cans of food. Rope. Chains. Hooks. Will's heart jumped as he heard movement down there, rustling, and he had to force himself not to jerk back.

Fierro asked, "Is it—"

Will put his finger to his lips, though he was pretty sure that the element of surprise was not on their side. Whoever was down there had seen the beam of the flashlight moving around. As if to reinforce this, Will heard a guttural sound from below, almost a moan. Was there another victim down there? He thought of the woman in the hospital. Anna. Will knew what electrical burns looked like. They stained the skin in a dark powder that never washed away. They stayed with you for a lifetime—that is, if you had a lifetime left in you.

Will took off his suit jacket and tossed it behind him. He reached toward Fierro's ankle and grabbed the revolver out of the holster. Before he could stop himself, Will swung his legs down into the hole.

"Jesus Christ," Fierro hissed. He looked over his shoulder at the dozens of cops who were a hundred feet away, no doubt realizing there was a better way to do this.

Will heard the sound from below again. Maybe an animal, maybe a human being. He turned off the flashlight and jammed it into the back of his pants. There was something he should have said, like "Tell my wife I love her," but he didn't want to give Angie the burden—or the satisfaction.

"Hold on," Fierro whispered. He wanted to get backup.

Will ignored him, shoving the revolver into his front pocket. Carefully, he tested his weight on the wobbly ladder, the heels of his shoes on the rungs so he could face the inside of the cavern as he descended. The space was narrow, his shoulders too broad. He had to keep one arm straight above his head so that he could fit down the hole. Dirt kept falling in clumps around him and roots scratched his face and neck. The wall of the shaft was just a few inches from his nose, bringing out a claustrophobia Will never knew he had. Every time he inhaled, he tasted mud in the back of his throat. He couldn't look down, because there was nothing to see, and he was afraid that if he looked up, he might reverse direction.

With each step, the smell got worse—feces, urine, sweat, fear. Maybe the fear was coming from Will. Anna had escaped from here. Maybe she had wounded her attacker in the process. Maybe the man was down there waiting with a gun or a razor or a knife.

Will's heart was beating so hard that he could feel it

choking his throat. Sweat was pouring off him, and his knees were shaky as he took step after interminable step down. Finally, his foot hit soft earth. He felt around with the toe of his shoe, finding the rope at the base of the ladder, hearing the chain rattle. He would have to crouch down to get inside, leaving himself completely exposed to whoever was waiting.

Will could hear panting, more mumbling. Fierro's revolver was in his hand. He wasn't sure how it had gotten there. The space was too tight for him to reach the flashlight, and it was falling down the back of his pants anyway. Will tried to make his knees bend, but his body would not comply. The panting was getting louder, and he realized it was coming from his own mouth. He looked up, seeing nothing but darkness. Sweat blurred his eyes. He held his breath, then dropped down in a squat.

No gun went off. His throat was not slit. Hooks were not jammed into his eyes. He felt a breeze from the shaft, or was that something in front of his face? Was someone standing in front of him? Had someone just brushed their hand in front of his face? He heard movement again, chattering.

"Don't move," Will managed. He held the gun in front of him, sweeping it back and forth like a pendulum in case someone was standing in front of him. With a shaking hand, he reached behind him for the flashlight. The panting was back, an embarrassing noise that echoed in the cave.

"Never . . ." a man murmured.

Will's hand was slick with sweat, but it held steady to the grooved metal grip of the flashlight. He jammed his thumb into the button, turning on the light.

Rats scattered—three big, black rats with plump bellies and sharp claws. Two of them went straight for Will. Instinctively, he backed up, slamming into the ladder, his feet tangling in the rope. He covered his face with his arms, and felt sharp claws dig into his skin as the rats bolted up the ladder. Will panicked, realizing he'd dropped the flashlight, and he snatched it up quickly, scanning the cave, looking for other occupants.

Empty.

"Crap . . ." Will exhaled, slumping to the ground. Sweat poured into his eyes. His arms throbbed where the rats had ripped the skin. He had to fight the overwhelming urge to escape up after them.

He used the flashlight to take in his surroundings, sending roaches and other insects scrambling. There was no telling where the other rat had gone, and Will wasn't going to go looking for him. The main part of the cavern was sunken, about three feet down from where Will was sitting. Whoever had designed the structure knew what they were doing. The depressed area would give a home-field advantage.

Will slowly lowered himself down, keeping the light trained in front of him so there wouldn't be any more surprises. The space was bigger than he had expected. It must have taken weeks to excavate the area, lifting out bucket after bucket of dirt, bringing down pieces of wood to keep the whole thing from caving in.

He guessed the main area was at least ten feet deep and six feet wide. The ceiling was about six feet overhead—tall enough for him to stand up if he kept stooped over, but he didn't trust his knees to lift him. The flashlight could not illuminate everything at once, so the space felt even more cramped than it was. Add to that the eeriness, the ungodly smells of Georgia clay mixed with blood and excrement, and everything started to feel smaller and darker.

Against one wall was a low bed that had been thrown together with what looked like recycled wood. A shelf overhead held supplies: water jugs, soup cans, implements of torture Will had only seen in books. The mattress was thin, bloodstained foam sticking out of the torn black cover. There were chunks of flesh on the surface, some of it already rotting. Maggots swirled like churning waters. Strands of rope were bunched up on the floor by the bed, enough to wrap around someone head to toe, almost like a mummy. Deep scratch marks clawed into the wood on the sides of the bed. There were sewing needles, fishing hooks, matches. Blood pooled onto the dirt floor, running underneath the bed frame like a slow leak in a faucet.

"Told . . ." a voice began, only to be drowned by static. There was a small television/radio sitting on a white plastic chair at the back of the cavern. Will kept down in a crouch as he moved toward the chair. He looked at the buttons, pressing a few before he managed to turn off the radio, remembering too late that he should have had his gloves on.

He followed the cord of the television with his eyes, finding a large marine battery. The plug had been cut off the cord, the bare red and black wires attached to the terminals. There were other wires, their ends stripped down to the copper. They were blackened, and Will caught the familiar scent of an electrical burn.

"Hey, Gomez?" Fierro called. His voice was all raw nerves.

"It's empty," Will told him.

Fierro made a hesitating noise.

"I'm serious," Will told him. He went back to the opening, craning up to see the man. "It's empty."

"Christ." Fierro's head disappeared from view, but not before Will saw his hand shoot up in the sign of the cross.

Will was ready to do some praying himself if he didn't get out of here. He shone the light on the ladder, seeing where his own shoe prints had smeared into the bloody footprints on the rungs. Will looked down at his scuffed shoes, the dirt floor, finding more bloody footprints that he had smeared. He crammed his shoulders back into the shaft and put his foot on the rung, trying not to mess up anything else. Forensics wasn't going to be happy with him, but there was nothing he could do about it now except apologize.

Will froze. Anna's feet had been cut, but the cuts were more like the nasty scrapes you get from stepping on sharp objects—pine needles, burrs, thorny vines. That was why he had assumed she had walked in the woods. She wasn't bleeding enough to leave bloody footprints that were so pronounced he could see the ridges of the sole in the dirt. Will stood there with his hand above him, one foot on the ladder, debating.

He gave a bone-weary sigh, then crouched back down, skipping the light along every corner of the cave. The rope was bothering him, the way it had been wrapped around the bed. His mind flashed on the image of Anna tied down, the rope wrapped in a continuous loop over and under the bed, securing her body to the frame. He pulled one of the lengths out from under the bed. The end was cut clean through, as were the others. He glanced around. Where was the knife now?

Probably with that last stupid rat.

Will pulled back the mattress, gagging from the smell, trying not to think about what his bare hands were touching. He kept the back of his wrist pressed under his nose as he pulled away slats of wood that supported the mattress, hoping to God the rat didn't spring up and claw out his eyes. He made as much noise as he could, dropping the slats in a pile on the floor. He heard a squeaking sound behind him, and turned to find the rat crouched down in the corner, its beady eyes reflecting the light. Will had a piece of wood in his hand, and he thought about hurling it at the beast, but he was worried his aim wouldn't be good enough in the narrow space. He was also worried it would piss off the rat.

He laid the plank onto the pile, keeping a wary eye on the creature. Something else got his attention. There were scratch marks on the bottom of the bed slats— deep bloody gouges that didn't look like they were made by an animal. Will shone the light into the opening under the bed. The dirt was excavated about six inches below the floor, running the length and width of the bed. Will reached down and picked up a small length of rope. Like the other pieces, this had been cut, too. Unlike the other pieces, there was a knot intact.

Will pulled back the rest of the slats. There were four metal bolts underneath the bed, one at each corner. A piece of rope was tied through one bolt. Pink blood stained the cord. He felt the rope with his fingers. It was wet. Something sharp scraped his thumb. Will leaned in closer, straining to see what had scratched him. He picked at the cord with his fingernails, prying out the object so he could examine it more closely in the flashlight beam. Bile hit the back of his throat when he saw what he was holding.

"Hey!" Fierro bellowed. "Gomez? You coming up or what?"

"Get a search team out here!" Will rasped.

"What're you talkin—"

Will looked at the piece of broken tooth in his hand. "There's another victim!"

CHAPTER THREE

FAITH SAT IN THE HOSPITAL CAFETERIA, THINKING SHE felt the same way she'd felt the night of her junior prom: unwanted, fat and pregnant. She looked at the wiry Rockdale County detective sitting across from her at the table. With his long nose and greasy hair hanging down over his ears, Max Galloway had the surly yet perplexed look of a Weimaraner. What's more, he was a poor sport. Every sentence he uttered to Faith alluded to the GBI taking away his case, beginning with his opening salvo when Faith asked to sit in on the interview with two of the witnesses: "I bet that bitch you work for is already primping her hair for the TV cameras."

Faith had held her tongue, though she couldn't imagine Amanda Wagner primping anything. Sharpening her claws, maybe, but her hair was a structure that defied primping.

"So," Galloway said to the two male witnesses. "You guys were just driving around, didn't see nothing, and then there's the Buick and the girl on the road?"

Faith struggled not to roll her eyes. She had worked homicide in the Atlanta Police Department for eight years before she had partnered with Will Trent. She knew what it was like to be the detective on the other side of that table, to have some arrogant jerk from the GBI waltz in and tell you he could run your case better than you could. She understood the anger and the frustration of being treated like an ignorant hick who couldn't detect your way out of a paper bag, but now that Faith herself was GBI, all she could think about was the pleasure she would feel when she snatched this case right out from under this particularly galling ignorant hick.

As for the paper bag, Max Galloway might as well have had one over his head. He had been interviewing Rick Sigler and Jake Berman, the two men who had come upon the car accident on Route 316, for at least half an hour and still hadn't noticed that both men were gay as handbags.

Galloway addressed Rick, the emergency medical technician who had helped the woman on the scene. "You said your wife's a nurse?"

Rick stared at his hands. He had a rose-gold wedding band around his finger and the most beautiful, delicate hands Faith had ever seen on a man. "She works nights at Crawford Long."

Faith wondered how the woman would feel knowing that her husband was out getting his knob polished while she was pulling the late shift.

Galloway asked, "What movie did y'all go see?"

He'd asked the two men this same question at least three times, only to be given the same answer. Faith was all for trying to trip up a suspect, but you had to have more intelligence than a russet potato to pull off that kind of thing—sadly, this was exactly the type of acumen that Max Galloway did not possess. From where Faith was sitting, it seemed like the two witnesses had just had the misfortune of finding themselves in the wrong place at the wrong time. The only positive aspect of their involvement was that the medic had been able to take care of the victim until the ambulance arrived.

Rick asked Faith, "Do you think she's going to be okay?"

Faith assumed the woman was still in surgery. "I don't know," she admitted. "You did everything you could to help her, though. You have to know that."

"I've been at a million car accidents." Rick looked back at his hands. "I've never seen anything like that before. It was . . . it was just awful."

In her normal life, Faith wasn't a touchy-feely person, but as a cop, she knew when a softer approach was needed. She felt the urge to lean across the table and put her hands over Rick's, to comfort him and draw him out, but she wasn't sure how Galloway would react and she didn't want to make herself any more of an enemy than she already was.

Galloway said, "Did y'all meet at the theater or did you take one car?"

Jake, the other man, shifted in his chair. He'd been very quiet from the beginning, only speaking when he was asked a direct question. He kept glancing at his watch. "I need to go," he said. "I have to get up for work in less than five hours."

Faith glanced at the clock on the wall. She hadn't realized it was coming up on one in the morning, probably because the insulin shot had given her a strange sort of second wind. Will had left two hours ago after giving her a quick rundown of what had happened, dashing off to the crime scene before she could offer to join him. He was persistent, and Faith knew that he would find a way to get this case. She just wished she knew what was taking him so long.

Galloway pushed a pad and pen toward the men. "Give me all your phone numbers."

The color drained from Rick's face. "Only call my cell. Please. Don't call me at work." He glanced nervously at Faith, then back at Galloway. "They don't like me to get personal calls at work. I'm out in the bus all day. All right?"

"Sure." Max sat back in the chair, arms crossed over his chest, staring at Faith. "You hear that, vulture?"

Faith gave the man a tight smile. She could take outright hate, but this passive-aggressive crap was getting on her last nerve.

She took out two business cards and handed one to each man. "Please call me if you think of anything else. Even something that doesn't seem important."

Rick nodded, tucking the card into his back pocket. Jake held on to his, and she imagined he was going to toss it into the first trashcan he came across. Faith's impression was that the men didn't know each other very well. They had been vague about details pertaining to their friendship, but each had presented a movie-ticket stub when asked. They had probably met in the theater, then decided to go somewhere more private.

A cell phone began to play "The Battle Hymn of the Republic." Faith corrected her initial assumption, thinking it was more than likely the University of Georgia fight song, as Galloway flipped open his phone, saying, "Yeah?"

Jake started to stand, and Galloway nodded to him, as if permission to leave had been asked and granted.

"Thank you," Faith told the two men. "Please call me if you think of anything else."

Jake was already halfway to the door, but Rick

lingered. "I'm sorry I wasn't much help. There was a lot going on, and—" Tears welled into his eyes. He was obviously still haunted by what had happened.

Faith put her hand on his arm, keeping her voice low. "I really don't care about what you guys were doing out there." Rick colored. "It's none of my business. All I care about is finding out who hurt this woman."

He looked away. Immediately, Faith knew that she had pushed him in exactly the wrong direction.

Rick gave a tight nod, still not meeting her eye. "I'm sorry I can't be more help."

Faith watched him leave, wanting to kick herself. Behind her, she heard Galloway mutter several curses. She turned as he pushed back from the table so hard that his chair clattered to the floor. "Your partner is a fucking lunatic. One hundred fucking percent."

Faith agreed—Will was never one to do things halfway—but she never badmouthed her partner unless it was to his face. "Is that just an observation, or are you trying to tell me something?"

Galloway tore off the page with the phone numbers and slapped it down on the table. "You got your case."

"What a surprising turn of events." Faith flashed him a smile, handing him a card. "If you could please fax all witness statements and preliminary reports to my office. Number's on the bottom."

He snatched the card, bumping into the table as he walked away, grumbling, "Keep smiling, bitch."

Faith leaned down and picked up the chair, feeling a bit woozy as she straightened. The nurse educator had been more of the former than the latter, and Faith was still unsure about what to do with all the diabetic instruments and supplies she had been given. She had notes, forms, a journal and all sorts of test results and papers to give to her doctor tomorrow. None of it made sense. Or maybe she was too shocked to process it all. She had always been very good at math, but the thought of measuring her food and calculating insulin made her brain go all fuzzy.

The final blow had been the result of the pregnancy test that had been kindly tagged on to all the other bloodwork. Faith had been clinging to the possibility that the over-the-counter tests were inaccurate—all three of them. How exact could the technology be for something that you peed on? She had vacillated daily between thinking she was pregnant and thinking that she had a stomach tumor, not exactly sure which news would be more welcome. When the nurse had happily informed her, "You're going to have a baby!" Faith had felt like she was going to pass out again.

There was nothing she could do about it now. She sat back down at the table, looking at Rick Sigler's and Jake Berman's phone numbers. She would have made a bet that Jake's was false, but Faith wasn't new to this game. Max Galloway had been annoyed when she had asked to see the men's driver's licenses and copied down the information in her notebook. Then again, maybe Galloway wasn't a total idiot. She'd seen him scribbling down his own copy of the phone numbers while he was on his cell. The thought of Galloway having to come ask Faith for Jake Berman's details made her smile.

She checked the clock again, wondering what was keeping the Coldfields. Galloway had told Faith the couple had been instructed to come to the cafeteria for their interviews as soon as the ER cleared them, but the couple seemed to be taking their own sweet time. Faith was also curious about what Will had done to make Max Galloway call him a lunatic. She would be the first person to admit that her partner was far from conventional. He certainly had his own way of doing things, but Will Trent was the best cop Faith had ever worked with— even if he had the social skills of an awkward toddler. For instance, Faith would've liked to have found out from her own partner that they were assigned to this case rather than hear it from an inbred Weimaraner from Rockdale County.

Maybe it was for the best that she had some time before she talked to Will. She had no idea how she was going to explain why she had passed out in the parking deck at the courthouse without actually having to tell him the truth.

She rifled through the plastic bag filled with diabetic supplies and pulled out the pamphlet the nurse had given her, hoping that this time she would be able to concentrate on it. Faith didn't get much further than *"So, you have diabetes"* before she was telling herself once again that there had been some kind of mistake. The insulin shot had made her feel better, but maybe just lying down for a few minutes had done the trick. Did she even have a history of this in her family? She should call her mother, but she hadn't even told Evelyn that she was pregnant. Besides, the woman was on vacation in Mexico, her first holiday in years. Faith wanted to make sure her mother was close to good medical care when she told her the news.

The person she should really call was her brother. Captain Zeke Mitchell was an Air Force surgeon stationed in Landstuhl, Germany. As a doctor, he would know everything about her condition, which was probably why she cringed at the thought of reaching out to him. When fourteen-year-old Faith announced that she was pregnant, Zeke was just hitting his senior year in high school. His mortification and humiliation had lasted twenty-four hours, seven days a week. At home, he had to watch his slut of a teenage sister swell up like a blimp, and at school, he had to listen to the crude jokes his friends made about her. It was no wonder he'd joined the military straight out of high school.

Then there was Jeremy. Faith had no idea how she would tell her son that she was pregnant. He was eighteen, the same age Zeke had been when she'd ruined his life. If boys did not want to know their sisters were having sex, they sure as hell didn't want to hear the news about their mothers.

Faith had done most of her growing up with Jeremy, and now that he was in college, their relationship was settling into a comfortable place where they could talk to each other as adults. Sure, she sometimes had flashes of her son as a child—the blanket he used to drag around with him everywhere, the way he constantly used to ask her when he was going to get too heavy for her to carry him—but she'd finally come to terms with the fact that her little boy was now a grown man. How could she pull the rug out from under her son now that he'd finally gotten settled? And it wasn't just that she was pregnant anymore. She had a *disease*. She had something that could be carried in families. Jeremy could be susceptible. He had a serious girlfriend now. Faith knew that they were having sex. Jeremy's children could become diabetic because of Faith.

"God," she mumbled. It wasn't the diabetes, but the

idea that she could end up being a grandmother before she hit thirty-four.

"How are you feeling?"

Faith looked up to find Sara Linton standing across from her with a tray of food.

"Old."

"Just from the pamphlet?"

Faith had forgotten it was in her hand. She indicated that Sara should sit. "Actually, I was questioning your medical abilities."

"You wouldn't be the first." She said it ruefully, and not for the first time, Faith wondered what Sara's story was. "My bedside manner could have been better with you."

Faith did not disagree. Back in the ER, she had wanted to hate Sara Linton on sight for no other reason than she was the type of woman you'd want to hate on sight: tall and thin with great posture, long auburn hair and that unusual kind of beauty that made men fall all over themselves when she entered a room. It didn't help matters that the woman was obviously smart and successful, and Faith had felt the same knee-jerk dislike she'd felt in high school when the cheerleaders had bounced by. She'd like to think a new strength of character, a spurt in maturity, had allowed her to overcome the petty response, but the truth was that it was hard for Faith to hate someone who was a widow, especially the widow of a cop.

Sara asked, "Have you had anything to eat since we talked?"

Faith shook her head, looking down at the doctor's food selection: a scrawny piece of baked chicken on a leaf of wilted lettuce and something that may or may not have been a vegetable. Sara used her plastic fork and knife to cut into the piece of chicken. At least she tried to cut into it. In the end, it was more like a tearing. She moved the roll off her bread plate and passed Faith the chicken.

"Thanks," Faith managed, thinking that the fudge brownies she had spotted when she walked in were much more appetizing.

Sara asked, "Are you officially on the case?"

Faith was surprised by the question, but then again, Sara had worked on the victim; she was bound to be curious. "Will managed to snag it for us." She checked the signal on her cell phone, wondering why he hadn't called yet.

"I'm sure the locals were very happy to step aside."

Faith laughed, thinking Sara's husband had probably been a good cop. Faith was a good cop, too, and she knew that it was one in the morning and Sara had said six hours ago that she was at the end of her shift. Faith studied the doctor. Sara had the unmistakable glow of an adrenaline junkie. The woman was here for information.

Sara offered, "I checked on Henry Coldfield, the driver." She hadn't eaten anything yet, but then she had come into the cafeteria to find Faith, not choke down a piece of chicken that had hatched just as Nixon was resigning. "The air bag bruised his chest, and the wife took a couple of stitches in her head, but they're both fine."

"That's actually what I'm waiting on." Faith checked the clock again. "They were supposed to meet me down here."

Sara looked confused. "They left at least half an hour ago with their son."

"What?"

"I saw them all talking to that detective with the greasy hair."

"Motherfucker." No wonder Max Galloway had looked so smug when he left the cafeteria. "Sorry," she told Sara. "One of the locals is smarter than I thought. He played me like a violin."

"Coldfield is an unusual name," Sara said. "I'm sure they're in the phone book."

Faith hoped so, because she didn't want to have to go crawling back to Max Galloway and give him the satisfaction of relaying the information.

Sara offered, "I could pull the address and phone number off the hospital intake form for you."

Faith was surprised by the offer, which usually required a subpoena. "That'd be great."

"It's not a problem."

"It's, uh—" Faith stopped, biting her tongue to keep from telling the other woman that she would be breaking the law. She changed the subject. "Will told me you worked on the victim when she came in."

"Anna," Sara supplied. "At least that's what I think she said."

Faith tested the waters. Will hadn't given her the gritty details. "What were your impressions?"

Sara sat back in her chair, arms folded. "She showed signs of severe malnutrition and dehydration. Her gums were white, her veins collapsed. Because of the nature of the healing and the way the blood was clotting, I would assume that the wounds were inflicted over a period of time. Her wrists and ankles showed signs of being bound. She was penetrated vaginally and anally; there were indications that a blunt object was used. I couldn't really do a rape kit before surgery, but I managed to examine her as best I could. I removed some splinters of wood from under her fingernails for your lab to look at—not pressure-treated from the look of it, but that will have to be confirmed by your guys."

She sounded like she was giving testimony in court. Every observation had supporting evidence, every educated guess was framed as an estimation. Faith asked, "How long do you think she was kept?"

"At least four days. Though gauging by how malnourished she was, it might be as much as a week to ten days."

Faith didn't want to think about the woman being tortured for ten days. "How are you so sure about the four days?"

"The cut on the breast here," Sara replied, indicating the side of her own breast. "It was deep, already septic, with signs of insect activity. You'd have to talk to an entomologist to pin down the pupation—the developmental stage of the insect—but considering she was still alive, that her body was relatively warm and there was a fresh blood supply to feed on, four days is a solid guess." She added, "I don't imagine they'll be able to save the tissue."

Faith kept her lips pressed tightly together, resisting the urge to put her hand over her own breast. How many pieces of yourself could you lose and still go on?

Sara kept talking, though Faith had not prompted her. "The eleventh rib, here"—she touched her abdomen—"that was recent, probably earlier today or late yesterday, and done with precision."

"Surgical precision?"

"No." She shook her head. "Confidence. There were no hesitation marks, no test cuts. The person was confident in what they were doing."

Faith thought the doctor seemed pretty confident herself. "How do you think it was done?"

Sara took out her prescription pad and started drawing a bunch of curved lines that only made sense when she explained, "The ribs are numbered in pairs starting at the top and going down, twelve each side, left and right." She tapped the lines with her pen. "Number one is just under the clavicle and twelve is the last one here." She looked up to make sure Faith was following. "Now, eleven and twelve at the bottom are considered to be 'floating,' because they don't have an anterior connection. They only connect at the back, not the front." She drew a straight line to indicate the spine. "The top seven ribs connect at the back and then attach to the sternum—like a big crescent. The next three rows connect roughly to the ribs above. They're called false ribs. All of this is very elastic so that you can breathe, and it's also why it's hard to break a rib with a direct blow— they bend quite a bit."

Faith was leaning forward, hanging on her every word. "So, this was done by someone with medical knowledge?"

"Not necessarily. You can feel your own ribs with your fingers. You know where they are in your body."

"But, still—"

"Look." She sat up straight, raising her right arm and pressing the fingers of her left hand into her side. "You run your hand down the posterior axillary line until you feel the tip of the rib—eleven, with twelve a little farther back." She picked up the plastic knife. "You slice the knife into the skin and cut along the rib—the tip of the blade could even scrape along the bone as a guide. Push back the fat and muscle, disarticulate the rib from the vertebra, snap it off, whatever, then grab hold and yank it out."

Faith felt queasy at the thought.

Sara put down the knife. "A hunter could do it in under a minute, but anyone could figure it out. It's not precision surgery. I'm sure you could Google up a better drawing than the one I've made."

"Is it possible that the rib was never there? That she was born without it?"

"A small portion of the population is born with one pair fewer, but the majority of us have twenty-four."

"I thought men were missing a rib?"

"You mean like Adam and Eve?" A smile curved Sara's lips, and Faith got the distinct impression the woman was trying not to laugh at her. "I wouldn't believe everything they told you in Sunday School, Faith. We all have the same number of ribs."

"Well, don't I feel stupid." It wasn't a question. "But you're sure about this, that the rib was taken out?"

"Ripped out. The cartilage and muscle were torn. This was a violent wrenching."

"You seem to have given this a lot of thought."

Sara shrugged, as if this was just the product of natural curiosity. She picked up the knife and fork again, cutting into the chicken. Faith watched her struggle with the desiccated meat for a few seconds before she put the utensils back down. She gave a strange smile, almost embarrassed. "I was a coroner in my previous life."

Faith felt her mouth open in surprise. The doctor had

said it the same way you might confide a hidden acrobatic talent or youthful indiscretion. "Where?"

"Grant County. It's about four hours from here."

"Never heard of it."

"It's well below the gnat line," Sara admitted. She leaned her arms on the table, a wistful tone to her voice when she revealed, "I took the job so that I could buy out my partner in our pediatric practice. At least I thought I did. The truth was that I was bored. You can only give so many vaccinations and stick so many Band-Aids on skinned knees before your mind starts to go."

"I can imagine," Faith mumbled, though she was wondering which was more alarming: that the doctor who had just diagnosed her with diabetes was a pediatrician or that she was a coroner.

"I'm glad you're on this case," Sara said. "Your partner is . . ."

"Strange?"

Sara gave her an odd look. "I was going to say 'intense.' "

"He's pretty driven," Faith agreed, thinking this was the first time since she'd met Will Trent that anyone's first impression of him had been so complimentary. He usually took a while to grow on you, like cataracts or shingles.

"He seemed very compassionate." Sara held up her hand to stop any protest. "Not that cops aren't compassionate, but they usually don't show it."

Faith could only nod. Will seldom showed any emotions, but she knew that torture victims cut him close to the bone. "He's a good cop."

Sara looked down at her tray. "You can have this if you want. I'm not really hungry."

"I didn't think you came in here to eat."

She blushed, caught.

"It's all right," Faith assured her. "But if you're still offering the Coldfields' information . . ."

"Of course."

Faith dug out one of her business cards. "My cell number is on the back."

"Right." She read the number, a determined set to her mouth, and Faith saw that not only did Sara know she was breaking the law, she obviously didn't care. "Another thing—" Sara seemed to be debating whether or not to speak. "Her eyes. The whites showed petechia, but there weren't any visible signs of strangulation. Her pupils wouldn't focus. It could be from the trauma or something neurological, but I'm not sure she could see anything."

"That might explain why she walked out in the middle of the road."

"Considering what she's been through . . ." Sara didn't finish the sentence, but Faith knew exactly what she meant. You didn't have to be a doctor to understand that a woman who'd been through that kind of hell might deliberately walk into the path of a speeding car.

Sara tucked Faith's business card into her coat pocket. "I'll call you in a few minutes."

Faith watched her leave, wondering how in the hell Sara Linton had ended up working at Grady Hospital. Sara couldn't be more than forty, but the emergency room was a young person's game, the sort of place you ran screaming from before you hit your thirties.

She checked her phone again. All six bars were lit, meaning the signal was bright and clear. She tried to give Will the benefit of the doubt. Maybe his phone had fallen apart again. Then again, every cop on the scene would have a cell phone, so maybe he really was an ass-hole.

It did occur to Faith as she got up from the table and made her way to the parking lot that she could call Will herself, but there was a reason Faith was pregnant and unmarried for the second time in less than twenty years, and it wasn't because she was good at communicating with the men in her life.

CHAPTER FOUR

WILL STOOD AT THE MOUTH OF THE CAVE, LOWERING
down a set of lights on a rope so that Charlie Reed
would have something better than a flashlight to help
him collect evidence. Will was soaked to the bone, even
though the rain had stopped half an hour ago. As dawn
approached, the air had turned chillier, but he would
rather stand on the deck of the *Titanic* than go down
into that hole again.

The lights hit the bottom and he saw a pair of hands
pull them into the cavern. Will scratched his arms. His
white shirt showed pinpoints of blood where the rats
had clawed their way over him, and he was wondering if
itching was a sign of rabies. It was the kind of question
he would normally ask Faith, but he didn't want to
bother her. She had looked awful when he'd left the hospital, and there was nothing she could do here but stand
in the rain alongside him. He would catch her up on the
case in the morning, after she'd had a good night's sleep.
This case wasn't going to be solved in an hour. At least
one of them should be well rested as they headed into
the investigation.

A helicopter whirred overhead, the chopping sound
vibrating in his ears. They were doing infrared sweeps,
looking for the second victim. The search teams had
been out for hours, carefully combing the area within a

two-mile radius. Barry Fielding had shown up with his search dogs, and the animals had gone crazy for the first half hour, then lost the scent. Uniformed patrolmen from Rockdale County were doing grid searches, looking for more underground caves, more clues that might indicate the other woman had escaped.

Maybe she hadn't managed to escape. Maybe her attacker had found her before she could reach help. Maybe she had died days or even weeks ago. Or maybe she had never existed in the first place. As the search wore on, Will was getting the impression that the cops were turning against him. Some of them didn't think there was a second victim at all. Some of them thought Will was keeping them out in the freezing cold rain for no reason other than he was too stupid to see that he was wrong.

There was one person who could clarify this, but she was still in surgery back at Grady Hospital, fighting for her life. The first thing you normally did in an abduction or murder case was put the victim's life under a microscope. Other than assuming her name was Anna, they knew nothing about the woman. In the morning, Will would pull all the missing persons reports in the area, but those were bound to be in the hundreds, and that was excluding the city of Atlanta, where on average, two people a day went missing. If the woman came from a different state, the paperwork would increase exponentially. Over a quarter of a million missing persons cases were reported to the FBI every year. Compounding the problem, the cases were seldom updated if the missing were found.

If Anna wasn't awake by morning, Will would send over a fingerprint technician to card her. It was a scattershot way of trying to find her identity. Unless she had committed an arrestable crime, her fingerprints would not be on file. Still, more than one case cracked open based on following procedure. Will had learned a long time ago that a slim chance was still a chance.

The ladder at the mouth of the cavern shook and Will steadied it as Charlie Reed made his way up. The clouds had passed with the rain, letting through some of the moonlight. Though the deluge had passed, there was the occasional drop, sounding like a cat smacking its lips. Everything in the forest had a strange, bluish hue to it, and there was enough light now that Will didn't need his flashlight to see Charlie. The crime-scene tech's hand reached out, slapping a large evidence bag on the ground at Will's feet as he climbed to the surface.

"Shit," Charlie cursed. His white clean suit was caked in mud. He unzipped it as soon as he was topside, and Will could see that he was sweating so badly his T-shirt was stuck to his chest.

Will asked, "You okay?"

"Shit," Charlie repeated, wiping his forehead with the back of his arm. "I can't believe . . . Jesus, Will." He leaned over, bracing his hands on his knees. He was breathing hard, though he was a fit man and the climb was not a difficult one. "I don't know where to start."

Will understood the feeling.

"There were torture devices . . ." Charlie wiped his mouth with the back of his hand. "I've only seen that kind of thing on television."

"There was a second victim," Will said, raising up his voice at the end so that Charlie would take his words as an observation that needed confirming.

"I can't make sense of anything down there." Charlie

squatted, resting his head in his hands. "I've never seen anything like it."

Will knelt down alongside him. He picked up the evidence bag. "What's this?"

He shook his head. "I found them rolled up in a tin can by the chair."

Will spread the bag flat on his leg and used the penlight from Charlie's kit to study the contents. There were at least fifty sheets of notebook paper inside. Each page was covered front to back in cursive pencil. Will squinted at the words, trying to make sense out of them. He had never been able to read well. The letters always tended to mix up and turn around. Sometimes, they blurred so much that he felt motion sickness just trying to decipher their meaning.

Charlie didn't know about Will's problem. Will tried to draw out some information from him, asking, "What do you make of these notes?"

"It's crazy, right?" Charlie was rubbing his thumb and forefinger along his mustache, a nervous habit that only came out during dire circumstances. "I don't think I can go back down there." He paused, swallowing hard. "It just feels . . . evil, you know? Just plain damn *evil*."

Will heard leaves rustling, branches snapping. He turned to find Amanda Wagner making her way through the woods. She was an older woman, probably in her sixties. She favored monochromatic power suits with skirts that hit below her knee and stockings that showed off the definition of what Will had to admit were remarkably good calves for a woman he often thought of as the Antichrist. Her high heels should have made it difficult for her to find her footing, but, as with most obstacles, Amanda conquered the terrain with steely determination.

Both men stood as she approached.

As usual, she didn't bother with pleasantries. "What's this?" She held out her hand for the evidence bag. Other than Faith, Amanda was the only person in the bureau who knew about Will's reading issues, something she both accepted and criticized at the same time. Will trained the penlight on the pages and she read aloud, " *'I will not deny myself. I will not deny myself.'* " She shook the bag, checking the rest of the pages. "Front and back, all the same sentence. Cursive, probably a woman's handwriting." She handed the notes back to Will, giving him a pointed look of disapproval. "So, our bad guy's either an angry schoolteacher or a self-help guru."

She addressed Charlie. "What else have you found?"

"Pornography. Chains. Handcuffs. Sexual devices."

"That's evidence. I need clues."

Will took over for him. "I think the second victim was bolted underneath the bed. I found this in the rope." He took a small evidence bag from his jacket pocket. It contained part of a front tooth, some of the root still attached. He told Amanda, "That's an incisor. The victim at the hospital had all of her teeth intact."

She scrutinized Will more than the tooth. "You're sure about this?"

"I was right in her face trying to get information," he answered. "Her teeth were chattering together. They were making a clicking sound."

She seemed to accept this. "What makes you think the tooth was recently lost? And don't tell me gut instinct, Will, because I've got the entire Rockdale County police force out here in the wet and cold, ready to lynch you for sending them on a wild-goose chase in the middle of the night."

"The rope was cut from underneath the bed," he told her. "The first victim, Anna, was tied down to the top of the bed. The second victim was underneath. Anna couldn't have cut the rope herself."

Amanda asked Charlie, "Do you agree with this?"

Still shaken up, he took his time answering. "Half of the cut ends of the rope were still under the bed. It would make sense that they would fall that way if they were cut from underneath. Cut from the top, the ends would be on the floor or still on top of the bed, not underneath it."

Amanda was still dubious. She told Will, "Go on."

"There were more pieces of rope tied to the eyebolts under the bed. Someone cut themselves away. They would still have the rope around their ankles and at least one wrist. Anna didn't have any rope on her."

"The paramedics could've cut it off," Amanda pointed out. She asked Charlie, "DNA? Fluids?"

"All over the place. We should get them back in forty-eight hours. Unless this guy's on the database . . ." He glanced at Will. They all knew that DNA was a shot in the dark. Unless their abductor had committed a crime in the past that caused his DNA to be taken, then logged into the computer, there was no way he would come up as a match.

Amanda asked, "What about the waste situation?"

Initially, Charlie didn't seem to understand the question, but then he answered, "There aren't any empty jars or cans. I guess they were taken away. There's a covered bucket in the corner that was used as a toilet, but from what I can tell, the victim—or victims—were tied up most of the time and didn't have a choice but to go where they were. I couldn't tell you if any of this points to one or two captives. It depends on when they were taken, how dehydrated they were, that kind of thing."

She asked, "Was there anything fresh underneath the bed?"

"Yes," Charlie answered, as if surprised by the revelation. "Actually, there was an area that tested positive for urine. It would be in the right place for someone lying down on their back."

Amanda pressed, "Wouldn't it take longer for liquid to evaporate underground?"

"Not necessarily. The high acidity would have a chemical reaction with the pH in the soil. Depending on the mineral content and the—"

Amanda cut him off. "Don't educate me, Charlie, just give me facts that I can use."

He looked at Will apologetically. "I don't know if there were two hostages at the same time. Someone was definitely kept under the bed, but it could have been that the abductor moved the same victim from place to place. The body fluids could've also drained off from above." He told Will, "You were down there. You saw what this guy is capable of." The color had drained from his face again. "It's awful," he mumbled. "It's just awful."

Amanda was her usual sympathetic self. "Man up, Charlie. Get back down there and find me some evidence I can use to catch this bastard." She patted him on the back, more of a shove to get him moving, then told Will, "Walk with me. We've got to find that pygmy detective you pissed off and make nice with him so he doesn't go crying to Lyle Peterson." Peterson was

Rockdale County's chief of police and no friend of Amanda's. By law, only a police chief, a mayor or a district attorney could ask the GBI to take over a case. Will wondered what strings Amanda had managed to pull and how furious Peterson was about it.

"Well." She held out her hands for balance as she stepped over a fallen limb. "You bought some good grace volunteering yourself to go down into that hole, but if you ever do anything that stupid again, I'll have you running stings in the men's bathroom at the airport for the rest of your natural born life. Do you hear me?"

Will nodded. "Yes, ma'am."

"Your victim doesn't look good," she told him, walking past a group of cops who had stopped for a cigarette break. They glared at Will. "There were some complications. I talked to the surgeon. Sanderson. He doesn't sound hopeful." She added, "He confirmed your observation about the teeth, by the way. They were fully intact."

This was typical Amanda, making him work for everything. Will didn't take it as an insult but as a sign that she might be on his side. "The soles of her feet were freshly cut," he said. "She didn't bleed from her feet when she was in the cave."

"Take me through your process."

Will had already relayed the highlights to her over the telephone, but he told her again about finding the sheet of plywood, going down into the hole. He went into more details this time around as he described the cavern, carefully giving her a sense of the atmosphere while trying not to reveal that he had been even more petrified than Charlie Reed. "The slats of the bed were clawed underneath," he said. "The second victim—her hands had to be unbound to make those marks. He wouldn't have left her hands free while she was alone because she could free herself and leave."

"You really think he kept one on top and one on bottom?"

"I think that's exactly what he did."

"If they were both tied up and one of them managed to get a knife, it would make sense that the woman on bottom would keep it hidden while they waited for the abductor to leave."

Will didn't respond. Amanda could be sarcastic and petty and downright mean, but she was also fair in her own way, and he knew that as much as she derided his gut instincts, she had learned over the years to trust him. He also knew better than to expect anything remotely resembling praise.

They had reached the road where Will had parked the Mini all those hours ago. Dawn was coming fast, and the blue cast of light had turned to sepia tones. Dozens of Rockdale County cruisers were blocking off the area. More men milled around, but the sense of urgency had been lost. The press was out there somewhere, too, and Will saw a couple of news helicopters hovering overhead. It was too dark to get a shot, but that probably was not stopping them from reporting every movement they saw on the ground—or at least what they thought they saw. Accuracy wasn't exactly part of the equation when you had to provide news twenty-four hours a day.

Will held out his hand to Amanda, helping her down the shoulder as they went into the opposite side of the forest. There were hundreds of searchers in the area, some from other counties, all spread out into groups. The Georgia Emergency Management Agency, or

GEMA, had called in the civilian canine corps, the people who had trained their dogs to scent corpses. The dogs had stopped barking hours ago. Most of the volunteers had gone home. It was mostly cops now, people who didn't have a choice. Detective Fierro was out there somewhere, probably cursing Will's name.

Amanda asked, "How's Faith?"

He was surprised by the question, but then, Amanda had a connection with Faith that went back several years. "She's fine," he said, automatically covering for his partner.

"I heard she passed out."

He feigned surprise. "Did you?"

Amanda raised her eyebrows at him. "She hasn't been looking good lately."

Will assumed she meant the weight gain, which was a little much for Faith's small frame, but he had figured out today that you did not discuss a woman's weight, especially with another woman. "She seems fine to me."

"She seems irritable and distracted."

Will kept his mouth shut, unsure whether Amanda was truly concerned or asking him to tattle. The truth was that Faith *had* been irritable and distracted lately. He had worked with her long enough to know her moods. For the most part, she was pretty even-keeled. Once every month, always around the same time, she carried her purse with her for a few days. Her tone would get snippy and she'd tend to favor radio stations that played women singing along to acoustic guitars. Will knew to just apologize a lot for everything he said until she stopped carrying her bag. Not that he would share this with Amanda, but he had to admit that lately, every day with Faith seemed like a purse day.

Amanda reached out her hand and he helped her step over a fallen log. "You know I hate working cases we can't clear," she said.

"I know you like solving cases no one else can."

She chuckled ruefully. "When are you going to get tired of me stealing all your thunder, Will?"

"I'm indefatigable."

"Putting that calendar to use, I see."

"It's the most thoughtful gift you've ever given me." Leave it to Amanda to give a functional illiterate a word-a-day calendar for Christmas.

Up ahead, Will saw Fierro making his way toward them. This side of the road was more densely forested, and there were limbs and vines everywhere. Will could hear Fierro cursing as his pant leg got caught in a prickly bush. He slapped his neck, probably killing an insect. "Nice of you to join this fucking waste of time, Gomez."

Will made the introductions. "Detective Fierro, this is Dr. Amanda Wagner."

Fierro tilted up his chin at her in greeting. "I've seen you on TV."

"Thank you," Amanda returned, as if he had meant it as a compliment. "We're dealing with some pretty salacious details here, Detective Fierro. I hope your team knows to keep a lid on it."

"You think we're a bunch of amateurs?"

Obviously, she did. "How is the search going?"

"We're finding exactly what's out here—nothing. Nada. Zero." He glared at Will. "This how you state guys run things? Come in here and blow our whole fucking budget on a useless search in the middle of the goddamn night?"

Will was tired and he was frustrated, and it came out in his tone. "We usually pillage your supplies and rape your women first."

"Ha-fucking-ha," Fierro grumbled, slapping his neck again. He pulled away his hand and there was a smear of bloody insect on his palm. "You're gonna be laughing your ass off when I take back my case."

Amanda said, "Detective Fierro, Chief Peterson asked us to intervene. You don't have the authority to take back this case."

"Peterson, huh?" His lip curled. "Does that mean you've been greasing his pole again?"

Will sucked in so much air that his lips made a whistling sound. For her part, Amanda looked unfazed, though her eyes narrowed, and she gave Fierro a single nod, as if to say his time would come. Will wouldn't be surprised if, at some future date, Fierro woke up to find a decapitated horse's head in his bed.

"Hey!" someone screamed. "Over here!"

All three stood where they were in various stages of shock, anger and unadulterated rage.

"I found something!"

The words got Will moving. He jogged toward the searcher, a woman who was furiously waving her hands in the air. She was Rockdale uniformed patrol, wearing a knit hat on her head and surrounded by tall switch-grass.

"What is it?" he asked.

She pointed toward a dense pack of low-hanging trees. He saw that the leaves underneath were disturbed, bare spots of earth showing in places. "Something caught my light," she said, turning on her Maglite and shining it into the shadowy area under the trees. Will didn't see anything. By the time Amanda had joined them, he was wondering if the patrolwoman was a little too tired, a little too anxious to find something.

"What is it?" Amanda asked, just as the light reflected back from the darkness. It was a small flash that lasted no more than a second. Will blinked, thinking maybe his tired brain had conjured it, too, but the patrolwoman found it again—a quick flash like a tiny burst of powder, approximately twenty feet away.

Will slipped on a pair of latex gloves from his jacket. He took the flashlight, carefully pushing back branches as he made his way into the area. The prickly bushes and limbs made it hard going, and he stooped down low to make forward progress. He shone the light on the ground, scanning for the object. Maybe it was a broken mirror or a chewing gum wrapper. All the possibilities ran through his mind as he tried to locate it: a piece of jewelry, a shard of glass, minerals in a rock.

A Florida state driver's license.

The license was about two feet from the base of the tree. Beside it was a small pocketknife, the thin blade so coated in blood that it blended in with the dark leaves around it. Close to the trunk, the branches thinned out. Will knelt down, picking up the leaves one at a time as he moved them off the license. The thick plastic had been folded in two. The colors and the distinctive outline of the state of Florida in the corner told him where the license had been issued. There was a hologram in the background to prevent forgeries. That must have been what the light had picked up on.

He leaned down, craning his neck so he could get a better look, not wanting to disturb the scene. One of the clearest fingerprints Will had ever seen was right in the middle of the license. Imprinted in blood, the ridges were practically jumping off the smooth plastic. The photograph showed a woman: dark hair, dark eyes.

"There's a pocketknife and a license," he told Amanda, his voice raised so that she could hear him. "There's a bloody fingerprint on the license."

"Can you read the name?" She put her hands on her hips, sounding furious.

Will felt his throat close up. He concentrated on the small print, making out a *J,* or maybe an *I,* before everything began to jumble around.

Her fury shot up exponentially. "Just bring the damn thing out."

There was a cluster of cops around her now, all looking confused. Even twenty feet away, Will could hear them mumbling about procedure. The purity of the crime scene was sacrosanct. Defense lawyers chewed apart irregularities. Photographs and measurements had to be taken, sketches made. The chain of custody could not be broken, or the evidence would be thrown out.

"Will?"

He felt a drop of rain hit the back of his neck. It was hot, almost like a burn. More cops were coming up, trying to see what had been found. They would wonder why Will didn't shout out the name from the license, why he didn't immediately send off someone to do a computer check. Was this how it was going to end? Was Will going to have to pick his way out of this dense covering and announce to a group of strangers that, at his best, he could only read at a second-grade level? If that information got out, he might as well go home and stick his head in the oven, because there wouldn't be a cop in the city who would work with him.

Amanda started making her way toward him, her skirt snagging on a prickly vine, various curses coming from her lips.

Will felt another drop of rain on his neck and wiped it away with his hand. He looked down at his glove. There was a fine smear of blood on his fingers. He thought maybe he had cut his neck on one of the limbs, but he felt another drop on the back of his neck. Hot, wet, viscous. He put his hand to the place. More blood.

Will looked up, into the eyes of a woman with dark brown hair and dark eyes. She was hanging upside down about fifteen feet above him. Her ankle was snagged in a patchwork of branches, the only thing keeping her from hitting the ground. She had fallen at an angle, face-first, snapping her neck. Her shoulders were twisted, her eyes open, staring at the ground. One arm hung straight down, reaching toward Will. There was an angry red circle around her wrist, the skin burned through. A piece of rope was knotted tightly around the other wrist. Her mouth was open. Her front tooth was broken, a third of it missing.

Another drop of blood dripped from her fingertips, this time hitting him on the cheek just below his eye. Will took off his latex glove and touched the blood. It was still warm.

She had died within the last hour.

DAY TWO

CHAPTER FIVE

PAULINE MCGHEE STEERED HER LEXUS LX RIGHT INTO the handicapped parking space in front of the City Foods Supermarket. It was five in the morning. All the handicapped people were probably still asleep. More important, it was too damn early to walk more than she had to.

"Come on, sleepy cat," she told her son, gently pressing his shoulder. Felix stirred, not wanting to wake up. She caressed his cheek with her hand, thinking not for the first time that it was a miracle that something so perfect had come out of her imperfect body. "Come on, sweet pea," she said, tickling his ribs until he curved up like a roly-poly worm.

She got out of the car, helping Felix climb out of the SUV behind her. His feet hadn't hit the ground before she went over the routine. "See where we're parked?" He nodded. "What do we do if we get lost?"

"Meet at the car." He struggled not to yawn.

"Good boy." She pulled him close as they walked toward the store. Growing up, Pauline had been told that she should find an adult if she ever got lost, but these days, you never knew who that adult might be. A security guard might be a pedophile. A little old lady might be a batty witch who spent her spare time hiding razor blades in apples. It was a sad state of affairs when the safest help for a lost six-year-old boy was an inanimate object.

The artificial lights of the store were a bit much for this time of morning, but it was Pauline's own fault for not already buying the cupcakes for Felix's class. She'd gotten the notice a week ago, but she hadn't anticipated all hell breaking loose at work in between. One of the interior design agency's biggest clients had ordered a custom-made sixty-thousand-dollar Italian brown leather couch that wouldn't fit in the damn elevator, and the only way to get it up to his penthouse was with a ten-thousand-dollar-an-hour crane.

The client was blaming Pauline's agency for not catching the error, the agency was blaming Pauline for designing the couch too big, and Pauline was blaming the dipshit upholsterer whom she had specifically told to go to the building on Peachtree Street to measure the elevator before making the damn couch. Faced with a ten-thousand-dollar-an-hour crane bill or rebuilding a sixty-thousand-dollar couch, the upholsterer was, of course, conveniently forgetting this conversation, but Pauline was damned if she was going to let him get away with it.

There was a meeting of all concerned at seven o'clock sharp, and she was going to be the first one there to get in her side of the story. As her father always said, shit rolls downhill. Pauline McGhee wasn't going to be the one smelling like a sewer when the day was over. She had evidence on her side—a copy of an email exchange with her boss asking him to remind the upholsterer about taking measurements. The critical part was Morgan's response: *I'll take care of it*. Her boss was pretending like the emails hadn't happened, but Pauline wasn't going to take the fall. Someone was going to lose their job today, and it sure as hell wasn't going to be her.

"No, baby," she said, pulling Felix's hand away from a package of Gummi Bears dangling from the shelf. Pauline swore they put those things at kid level just so their parents would be bullied into buying them. She had seen more than one mother relent to a screaming kid just so he'd shut up. Pauline didn't play that game, and Felix knew it. If he tried anything, she would snatch him up and leave the store, even if that meant abandoning a half-filled shopping cart.

She turned down the bakery aisle, nearly smacking into a grocery cart. The man behind the buggy laughed good-naturedly, and Pauline managed a smile.

"Have a good day," he said.

"You, too," she returned.

That, she thought, was the last time she was going to be nice to anybody this morning. She'd tossed and turned all night, then gotten up at three so she could run on the treadmill, put her face on, fix breakfast for Felix and get him ready for school. Long gone were her single days when she could spend all night partying, go home with whomever looked good, then roll out of bed the next morning twenty minutes before it was time to get to work.

Pauline ruffled Felix's hair, thinking she didn't miss it a bit. Though getting laid every now and then would've been a damn gift from heaven.

"Cupcakes," she said, relieved to find several stacks lined up along the front of the bakery counter. Her relief quickly left when she saw that every single one was pastel with Easter bunnies and multicolored eggs on top. The note she'd gotten from the school had specified nondenominational cupcakes, but Pauline wasn't sure what that meant, other than Felix's extremely expensive private school was brimming with politically correct bullshit. They wouldn't even call it an Easter Party—it was a Spring Party that just happened to fall a few days before Easter Sunday. What religion didn't celebrate Easter? She knew the Jews didn't get Christmas, but for the love of God, Easter was all about them. Even the pagans got the bunny.

"All right," Pauline said, handing Felix her purse. He slung it over his shoulder the same way she did, and Pauline felt a pang of angst. She worked in interior design. Just about every man in her life was a flaming mo. She'd have to make an effort to meet some straight men soon for both their sakes.

There were six cupcakes in each box, so Pauline scooped up five boxes, thinking the teachers would want some. She couldn't stand most of the faculty at the school, but they loved Felix, and Pauline loved her son, so what was an extra four seventy-five to feed the fat cows who took care of her baby?

She carried the boxes to the front of the store, the smell making her feel hungry and nauseated at the same time, like she could eat every one of them until it made her sick enough to spend the next hour in the toilet. It was too early to smell anything with frosting, that was for sure. She turned around and checked on Felix, who was dragging his feet behind her. He was exhausted, and it was her fault. She contemplated getting him the bag of Gummi Bears he'd wanted, but her cell phone started ringing as soon as she put the cupcakes on the checkout belt and all was forgotten when she recognized the number.

"Yeah?" she asked, watching the boxes slowly make their way down the belt toward the slope-shouldered cashier. The woman was so large that her hands barely met in the middle, like a T. Rex or a baby seal.

"Paulie." Morgan, her boss, sounded frantic. "Can you believe this meeting?"

He was acting like he was on her side, but she knew he'd stab her in the back the minute she let her guard down. She'd enjoy watching him pack up his office after she produced the email at the meeting. "I know," she commiserated. "It's horrible."

"Are you at the grocery store?"

He must have heard the beeps from the scanner. The T. Rex was ringing up each box individually, even though they were all the same. If Pauline hadn't been on the phone, she would have jumped over the counter and scanned them herself. She moved to the end of the checkout and grabbed a couple of plastic bags to expedite the operation. Cradling her phone between her ear and shoulder, she asked, "What do you think's gonna happen?"

"Well, it's clearly not your fault," he said, but she would've bet her right one that the bastard had told his boss that very thing.

"It's not yours, either," she countered, though Morgan had recommended the upholsterer in the first place, probably because the guy looked thirteen and waxed his gym-toned legs to shiny perfection. She knew the little tart was working the gay connection with Morgan, but he was dead wrong if he thought Pauline was going to be the odd girl out. It had taken her sixteen years to work her way up from secretary to assistant to designer. She'd spent endless nights at the Atlanta School of Art and Design getting her degree, dragging into work every morning so she could pay the rent, finally getting to a position where she could breathe a little, could afford to bring a kid into the world the right way—and then some. Felix had all the right clothes, all the good toys, and he went to one of the most expensive schools in the city. Pauline hadn't stopped with her boy, either. She'd gotten her teeth fixed and laser-corrected her eyes. Every week she got a massage, every other week she got a facial and there wasn't a damn root in her hair that showed anything but sassy brown thanks to the girl she saw in Peachtree Hills every month and a half. There was no way in hell she was giving up any of that. Not by a long shot.

It would serve Morgan well to remember where Pauline had started. She'd worked the secretarial pool back before wire transfers and online banking, when they kept all the checks in a wall safe until they could be deposited at the end of the day. After the last office remodel, Pauline had taken a smaller office just so the safe would end up in her space. Just in case, she'd even had a locksmith come in after hours to reset the combination, and she was the only one who knew it. It drove Morgan crazy that he didn't know the combination, and it was a damn good thing he didn't, because the copy of the email covering her ass was locked behind that steel door. For days, she had conjured countless scenarios of herself opening the safe with a flourish, shoving the email in Morgan's face, shaming him in front of their boss and the client.

"What a mess," Morgan sighed, going for the dramatic. "I just can't believe—"

Pauline took her purse from Felix and dug around

for her wallet. He stared longingly at the candy bars as she slid her debit card through the reader and went through the motions. "Uh-huh," she said as Morgan yapped in her ear about what a bastard the client was, how he wouldn't stand by while Pauline's good name was dragged through the mud. If anyone had been around to appreciate it, she would've feigned gagging herself.

"Come on, baby," she said, gently pushing Felix toward the door. She cradled the phone to her ear as she took the bags by the handles, then wondered why she had bothered to bag the boxes in the first place. Plastic boxes, plastic bags; the women at Felix's school would be horrified on behalf of the environment. Pauline stacked the cupcakes back together, pressing against the top box with her chin. She dropped the empty bags in the trash, and used her free hand to dig into her purse for her car keys as she walked through the sliding doors.

"This is absolutely the worst thing that's ever happened to me in my career," Morgan groaned. Despite the crick in her neck, Pauline had forgotten she was still on the phone.

She pressed the button on the remote to open the trunk of the SUV. It slid up with a sigh, and she thought about how much she loved the sound of that tailgate lifting, what a luxury it was to make enough money so that you didn't even have to open your own trunk. She wasn't going to lose it all because of some pretty-boy butt waxer who couldn't be bothered to measure a fucking elevator.

"It's true," she said into the phone, though she hadn't really paid attention to what Morgan was stating as the God's honest. She put the boxes in the back, then pressed the button on the bottom of the trunk to make it close. She was in her car before she realized that Felix wasn't with her.

"Fuck," she whispered, closing the phone. She was out of the car in a flash, scanning the parking lot, which had filled up considerably since she'd been inside the store.

"Felix?" She circled the car, thinking he must be hiding on the other side. He wasn't there.

"Felix?" she called, running back toward the store. She nearly slammed into the sliding doors because they didn't open quickly enough. She asked the cashier, "Did you see my son?" The woman looked confused, and Pauline tersely repeated, "My son. He was just with me. He's got dark hair, he's about this tall, he's six years old?" She gave up, mumbling, "For fucksakes." She ran back to the bakery, then up and down the aisles.

"Felix?" she called, her heart beating so loud she couldn't hear herself speak. She went up and down every aisle, jogging, then running like a madwoman through the store. She ended up at the bakery, about to lose her shit. What had she dressed him in today? His red sneakers. He always wanted to wear his red sneakers because they had Elmo on the soles. Was he in the white shirt or the blue one? What about his pants? Had she pressed his cargo pants this morning or put him in jeans? Why couldn't she remember this?

"I saw a child outside," someone said, and Pauline bolted for the doors again.

She saw Felix walking around the back of the SUV toward the passenger side. He was wearing his white shirt, his cargo pants and his red Elmo sneakers. His hair was still wet in the back where she had smoothed down the cowlick this morning.

Pauline slowed her pace to a fast walk, patting her hand to her chest as if she could calm her heart. She wasn't going to yell at him, because he wouldn't understand and it would only make him scared. She was going to grab him up and kiss every single inch of his body until he started to squirm and then she was going to tell him that if he ever left her side again she was going to throttle his precious little neck.

She wiped away tears as she rounded the rear of the car. Felix was in the Lexus, the door open, his legs dangling down. He wasn't alone.

"Oh, thank you," she gushed to the stranger. She reached out to Felix, saying, "He got lost in the store and—"

Pauline felt an explosion in her head. She collapsed to the pavement like a rag doll. The last thing she saw when she looked up was Elmo laughing down at her from the bottom of Felix's shoe.

CHAPTER SIX

SARA WOKE WITH A START. SHE HAD A MOMENT OF disorientation before she realized that she was in the ICU, sitting in a chair beside Anna's bed. There were no windows in the room. The plastic curtain that acted as a door blocked out all the light from the hallway. Sara leaned forward, looking at her watch in the glow of monitors, and saw that it was eight in the morning. She had worked a double shift yesterday so that she could take off today and catch up on her life: the refrigerator was empty, bills needed to be paid and the dirty laundry was piled so high on the floor of her closet that she could no longer close the door.

And yet, here she was.

Sara sat up in her chair, wincing as her spine adjusted to a position that did not resemble a C. She pressed her fingers to Anna's wrist, though the rhythmic beat of her heart, along with every in and out of breath, was announced by the machines. Sara had no idea if Anna could feel her touch or even knew that Sara was there, but it made her feel better to have the contact.

Maybe it was for the best that Anna was not awake. Her body was fighting against a raging infection that had sent her white blood cell count into the danger zone. Her arm was in an open splint, her right breast removed. Her leg was in traction, metal pins holding together what the car had ripped apart. A plaster cast kept her hips in a fixed position so that the bones would stay aligned as they healed. The pain would be unimaginable, though considering what torture the poor woman had been through, it might not even matter anymore.

What Sara could not get past was the fact that, even in her current state, Anna was an attractive woman—probably one of the qualities that had first caught her abductor's eye. She wasn't movie-star beautiful, but there was something striking about her features that must have garnered a fair share of attention. Probably Sara had watched too many sensational cases on the news, but it didn't make sense that someone as noticeable as Anna would go missing without another person in the world noticing. Whether it was Laci Peterson or Natalee Holloway, the world seemed to pay more attention when a beautiful woman disappeared.

Sara didn't know why she was thinking about such things. Figuring out what happened was Faith Mitchell's job. Sara wasn't involved in the case, and there really had been no reason for her to stay at the hospital last night. Anna was in good hands. The nurses and doctors were down the hallway. Two cops stood guard by the door. Sara should have gone home and climbed into bed, listening to the soft rain, waiting for sleep to come. The problem was that sleep seldom came peacefully, or—worse still—sometimes it came too deeply, and Sara would find herself caught up in a dream, living back in the before time when Jeffrey was alive and her life was everything she had wanted it to be.

Three and a half years had passed since her husband was killed, and Sara could not recall a minute since that some thought of him, some piece of him, did not linger in her mind. In the days after he was gone, Sara had been terrified she would forget something important about Jeffrey. She had made endless lists of everything she had loved about him—the way he smelled when he got out of the shower. The way he liked to sit behind her and brush her hair. The way he tasted when she kissed him. He always carried a handkerchief in his back pocket. He used oatmeal-scented lotion to keep his hands soft. He was a good dancer. He was a good cop. He took care of his mother. He loved Sara.

He *had* loved Sara.

The lists became exhaustive, and turned at times into endless itemizations: songs she could no longer listen to, movies she could no longer see, places she could no longer go. There was page after page of books they had read and holidays they had taken and long weekends spent in bed and fifteen years of a life she knew she would never get back.

Sara had no idea what happened to the lists. Maybe her mother had put them in a box and taken them to her father's storage unit, or maybe Sara had never really made them at all. Maybe in those days after Jeffrey's death, when she had been so distraught that she had welcomed sedation, Sara had simply dreamed up the lists, dreamed up sitting in her dark kitchen for hours on end, recording for posterity all of the wonderful things about her beloved husband.

Xanax, Valium, Ambien, Zoloft. She had nearly poisoned herself trying to make it through each day. Sometimes she would lie in bed, half conscious, and conjure Jeffrey's hands, his mouth, on her body. She would dream of the last time they were together, the way he had stared into her eyes, so sure of himself as he slowly brought her to the edge. Sara would wake to find herself writhing, fighting against the urge to rouse in hopes of a few more moments in that other time.

She wasted hours dwelling on memories of sex with him, recalling every sensation, every inch of his body, in lurid detail. For weeks, she could think only about the first time they made love—not the first time they'd had sex, which was a frenzied, wanton act of passion that had caused Sara to sneak out of her own house in shame the next morning—but the first time they had really held each other, had caressed and touched and cherished each other's bodies the way that lovers do.

He was gentle. He was tender. He always listened to her. He opened the door for her. He trusted her judgment. He built his life around her. He was always there when she needed him.

He used to be there.

After a few months, she remembered stupid things: a fight they had had over which way the toilet paper roll should go on the holder. A disagreement about the time they were supposed to meet at a restaurant. Their second anniversary, when he'd thought driving to Auburn to see a football game was a romantic weekend. A beach trip where she had gotten jealous over the attention a woman at the bar was giving him.

He knew how to fix the radio in the bathroom. He loved reading to her on long trips. He put up with her cat, who urinated in his shoe the first night he officially moved into her house. He was getting laugh lines around his eyes, and she used to kiss them and think about how wonderful it was to be growing older with this man.

And now, when she looked in the mirror and saw a

new line on her own face, a new wrinkle, all she could think was that she was growing old without him.

Sara still wasn't sure how long she had grieved—or if, in fact, she had ever stopped at all. Her mother had always been the strong one, never stronger than when her daughters needed her. Tessa, Sara's sister, had sat with her for days, sometimes holding her, rocking Sara back and forth as if she were a child who needed soothing. Her father fixed things around the house. He took out the trash and walked the dogs and went to the post office to get her mail. Once, she found him sobbing in the kitchen, whispering, "My child . . . My own child . . ." Not for Sara, but for Jeffrey, because he had been the son that her father never had.

"She's just come undone," her mother had whispered on the phone to her aunt Bella. It was an old colloquialism, the sort of thing you didn't think people still said. The phrase fit Sara so completely that she had found herself surrendering to it, imagining her arms, her legs, detaching from her body. What did it matter? What did she need arms or legs or hands or feet for if she could not run to him, if she could not hold him and touch him anymore? Sara had never thought of herself as the type of woman who needed a man to complete her life, but somehow, Jeffrey had come to define her, so that without him, she felt untethered.

Who was she without him, then? Who was this woman who did not want to live without her husband, who just gave up? Maybe that was the real genesis of the grief she felt—not just that she had lost Jeffrey, but that she had lost herself.

Every day, Sara told herself she would stop taking the pills, stop trying to sleep away every painful minute that passed so slowly she was sure weeks had gone by when it was only hours. When she managed to stop taking the pills, she stopped eating. This wasn't a choice. Food tasted rotten in her mouth. Bile would rise in her throat no matter what her mother brought her. Sara stopped leaving the house, stopped taking care of herself. She wanted to stop existing, but she didn't know how to make it happen without compromising everything that she had once believed in.

Finally, her mother had come to her and begged, "Make up your mind. Either live or die, but don't force us to watch you waste away like this."

With a cold eye, Sara had considered her alternatives. Pills. Rope. A gun. A knife. None of them would bring back Jeffrey, and none of them would change what had happened.

More time passed, the clock ticking forward when she longed for it to go back. Sara was coming up on the one-year anniversary when she had realized that if she were gone, then her memories of Jeffrey would be gone, too. They had no children together. They had no lasting monument to their married life. There was just Sara, and the memories that were locked in Sara's mind.

And so she had had no choice but to pull herself back together, to turn back the process of coming undone. Slowly, a lesser shadow of Sara started to go through the motions. She was getting up in the morning, going for a run, working part-time, trying to live the life she had had before, but without Jeffrey. She had valiantly tried to trudge through this semblance of her earlier life, but she simply couldn't do it. She couldn't be in the house where they had loved each other, the town where they had lived together. She couldn't even attend a typical

Sunday dinner at her parents' because there would always be that empty chair beside her, that vacancy that would never be filled.

The job notice at Grady Hospital had been emailed to her by a fellow Emory grad who had no idea what had happened to Sara. He had sent it as a joke, as if to say, "Who would go back to this hellhole?" but Sara had called the hospital administrator the next day. She had interned at Grady in the ER. She knew the great, creaking beast that was the public health system. She knew that working in an emergency room took over your life, your soul. She had rented out her house, sold her pediatric practice, given away most of her furniture, and moved to Atlanta a month later.

And here she was. Two more years had passed and Sara was still stagnating. She didn't have many friends outside of work, but then she'd never been a social person. Her life had always revolved around her family. Her sister Tessa had always been her best friend, her mother her closest confidante. Jeffrey was the chief of police for Grant County. Sara was the coroner. They had worked together more often than not, and she wondered now if their relationship would have been as close if they had each gone their separate ways every day and only glimpsed one another over the dinner table.

Love, like water, always flowed down the path of least resistance.

Sara had grown up in a small town. The last time she had seriously dated, girls were not allowed to call boys on the telephone and boys were required to ask the girl's father for permission to date his daughter. Those practices were quaint now, almost laughable, but Sara found herself wishing for them. She didn't understand the nuances of adult dating, but she had forced herself to try, to see if that part of her had died with Jeffrey, too.

There had been two men since she moved to Atlanta, both fixed up through nurses at the hospital and both exhaustingly unremarkable. The first man had been handsome and smart and successful, but there was nothing else behind his perfect smile and good manners, and he hadn't called back after Sara had burst into tears the first time they'd kissed. The second man had been three months ago. The experience was a little better, or maybe she was fooling herself. She had slept with him once, but only after four glasses of wine. Sara had gritted her teeth the entire time as if the act was a test she was determined to pass. The man had broken it off with her the next day, which Sara had not realized until she checked her voicemail at home a week later.

If she had only one regret about her life with Jeffrey, it would be this one: Why hadn't she kissed him more? Like most married couples, they had developed a secret language of intimacy. A long kiss usually signaled the desire for sex, not simple affection. There were the odd pecks on the cheek and the quick smacks before they went to work, but nothing like when they had first started seeing each other—when passionate kisses were titillating and exotic gifts that didn't always lead to ripping off each other's clothes.

Sara wanted to be back at that beginning, to enjoy those long hours on the couch with Jeffrey's head in her lap, kissing him deeply, her fingers running through his soft hair. She longed for those stolen moments in parked cars and in hallways and movie theaters when Sara thought she would stop breathing if she didn't feel his mouth pressed to hers. She wanted that surprise of seeing him at work, that thump in her heart when she caught sight of him walking down the street. She wanted that thrill in her stomach when the phone rang and she heard his voice on the line. She wanted that rush of blood to her center when she was driving alone in her car or walking down the aisle at the drugstore and smelled him on her skin.

She wanted her lover.

The vinyl curtain slid back, squeaking on the rail. Jill Marino, one of the ICU nurses, flashed Sara a smile as she put Anna's chart on the bed.

"Have a good night?" Jill asked. She bustled around the room, checking the leads, making sure the IV was running. "Blood gases came back."

Sara opened the chart and checked the numbers. Last night, the pulse oximeter on Anna's finger kept detecting low oxygen levels in her blood. They seemed to have leveled out on their own this morning. Sara was constantly humbled by the human body's ability to heal itself. "Makes you feel superfluous, doesn't it?"

"Maybe doctors," Jill teased. "Nurses?"

"Good point." Sara stuck her hand into her lab coat pocket, feeling the letter inside. She had changed into fresh scrubs after working on Anna last night, automatically moving the letter to the pocket of the clean coat. Maybe she should open it. Maybe she should sit down and rip it open and get it over with once and for all.

Jill asked, "Something wrong?"

Sara shook her head. "No. Thanks for putting up with me last night."

"You made my job a little easier," the nurse admitted. The ICU was, as usual, packed to the rafters. "I'll call you if anything changes." Jill put her hand to

Anna's cheek, smiling down at the woman. "Maybe our girl will wake up today."

"I'm sure she will." Sara didn't think Anna could hear her, but it made her feel good to hear the words said.

The two cops stationed outside the room tipped their hats to Sara as she left the room. She could feel their eyes follow her as she walked down the hall—not because they thought she was attractive, but because they knew she was a cop's widow. Sara had never discussed Jeffrey with anyone at Grady, but there were enough cops in and out of the ER every day that the news had spread. It quickly became one of those known secrets that everyone talked about, just not in front of Sara. She hadn't intended to become a tragic figure, but it kept people from asking questions, so she did not complain.

The great mystery was why she had so easily talked about Jeffrey with Faith Mitchell. Sara liked to think that Faith was just a really good detective rather than admit what was probably closer to the truth, which was that Sara was lonely. Her sister was living halfway around the world, her parents were four hours and a lifetime away, and Sara's days were filled with little more than work and whatever was on television when she got home.

What's worse, she had a nagging suspicion that it wasn't Faith she'd found enticing, but the case. Jeffrey had always used Sara as a sounding board during his investigations, and she missed having that part of her brain engaged.

Last night, for the first time in forever, the last thing on Sara's mind before she fell asleep had not been Jeffrey, but Anna. Who had abducted her? Why had she been chosen? What clues had been left on her body that might explain the motivations of the animal who'd hurt her? Talking to Faith in the cafeteria last night, Sara had finally felt like her brain was doing something more useful than just keeping her alive. And it was probably the last time she would feel that way again for a very long while.

Sara rubbed her eyes, trying to wake herself up. She had known that life without Jeffrey would be painful. What she wasn't prepared for was that it would be so damn irrelevant.

She was almost to the elevators when her cell phone rang. She turned on her heel, walking back toward Anna's room as she opened the phone. "I'm on my way."

Mary Schroder said, "Sonny's about ten minutes out."

Sara stopped, her heart dropping in her chest at the nurse's words. Sonny was Mary's husband, a patrolman who worked the early shift. "Is he all right?"

"Sonny?" she asked. "Of course he is. Where are you?"

"I'm upstairs in the ICU." Sara changed course, heading back toward the elevator. "What's going on?"

"Sonny got a call about a little boy abandoned at the City Foods on Ponce de Leon. Six years old. Poor thing was left in the back of the car for at least three hours."

Sara punched the button for the elevator. "Where's the mother?"

"Missing. Her purse is on the front seat, the keys are in the ignition and there's blood on the ground beside the car."

Sara felt her heart speed back up. "Did the boy see anything?"

"He's too upset to talk, and Sonny's useless. He

doesn't know how to deal with kids that age. Are you on your way down?"

"I'm waiting for the elevator." Sara double-checked the time. "Is Sonny sure about the three hours?"

"The store manager noticed the car when he came into work. He said the mother was there earlier, freaking out because she couldn't find her kid."

Sara jammed the button again, knowing full well the gesture was useless. "Why did he take three hours to call it in?"

"Because people are assholes," Mary answered. "People are just plain, goddamn assholes."

CHAPTER SEVEN

FAITH'S RED MINI WAS PARKED IN HER DRIVEWAY when she woke up that morning. Amanda must have followed Will here, then taken him home. He had probably thought he was doing Faith a favor, but Faith still wanted to rake him over the coals. When Will had called this morning to tell her that he would pick her up at their usual eight-thirty, she had snapped a "Fine" that seemed to float over his head.

Her anger had evened out somewhat when Will had told her what had happened last night—his idiotic foray into the cave, finding the second victim, dealing with Amanda. The last part sounded particularly challenging: Amanda never made things easy. Will had sounded exhausted, and Faith's heart went out to him as he described the woman hanging in the tree, but as soon as she got off the phone, she was furious with him all over again.

What was he doing going down into that cave alone with no one but that idiot Fierro topside? Why the hell hadn't he called Faith to come help search for the second victim? Why in God's name did he think he was doing her a favor by actively preventing her from doing her job? Did he think she wasn't capable, wasn't good enough? Faith wasn't some useless mascot. Her mother had been a cop. Faith had worked her way up from patrol to homicide detective faster than anyone else on the squad. She hadn't been picking daisies when Will stumbled across her. She wasn't damn Watson to his Sherlock Holmes.

Faith had forced herself to take a deep breath. She was just sane enough to realize that her level of fury might be out of proportion. It wasn't until she sat down at the kitchen table and measured her blood sugar that she realized why. She was hovering around one-fifty again, which, according to *Your Life with Diabetes,* could make a person nervous and irritable. It didn't help her nervousness and irritability one whit when she tried to inject herself with the insulin pen.

Her hands were steady as she turned the dial for what she hoped were the correct units, but her leg started shaking as she tried to stick herself with the needle, so that she looked like a dog who was enjoying a particularly good scratch. There had to be some part of her unconscious brain that kept her hand hovering frozen over her shaking thigh, unable to willfully inflict pain on herself. It was probably somewhere near that damaged region that made it impossible for Faith to enter into a long-term relationship with a man.

"Screw it," she had said, almost like a sneeze, jamming the pen down, pressing the button. The needle burned like hellfire, even though the literature on the device claimed it was virtually pain-free. Maybe after sticking yourself six zillion times a week, a needle jamming into your leg or your abdomen felt relatively painless, but Faith wasn't to that point yet and she couldn't imagine herself ever being there. She was sweating so badly by the time she pulled out the needle that her underarms were sticky.

She spent the next hour dividing her time between the phone and the Internet, reaching out to various governmental organizations to get the investigation moving while scaring the ever-loving shit out of herself by investiGoogling type 2 diabetes on her laptop computer. The first ten minutes were spent on hold with the Atlanta Police Department while she looked for an alternate diagnosis in case Sara Linton was wrong. That proved to be a pipe dream, and by the time Faith was on hold with the GBI's Atlanta lab, she had stumbled upon her first diabetic blog. She found another, then another— thousands of people letting loose about the travails of living with a chronic disease.

Faith read about pumps and monitors and diabetic retinopathy and poor circulation and loss of libido and all the other wonderful things diabetes could bring into your life. There were miracle cures and device reviews and one nut who claimed that diabetes was a government plot to extract billions of dollars from the unsuspecting public in order to wage the war for oil.

As Faith waded through the conspiracy pages, she was ready to believe anything that might get her out of having to live the rest of her life under constant measurement. A lifetime of following every fad diet *Cosmo* could spit out had taught her to count carbs and calories, but the thought of turning into a human pincushion was almost too much to bear. Thoroughly depressed— and on hold with Equifax—she had quickly clicked back to the pharmaceutical pages with their images of smiling, healthy diabetics riding bicycles and doing yoga and playing with puppies, kittens, small children, kites, sometimes a combination of all four. Surely, the woman swinging around the adorable toddler wasn't suffering from vaginal dryness.

Surely, after spending all morning on the telephone, Faith could have called the doctor's office and scheduled an appointment for later this afternoon. She had the number Sara had scribbled down at her elbow—of course she'd done a search on Delia Wallace, checking to see if she'd been sued for malpractice or had a history of drunk driving. Faith knew every detail of the doctor's education as well as her driving record, but still could not make the call.

Faith knew she was looking at desk time because of the pregnancy. Amanda had dated Faith's uncle Ted until the relationship had petered out around the time Faith had entered junior high. Boss Amanda was very different from Aunt Amanda. She was going to make Faith's life miserable in the way that only a woman can make another woman miserable for doing the things that most women do. That sort of living hell Faith was prepared for, but would Faith be allowed to return to her job even though she had diabetes?

Could she go out in the field, carry a gun and round up the bad guys if her blood sugar was out of whack? Exercise could lead to a precipitous drop. What if she was chasing a suspect and fainted? Emotional moments could stress her blood sugar as well. What if she was interviewing a witness and didn't realize she was acting crazy until internal affairs was called in? And what about Will? Could she be trusted to have his back? For all her complaints about her partner, Faith had a deep devotion to the man. She was at times his navigator, his buffer against the world and his big sister. How could she protect Will if she couldn't protect herself?

Maybe she wouldn't even have a choice in the matter.

Faith stared at her computer screen, contemplating doing another search to see what the standard policy was for diabetics in law enforcement. Were they shoved behind desks until they atrophied or quit? Were they fired? Her hands went to the laptop, her fingers resting on the keyboard. As with the insulin pen, her brain froze her muscles, not letting her press the keys. She tapped her finger lightly on the *H* in a nervous tick, feeling the flop sweat come back. When the phone rang, she nearly jumped out of her skin.

"Good morning," Will said. "I'm outside when you're ready."

Faith shut down the laptop. She gathered up the notes she had taken from her phone calls, loaded her diabetes paraphernalia into her purse and walked out the front door without a look back.

Will was in an unmarked black Dodge Charger, what they called a G-ride, slang for government-issued car. This particular beauty had a key scratch cutting along the panel over the back tire and a large antenna mounted on a spring so the scanner could pick up all signals within a hundred-mile area. A blind three-year-old would've been able to tell it was a cop car.

She opened the door and Will said, "I've got Jacquelyn Zabel's Atlanta address."

He meant the second victim, the woman who had been hanging upside down in the tree.

Faith got in the car and buckled her seatbelt. "How?"

"The Walton Beach sheriff called me back this morning. They checked with her neighbors down there. Apparently, her mother just went into a retirement home and Jacquelyn was up here packing up the house to sell it."

"Where's the house?"

"Inman Park. Charlie's going to meet us there. I've reached out to the Atlanta police for some feet on the ground. They say they can give me two patrols for a couple of hours." He reversed the car down the driveway, glancing at Faith. "You look better. Did you get some sleep?"

Faith didn't answer his question. She pulled out her notebook, going through the list of things she had accomplished on the phone this morning. "I had the splinters of wood that were taken from underneath Anna's fingernails transferred to our lab. I sent a tech to fingerprint her at the hospital first thing. I put out a statewide APB for any missing women matching Anna's age and description—they're going to try to send over a sketch artist for a drawing. Her face is pretty bruised. I'm not sure anyone would recognize her from a photograph."

She flipped to the next page, skimming her notes. "I checked the NCIC and VICAP for comparable cases—the FBI isn't tracking anything similar, but I put our details into the database just in case something hits." She went to the next page. "I put an alert on Jacquelyn Zabel's credit cards so we'll know if someone tries to use them. I called the morgue; the autopsy is scheduled to start around eleven. I put in a call to the Coldfields—the man and wife in the Buick that hit Anna. They said we could come by and talk to them at the shelter where Judith volunteers, even though they've already told that nice Detective Galloway everything they know, and speaking of that prick, I woke up Jeremy at school this morning and made him leave a message on Galloway's voicemail saying he was from the IRS and needed to talk to him about some irregularities."

Will chuckled at this last bit.

"We're waiting on Rockdale County to fax over the crime-scene reports and whatever witness statements they have. Other than that, that's all I've got." Faith closed her notebook. "So, what did you do this morning?"

He nodded toward the cup holder. "I got you some hot chocolate."

Faith stared longingly at the takeout cup, dying to lick off the foamy puddle of whipped cream that had squirted through the slit in the lid. She had lied to Sara Linton about her usual diet. The last time Faith had jogged anywhere, she had been rushing from her car to the front door of Zesto's, hoping to get a milk shake before they closed. Breakfast was usually a Pop-Tart and a Diet Coke, but this morning, she had eaten a boiled egg and a piece of dry toast, the kind of thing they served at the county jail. The sugar in the hot chocolate would probably kill her, though, and she said, "No, thanks," before she could change her mind.

"You know," he began, "if you're trying to lose weight, I could—"

"Will," she interrupted. "I've been on a diet for the last eighteen years of my life. If I want to let myself go, I'm going to let myself go."

"I didn't say—"

"Besides, I've only gained five pounds," she lied. "It's not like I need a Goodyear sign strapped to my ass."

Will glanced at the purse in her lap, his mouth drawn. Finally, he said, "I'm sorry."

"Thank you."

"If you're not going to . . ." He let his words trail off, taking the cup out of the holder. Faith turned on the radio so she wouldn't have to listen to him swallow. The volume was low, and she heard the dull murmur of news coming from the speakers. She pressed the buttons until she found something soft and innocuous that wouldn't get on her nerves.

She felt the seatbelt tense as Will slowed for a pedestrian darting across the road. Faith had no excuse for snapping at him, and he wasn't a stupid man—he obviously knew that something was wrong but, as usual, didn't want to push. She felt a pang of guilt for keeping secrets, but then again, Will wasn't exactly known for sharing. It had only been by accident that she'd stumbled onto the realization that he was dyslexic. At least, she thought it was dyslexia. There was certainly some reading issue there, but God knew what it was. Faith had figured out from watching him that Will could make out some words on his own, but it took forever, and he was wrong more often than not about the content. When she'd tried to ask him about the diagnosis, Will had shut her down so tersely that Faith had felt her face flush in embarrassment for asking the question in the first place.

She hated to admit that he was right to hide the problem. Faith had worked on the force long enough to know that most police officers were barely out of the primordial ooze. They tended to be a conservative lot, and they didn't exactly embrace the unusual. Maybe dealing with the most freakish elements society had to offer made them reject any semblance of abnormality in their own ranks. Whatever the reason, Faith knew that if word of Will's dyslexia got out, there wasn't a cop around who would let it pass. He already had trouble fitting in. This would make him a permanent outsider.

Will took a right on Moreland Avenue, and she wondered how he knew which way to go. Directions were an issue for him, left and right an insurmountable problem. Despite this, he was incredibly adept at hiding his disability. For those times when his shockingly good memory wouldn't suffice, he had a digital recorder that he kept in his pocket the way that most cops kept a notebook. Sometimes he slipped up and made a mistake, but most of the time, Faith found herself in awe of his accomplishments. He had gotten through school and then college with no one recognizing there was a problem. Growing up in an orphanage hadn't exactly given him a good start in life. His success was a lot to be proud of, which made the fact that he had to hide his disability even more heartbreaking.

They were in the middle of Little Five Points, an eclectic part of the city that blended seedy bars and fashionably overpriced boutiques, when Will finally spoke. "You okay?"

"I was just thinking," Faith began, though she didn't share her actual thoughts. "What do we know about the victims?"

"Both of them have dark hair. Both are fit, attractive. We think the woman at the hospital's name is Anna. The license says the one hanging in the tree is Jacquelyn Zabel."

"What about fingerprints?"

"There was a latent on the pocketknife that belongs to Zabel. The print on her license came back unknown—it doesn't match Zabel and there's no match on the computer."

"We should compare it to Anna's fingerprints and see if she's the one who made it. If Anna touched the license, then that puts both Anna and Jacquelyn Zabel in the cave together."

"Good idea."

Faith felt like she was pulling teeth, though she couldn't blame Will for being gun-shy, considering how mercurial her mood was lately. "Have you found out anything else about Zabel?"

He shrugged, as if there wasn't much, but reeled off, "Jacquelyn Zabel is thirty-eight, unmarried, no children. The Florida Law Enforcement Bureau is giving us an assist—they're going to go through her place, do a phone dump, try to find next of kin other than the mother who was living in Atlanta. The sheriff says no one in town knows Zabel that well. She has one sort-of friend next door who's been watering her plants but doesn't know anything about her. There's been an ongoing feud with some of the other neighbors about people leaving out their trashcans on the street. The sheriff said Zabel's made a few nuisance complaints in the past six months over loud noises from pool parties and cars being parked in front of her house."

Faith bit back the urge to ask him why he hadn't told her all this in the first place. "Has the sheriff ever met Zabel?"

"He said he took a couple of the nuisance calls himself and didn't find her to be a very pleasant person."

"You mean, he said she was a bitch," Faith clarified. For a cop, Will had a surprisingly clean vocabulary. "What did she do for a living?"

"Real estate. The market's been off, but she looks

pretty set—house on the beach, BMW, a boat at the marina."

"Wasn't the battery you found in the cave for marine use?"

"I had the sheriff check her boat. The battery's still there."

"It was worth a shot," Faith mumbled, thinking they were still grasping at straws.

"Charlie says the battery we found in the cave is at least ten years old. All the numbers are worn off. He's going to see if he can get some more information on it, but chances are it's a wash. You can pick up those things at yard sales." Will shrugged, adding, "The only thing it tells us is that the guy knew what he was going to do with it."

"Why is that?"

"A car battery is designed to deliver a short, large current like you need to crank your car. Once the car starts, the alternator takes over, and the battery isn't needed again until the next time you need to start the engine. A marine battery like from the cave is what's called a deep-cycle battery, meaning it gives a steady current over a long period of time. You'd ruin a car battery pretty quickly if you tried to use it the way our guy was. The marine battery would last for hours."

Faith let his words hang in the air, her brain trying to make sense of them. There was no way to make sense of it, though: What had been done to those women was not the product of a sound mind.

She asked, "Where's Jacquelyn Zabel's BMW?"

"Not in her driveway in Florida. And not at her mother's house."

"Did you put out an APB on the car?"

"In both Florida and Georgia." He reached around to the back seat and pulled out a handful of folders. They were all color-coded, and he thumbed through until he found the orange one, which he handed to Faith. She opened it to find a printout from the Florida Department of Motor Vehicles. Jacquelyn Alexandra Zabel's driver's license stared back at her, the picture showing a very attractive woman with long dark hair and brown eyes. "She's pretty," Faith said.

"So's Anna," Will provided. "Brown hair, brown eyes."

"Our guy has a type." Faith turned to the next page and read aloud from the woman's driving record, "Zabel's car is a 2008 red BMW 540i. Speeding ticket six months ago for going eighty in a fifty-five. Running a stop sign in a school zone last month. Failure to stop at a roadblock two weeks ago, refused to take a Breathalyzer, court date pending." She thumbed through the pages. "Her record was pretty clean until recently."

Will absently scratched his forearm as he waited for another light to change. "Maybe something happened."

"What about the notes Charlie found in the cave?"

" 'I will not deny myself,' " he recalled, taking out the blue folder. "The pages are being fingerprinted. They're from a standard spiral notebook, written in pencil, probably by a woman."

Faith looked at the copy, the same sentence written over and over again like she'd done many times herself as punishment back in junior high school. "And the rib?"

He was still scratching his arm. "No sign of the rib in the cave or the immediate area."

"A souvenir?"

"Maybe," he said. "Jacquelyn didn't have any cuts on

her body." He corrected, "I mean, any deep cuts like what Anna had where the rib was removed. Both of them looked like they'd been through the same kind of stuff, though."

"Torture." Faith tried to put herself in the mind of their perpetrator. "He keeps one woman on the top of the bed and one woman underneath. Maybe he trades them out—does one horrible thing to Anna, then swaps her out for Jacquelyn and does the horrible thing to her."

"Then trades them back," Will said. "So, maybe Jacquelyn heard what happened to Anna with the rib, knew what was coming and chewed her way through the rope around her wrist."

"She must have found the penknife, or had it with her under the bed."

"Charlie examined the slats under the bed. He put them back together in sequence. The tip of a very sharp knife ran in the center of each slat where someone cut the rope from underneath the bed, head to foot."

Faith suppressed a shudder as she stated the obvious. "Jacquelyn was under the bed while Anna was being mutilated."

"And she was probably alive while we were searching the woods."

Faith opened her mouth to say something along the lines of "It's not your fault," but she knew the words were useless. She felt guilt herself for not being out there during the search. She could not imagine how Will was feeling, considering he'd been blundering around in the woods while the woman was dying.

Instead, she asked, "What's wrong with your arm?"

"What do you mean?"

"You keep scratching it."

He stopped the car and squinted up at the street signs. "Hamilton," Faith read.

He checked his watch, a ploy he used for telling left from right. "Both victims were probably well-off," he said, taking a right onto Hamilton. "Anna was malnourished, but her hair was nice—the color, I mean—and she'd had a manicure recently. The polish on her nails was chipped, but it looked professionally done."

Faith didn't press him on how he knew a professional manicure from an amateur one. "These women weren't prostitutes. They had homes and probably jobs. It's unusual for a killer to choose victims who will be missed."

"Motive, means, opportunity," he listed, stating the foundation for any investigation. "Motive is sex and torture and maybe taking the rib."

"Means," Faith said, trying to think of ways the killer might have abducted his victims. "Maybe he rigs their cars to break down? He could be a mechanic."

"BMWs are equipped with driver assist. You just press a button and they're on the phone with you and they send out a tow truck."

"Nice," Faith said. The Mini was a poor man's BMW, which meant you had to use your own phone if you got stuck. "Jacquelyn's moving her mother's house. That means she probably contracted with a moving company or liquidation agent."

"She'd need a termite letter to sell the house," Will added. You couldn't get a mortgage on a house in most of the South without first proving that termites weren't feasting on the foundation. "So, our bad guy could be an exterminator, a contractor, a mover . . ."

Faith got out a pen and started a list on the back of

the orange folder. "Her real estate license wouldn't transfer up here, so she'd have to have an Atlanta agent to sell the house."

"Unless she did a for-sale-by-owner, in which case she could have had open houses, could've had strangers in and out all the time."

"Why didn't anyone notice she was missing?" Faith asked. "Sara said Anna was taken at least four days ago."

"Who's Sara?"

"Sara Linton," Faith said. He shrugged, and she studied him carefully. Will never forgot names. He never forgot anything. "The doctor from yesterday?"

"Is that her name?"

Faith resisted a "Come on."

He asked, "How would she know how long Anna was kept?"

"She used to be a coroner in some county way down South."

Will's eyebrows went up. He slowed to look at another sign. "A coroner? That's weird."

He was one to talk. "She was a coroner *and* a pediatrician."

Will mumbled as he tried to make out the sign. "I took her for a dancer."

"Woodland," Faith read. "A dancer? She's twenty feet tall."

"Dancers can be tall."

Faith clenched her teeth together so that she would not laugh out loud.

"Anyway." He didn't add anything else, using the word to indicate an end to that part of the conversation.

She studied his profile as he turned the wheel, the way he stared so intently at the road ahead. Will was an attractive man, arguably handsome, but he was about as self-aware as a snail. His wife, Angie Polaski, seemed to see beyond his quirks—among them his painful inability to conduct small talk and the anachronistic three-piece suits he insisted on wearing. In return, Will seemed to overlook the fact that Angie had slept with half the Atlanta police force, including—if graffiti in the ladies' toilet on the third floor was to be believed—a couple of women. They had met each other at the Atlanta Children's Home, and Faith supposed this was the connection that bound them together. They were both orphans, both abandoned by, presumably, crappy parents. As with everything in his personal life, Will did not share the details. Faith hadn't even known that he and Angie were officially married until Will showed up one morning wearing a wedding band.

And she had never known Will to even give a passing glance to another woman until now.

"This is it," he said, taking a right down a narrow, tree-lined street. She saw the white crime-scene van parked in front of a very small house. Charlie Reed and two of his assistants were already going through the trash on the side of the road. Whoever had taken out the trash was the neatest person in the world. There were boxes stacked up on the curb, three rows of two, each labeled with the contents. Beside these were a bunch of large black garbage bags lined up like a row of sentries. On the other side of the mailbox were a precisely aligned mattress and box spring, and a couple of pieces of furniture that the local trash trollers hadn't spotted yet. Behind Charlie's van were two empty Atlanta police cruisers, and Faith assumed the patrolmen Will had requested were already canvassing the neighborhood.

Faith said, "Her husband was a cop. Sounds like he was killed in the line of duty. I hope they fried the bastard."

"Whose husband?"

He knew damn well who she was talking about. "Sara Linton's. The dancing doctor."

Will put the car in park and cut the engine. "I asked Charlie to hold off on processing the house." He took two pairs of latex gloves out of his jacket pocket and handed one to Faith. "My guess is that it's packed up for the move, but you never know."

Faith got out of the car. Charlie would have to close off the house as a crime scene as soon as he started collecting evidence. Letting Will and Faith check it out first meant that they wouldn't have to wait for everything to be processed before they started following up on clues.

"Hey there," Charlie called, tossing them an almost cheery wave. "Got here just in time." He indicated the bags. "Goodwill was about to cart it off when we pulled up."

"What've you got?"

He showed them the tags on the bags where the contents had been neatly labeled. "Clothes, mostly. Kitchen items, old blenders, that sort of thing." He flashed a smile. "Beats the hell out of that hole in the ground."

Will asked, "When do you think we'll have the analysis back from the cave?"

"Amanda put a rush on it. There was a lot of shit down there, literally and figuratively. We prioritized the pieces we thought might be more important. You know that DNA from the fluids will take forty-eight hours. Fingerprints are run through the computer as they're developed. If there's something earth-shattering down there, we'll know by tomorrow morning at the latest." He mimed holding a telephone receiver to his ear. "You'll be the first call."

Will indicated the garbage bags. "Find anything useful?"

Charlie handed him a packet of mail. Will snapped off the rubber band and looked at each envelope before handing it to Faith. "Postmark's recent," he noticed. He could easily read numbers, if not words, which was one of the many useful tools he used to conceal his problem. He was also good at recognizing company logos. "Gas bill, electric, cable . . ."

Faith read the name of the addressee: "Gwendolyn Zabel. That's a lovely old name."

"Like Faith," Charlie said, and she was a little surprised to hear him utter something so personal. He hastily covered for it, saying, "And she lived in a lovely old house."

Faith wouldn't have called the small bungalow lovely, but it was certainly quaint with its gray shingles and red trim. Nothing had been done to update the place, or even simply keep it up. The gutters sagged from years of leaves and the roofline resembled a camel's back. The grass was neatly trimmed, but there were no flower beds or carefully sculpted shrubs typical of Atlanta homes. All the other houses on the street but one had a second story added on or had simply been torn down to make way for a mansion. Gwendolyn Zabel must have been one of the last holdouts, the only two-bedroom, one-bath in the area. Faith wondered if the neighbors were glad to see the old woman go. Her daughter must have been happy to have the check from the sale. A house like this had probably cost around thirty thousand dollars when it was first built. Now the land alone would be worth around half a million.

Will asked Charlie, "Did you get the door unlocked?"

"It was unlocked when I got here," he told them. "Me and the guys took a look around. Nothing jumped out, but you've got first dibs." He indicated the trash pile in front of him. "This is just the tip of the iceberg. The place is a freakin' mess."

Will and Faith exchanged a look as they walked toward the house. Inman Park was far from Mayberry. You didn't leave your door unlocked unless you were hoping for an insurance claim.

Faith pushed open the front door, walking back into the 1970s as she crossed the threshold. The green shag carpet on the floor was deep enough to cup her tennis shoes, and the mirrored wallpaper was kind enough to remind her that she'd put on fifteen pounds in the last month.

"Wow," Will said, glancing around the front room. It was packed with untold amounts of crap: stacks of newspapers, paperback books, magazines.

"This can't be safe to live in."

"Imagine how it looked with all the stuff on the street back inside." Faith picked up a rusted hand blender sitting on top of a stack of *Life* magazines. "Sometimes old people start collecting things and they can't stop."

"This is crazy," he said, wiping his hand along a stack of old forty-fives. Dust flew into the stale air.

"My grandmother's house was worse than this,"

Faith told him. "It took us a whole week just to be able to walk through to the kitchen."

"Why would someone do this?"

"I don't know," she admitted. Her grandfather had died when Faith was a child, and her granny Mitchell had lived on her own for most of her life. She had started collecting things in her fifties, and by the time she was moved into a nursing home, the house had been filled to the rafters with useless things. Looking around another lonely old woman's house, seeing a similar accumulation, made Faith wonder if someday Jeremy would be saying the same thing about Faith's housekeeping.

At least he would have a little brother or sister to help him. Faith put her hand to her stomach, wondering for the first time about the child growing inside of her. Was it a girl or a boy? Would it have her blonde hair or its father's dark Latino looks? Jeremy looked nothing like his father, thank God. Faith's first love had been a gangly hillbilly with a build that was reminiscent of Spike from the Peanuts cartoon. As a baby, Jeremy had been almost delicate, like a thin piece of porcelain. He'd had the sweetest little feet. Those first few days, Faith had spent hours staring at his tiny toes, kissing the bottoms of his heels. She had thought that he was the most remarkable thing on the face of the earth. He had been her little doll.

"Faith?"

She dropped her hand, wondering what had come over her. She'd taken enough insulin this morning. Maybe she was just feeling the typical hormonal swings of pregnancy that had made being fourteen such a pleasure for Faith as well as everyone around her. How on earth was she going to go through this again? And how was she going to do it alone?

"Faith?"

"You don't have to keep saying my name, Will." She indicated the back of the house. "Go check the kitchen. I'll take the bedrooms."

He gave her a careful look before heading into the kitchen.

Faith walked down the hallway toward the back rooms, picking her way through broken blenders and toasters and telephones. She wondered if the old woman had scavenged for these things or if she had accumulated them over a lifetime. The framed photographs on the walls looked ancient, some of them in sepia and black-and-white. Faith scanned them as she made her way back, wondering when people had started smiling for photographs, and why. She had some older photos of her mother's grandparents that were particularly treasured. They had lived on a farm during the Depression, and a traveling photographer had taken a shot of their small family as well as a mule that was called Big Pete. Only the mule had been smiling.

There was no Big Pete on Gwendolyn Zabel's wall, but some of the color photographs showed not one but two different young girls, both with dark brown hair hanging down past their pencil-thin waists. They were a few years apart in age, but definitely sisters. None of the more recent photographs showed the two posing together. Jacquelyn's sister seemed to prefer desert settings for the shots she sent her mother, while Jacquelyn's photos tended to show her posing on the beach, a bikini low across her boyishly thin hips. Faith could not help but think if she looked that great at thirty-eight years old, she'd be taking pictures of herself wearing a bikini, too. There were very few recent pictures of the sister, who appeared to have grown plumper with age. Faith hoped she had kept in touch with her mother. They could do a reverse trace on the telephone and find her that way.

The first bedroom did not have a door. Stacks of debris filled the room—more newspapers and magazines. There were some boxes, but for the most part, the small bedroom was filled with so much trash it was impossible to go more than a few feet in. A musty odor filled the air, and Faith remembered a story she'd seen on the news many years ago about a woman who'd gotten a paper cut from an old magazine and ended up dying from some strange disease. She backed out of the room and glanced into the bathroom. More junk, but someone had cleared a path to the toilet and scrubbed it clean. A toothbrush and some other toiletries were lined up on the sink. There were piles of garbage bags in the bathtub. The shower curtain was almost black with mold.

Faith had to turn sideways to get past the door to the master bedroom. She saw the reason as soon as she was inside. There was an old rocking chair near the door, so piled with clothes that it was ready to topple over except for the door propping it up. More clothes were scattered around the room, the sort of stuff that would be called vintage and sold for hundreds of dollars down the street in the funky clothing stores of Little Five Points.

The house was warm, which made it more difficult for Faith to get her sweaty hands into the latex gloves. She ignored the pinprick of dried blood on the tip of her finger, not wanting to think about anything else that would turn her into a sobbing mess.

She started on the chest of drawers first. All of the

drawers were open, so it was just a matter of pushing around clothes, looking for stashed letters or an address book that might list family relations. The bed was neatly made, the only item in the house about which "neat" could be said to describe it. There was no telling if Jacquelyn Zabel had slept in her mother's bedroom or if she had opted for a hotel downtown.

Or maybe not. Faith saw an open duffel bag sitting beside a laptop case on the floor. She should have spotted the items immediately, because they were both obviously out of place, with their distinctive designer logos and soft leather shells. Faith checked the laptop case, finding a MacBook Air that her son would've killed for. She booted it up, but the welcome screen asked for a username and password. Charlie would have to send it through the proper channels to try to crack it, but in Faith's experience, Macs that had been password-protected were impossible to decode, even by the manufacturer.

Next, Faith looked through the duffel. The clothes inside were designer—Donna Karan, Jones of New York. The Jimmy Choos were particularly impressive, especially to Faith, who was wearing a skirt that was the equivalent of a camping tent, since she couldn't find any pants in her closet that would button anymore. Jacquelyn Zabel apparently suffered no such sartorial quandaries, and Faith wondered why someone who could obviously afford otherwise chose to stay in this awful house.

So, Jacquelyn had apparently been sleeping in the room. The neatly made bed, a glass of water and a pair of reading glasses on the table beside it all pointed to a recent inhabitant. There was also a giant, hospital-size bottle of aspirin. Faith opened the container and found it half empty. She would probably need some aspirin herself if she were packing up her mother's home. Faith had seen the heartbreak her father suffered when he'd had to put his mother in an assisted-living facility. The man had passed away years ago, but Faith knew that he had never gotten over having to put his mother in a home.

Unbidden, Faith felt her eyes fill with tears. She let out a groan, wiping her eyes with the back of her hand. Since she'd seen a plus sign on the pregnancy test, a day hadn't gone by without Faith's brain conjuring some story to make her burst into tears.

She returned to the duffel. She was feeling around for pieces of paper—a notebook, a journal, a plane ticket—when she heard yelling coming from the other side of the house. Faith found Will in the kitchen. A very large and very angry woman was screaming in his face.

"You pigs have no right to be here!"

Faith thought the woman looked just like the type of aging hippie who would use the word "pigs." Her hair was braided down her back and she was wearing a horse-blanket shawl around her body in lieu of a shirt. Faith guessed that the woman was officially the last holdout in the neighborhood, soon to be the crappiest house on the street. She didn't look like the yoga-loving mommies who probably lived in the renovated mansions.

Will remained remarkably cool, leaning against the refrigerator with a hand in his pocket. "Ma'am, I need you to calm down."

"Fuck you," she shot back. "Fuck you, too," she added, seeing Faith in the doorway. Close up, Faith thought the woman was in her late forties. It was hard to tell, though, since her face was twisted into an angry red knot. She had the sort of features that seemed built for fury.

Will asked, "Did you know Gwendolyn Zabel?"

"You have no right to question me without a lawyer."

Faith rolled her eyes, reveling in the sheer childish joy of the gesture.

Will was more mature in his approach. "Can you tell me your name?"

She turned instantly reticent. "Why?"

"I'd like to know what to call you."

She seemed to scroll through her options. "Candy."

"All right, Candy. I'm Special Agent Trent with the Georgia Bureau of Investigation, this is Special Agent Mitchell. I'm sorry to tell you that Mrs. Zabel's daughter has been in an accident."

Candy pulled the blanket closer. "Was she drinking?"

Will asked, "Did you know Jacquelyn?"

"Jackie." Candy shrugged her shoulders. "She was here for a few weeks to get her mother's house sold. We talked."

"Did she use a real estate agent or sell it herself?"

"She used a local agent." The woman shifted her stance, blocking Faith from her view. "Is Jackie okay?"

"I'm afraid she's not. She was killed in the accident."

Candy put her hand to her mouth.

"Have you seen anyone hanging around the house? Anyone suspicious?"

"Of course not. I'd call the police."

Faith suppressed a snort. The ones who screamed

about the pigs were always the ones who called the police for help at the first whiff of trouble.

Will asked, "Does Jackie have any family we can get in touch with?"

"Are you fucking blind?" Candy demanded. She jerked her head toward the refrigerator. Faith could see a list of names and phone numbers taped to the door that Will was leaning against. The words EMERGENCY NUMBERS were typed in bold print at the top, less than six inches away from his face. "Christ, don't they teach you people to *read*?"

Will looked absolutely mortified, and Faith would have slapped the woman if she had been standing close enough. Instead, she said, "Ma'am, I'm going to need you to go downtown and make a formal statement."

Will caught her eye, shook his head, but Faith was so furious she struggled to keep her voice from shaking. "We'll get a cruiser to take you to City Hall East. It'll only take a few hours."

"Why?" the woman demanded. "Why do you need me to—"

Faith took out her cell phone and dialed her old partner at the Atlanta Police Department. Leo Donnelly owed her a favor—make that several favors—and she intended to use them to make this woman's life as difficult as possible.

Candy said, "I'll talk to you here. You don't need to take me downtown."

"Your friend Jackie is dead," Faith said, her anger making her tone sharp. "Either you're helping our investigation or you're obstructing it."

"Okay, okay," she said, holding up her hands in surrender. "What do you want to know?"

Faith glanced at Will, who was looking at his shoes. She pressed her thumb on the end button, disconnecting the call to Leo. She asked Candy, "When's the last time you saw Jackie?"

"Last weekend. She came over for some company."

"What kind of company?"

Candy equivocated, and Faith started to dial Leo's number again.

"All right," the woman groaned. "Jesus. We smoked some weed. She was freaked out about all this shit. She hadn't visited her mom in a while. None of us knew how bad it had gotten."

" 'None of us' meaning who?"

"Me and a couple of the neighbors. We kept an eye on Gwen. She's an old woman. Her daughters live out of state."

They must have not kept too close an eye on her if they hadn't realized she was living in a firetrap. "Do you know the other daughter?"

"Joelyn," she answered, nodding toward the list on the fridge. "She doesn't visit. At least, she hasn't in the ten years I've lived here."

Faith glanced at Will again. He was staring somewhere over Candy's shoulder. She asked the woman, "The last time you saw Jackie was a week ago?"

"That's right."

"What about her car?"

"It was in the driveway until a couple of days ago."

"A couple as in two?"

"I guess it's closer to four or five. I've got a life. It's not like I track the comings and goings of the neighborhood."

Faith ignored the sarcasm. "Have you seen anyone suspicious hanging around?"

"I told you no."

"Who was the real estate agent?"

She named one of the top Realtors in town, a man who advertised on every available bus stop in the city. "Jackie didn't even meet him. They handled it all on the phone. He had the house sold before the sign even went up in the yard. There's a developer who has a standing offer on all the lots, and he closes in ten days with cash."

Faith knew this was not uncommon. Her own poor house had been subject to many such offers over the years—none of them worth taking because then she wouldn't be able to afford a new house in her own neighborhood. "What about movers?"

"Look at all this shit." Candy slapped her hand against a crumbling pile of papers. "The last thing Jackie told me was that she was going to have one of those construction Dumpsters delivered."

Will cleared his throat. He wasn't looking at the wall anymore, but he wasn't exactly looking at the witness, either. "Why not just leave everything here?" he asked. "It's mostly trash. The builder is going to bulldoze it anyway."

Candy seemed appalled by the prospect. "This was her mother's house. She grew up here. Her childhood is buried under all this shit. You can't just throw that all away."

He took out his phone as if it had rung. Faith knew the vibration feature was broken. Amanda had nearly gutted him in a meeting last week when it had started ringing. Still, Will looked at the display, then said,

"Excuse me." He left by the back door, using his foot to move a pile of magazines out of the way.

Candy asked, "What's his problem?"

"He's allergic to bitches," Faith quipped, though if that were true, Will would be covered in a head-to-toe rash after this morning. "How often did Jackie visit her mother?"

"I'm not her social secretary."

"Maybe if I take you downtown, it'll jog your memory."

"Jesus," she muttered. "Okay. Maybe a couple of times a year—if that."

"And you've never seen Joelyn, her sister, visit?"

"Nope."

"Did you spend much time with Jackie?"

"Not much. I wouldn't call us friends or anything."

"What about when you smoked together last week? Did she say anything about her life?"

"She told me the nursing home she sent her mom off to cost fifty grand a year."

Faith suppressed the urge to whistle. "There goes any profit from the house."

Candy didn't seem to think so. "Gwen's been failing for a while now. She won't last the year. Jackie said might as well get her something nice on her way out."

"Where's the home?"

"Sarasota."

Jackie Zabel lived on the Florida Panhandle, about five hours' drive away from Sarasota. Not too close and not too far. Faith said, "The doors weren't locked when we got here."

Candy shook her head. "Jackie lived in a gated community. She never locked her doors. One night, she left her keys in her car. I couldn't believe it when I saw them in the ignition. It was dumb luck that it wasn't stolen." She added ruefully, "But Jackie was always pretty lucky."

"Was she seeing anyone?"

Candy turned reticent again.

Faith waited her out.

Finally, the woman said, "She wasn't that nice, okay? I mean, she was fine to get stoned with, but she was kind of a bitch about things, and men wanted to fuck her, but they didn't want to talk to her afterward. You know what I mean?"

Faith wasn't in a position to judge. "What things was she a bitch about?"

"The best way to drive up from Florida. The right kind of gas to put in your car. The proper way to throw out the freaking trash." She indicated the cluttered kitchen. "That's why she was doing this all by herself. Jackie's loaded. She could afford to pay a crew to clean out this place in two days. She didn't trust anyone else to do it the right way. That's the only reason she's been staying here. She's a control freak."

Faith thought about the neatly tied bundles out by the street. "You said she wasn't seeing anyone. Were there any men in her life—ex-husbands? Ex-boyfriends?"

"Who knows? She didn't confide in me much and Gwen hasn't known the day of the week for the last ten years. Honestly, I think Jackie just needed a couple of tokes to take off the edge, and she knew I was holding."

"Why'd you let her?"

"She was okay when she unclenched."

"You asked if she'd been in a drunk-driving accident."

"I know she got stopped in Florida. She was really pissed about that." Candy was sure to add, "Those stops are completely bogus. One measly glass of wine and they're cuffing you like you're some kind of criminal. They just want to make their quota."

Faith had done many of those stops herself. She knew she had saved lives just as sure as she knew Candy had probably had her own run-ins with the cops. "So, you didn't like Jackie, but you spent time with her. You didn't know her well but you knew she was fighting a DUI rap. What's going on here?"

"It's easier to go with the flow, you know? I don't like causing trouble."

She certainly seemed fine with causing it for other people. Faith took out her notebook. "What's your last name?"

"Smith."

Faith gave her a sharp look.

"I'm serious. It's Candace Courtney Smith. I live in the only other shitty house on the street." Candy glanced out the window at Will. Faith saw that he was talking to one of the uniformed patrolmen. She could tell from the way the other man was shaking his head that they hadn't found anything useful.

Candy said, "I'm sorry I snapped. I just don't like the police around."

"Why is that?"

She shrugged. "I had some problems a while back."

Faith had already guessed as much. Candy certainly had the angry disposition of a person who had sat in the back of a squad car on more than one occasion. "What kind of problems?"

She shrugged again. "I'm only saying this because you're going to find out about it and come running back here like I'm an ax murderer."

"Go on."

"I got picked up on a solicitation when I was in my twenties."

Faith was unsurprised. She guessed, "You met a guy who got you hooked on drugs?"

"Romeo and Juliet," Candy confirmed. "Asshole left me holding his stash. He said I wouldn't go down for it."

There had to be a mathematical formula out there that calculated to the second how long it took a woman whose boyfriend got her hooked on drugs to get turned out on the street in order to support both their habits. Faith imagined the equation involved a lot of zeroes behind the decimal point.

Faith asked, "How long were you in for?"

"Shit," she laughed. "I flipped on the asshole *and* his dealer. I didn't spend day one in prison."

Still not surprised.

The woman said, "I stopped the hard stuff a long time ago. The weed just keeps me mellow." She glanced at Will again. Obviously, there was something about him that was making her nervous.

Faith called her on it. "What are you so worried about?"

"He doesn't look like a cop."

"What does he look like?"

She shook her head. "He reminds me of my first boyfriend, all quiet and nice, but his temper—" She smacked her hand into her palm. "He beat me pretty bad. Broke my nose. Broke my leg once when I didn't earn out for him." She rubbed her knee. "Still hurts me when it's cold."

Faith saw where this was going. It wasn't Candy's fault that she'd tricked herself out to get high and more than likely failed her share of Breathalyzers. The evil boyfriend was to blame, or the stupid cop meeting his quota, and now Will was getting his turn as the bad guy, too.

Candy was a skilled enough manipulator to know when she was losing her audience. "I'm not lying to you."

"I don't care about the sordid details of your tragic past," Faith stated. "Tell me what you're really worried about."

She debated for a few seconds. "I take care of my daughter now. I'm straight."

"Ah," Faith said. The woman was worried her child would be taken away.

Candy nodded toward Will. "He reminds me of those bastards from the state."

Will as a social worker certainly was a better fit than Will as an abusive boyfriend. "How old is your daughter?"

"She's almost four. I didn't think I'd be able to— All the shit I've been through." Candy smiled, her face changing from an angry fist into something that might be called a moderately attractive plum. "Hannah's a little sweetheart. She loved Jackie a lot, wanted to be like her with her nice car and her fancy clothes."

Faith didn't think Jackie sounded like the kind of woman who wanted a three-year-old pawing her Jimmy

Choos, not least of all because kids tended to be sticky at that age. "Did Jackie like her?"

Candy shrugged. "Who doesn't like kids?" She finally asked the question that a less self-absorbed person would've asked ten minutes ago. "So, what happened? Was she drunk?"

"She was murdered."

Candy opened her mouth, then closed it. "Killed?"

Faith nodded.

"Who would do that? Who would want to hurt her?"

Faith had seen this enough times to know where it was heading. It was the reason she had held back the true cause of Jacquelyn Zabel's death. No one wanted to speak ill of the dead, even a fried-out hippie wannabe with an anger problem.

"She wasn't bad," Candy insisted. "I mean, she was good deep down."

"I'm sure she was," Faith agreed, though the opposite was more likely true.

Candy's lip quivered. "How am I gonna tell Hannah that she's dead?"

Faith's phone rang, which was just as well because she did not know how to answer the question. Worse, part of her didn't care, now that she'd wrung out all the information she needed. Candy Smith was hardly number one on the list of horrible parents, but she wasn't a stellar human being, either, and there was a three-year-old child out there who was probably paying for it.

Faith answered the phone. "Mitchell."

Detective Leo Donnelly asked, "Did you just call me?"

"I hit the wrong button," she lied.

"I was about to call you anyway. You put out that BOLO, right?"

He meant the Be On the Look Out Faith had sent around to all the zones this morning. Faith held up her finger to Candy, asking for a minute, then walked back into the family room. "What've you got?"

"Not exactly a miss-per," he said, meaning a missing person. "Uniform patrol found a kid asleep in an SUV this morning, mom nowhere to be found."

"And?" Faith asked, knowing there had to be more. Leo was a homicide detective. He didn't get called out to coordinate social services.

"Your BOLO," he said. "It kind of matches the mom's description. Brown hair, brown eyes."

"What's the kid saying?"

"Fuck-all," he admitted. "I'm at the hospital with him now. You've got a kid. You wanna come see if you can get anything out of him?"

CHAPTER EIGHT

MEMBERS OF THE PRESS WERE CLUSTERED AROUND the entrance of Grady Hospital, momentarily displacing the pigeons but not the homeless people, who appeared determined to be included in every background shot. Will pulled into one of the reserved parking spots out front, hoping they could sneak in unnoticed. The prospect did not seem likely. News vans had their satellite dishes pointed skyward, and perfectly pressed reporters stood with mikes in their hands, breathlessly reporting the tragic story of the child who was abandoned at City Foods this morning.

Will got out of the car, telling Faith, "Amanda thought the kid would take the heat off us for a while. She's going to go ballistic when she finds out they might be connected."

Faith offered, "I'll tell her if you want me to."

He tucked his hands into his pockets as he walked beside her. "If I get a vote here, I'd rather you snap at me than feel sorry for me."

"I can do both."

He chuckled, although the fact that he'd missed the list of emergency numbers taped to the refrigerator was about as funny as his inability to read Jackie Zabel's name off her driver's license while the woman hung lifeless over his head. "Candy's right, Faith. She called it in one."

"You would have shown the list to me," Faith defended. "Jackie Zabel's sister wasn't even home. I doubt a five-minute delay in leaving a message on her answering machine will make a huge difference."

Will kept his mouth shut. They both knew she was stretching things. In some cases, five minutes made all the difference in the world.

Faith continued, "And if you hadn't stayed under that tree with the license last night, you might not have found the body until daylight. If ever."

Will saw the reporters were studying each person who walked to the front entrance of the hospital, trying to ascertain whether or not they were important to their story.

He told Faith, "One day, you're going to have to stop making excuses for me."

"One day, you're going to have to get your head out of your ass."

Will kept walking. Faith was right about one thing—she could snap at him and feel sorry for him at the same time. The revelation brought him no comfort. Faith's blood ran blue—not the old-money kind, but the cop kind—and she had the same knee-jerk response that had been drilled into Angie every single day at the police academy, every single second on the street. When your partner or your squad was attacked, you defended him no matter what. Us against them, damn the truth, damn what was right.

"Will—" Faith was cut off as the reporters swarmed around her. They had pegged Faith for a cop as she walked across the parking lot while Will, as usual, had gotten a free pass.

Will held out his hand, blocking a camera, using his

elbow to push away a photographer with an *Atlanta Journal* logo on the back of his jacket.

"Faith? Faith?" a man called.

She turned around, spotting a reporter, and shook her head as she kept walking.

"Come on, babe!" the man called. Will thought that with his scruffy beard and rumpled clothes, he looked just like the kind of guy who could get away with calling a woman "babe."

Faith turned away, but she kept shaking her head as she walked toward the entrance.

Will waited until they were inside the building, past the metal detectors, to ask, "How do you know that guy?"

"Sam works for the *Atlanta Beacon*. He did a ride-along with me when I was working patrol."

Will seldom thought about Faith's life before him, the fact that she had worn a uniform and driven a squad car before she became a detective.

Faith gave a laugh Will didn't quite understand. "We were hot and heavy for a few years."

"What happened?"

"He didn't like that I had a kid. And I didn't like that he was an alcoholic."

"Well . . ." Will tried to think of something to say. "He seems all right."

"He does seem that way," she answered.

Will watched the reporters press their cameras against the glass, trying desperately for a shot. Grady Hospital was a public area, but the press needed permission to film inside the building and they had all learned at one time or another that the security guards had no qualms about tossing them out on their ears if they started to bug the patients or—worse—the staff.

"Will," Faith said, and he could tell from her voice that she wanted to go back to talking about the list on the fridge, Will's glaring illiteracy.

He said something that he knew would sidetrack her. "Why did Dr. Linton tell you all that stuff?"

"What stuff?"

"About her husband and being a coroner down South."

"People tell me things."

That was true enough. Faith had the cop's gift of being quiet so that other people talked just to fill the silence. "What else did she say?"

She smiled like a cat. "Why? Do you want me to put a note in her locker?"

Will felt stupid again, but this kind of stupid was far worse.

Faith asked, "How's Angie doing?"

He shot back, "How's Victor?"

And they were quiet the rest of the journey through the lobby.

"Hey, hey!" Leo held out his arms as he walked toward Faith. "Look at the big GBI girl!" He gave her a bear hug that, surprisingly, Faith allowed. "You're looking good, Faith. Real good."

She waved him off with a disbelieving laugh that would've seemed girlish if Will hadn't known her better.

"Good to see you, man," Leo boomed, shooting out his hand.

Will tried not to wrinkle his nose at the stench of cigarette smoke coming off the detective. Leo Donnelly was of average height and average build and, unfortunately, was a well-below-average cop. He was good at following orders, but thinking on his own was something the man just didn't want to do. While this was hardly surprising in a homicide detective who had come up in the 1980s, Leo represented exactly the kind of cop that Will hated: sloppy, arrogant, not afraid to use his hands if a suspect needed loosening up.

Will tried to keep things pleasant, shaking the man's hand, asking, "How's it going, Leo?"

"Can't complain," he answered, then started to do exactly that as they walked toward the emergency room. "I'm two years away from full retirement and they're trying to push me out. I think it's the medical— y'all remember that problem I had with my prostate." Neither one of them responded, but that didn't stop Leo. "Fucking city insurance is refusing to pay for some of my medication. I'm telling you, don't get sick or they'll screw you six ways to Sunday."

"What medication?" Faith asked. Will wondered why she was encouraging him.

"Fucking Viagra. Six bucks a pill. First time in my life I've ever had to pay for sex."

"I find that hard to believe," Faith commented. "Tell us about this kid. Any leads on the mom?"

"Zilch. Car's registered to a Pauline McGhee. We found blood at the scene—not a lot but enough, you know? This wasn't a nosebleed."

"Anything in the car?"

"Just her purse, her wallet—license confirms it's McGhee. Keys were in the ignition. The kid—Felix— was sleeping in the back."

"Who found him?"

"A customer. She spotted him sleeping in the car, then got the manager."

"He was probably exhausted from fear," Faith murmured. "What about video?"

"The only working camera outside sweeps back and forth across the front of the building."

"What happened to the other cameras?"

"Bad guys shot them out." Leo shrugged, as if this was to be expected. "The SUV was just out of the frame, so we've got no footage of the car. We've got McGhee walking in with her kid, walking out alone, running back in, running back out. My guess is she didn't notice the kid was gone until she got to her car. Maybe somebody outside kept him hidden, then used him as bait to lure her close enough, then smash and grab."

"Anyone else on the camera coming out of the store?"

"It pans left to right. The kid was definitely in the store. I'm guessing whoever snatched him was watching the camera. They sneaked by when it swept the other side of the lot."

Faith asked, "Do you know what school Felix goes to?"

"Some fancy private school in Decatur. I called them already." He took out his notebook and showed it to Faith so she could write down the information. "They said the mom doesn't have an emergency contact listed. The dad jerked off in a cup; end of involvement. No grandparents have ever shown up. FYI, personal observation, folks at her job ain't too crazy about the chick. Sounded like they thought she was a real bitch." He took a folded sheet of paper out of his pocket and showed it to Faith. "Here's a copy of her license. Good-lookin' broad."

Over her shoulder Will looked at the picture. It was black-and-white, but he took a good guess. "Brown hair. Brown eyes."

"Just like the others," Faith confirmed.

Leo said, "We already got guys at McGhee's house. None of the neighbors seem to know who the hell she is or really care that she's gone. They say she kept to herself, never waved, never went to the block parties or whatever they did. We're gonna try her work—it's some hoity toity design firm on Peachtree."

"You run a credit check on her?"

"She's flush," Leo answered. "Mortgage looks good. Car's paid for. Has money in the bank, the market and an IRA. She's obviously not working off a cop's salary."

"Any recent activity on her credit cards?"

"Everything was still in her purse—wallet, cards, sixty bucks cash. Last time she used her debit card was at the City Foods this morning. We put a flag on everything in case somebody wrote the numbers down. I'll let you know if we get a hit." Leo glanced around. They were standing outside the emergency room entrance. He lowered his voice. "Is this related to your Kidney Killer?"

"Kidney Killer?" Will and Faith asked in unison.

"Y'all are cute," Leo said. "Like the Bobbsey Twins."

"What are you talking about, the Kidney Killer?" Faith sounded as puzzled as Will felt.

"Rockdale County's leaking worse than my prostate," Leo confided, obviously delighted to be spreading the news. "They're saying your first victim had her kidney removed. I guess this is some kind of organ-harvesting thing. A cult maybe? I hear you can make big bucks for a kidney, around a hundred grand."

"Jesus Christ," Faith hissed. "That's the stupidest thing I've ever heard."

"Her kidney wasn't taken?" Leo seemed disappointed.

Faith didn't answer, and Will wasn't about to give Leo Donnelly any information that he could take back to the squad room. He asked, "Has Felix said anything?"

Leo shook his head, flashing his badge so they'd be buzzed back into the ER. "The kid clammed up. I called in social services, but they got fuck-all out of him. You know how they are at that age. Little thing's probably retarded."

Faith bristled. "He's probably upset because he saw his mother abducted. What do you expect?"

"Who the hell knows? You've got a kid. I figured you'd be better at talking to him."

Will had to ask Leo, "Don't you have kids?"

Leo shrugged. "Do I look like the kind of man who has a good relationship with his children?"

The question did not really need an answer. "Was anything done to the boy?"

"The doc says he's okay." His elbow dug into Will's ribs. "Speaking of the doc, shit, she's something else. Fucking gorgeous. Red hair, legs up to here."

Faith had a smile on her lips, and Will would have asked her about Victor Martinez again if Leo hadn't been standing there with his elbow jammed into Will's liver.

There was a loud beeping from one of the rooms, and nurses and doctors ran past, crash carts and stethoscopes flying. Will felt his gut tighten at the familiar sights and sounds. He had always dreaded doctors—especially the Grady docs who had served the kids at the children's home where Will grew up. Every time he'd been taken out of a foster home, the cops had brought him here. Every scrape, every cut, every burn and bruise, had to be photographed, catalogued and detailed. The nurses had been doing it long enough to know that there was a certain detachment needed for the job. The doctors weren't as practiced. They would yell and scream at social services and make you think that for once, something was going to change, but then you found yourself right back in the hospital a year later, a new doc railing and screaming the same things.

Now that Will was in law enforcement, he understood how their hands were tied, but that still didn't change the way his gut twisted every time he walked into the Grady emergency room.

As if he sensed the ability to make the situation worse, Leo patted Will on the arm, saying, "Sorry about Angie splitting, man. Probably for the best."

Faith was silent, but Will felt lucky she wasn't capable of shooting flames from her eyes.

Leo said, "I'll go find out where the doc is. They were keeping the kid in the lounge, trying to get him to calm down."

He left, and Faith's continued silence as she stared at Will spoke volumes. He tucked his hands in his pockets, leaning against the wall. The emergency room wasn't as busy as it had been last night, but there were still enough people milling around to make it difficult to have a private chat.

Faith didn't seem to mind. "How long has Angie been gone?"

"A little under a year."

Her breath caught. "You've only been married for nine months."

"Yeah, well." He glanced around, not wanting to have this conversation here or anywhere else. "She only married me to prove that she actually was going to marry me." He felt himself smiling despite the situation. "It was more to win an argument than to actually get married."

Faith shook her head as if she could make no sense of what he was saying. Will wasn't sure he could help her. He had never understood his relationship with Angie Polaski. He had known her since he was eight years old and there wasn't much he had figured out in the ensuing years, except that the minute she felt too close to him, she headed for the door. That she always eventually came back was a pattern Will had come to appreciate for its simplicity.

He told her, "She leaves me a lot, Faith. It wasn't a surprise."

She kept her mouth shut, and he couldn't tell if she was mad or just too shocked to speak.

He said, "I want to check on Anna upstairs before we leave."

She nodded.

He tried again. "Amanda asked me how you were doing last night."

Faith suddenly gave him her full attention. "What did you tell her?"

"That you're fine."

"Good, because I am."

He stared his meaning into her: Will wasn't the only one holding back information.

"I *am* fine," she insisted. "At least I will be, okay? So don't worry about me."

Will pressed his shoulders into the wall. Faith was silent, and the low hum of the emergency room was like static in his ears. Within minutes, he found himself fighting the urge to close his eyes. Will had fallen into bed around six that morning, thinking that he'd manage at least two hours' sleep before he had to go pick up Faith. He'd negotiated down the morning's activities as each hour passed, thinking first that he'd skip taking the dog for a walk, then taking off eating breakfast from the list, then finally removing his usual coffee. The clock had ticked off each hour with excruciating slowness, which he marked every twenty minutes when his eyes shot open, his heart in his throat, his head still thinking he was trapped back in that cave.

Will felt his arm itching again, but he didn't scratch it for fear of drawing Faith's attention to the gesture. Every time he thought about the cave, those rats using the flesh on his arms for a ladder, he felt his skin start to crawl. Considering how many scars Will had on his body, it was foolish to obsess about a couple of scratches that would eventually heal without leaving a mark, but it kept troubling his mind, and the more his mind was troubled, the more he itched.

He asked Faith, "You think this Kidney Killer thing has already hit the news?"

"I hope it has so when the real story comes out, those Rockdale County idiots look like the ignorant pricks they are."

"Did I tell you what Fierro said to Amanda?"

She shook her head, and he relayed Fierro's ill-timed

accusation involving the Rockdale County chief of police's pole.

Faith's voice was little more than a shocked whisper. "What did she do to him?"

"He just disappeared," Will said, taking out his cell phone. "I don't know where he went, but I never saw him again." He checked the time on his phone. "The autopsy's in an hour. If nothing comes out of this kid, let's go to the morgue and see if we can get Pete to start early."

"We're supposed to meet the Coldfields at two. I can call them and see if we can make it closer to noon."

Will knew Faith hated sitting in on autopsies. "Do you want to split up?"

She obviously did not appreciate the offer. "We'll see if they can move up the time. Our part of the post-mortem should be fairly quick."

Will hoped so. He didn't relish the idea of lingering over the morbid details of the torture Jacquelyn Zabel had endured before she'd managed to escape to safety, only to fall and break her neck while waiting for help. "Maybe we'll have something more to go on by then. A connection."

"You mean other than both women were single, attractive, successful and pretty much hated by everyone who came into contact with them?"

"A lot of successful women are hated," Will said, realizing the moment that the words came out of his mouth that he sounded like a sexist pig. "I mean, a lot of men feel threatened by—"

"I get it, Will. People don't like successful women." She added ruefully, "Sometimes other women are worse than men."

He knew that she was probably thinking about Amanda. "Maybe that's what's motivating our killer. He's angry that these women are successful and they don't need men in their lives."

Faith crossed her arms, obviously considering the angles. "Here's the trick: He's picked two women who won't be missed, Anna and Jackie Zabel. Actually, three women, if you count Pauline McGhee."

"She's got long dark hair and brown eyes like the other two victims. Usually, these guys like a pattern, a certain type."

"Jackie Zabel's successful. You said Anna was well put together. McGhee drives a Lexus and had a kid on her own, which, take it from me, is not easy." She was silent for a beat, and he wondered if she was thinking about Jeremy. Faith didn't give him time to ask. "It's one thing to kill prostitutes—you've got to go through at least four or five before anyone notices. He's targeting women who have real power in the world. So we can assume he's been watching them."

Will hadn't considered that, but she was probably right.

Faith continued, "Maybe he thinks of it as part of the hunt—doing reconnaissance on them, finding out about their lives. He stalks them, then he takes them."

"So, what are we talking about here—a guy who works for a woman he's not particularly fond of? A loner who felt abandoned by his mother? A cuckold?" Will stopped trying to profile their suspect, thinking the characteristics were a little too close to home.

"It can be anyone," Faith said. "That's the problem—it can be anyone."

Will felt the frustration he heard in her voice. They

both knew that the case was reaching a critical point. Stranger abductions were the hardest crimes to solve. The victims were usually randomly chosen, the abductor a practiced hunter who knew how to cover his tracks. It was sheer luck finding the cave last night, but Will had to hope that the kidnapper was getting sloppy; two of his victims had escaped. He might be feeling desperate, off his game. Luck had to be on their side, if they were going to catch him.

Will tucked his phone back into his pocket. They were less than twelve hours out and close to hitting a brick wall. Unless Anna woke up, unless Felix could offer them a solid lead or one of the crime scenes revealed a clue they could follow up on, they were still solidly on square one with nothing to do but wait until another body showed up.

Faith was obviously considering the same problems. "He would need another place to hold a new victim."

"I doubt it's another cave," Will said. "It would've been pretty hard to dig. I nearly killed myself digging the hole for that pond I put in my backyard last summer."

"You have a pond in your backyard?"

"Koi," he provided. "It took me two full weekends."

She was silent for a few beats, as if she was considering his pond. "Maybe our suspect might have had help digging the cave."

"Serial killers usually work alone."

"What about those two guys in California?"

"Charles Ng and Leonard Lake." Will knew about the case, mostly because it was one of the lengthiest and most expensive in California's history. Lake and Ng had built a cinderblock bunker in the hills, fitting the chamber with various torture devices and other implements to help them act out their sick fantasies. Both men had filmed themselves taking turns with the victims—men, women and children, some whom had never been identified.

Faith continued, "The Hillside Stranglers worked together, too."

The two cousins had hunted women on the margins, prostitutes and runaways.

Will said, "They had a fake police badge. That's how they got the women to trust them."

"I don't even want to consider the possibility."

Will felt the same way, but it was something to keep in mind. Jackie Zabel's BMW was missing. The woman at City Foods this morning had been abducted right beside her car. Someone posing as a police officer could have easily fabricated a scenario to approach their vehicles.

Will said, "Charlie didn't find evidence of two different attackers being in the cave." He had to add, "Then again, he wasn't exactly eager to stay down there any longer than he had to."

"What was your impression when you were down there?"

"That I needed to get out of there before I had a heart attack," Will admitted, feeling the rat scratches on his arms start itching again. "It's not the kind of place you want to linger."

"We'll look at the photos. Maybe there's something you and Charlie didn't see in the heat of the moment."

Will knew that this was a distinct possibility. The photos of the cave would probably be on his desk by the time they got back to the office. They could examine the scene at leisure, the claustrophobia of the surroundings kept safely at arm's length.

"Two victims, Anna and Jackie. Maybe two abductors?" Faith made the next connection. "If that's their pattern, and Pauline McGhee is another victim, then they need a second victim."

"Hey," Leo called, waving them back. He stood at a door with a large sign on it.

" 'Doctors' Lounge,' " Faith read, a habit she'd gotten into that Will both loathed and appreciated in unequal parts.

"Good luck," Leo said, patting Will on the shoulder.

Faith asked, "You're leaving?"

"The doc just handed me my ass on a platter." Leo did not look particularly bothered by the fact. "You guys can talk to the kid, but unless this breaks toward your case, I need you to stay away."

Will was slightly surprised by his words. Leo had always been more than happy to let other people do his work.

The detective said, "Trust me, I'd love to hand this over to you, but I got my bosses breathing down my neck. They're looking for any reason to kick me. I'll need a solid connection before I send this up the chain to get y'all on the case, all right?"

"We'll make sure you're covered," Faith promised. "Can you still keep a lookout for us on missing persons? White, midthirties, dark brown hair, successful, but not someone who's got a lot of friends who will miss her."

"Brown and bitchy." He gave her a wink. "What else I gotta do except gumshoe your case?" He seemed okay with it. "I'll be at the City Foods if anything comes up. You've got my numbers."

Will watched him go, asking, "Why are they pushing Leo out? I mean, other than the obvious reasons."

Faith had been Leo's partner for a few years, and Will could see her struggling with the desire to defend him. Finally, Faith said, "He's at the top of his pay scale. It's cheaper to have some fresh-faced kid just off patrol doing his job for half the pay. Plus, if Leo takes early retirement, he leaves twenty percent of his pension on the table. Throw in the medical, and it gets even more expensive to keep him around. The bosses look at that kind of thing when they're doing their budgets."

Faith was about to open the door, but stopped when her cell phone started ringing. She checked the caller ID and told Will, "Jackie's sister." She answered the phone, nodding for Will to go ahead without her.

Will's hand was sweating when he pressed his palm to the wooden door. His heart did something weird— almost a double beat—that he put down to lack of sleep and too much hot chocolate this morning. Then he saw Sara Linton, and it did it again.

She was sitting in a chair by the window, holding Felix McGhee in her lap. The boy was almost too big to be held, but Sara seemed to be managing it well. One arm was wrapped around his waist, the other around his shoulders. She used her hand to stroke his hair as she whispered sounds of comfort in his ear.

Sara had looked up when Will entered the room, but didn't let his presence disturb the scene. Felix stared blankly out the window, his lips slightly parted. Sara nodded toward a chair opposite, and Will guessed from the fact that it was less than six inches from Sara's knee that Leo had been sitting there. He pulled the chair back a few feet and sat down.

"Felix." Sara's voice calm and in control, the same tone she had used with Anna the night before. "This is Agent Trent. He's a policeman, and he's going to help you."

Felix kept staring out the window. The room was cool, but Will could see the boy's hair was damp with perspiration. A bead of sweat rolled down his cheek, and Will took out his handkerchief to wipe it away. When he looked back at Sara, she was staring at him as if he'd pulled a rabbit out of his pocket.

"Old habit," Will mumbled, embarrassed as he folded the cloth in two. He had been made well aware over the years that only old men and dandies carried handkerchiefs, but all the boys at the Atlanta Children's Home had been made to carry them, and Will felt naked without one.

Sara shook her head, as if to say she didn't mind. Her lips pressed to the top of Felix's head. The child didn't move, but Will had seen his eyes dart to the side, checking out Will, trying to see what he was doing.

"What's this?" Will asked, noticing a book bag beside Sara's chair. He guessed from the cartoon characters and bright colors that the bag belonged to Felix. Will slid it toward him and opened the zip, brushing away stray pieces of colored confetti as he explored the contents.

Leo would've already gone through everything in the bag, but Will took out each item as if he was carefully examining it for clues. "Nice pencils." He held up a packet of colored pencils. The packaging was black, not the kind of thing you usually saw on children's items. "These are for grown-ups. You must be a very good artist."

Will didn't expect a response, and Felix didn't give

one, but the boy's eyes were watching carefully now, as if he wanted to make sure Will didn't take anything from his bag.

Next, Will opened up a folder. There was an ornate crest on the front, probably from Felix's private school. Official-looking documents from the school were in one pocket. What looked like Felix's homework was in the other. Will couldn't make out the school memos, but he could tell from the double-lined paper on the homework side that Felix was learning how to write on a straight line.

He showed this to Sara. "His letters are pretty good."

"They are," Sara agreed. She was watching Will as carefully as Felix was, and Will had to put her out of his mind so he didn't forget how to do his job. She was too beautiful, and too smart, and too much of everything Will was not.

He put the folder back in the book bag and pulled out three slim books. Even Will could make out the first three letters of the alphabet that adorned the jacket of the first book. The other two were a mystery to him, and he held them up to Felix, saying, "I wonder what these are about?" When Felix didn't answer, Will looked back at the jackets, squinting at the images. "I guess this pig works at a restaurant, because he's serving people pancakes." Will looked at the next book. "And this mouse is sitting in a lunchbox. I guess somebody's going to eat him for lunch."

"No." Felix spoke so quietly that Will wasn't sure the boy had said anything at all.

"No?" Will asked, looking back at the mouse. The great thing about being around kids was you could be absolutely honest and they thought you were just teasing them. "I can't read very well. What does this say?"

Felix shifted, and Sara helped him turn toward Will. The child reached for the books. Instead of answering, Felix held the books close to his chest. His lip started to tremble, and Will guessed, "Your mom reads to you, doesn't she?"

He nodded, big fat tears rolling down his cheeks.

Will leaned forward, his elbows on his knees. "I want to find your mommy."

Felix swallowed, as if he was trying to choke down his grief. "The big man took her."

Will knew that to a kid, all adults were big. He sat up straight, asking, "As big as me?"

Felix really looked at Will for the first time since he'd walked into the room. He seemed to consider the question, then shook his head.

"What about the detective who was just in here—the stinky one? Was the man as tall as him?"

Felix nodded.

Will tried to keep the pace slow, casual, so Felix would keep answering the questions without feeling like he was being interrogated. "Did he have hair like mine, or was it darker?"

"Darker."

Will nodded, scratching his chin as if he was deliberating possibilities. Kids were notoriously unreliable witnesses. They either wanted to please the adults who questioned them or they were so open to suggestion that you could pretty much plant any idea in their heads and have them swear that it actually happened.

Will asked, "What about his face? Did he have hair on his face? Or was it smooth like mine?"

"He had a mustache."

"Did he speak to you?"

"He told me that my mommy said to stay in the car."

Will treaded carefully. "Was he wearing a uniform like a janitor or a fireman or a police officer?"

Felix shook his head. "Just normal clothes."

Will felt a rush of heat to his face. He knew Sara was staring at him. Her husband had been a cop. She wouldn't like the implication.

Will asked, "What color were his clothes?"

Felix shrugged, and Will wondered if the boy was finished answering questions or if he really didn't remember.

Felix picked at the edge of his book. "He wore a suit like Morgan."

"Morgan is a friend of your mommy's?"

He nodded. "He's at her work, but she's mad at him because he's lying and he's trying to get her into trouble, but she's not going to let him get away with it because of the safe."

Will wondered if Felix had overheard some phone calls or if Pauline McGhee was the type of woman to vent her problems to a six-year-old boy. "Do you remember anything else about the man who took your mommy?"

"He said he would hurt me if I told anybody about him."

Will kept his face blank, as did Felix. "You're not scared of the man," he said, not a question but a statement.

"My mommy says that she'll never let anybody hurt me."

He seemed so sure of himself that Will couldn't help

but feel a great deal of respect for Pauline McGhee's parenting skills. Will had interviewed a lot of children in his time, and while most of them loved their parents, not many of them exhibited this kind of blind trust.

Will said, "She's right. No one is going to hurt you."

"My mommy will protect me," Felix insisted, and Will started to wonder about his certainty. You usually didn't reassure a kid of something unless there was a real fear you were trying to combat.

Will asked, "Was your mom worried that someone might hurt you?"

Felix picked at the book jacket again. He gave an almost imperceptible nod.

Will waited, trying not to rush his next question. "Who was she afraid of, Felix?"

He spoke quietly, his voice little more than a whisper. "Her brother."

A brother. This could be some kind of family dispute after all. Will asked, "Did she tell you his name?"

He shook his head. "I never met him, but he was bad."

Will stared at the boy, wondering how to phrase his next question. "Bad how?"

"Mean," Felix said. "She said he was mean, and that she would protect me from him because she loves me more than anybody in the world." There was a finality to his tone, as if that was all he was willing to say on the matter. "Can I go home now?"

Will would've preferred a knife to his chest rather than have to answer this question. He glanced at Sara for support, and she took over, saying, "Remember that lady you met earlier? Miss Nancy?"

Felix nodded.

"She's going to find someone to take care of you until your mom comes to get you."

The boy's eyes filled with tears. Will couldn't blame him. Miss Nancy was probably from social services. She would be a far cry from the women at Felix's private school and his mother's well-heeled friends.

He said, "But I want to go home."

"I know, sweetheart," Sara soothed. "But if you go home, you'll be all alone. We need to make sure that you're safe until your mom comes to get you."

He didn't seem convinced.

Will got down on one knee so that he was face-to-face with the boy. He wrapped his hand around Felix's shoulder, his fingers accidentally brushing Sara's arm in the process. Will felt a lump rise in his throat, and he had to swallow before he could speak. "Look at me, Felix." He waited until the child complied. "I'm going to make sure your mom comes back to you, but I need you to be brave for me while I'm working to make that happen."

Felix's face was so open and trusting that it was painful to look at him. "How long will it take?" There was a wobble in his voice as he asked the question.

"Maybe a week at the most," Will said, fighting the urge to break eye contact. If Pauline McGhee was gone longer than a week, she would be dead, and Felix would be an orphan. "Can you give me a week?"

The boy kept staring at Will as if to judge whether or not he was being told the truth. Finally, he nodded.

"All right," Will said, feeling as if an anvil had been placed on his chest. He saw that Faith was sitting in a chair by the door and wondered when she had come into the room. She stood, nodding for him to follow her outside. Will patted Felix on the leg before joining Faith in the hallway.

"I'll tell Leo about the brother," Faith said. "Sounds like a family dispute."

"Probably." Will glanced back at the closed door. He wanted to go back in there, but not because of Felix. "What'd Jackie's sister say?"

"Joelyn," Faith provided. "She's not exactly torn up about her sister being killed."

"What do you mean?"

"Bitch runs in the family."

Will felt his eyebrows go up.

"I'm just having a bad day," Faith said, but that was hardly an explanation. "Joelyn lives in North Carolina. She said it'll take her about five hours to drive down." Almost as an afterthought, Faith added, "Oh, and she's going to sue the police and get us fired if we don't find out who killed her sister."

"One of those," Will said. He didn't know which was worse—family members who were so torn up with grief that you felt like they were reaching into your chest and squeezing your heart or family members who were so angry that you felt like they were squeezing you a little farther down.

He said, "Maybe you should have another go at Felix."

"He seemed pretty tapped out to me," Faith replied. "I probably couldn't get any more out of him than you did."

"Maybe talking to a woman—"

"You're good with kids," Faith interrupted, a hint of surprise in her tone. "More patient than me right now, anyway."

Will shrugged. He had helped out with some of the younger kids at the children's home, mostly to keep the new ones from crying all night and keeping everyone awake. He asked, "Did you get Pauline's work number from Leo?" Faith nodded. "We need to call and see if there's a Morgan there. Felix says the abductor dressed like him—maybe there's a kind of suit that Morgan favors. Also, our guy's about five-six with dark hair and a mustache."

"The mustache could be fake."

Will admitted as much. "Felix is smart for his age, but I'm not sure he can tell the difference between real and fake. Maybe Sara got something out of him?"

"Let's give them a few more minutes alone," Faith suggested. "You sound like you think Pauline's one of our victims."

"What do you think?"

"I asked you first."

Will sighed. "My gut is pointing that way. Pauline's well-off, well employed. She's got brown hair, brown eyes." He shrugged, contradicting himself. "That's not much to hang your hat on."

"It's more than we had when we got up this morning," she pointed out, though he couldn't tell if she was agreeing with his gut or clutching at straws. "Let's be careful about this. I don't want to get Leo in trouble by snooping around his case, then leaving him hanging out to dry when nothing comes out of it."

"Agreed."

"I'll call Pauline McGhee's work and ask about Morgan's suits. Maybe I can get some information out of them without stepping on Leo's toes." Faith took out her phone and looked at the screen. "My battery is dead."

"Here." Will offered his. She took it gently in both hands and dialed a number from her notebook. Will wondered if he looked as silly as Faith did holding the two pieces of the phone to his face and figured he probably looked even more so. Faith was not really his type, but she was an attractive woman, and attractive women could get away with a lot. Sara Linton, for instance, could probably get away with murder.

"Sorry," Faith said into the phone, her voice raised. "I'm having trouble hearing you." She shot Will a look, as if this was his fault, before heading down the hall where the reception was better.

Will leaned his shoulder against the doorjamb. Replacing the phone represented a seemingly insurmountable problem—the sort of problem that Angie usually handled for him. He'd tried to get the device replaced by calling the cell phone company, but they had told him he would have to go to the store and fill out paperwork. Assuming that miracle occurred, Will would then have to figure out the new features on the phone—how to set the ring tone to something that wouldn't annoy him, how to program in the numbers he needed for work. Will supposed he could ask Faith, but his pride kept getting in the way. He knew that she would gladly help him, but she would want to have a conversation about it.

For the first time in his adult life, Will found himself wishing that Angie would come back to him.

He felt a hand on his arm, then heard an "Excuse me" as a thin brunette opened the door to the doctors' lounge. He guessed she was Miss Nancy from social services, come to collect Felix. The day was early enough that the boy wouldn't immediately be taken to a shelter. There might be a foster family who could look after him for a while. Hopefully, Miss Nancy had been at this job long enough so that she had some good families who owed her favors. It was hard to place children who were in limbo. Will had been in limbo himself, just long enough to get to that age where adoption was almost impossible.

Faith was back. She had a disapproving frown on her face as she handed Will back his phone. "You should get that replaced."

"Why?" he asked, pocketing the phone. "It works fine."

She ignored his obvious lie. "Morgan only wears Armani, and he seemed pretty convinced that he's the only man in Atlanta with enough style to pull it off."

"So, we're talking anywhere from twenty-five hundred to five thousand dollars for a suit."

"I'd bet it's on the high end, judging by his haughty tone. He also told me that Pauline McGhee is estranged from her family, going back at least twenty years. He says she ran away at seventeen and never looked back. He's never heard her mention a brother before."

"How old is Pauline now?"

"Thirty-seven."

"Did Morgan know how to get in touch with her family?"

"He doesn't even know what state she's from. She didn't talk about her past much. I left a message on Leo's cell. I'm pretty sure he'll track down the brother before the day is out. He's probably already running all the fingerprints from her SUV."

"Maybe she's living under an alias? You don't run

away from home at seventeen without a reason. Pauline's obviously doing pretty well for herself financially. Maybe she had to change her name to make that happen."

"Obviously, Jackie's been in touch with her family and hasn't changed her name. Her sister was going by Zabel, too." Faith laughed, pointing out, "All of their names rhyme—Gwendolyn, Jacquelyn, Joelyn. It's kind of weird, don't you think?"

Will shrugged. He'd never been able to recognize words that rhymed, a problem he thought might be coupled with his reading issues. Fortunately, it wasn't the sort of thing that came up much.

Faith continued, "I don't know what it is, but something about having a baby makes you think the stupidest names are beautiful." She sounded wistful. "I almost named Jeremy Fernando Romantico after one of the guys from Menudo. Thank God my mother put her foot down."

The door opened. Sara Linton joined them in the hallway, looking exactly how you'd expect someone to look if they felt like they'd just abandoned a child to social services. Will wasn't one to rail against the system, but the reality was that no matter how nice the social workers were, or how hard they tried, there weren't enough of them and they didn't get nearly the support they needed. Add to that the fact that foster parents were either the salt of the earth or money-hungry, child-hating sadists, and you quickly understood how soul-killing the entire enterprise could be. Unfortunately, it was Felix McGhee's soul that would pay the most.

Sara told Will, "You were good in there."

He fought the urge to smile like a kid who'd just been patted on the head.

Faith asked, "Did Felix say anything else?"

Sara shook her head. "How are you feeling?"

"Much better," Faith answered, a defensive edge to her tone.

Sara said, "I heard about the second victim you found last night."

"Will found her." Faith paused a moment, as if to draw out the information. "This isn't for public consumption, but she snapped her neck when she fell from a tree."

Sara frowned. "What was she doing in a tree?"

Will took over the story. "She was waiting for us to find her. Apparently, we didn't get there quickly enough."

"You have no way of knowing how long she was in the tree," Sara told him. "Time of death isn't an exact science."

"Her blood was warm," he returned, feeling that same darkness come as he thought about the hot liquid hitting the back of his neck.

"There are other reasons the blood might still be warm. If she was in a tree, then the leaves could've acted as an insulation from the cold. She could've been medicated by her abductor. Several pharmaceuticals can raise the body's core temperature and keep it high even after death."

He countered, "The blood hadn't had time to clot."

"Something as simple as a couple of aspirin could keep it from coagulating."

Faith provided, "Jackie had a large bottle of aspirin by her bed. It was half empty."

Will was unconvinced, but Sara had moved on. She asked Faith, "Is Pete Hanson still the coroner for this region?"

"You know Pete?"

"He's a good ME. I did a couple of courses with him when I first got elected."

Will had forgotten that in small towns, the medical examiner's job was an elected position. He couldn't picture Sara's face on a yard sign.

Faith said, "We were actually about to head over there for the autopsy on the second victim."

Sara seemed to take on an air of uncertainty. "Today's my day off."

"Well," Faith began, again drawing out the moment. "I hope you enjoy your day." She said it as a parting shot, but didn't make a move to leave.

Will noticed that the hallway had gone quiet enough to hear the clacking of high heels on the tiles behind him. Amanda Wagner walked briskly toward them. She looked well rested despite the fact that she had stayed out in the forest as late as Will. Her hair was in its usual unmoving helmet and her pantsuit was a muted dark purple.

As usual, she jumped right into the middle of things. "The bloody fingerprint on Jacquelyn Zabel's Florida driver's license belongs to our first victim. Are you still calling her Anna?" She didn't give them time to answer. "Is this grocery store abduction related to our case?"

Will told her, "It could be. The mother was abducted around five-thirty this morning. The kid, Felix, was found sleeping in his mother's car. We've got a sketchy description from him, but he's only six years old. The

Atlanta police are cooperating. As far as I know, they haven't asked for help."

"Who's on point?"

"Leo Donnelly."

"Worthless," Amanda grumbled. "We'll let him keep his case for the time being, but I want a very tight leash on him. Let Atlanta do the footwork and pay for the forensics, but if he starts to screw things up, yank him off."

Faith said, "He's not going to like that."

"Do I look like I give a damn?" She didn't wait for a response. "Our friends in Rockdale County apparently have some regrets about turning over their case," she informed them. "I've called a press conference outside in five minutes and I want you and Faith flanking me, looking reassuring as I explain to the public at large that their kidneys are safe from the hands of vicious organ harvesters." She held out her hand to Sara. "Dr. Linton, I suppose it's not a stretch to say we're meeting under better circumstances this time around."

Sara shook her hand. "For me, at least."

"It was a moving service. A fitting tribute to a great officer."

"Oh . . ." Sara's voice trailed off, confused. Tears welled into her eyes. "I didn't realize you were . . ." She cleared her throat, and tried to collect herself. "That day is still a blur for me."

Amanda gave her a close look of appraisal, and her tone was surprisingly soft when she asked, "How long has it been?"

"Three and a half years."

"I heard about what happened at Coastal." Amanda was still holding Sara's hand, and Will could see her give the woman a reassuring squeeze. "We take care of our own."

Sara wiped her eyes, glancing at Faith as if she felt foolish. "I was actually about to offer my services to your agents."

Will saw Faith's mouth open, then close just as quickly.

Amanda said, "Go on."

"I worked on the first victim—Anna. I didn't have the opportunity to do a full exam, but I had time with her. Pete Hanson is one of the finest medical examiners I've ever met, but if you want me to sit in on the autopsy of the second victim, I might be able to offer a perspective on the differences and similarities between the two."

Amanda didn't waste time thinking over the decision. "I'll take you up on that offer," she said. "Faith, Will, come with me. Dr. Linton, my agents will meet you at City Hall East in an hour." When no one moved, she clapped her hands. "Let's go." She was halfway down the hall before Faith and Will found it in themselves to follow.

Will walked behind Amanda, keeping his stride short so he wouldn't run her over. She walked fast for such a small woman, but his height always made him feel a bit like the Green Giant as he tried to keep a respectful distance. Looking down at the back of her head, he wondered whether their killer worked for a woman like Amanda. Will could see where a different kind of man might feel outright hatred instead of the mix of exasperation with a dash of burning desire to please that Will felt toward the older woman.

Faith put her hand on his arm, pulling him back. "Can you believe that?"

"Believe what?"

"Sara elbowing in on our autopsy."

"She had a point about seeing both victims."

"*You* saw both victims."

"I'm not a coroner."

"Neither is she," Faith shot back. "She's not even a real doctor. She's a pediatrician. And what the hell was Amanda talking about at Coastal?"

Will was curious about what had happened at Coastal State Prison, too, but mostly he wondered why Faith was so angry about it all.

Amanda called over her shoulder, "You're to take any and all help Sara Linton is willing to offer." She had obviously heard them whispering. "Her husband was one of the finest cops in this state, and I'd stake any investigation on Sara's medical skills."

Faith didn't bother hiding her curiosity. "What happened to him?"

"Line of duty," was all Amanda would say. "How are you doing after your tumble, Faith?"

Faith sounded unusually chipper. "Perfect."

"Doctor cleared you?"

She got even chippier. "One hundred percent."

"We're going to have a talk about that." Amanda waved the security guards away as they entered the lobby, telling Faith, "I've got a meeting after this with the mayor, but I'll expect you in my office by the end of the day."

"Yes, ma'am."

Will wondered if he was turning more stupid by the

minute or if the women in his life were just getting more obtuse. Now was not the time to figure it out, though. He reached ahead of Amanda and opened the glass entrance door. There was a podium outside, a small carpet behind it for Amanda to stand on. Will took his usual spot to the side, safe in the knowledge that the cameras would capture his chest and maybe the knot in his tie as they went in for the tight focus on Amanda. Faith obviously knew she would not be as lucky, and she perfected a scowl as she stood behind her boss.

The cameras flashed. Amanda stepped up to the microphones. Questions were shouted, but she waited for the ruckus to die down before taking out a folded sheet of paper from her jacket pocket and smoothing it flat on the platform. "I'm Dr. Amanda Wagner, deputy director of the Georgia Bureau of Investigation's Atlanta regional office." She paused for effect. "Some of you have heard the spurious rumors about the so-called Kidney Killer. I am here to set the record straight that this rumor is false. There is no such killer in our midst. The victim's kidney was not removed; there was no surgical interference whatsoever. The Rockdale County Police Department has denied starting said rumors, and we have to trust that our colleagues are being honest in this matter."

Will didn't have to look at Faith to know she was fighting the urge to smile. Detective Max Galloway had certainly gotten under her skin, and Amanda had just slammed the entire Rockdale County police force on camera.

One of the reporters asked, "What can you tell us

about the woman who was brought into Grady last night?"

Not for the first time, Amanda knew more about their case than Will or Faith had told her. She responded, "We should have a sketch of the victim for you by one o'clock this afternoon."

"Why no photographs?"

"The victim suffered some blows to the face. We want to give the public their best chance to identify her."

A woman from CNN asked, "What's her prognosis?"

"Guarded." Amanda moved on, pointing to the next person with his hand up. It was Sam, the guy who had called to Faith when they first entered the hospital. He was the only reporter Will could see who was taking notes the old-fashioned way instead of using a digital recorder. "Do you have a comment about the statement from Jacquelyn Zabel's sister, Joelyn Zabel?"

Will felt his jaw tighten as he forced himself to stare impassively ahead. He imagined Faith was doing the same thing, because the crowd of reporters was still focused on Amanda instead of the two shocked agents behind her.

"The family is obviously very upset," Amanda answered. "We're doing everything we can do to solve this case."

Sam pressed, "You can't be pleased that she's using such harsh language about your agency."

Will could imagine Amanda's smile just by the look on Sam's face. They were both playing a game, because the reporter obviously knew full well that Amanda had no idea what he was talking about.

She said, "You'll have to ask Ms. Zabel about her statements. I have no further comment on the matter." Amanda took two more questions, then wrapped up the press conference with the usual request for anyone with information to come forward.

The reporters started to dissipate, off to file their stories—though Will was fairly certain that none of them would take responsibility for failing to fact-check their reports before running the specious rumor about the so-called Kidney Killer.

Amanda's voice was a low grumble that Will could barely make out when she told Faith, "Go."

Faith didn't need an explanation, nor did she need backup, but she still grabbed Will by the arm as she walked toward the crowd of reporters. She brushed past Sam, and she must've said something to him because the man started following her toward a narrow alley between the hospital and the parking garage.

Sam said, "Caught the dragon off guard, didn't I?"

Faith indicated Will. "Agent Trent, this is Sam Lawson, professional asshole."

Sam flashed him a smile. "Pleased to meet you."

Will didn't offer a response, and Sam didn't appear to mind. The reporter was more interested in Faith, and he was looking at her in such a predatory way that Will felt a caveman urge to punch the guy squarely in the jaw.

Sam said, "Damn, Faith, you're looking really hot."

"Amanda's pissed at you."

"Isn't she always?"

"You don't want to be on her bad side, Sam. You remember what happened last time."

"The great thing about drinking so much is that I don't." He was grinning again, looking her up and down. "You look really good, babe. I mean—just fantastic."

She shook her head, though Will could tell she was softening. He'd never seen her look at a man the way she was looking at Sam Lawson. There was definitely something unresolved between them. Will had never felt more like a third wheel in his life.

Thankfully, Faith seemed to realize she was here for a reason. "Did Rockdale give you Zabel's sister?"

"Reporters' sources are confidential," Sam answered, all but confirming her guess.

Faith asked, "What's Joclyn's statement?"

"In a nutshell, she said you guys stood around with your thumbs up your asses for three hours arguing about who would get the case while her sister was dying up in a tree."

Faith's lips were a thin white line. Will felt physically ill. Sam must have talked to the sister right after Faith had, which explained why the reporter had been so sure Amanda was in the dark.

Finally, Faith asked, "Did you feed Zabel that information?"

"You know me better than that."

"Rockdale fed her the information, then you got her on the record."

He shrugged another confirmation. "I'm a reporter, Faith. I'm just doing my job."

"That's a pretty shitty job—ambushing grieving family members, trashing the cops, printing what you know are lies."

"Now you know why I was a drunk for so many years."

Faith tucked her hands into her hips, gave a heavy, frustrated sigh. "That's not what happened with Jackie Zabel."

"I figured it wasn't." Sam took out his notepad and pen. "So give me something else to lead with."

"You know I can't—"

"Tell me about the cave. I heard he had a boat battery down there so he could burn them."

The boat battery was what they called "guilty knowledge," the sort of information only the killer would know. There were a handful of people who had seen the evidence Charlie Reed had collected belowground, and they all wore badges. At least for now.

Faith said what Will was thinking. "Either Galloway or Fierro is feeding you inside information. They get to screw us over, and you get your front-page story. Win-win, right?"

Sam's toothy grin confirmed her speculation. Still he said, "Why would I talk to Rockdale when you're my inside man on this case?"

Will had seen Faith's temper turn on a dime over the last few weeks, and it was nice to not be on the receiving end of her anger for a change. She told Sam, "I'm not your inside anything, asshole, and your facts are wrong."

"Set me straight, babe."

She seemed about to, but sanity caught up with her at the last minute. "The GBI has no official comment on Joelyn Zabel's statement."

"Can I quote you on that?"

"Quote this, *babe*."

Will followed Faith to the car, but not before flashing a smile at the reporter. He was pretty sure the gesture Faith had made was not something you could put in a newspaper.

CHAPTER NINE

Sara had spent the last three and a half years perfecting her denial skills, so it shouldn't have come as a surprise that it took a solid hour before she realized what a horrible mistake she had made by offering her services to Amanda Wagner. In that hour, she'd managed to drive home, shower, change her clothes and get all the way to the basement of City Hall East before the truth hit her like a sledgehammer. She had put her hand to the door marked GBI MEDICAL EXAMINER, then stopped, unable to open it. Another city. Another morgue. Another way to miss Jeffrey.

Was it wrong to say that she had loved working with her husband? That she had looked at him over the body of a gunshot victim or drunken driver and felt like her life was complete? It seemed macabre and foolish and all the things that Sara had thought she'd put behind her when she moved to Atlanta, but here she was again, her hand pressed against a door that separated life and death, incapable of opening it.

She leaned her back against the wall, staring at the painted letters on the opaque glass. Wasn't this where they had brought Jeffrey? Wasn't Pete Hanson the man who had dissected her husband's beautiful body? Sara had the coroner's report somewhere. At the time, it had seemed of vital importance that she have all the information pertaining to his death—the toxicology, the weights and measures of organ, tissue and bone. She had watched Jeffrey die back in Grant County, but this place, this basement under City Hall, was where everything that had made him a human being had been reduced, removed, redacted.

What was it, exactly, that had convinced Sara to bring herself to this place? She thought about the people she had come into contact with over the last few hours: Felix McGhee—the lost look on his pale face, his lower lip trembling as he searched the hospital corridors for his mother, insisting she would never leave him alone. Will Trent offering the child his handkerchief. Sara had thought that her father and Jeffrey were the only two men left on earth who carried them around anymore. And then Amanda Wagner, commenting on the funeral.

Sara had been so sedated the day Jeffrey was buried that she'd barely been able to stand. Her cousin had kept his arm around her waist, literally holding her up so that she could walk to Jeffrey's grave. Sara had held her hand over the coffin that lay in the ground, her fingers refusing to release the clump of dirt she held. Finally, she had given up, clutching her fist to her chest, wanting to smooth the dirt onto her face, inhale it, climb into the earth with Jeffrey and hold him until her lungs could no longer draw breath.

Sara put her hand in the back pocket of her jeans, felt the letter there. She had folded it so many times that the envelope was tearing at the crease, showing the bright yellow of the legal paper inside. What would she do if one day it suddenly opened? What would she do if she happened to glance down one morning and saw the neat scrawl, the pained explanations or blatant excuses from the woman whose actions had led to Jeffrey's death?

"Sara Linton!" Pete Hanson boomed as his foot hit the bottom stair. He was wearing a bright Hawaiian shirt, a style she recalled that he favored, and the expression on his face was a mix of delight and curiosity. "To what do I owe this tremendous pleasure?"

She told him the truth. "I managed to worm my way onto one of your cases."

"Ah, the student taking over for the teacher."

"I don't think you're ready to give all this up."

He gave her a bawdy wink. "You know I've got the heart of a nineteen-year-old."

Sara recognized the setup. "Still keep it in a jar over your desk?"

Pete guffawed as if he was hearing the line for the first time.

Sara thought she should explain herself, offering, "I saw one of the victims at the hospital last night."

"I heard about her. Torture, assault?"

"Yes."

"Prognosis?"

"They're trying to get the infection under control." Sara didn't elaborate, but she didn't need to. Pete saw his share of hospital patients who'd not responded to antibiotic treatment.

"Did you get a rape kit?"

"There wasn't enough time pre-op, and post—"

"Spoils the chain of evidence," he provided. Pete was up on his case law. Anna had been doused in Betadine, exposed to countless different environments. Any good defense attorney could find an expert witness who would argue that a rape kit taken after a victim had undergone the rigors of surgery was too contaminated to use as evidence.

Sara told him, "I managed to remove some splinters from under her nails, but I thought the best thing I could offer is a forensic comparison between the two victims."

"Rather dubious reasoning, but I'm so happy to see you that I'll overlook your faulty logic."

She smiled; Pete had always been blunt in that polite, southern way—one of the reasons he made such a great teacher. "Thank you."

"The pleasure of your company is more than enough reward." He opened the door, ushering her inside. Sara hesitated, and he pointed out, "Hard to see from the hallway."

Sara put on what she thought of as her game face as she followed him into the morgue. The smell hit her first. She had always thought the best way to describe it would be cloying, a word that made no sense until you smelled something cloying for yourself. The predominant odor wasn't from the dead but from the chemicals used around them. Before scalpel touched flesh, the deceased were catalogued, X-rayed, photographed, stripped and washed down with disinfectant. A different cleaner was used to swab the floors, another to wash down the stainless steel tables; yet another chemical cleaned and sterilized the tools of autopsy. Together, they created an unforgettable, overly sweet smell that permeated your skin, lived in the back of your nose so that you didn't realize it was there until you had been away from it for a while.

Sara followed Pete to the back of the room, feeling caught in his wake. The morgue was as far from the constant hustle of Grady as Grant County was from Grand Central. Unlike the endless treadmill of cases in the ER, an autopsy was a contained question that almost always had an answer. Blood, fluid, organ, tissue—each component contributed a piece to the puzzle. A body could not lie. The dead could not always take their secrets to the grave.

Almost two and a half million people die in America each year. Georgia is responsible for about seventy thousand of these deaths, less than a thousand of which are homicides. By state law, any unattended death— which is to say a person who dies outside of a hospital or nursing home—has to be investigated. Small towns that do not often see violent death, or communities that are so strapped for cash that the local funeral director fills in for the job of coroner, usually let the state handle their criminal cases. The majority of them end up in the Atlanta morgue. Which explained why half the tables were occupied with corpses in various stages of autopsy.

"Snoopy," Pete said, calling to an elderly black man in scrubs. "This is Dr. Sara Linton. She's going to be assisting me on the Zabel case. Where are we?"

The man didn't acknowledge Sara as he told Pete, "X-rays are on the screen. I can bring her out now if you want."

"Good man." Pete went to the computer and tapped the keyboard. A series of X-rays came onto the screen. "Technology!" Pete exclaimed, and Sara could not help but be impressed. Back in Grant County, the morgue had been in the basement of the hospital, almost an afterthought. The X-ray machine was designed for living humans, unlike the setup here, where it didn't really matter how much radiation shot into the dead body.

The films were pristine, read on a twenty-four-inch flat-panel monitor instead of a lightbox that flickered enough to cause an epileptic fit. The single porcelain table Sara had used in Grant was no match for the rows of stainless steel gurneys behind her. She could see junior coroners and medical investigators bustling back and forth in the glassed-off hallway running beside the morgue. She realized that she and Pete were alone, the only living beings in the main autopsy suite.

"We cleared out all the other cases when we brought him in," Pete said, and for a moment, Sara did not understand what he meant.

He pointed to an empty gurney, the last in the row. "This is where I worked on him."

Sara stared at the empty table, wondering why the image didn't flash in her head, that horrible vision of the last time she had seen her husband. Instead, all she saw was a clean gurney, the overhead light bouncing off the dull stainless steel. This is where Pete collected the evidence that had led to Jeffrey's killer. This is where the case broke open, proving without a shadow of a doubt who was involved in his murder.

Standing here now, Sara had expected her memories to overwhelm her, but there was only calmness, a certainty of purpose. Good things were done here. People were helped, even in death. Particularly in death.

Slowly, she turned back to Pete, still not seeing Jeffrey, but feeling him, as if he was in the room with her. Why was that? Why was it that after three and a half years of begging her brain to come up with some sensation that might replicate what it felt like to have Jeffrey with her, being in the morgue had brought him to her in a flash?

Most cops hated sitting in on an autopsy, and Jeffrey was no exception, but he considered his attendance a sign of respect, a promise to the victim that he would do everything he could to bring the killer to justice. That was why he had become a cop—not just to help the innocent, but to punish the criminals who preyed upon them.

In all honesty, that was why Sara had taken the coroner's job. Jeffrey hadn't even heard of Grant County the first time she had walked into the morgue under the hospital, examined a victim, helped break a case. Many years ago, Sara had seen violence firsthand, had herself been the victim of a horrific assault. Every Y-incision she made, every sample she collected, every time she testified in court to the horrors she had documented, she had felt a righteous revenge burning in her chest.

"Sara?"

She realized she'd gone quiet. She had to clear her throat before she could tell Pete, "I had Grady send over the films of our Jane Doe from last night. She was able to speak before she went under. We think her name is Anna."

He clicked through to the file, pulling up Anna's X-rays on-screen. "Is she conscious?"

"I called the hospital before I got here. She's still out."

"Neurologic damage?"

"She pulled through the surgery, which is more than anyone expected. Reflexes are good, pupils are still nonreactive. There's some swelling in her brain. They've got a scan scheduled for later today. It's the infection that's the real concern. They're doing some cultures, trying to figure out the best way to treat it. Sanderson called in the CDC."

"Oh, my." Pete was studying the X-ray. "How much hand strength do you think that would take, ripping out the rib?"

"She was starved, dehydrated. I suppose that would've made it easier."

"Tied down—couldn't have put up much of a fight. But, still . . . goodness. Reminds me of the third Mrs. Hanson. Vivian was a body builder, you know. Biceps as big around as my leg. Quite a woman."

"Thank you, Pete. Thank you for taking care of him."

He gave her another wink. "You earn respect by giving it to others."

She recognized the dictum from his lectures.

"Snoopy," Pete pronounced as the man pushed a gurney through the double doors. Jacquelyn Zabel's head showed above a white sheet, her skin purple with lividity from hanging upside down in the tree. The color was even darker around the woman's lips, as if someone had smeared a handful of blueberries over her mouth. Sara noticed that the woman had been attractive, with only a few fine lines at the edges of her eyes to show age. Again, she was reminded of Anna, the fact that she, too, was a striking woman.

Pete seemed to be thinking the same thing. "Why is it that the more beautiful the woman, the more horrendous the crime?"

Sara shrugged. It was a phenomenon she'd seen as a coroner back in Grant County. Beautiful women tended to pay a heavier price where homicide was concerned.

"Put her in my spot," Pete told his assistant.

Sara watched the expressionless way Snoopy approached his job, the methodical care he took as he angled the body toward an empty slot in the row. Pete was in the minority here; most of the people working in the morgue were either African-American or women. It was the same at Grady Hospital, which made sense, because Sara had noticed that the more horrible the job, the more likely a woman or minority was to do it. The irony was not lost on Sara that she was included in this mix.

Snoopy kicked down the brakes on the wheels and started to organize the various scalpels, knives and saws Pete would need over the next few hours. He had just pulled out a pair of large pruning shears that you normally find in the gardening section of a hardware store when Will and Faith walked into the room.

Will seemed unfazed as they passed by open bodies. Faith, on the other hand, looked worse than she had when Sara had first seen her in the hospital. The woman's lips were white, and she stared straight ahead as she walked past a man with his face peeled from his skull so the doctor could check for contusions.

"Dr. Linton," Will began. "Thank you for coming. I know this is supposed to be your day off."

Sara could only smile and nod, wondering at his formal tone. Will Trent sounded more like a banker with every passing minute. She was still having trouble reconciling the man with his job.

Pete held out a pair of gloves to Sara, but she demurred, saying, "I'm just here to observe."

"Don't want to get your hands dirty?" He blew into the glove to open it, sliding in his hand. "Wanna go to lunch after this? There's a great new Italian place on Highland. I can print out a coupon from the web."

Sara was about to beg off when Faith made a noise that caused them all to look her way. She waved her hand in front of her face, and Sara guessed that it was nothing more nefarious than her presence in the morgue that was causing Faith Mitchell's skin to go ashen.

Pete ignored the reaction, telling Will and Faith, "Found plenty of sperm and fluids on the skin before we scrubbed her down. I'll bag them with the rape kit and send them off."

Will scratched his arm under his jacket sleeve. "I doubt our guy's been caught before, but we'll see what the computer kicks back."

For the sake of procedure, Pete turned on the Dictaphone, giving the time and date, then saying, "This is the body of Jacquelyn Alexandra Zabel, a malnourished female, reportedly thirty-eight years of age. She was found in a wooded area near Route 316 in Conyers, which is located in the Georgia county of Rockdale, in the early hours of Saturday, April fourth. The victim was hanging from a tree, upside down, her right foot caught in the branches. There is an obvious broken neck and signs of severe torture. Performing the procedure is Pete Hanson. Attending are Special Agents Will Trent and Faith Mitchell, and the inimitable Dr. Sara Linton."

He pulled back the sheet and Faith gasped. Sara realized that this was the first time she had seen the abductor's handiwork. In the harsh light of the morgue, every injustice was on display: the dark bruises and welts, the rips in the skin, the black electrical burns that looked like powder but could never be wiped off. The body had been washed prior to examination, the blood scrubbed away, so that the waxy white of the skin stood in stark contrast to the injuries. Shallow slices crisscrossed the victim's flesh, each cut deep enough to bleed but not bring about mortality. Sara guessed the cuts had been made by a razor blade or a very sharp, very thin knife.

"I need to—" Faith didn't finish the sentence. She just turned on her heel and left. Will watched her go, shrugging an apology to Pete.

"Not her favorite part of the job," Pete noted. "She's a bit thin. The victim, that is."

He was right. Jacquelyn Zabel's bones were pronounced under her skin.

Pete asked Will, "How long was she held?"

He shrugged. "We're hoping you can tell us."

"Could be from dehydration," Pete mumbled, pressing his fingers against the woman's shoulder. He asked Sara, "What do you think?"

"The other victim, Anna, was in the same physical condition. He could have been giving them diuretics, withholding food and water. Starvation isn't an unusual form of torture."

"He certainly tried every other kind." Pete sighed, puzzled. "The blood should tell us more."

The examination continued. Snoopy laid down a ruler by the cuts and took photographs as Pete drew hatches on the sketch for the autopsy report, trying to approximate the damage. Finally, he put down the pen, peeling back the eyelids to check the color.

"Interesting," he murmured, indicating Sara should look for herself. Absent a moist environment, the organs of a decomposing body would shrink, the flesh contracting away from any wounds. Sara found several holes in the sclera as she examined the eyes, tiny red dots that opened in perfect round circles.

"Needles or straight pins," Pete guessed. "He pierced each eyeball at least a dozen times."

Sara checked the woman's eyelids, saw the holes went clean through. "Anna's pupils were fixed and dilated," she told him, taking a pair of gloves off the tray, slipping them on as she looked into the woman's bloody ears. Snoopy had cleaned away the clots, but the canals were still coated in dried blood. "Do you have a—"

Snoopy handed her an otoscope. Sara pressed the tip into Zabel's ear, finding the sort of damage she had seen only in child abuse cases. "The drum has been punctured." She turned the head to check the other ear, hearing the broken vertebrae in the neck crunch from the movement. "This one, too." She handed the scope to Pete so he could see.

"Screwdriver?" he asked.

"Scissors," she suggested. "See the way the skin at the opening of the canal has been shaved off?"

"The pattern slants upwards, deeper at the top."

"Right, because the scissors narrow at the point."

Pete nodded, making more notes. "Deaf and blind."

Sara made the obvious leap, opening the woman's mouth. The tongue was intact. She pressed her fingers against the outside of the trachea, then used the laryngoscope Snoopy handed her to look down the throat. "The esophagus is raw. Smell that?"

Pete leaned down. "Bleach? Acid?"

"Drain cleaner."

"I had forgotten your father is a plumber." He pointed to a dark staining around the woman's mouth. "See this?"

Blood always pooled to the lowest point of a dead body, leaving a stain on the skin called lividity. The face was a deep, dark purple from hanging upside down. It was hard to isolate the rash around her lips, but once Pete pointed it out, Sara could see where liquid had been poured into the mouth and dripped down the sides of the face as the victim gagged.

Pete palpated the neck. "Lots of damage here. It definitely looks like he had her drink some kind of astringent. We'll see if it made it to her stomach when we cut her open."

Sara startled when Will spoke; she had forgotten he was there. "It looked like she broke her neck in the fall. That she slipped."

Sara remembered their earlier conversation, his certainty that Jacquelyn Zabel had been hanging in the tree while he looked for her on the ground. He had told her the woman's blood was still warm. She asked, "Were you the one who took her down?"

Will shook his head. "They had to photograph her."

"You checked her carotid for a pulse?" Sara asked.

He nodded. "The blood was dripping from her fingers. It was hot."

Sara checked the woman's hands, saw the fingernails had been broken, some ripped straight out of the nail beds. Per routine, photographs had been taken of the body before Snoopy had cleaned it. Pete knew what Sara was thinking. He indicated the computer monitor. "Snoopy, do you mind pulling up the pre-wash photos?"

The man did as he was asked, Pete and Sara standing over either shoulder. Everything was on the database, from the initial crime-scene photos to the more recent ones taken at the morgue. Snoopy had to click through them all, and Sara saw the original scene in quick succession, Jacquelyn Zabel hanging from the tree, her neck awkwardly bent to the side. Her foot was so firmly caught in the branches that they probably had to cut the limbs to get her down.

Snoopy finally reached the autopsy series. Blood caked the face, the legs, the torso. "There," Sara said, pointing to the chest. They both returned to the body, and Sara stopped herself before reaching down. "Sorry," she apologized. This was Pete's case.

His ego seemed unharmed. He lifted the breast, exposing another crisscrossed wound. This one was deeper in the center of the X. Pete pulled down the overhead light, trying to get a closer look as he pressed the skin apart. Snoopy handed him a magnifying glass, and Pete leaned in even closer, asking Will, "You found a pocket-knife at the scene?"

Will provided, "The only print was the victim's, a latent on the case of the knife."

Pete handed Sara the magnifying glass so she could see for herself. He asked Will, "Left or right hand?"

"I—" Will stopped, glancing back toward the door for Faith. "I don't remember."

"Was the print a thumb? Index?"

Snoopy had gone to the computer to pull up the information, but Will said, "Partial thumb on the butt of the knife."

"Three-inch blade?"

"About."

Pete nodded to himself as he made the notation on his diagram, but Sara wasn't going to make Will wait for him to finish. "She stabbed herself," she told him, holding the magnifying glass over the site, motioning him over. "See the way the wound is V-shaped at the bottom and flat on the top?" Will nodded. "The blade was upside down and moved in an upward trajectory." Sara made the motion, stabbing herself in the chest. "Her thumb was on the butt of the knife, driving it in deeper. She must have dropped it, then fallen. Look at her ankle." She indicated the slight marks around the base of the fibula. "The heart had stopped beating when her foot caught. The bones were broken, but there's no swelling, no sign of trauma. There would be serious bruising if the blood was still circulating when she fell."

Will shook his head. "She wouldn't have—"

"The facts bear it out," Sara interrupted. "The wound was self-inflicted. It would've been fast. She didn't suffer for long." Sara felt the need to add, "Or much longer than she already had."

Will's eyes locked with hers, and Sara had to force herself not to look away. The man may not have looked like a cop, but she was certain he thought like one. Whenever an open case stopped moving forward, any policeman worth his salt took the time to beat himself up for making an ill-timed decision, missing an obvious clue. Will Trent would be doing that now—searching for ways to blame himself for the death of Jacquelyn Zabel.

Sara said, "Your time to help her is now. Not back in that forest."

Pete put down his pen. "She's right." He pressed his hands against the chest. "Feels like there's a lot of blood in here, and she made a damn lucky guess about where to sink the blade. Probably hit the heart immediately. I'd agree that the break in the foot as well as the neck came postmortem." He slipped off a glove as he walked to the computer and pulled up the crime-scene photos. "Look at how her head seems to be resting against the branches, tilted. That's not what happens when you snap your neck during a fall. It would be pressed hard against the offending object. When you're alive, your muscles are taught to prevent such an injury. It's a violent event, not a gentle twisting. Good call, kiddo."

Pete beamed at Sara, and she felt herself blush with a student's pride.

"Why would she kill herself?" Will asked, as if the tortured woman had had everything to live for.

Pete supplied, "She was probably blind, most certainly deaf. I'm surprised she was able to make it up the tree. She wouldn't have heard the searchers, would have no idea that you were looking for her."

"But she—"

"The infrared on the helicopters didn't pick up her signature," Pete interrupted. "But for you being out there, just happening to look up, I imagine the only way you would have found her body is tracking down a DRT call come deer season."

Dead Right There, he meant. All police agencies had their slang, some of it more colorful than others. Hunters were notorious for calling in bodies they'd found DRT.

Pete turned to Sara. "Do you mind?" he asked, nodding toward the bag for the rape kit. Snoopy was an excellent assistant, but Sara got the message: She was back to being an observer. She peeled off her gloves and opened the kit, laying out the swabs and vials. Pete picked up the speculum, pressing open the legs so he could insert it into the vagina.

As with some violent rapes that resulted in homicide, the vaginal walls had stayed clenched postmortem, and the plastic speculum broke as Pete tried to pry it open. Snoopy handed him a metal speculum, and Pete tried again, his hands shaking as he forced open the clamp. It was rough to watch, and Sara was glad that Faith was not there as the wrenching sound of metal parting flesh filled the room. Sara handed Pete a swab, and he inserted the cotton-tipped stick, only to meet resistance.

Pete bent over, trying to find the obstruction. "Dear Lord," he mumbled, his hand scattering the tray of tools as he snatched up a pair of thin-nosed forceps. His voice was absent any charm as he told Sara, "Glove up—help me with this."

Sara snapped on the gloves, wrapping her hands around the speculum as he reached in with the forceps, which were nothing more than a long pair of tweezers. The tips grabbed something, and he pulled back his arm. A long, single piece of white plastic came out, like a silk cloth from a magician's sleeve. Pete kept pulling, layering the plastic into a large bowl. Section after section came, each streaked in dark, black blood, each connected to the next in a perforated line.

"Trash bags," Will said.

Sara could not breathe. "Anna," she said. "We need to check Anna."

CHAPTER TEN

WILL'S OFFICE ON THE THIRD FLOOR OF CITY HALL East was little more than a storage closet with a window that looked down onto a pair of abandoned railroad tracks and a Kroger grocery store parking lot that seemed to be the meeting place for many suspicious-looking people in very expensive cars. The back of Will's chair was pressed so tightly against the wall that it gouged the sheetrock every time he turned. Not that he needed to turn. He could see the entire office without moving his head. Even getting into the chair was difficult because Will had to squeeze between his desk and the window in order to reach it—a maneuver that made him glad he wasn't planning on having children.

He leaned on his elbow as he watched his computer boot up, the screen flickering, the little icons flashing into place. Will opened his email first, tucking a pair of headphones into his ears so he could hear them through the SpeakText program he'd installed a few years ago. After deleting a couple of sexual enhancement offers and a plea from a deposed Nigerian president, he found a note from Amanda and a policy-change notice on the state health insurance plan that he sent to his private email so he could muddle through his loss of covered items from the comfort of his own home.

Amanda's email needed no such study. She always

wrote in all caps and she seldom bothered with proper sentence construction. UPDATE ME was plastered across the screen in a thick, bold font.

What could he tell her? That their victim had eleven kitchen garbage bags shoved up inside her? That Anna, the victim who had survived, had the same number inside of her? That twelve hours had passed and they were no closer to finding out who had taken the women, let alone what pattern connected the two victims?

Blind, possibly deaf, possibly mute. Will had been in the cave where the women were kept. He could not imagine the horrors they experienced. Seeing the torturer's instruments had been bad enough, but he imagined not seeing them would be worse. At least the burden of Jackie Zabel's death was off his shoulders, though knowing that the woman had chosen death when help was so nearby brought him no comfort.

Will could still hear the compassionate tone Sara Linton had used as she'd explained how Zabel had taken her life. He could not remember the last time a woman had talked to him that way—tried to throw him a life vest instead of yelling at him to swim harder the way Faith did or, worse, grabbing onto his legs and pulling him farther down the way Angie always tried.

Will slumped back in his chair, knowing he should put Sara out of his mind. There was a case in front of him that needed his undivided attention, and Will made himself focus on the women he could actually have an impact on.

Both Anna and Jackie had probably escaped from the cave at the same time, Jackie unable to hear or see, Anna most probably blind. There would have been no way for the two damaged women to communicate with each other except through touch. Had they held hands, stumbling together blindly as they'd tried to find their way out of the forest? Somehow, they'd been separated, lost from each other. Anna must have known she was on a road, felt the cool asphalt on the soles of her bare feet, heard the roar of an approaching car. Jackie had gone the other way—finding a tree, climbing to what must have felt like safety. Waiting. Every creak of the tree, every movement of the branches, sending panic through her body as she waited for her abductor to find her and take her back to that cold, dark place.

She would have been holding her license, her identity, in one hand and the means of her death in the other. It was an almost incomprehensible choice. Climb down, walk aimlessly to look for help, risking possible capture? Or plunge the blade into her chest? Fight for her life? Or seize control and end it on her own terms?

The autopsy bore witness to her decision. The blade had pierced her heart, severing the main artery, filling the chest with blood. According to Sara, Jackie had probably passed out almost instantly, her heart stopping even as she fell from the tree. Knife dropping. Driver's license dropping. They had found aspirin in her stomach. It had thinned her blood so that it was still dripping long after her death. This was the hot splatter on Will's neck. Looking up, seeing her hand reaching down, he had thought she was grasping for freedom, but she had actually managed to find it on her own.

He opened a large folder on his desk and fanned out the photos of the cave. The torture devices, the marine battery, the unopened cans of soup—Charlie had documented all of it, recording the descriptions on a master list. Will thumbed through the photographs, finding the best view of the cave. Charlie had squatted at the base of the ladder the same way Will had last night. Xenon lights pulled every nook and cranny out of shadow. Will found another photo, this one showing the sexual devices laid out like artifacts at an archaeological dig. He could figure out from first glance how most of them were used, but some were so complicated, so horrific, that his mind could not grasp how they operated.

Will was so lost in thought that his brain took its time registering the fact that his cell phone was ringing. He opened the pieces, saying, "Trent."

"It's Lola, baby."

"Who?"

"Lola. One of Angie's girls."

The prostitute from last night. Will tried to keep his tone even, because he was more furious with Angie than the hooker, who was just doing what bottom feeders always did—trying to exploit an angle. Will wasn't Angie's angle, though, and he was sick of these girls trying to play him. He said, "Listen, I'm not getting you out of jail. If you're one of Angie's girls, then get Angie to help you."

"I can't get ahold of her."

"Yeah, well, I can't either, so stop calling me for help when I don't even know her phone number. Understand?" He didn't give her time to respond. He ended the call and gently put his cell phone on his desk. The tape was starting to peel, the string coming loose. He had asked Angie to help him with the phone before she left, but, like a lot of things regarding Will, it hadn't been a priority.

He looked down at his hand, the wedding ring on his finger. Was he stupid or just pathetic? He couldn't tell the difference anymore. He bet Sara Linton wasn't the sort of woman who pulled this kind of crap in a relationship. Then again, Will bet Sara's husband hadn't been the kind of pussy who would let it happen.

"God, I hate autopsies." Faith pushed her way into his office, her color still off. Will knew she hated autopsies—it was an obvious aversion—but this was the first time he'd ever heard Faith admit to it. "Caroline left a message on my cell." She meant Amanda's assistant. "We can't talk to Joelyn Zabel without counsel present."

Jackie Zabel's sister. "Is she really going to sue the department?"

She dropped her purse on his desk. "As soon as she finds a lawyer in the Yellow Pages. Are you ready to go?"

He looked at the time on the computer. They were supposed to meet the Coldfields in half an hour, but the shelter was less than ten minutes away. "Let's talk this through a little bit more," he suggested.

There was a folding chair against the wall, and Faith had to close the door before she could sit down. Her own office was not much larger than Will's, but you could at least stretch your legs out in front of you without your feet hitting a wall. Will wasn't sure why, but they always ended up back in his office. Maybe it was because Faith's office had, in fact, been a storage closet. There was no window and it still held the lingering scent of urine cake and toilet cleaner. The first time she had closed the door, she'd nearly passed out from the fumes.

Faith nodded toward the computer. "What've you got?"

Will turned the monitor around so that Faith could read Amanda's email.

Faith squinted at the screen, scowling. He kept the background bright pink and the letters navy blue, which for some reason made it easier for him to make out the words. She mumbled under her breath as she adjusted the colors, then slid over the keyboard so she could type a reply. The first time she had done this, Will had complained, but over the last few months, he'd come to realize that Faith was just plain bossy, no matter who she was dealing with. Maybe it came from being a mother since the age of fifteen, or maybe it was just a natural inclination, but she wasn't comfortable unless she was doing everything herself.

With Jeremy off to college and Victor Martinez apparently out of the picture, Will was taking the brunt of her bossiness. He supposed this was what it was like to have an older sister. But then again, Angie acted the same way with Will and he was sleeping with her. When she was around.

Faith said, "Amanda should already have the autopsy report on Jacquelyn Zabel by now." She typed as she talked. "What do we have? No fingerprints or trace evidence to follow. Plenty of DNA in sperm and blood, but no matches so far. No ID or even last name on Anna. An attacker who blinds his victims, punches out their eardrums, makes them drink Drano. The trash bags . . . shit, I can't even begin to understand that. He tortures them with God knows what. One had a rib removed . . ." She hit the arrow key, going back to add something earlier in the line. "Zabel was probably going to be next."

"The aspirin," Will said. The aspirin found in

Jacquelyn Zabel's stomach was ten times more than the average person would take.

"Nice of him to give them something for their pain." Faith arrowed back down the screen. "Can you imagine? Trapped in that cave, can't hear him coming, can't see what he's doing, can't scream for help." Faith clicked the mouse, sending the email, then sat back in the chair. "Eleven trash bags. How did Sara miss that on the first victim?"

"I don't imagine you stop to do a pelvic exam when a woman comes in with nearly every bone in her body broken and one foot in the grave."

"Don't get testy with me," she said, though Will didn't think he was being testy at all. "She doesn't belong in the middle of this case."

"Who?"

Faith rolled her eyes, using the mouse to click open the browser.

"What are you doing?" he asked.

"I'm going to look her up. Her husband was a cop when he died. I'm sure whatever happened to him made the news."

"That's not fair."

"Fair?" Faith tapped the keyboard. "What do you mean, 'fair'?"

"Faith, don't intrude in her personal—"

She hit the enter key. Will didn't know what else to do, so he reached down and unplugged the computer. Faith jiggled the mouse, then pressed the space bar. The building was old—the power was always going off. She glanced up, noticing the lights were still on.

"Did you turn off the computer?"

"If Sara Linton wanted you to know the details of her personal life, then she would tell you."

"You'd think you'd have better posture with that stick up your ass." Faith crossed her arms, giving him a sharp look. "Don't you think it's weird how she's inserting herself into our investigation? I mean, she's not a coroner anymore. She's a civilian. If she wasn't so pretty, you'd see how strange—"

"What does her beauty have to do with anything?"

Faith was kind enough to let his words hang over their heads like a neon sign flashing *idiot*. She gave it almost a full minute to burn out before saying, "Don't forget I have a computer in my office. I can look her up there just as easily."

"Whatever you find out, I don't want to know."

Faith rubbed her face with her hands. She stared at the gray sky outside the window for another solid minute. "This is crazy. We're spinning our wheels here. We need a break, something to follow."

"Pauline McGhee—"

"Leo is drawing a blank on the brother. He says her house is clean—no documents, no indication of parents, relatives. No record of an alias, but that's easy enough to hide if you pay the right people enough money. Pauline's neighbors haven't changed their story, either: They either don't know her or don't like her. Either way, they can't tell us anything about her life. He talked to the teachers at the kid's school. Same thing. I mean, Christ, her son is in care right now because the mother doesn't have any close friends who are willing to take him."

"What's Leo doing now?"

She checked her watch. "Probably trying to figure

out how to knock off early." She rubbed her eyes again, obviously tired. "He's running McGhee's fingerprints, but that's a long shot unless she's ever been arrested."

"Is he still worried about us treading on his case?"

"Even more so than before." Faith pressed her lips together. "I bet it's because he's been sick. They do that, you know—look at what your insurance is costing, try to push you out if you're too much of a drain on the system. God forbid you have a chronic disease that requires expensive medication."

Thankfully, that wasn't something Will or Faith had to worry about yet. He said, "Pauline's abduction could be separate from our case, something as simple as an argument that set off her brother, or a stranger abduction. She's an attractive woman."

"If she's not connected to our case, it's more likely someone she knew is involved."

"So, that's the brother."

"She wouldn't have warned the kid about him unless she was worried." Faith added, "Of course, there's also that Morgan guy—arrogant bastard. I was ready to slap him through the phone when I talked to him. Maybe there was something going on between him and Pauline."

"They worked together. She could've pushed him too far and he snapped. That happens a lot when men work with bossy women."

"Ha-ha," Faith allowed. "Wouldn't Felix recognize Morgan if he was the abductor?"

Will shrugged. Kids could block out anything. Adults weren't bad at it, either.

Faith pointed out, "Neither of our two known victims has children. Neither of them has been reported missing, as far as we know. Jacquelyn Zabel's car is gone. We have no idea if Anna has a car, since we don't even know her last name." Her tone was getting sharper as she ticked off each dead end. "Or her first name. It could be something other than Anna. Who knows what Sara heard?"

"I heard it," Will defended. "I heard her say 'Anna.' "

Faith skipped over his response. "Do you still think there might be two abductors?"

"I'm not sure about anything right now, except that whoever is doing this is no amateur. His DNA is everywhere, which means he probably doesn't have a criminal record he's worried about. We don't have any clues because he didn't leave any. He's good at this. He knows how to cover his tracks."

"A cop?"

Will let the question go unanswered.

Faith reasoned it out. "There's something he's doing that makes women trust him—lets him get close enough to snatch them without anyone seeing."

"The suit," Will said. "Women—men, too—are more likely to trust a well-dressed stranger. It's a class judgment, but it's true."

"Great. We just need to round up all the men in Atlanta who were wearing suits this morning." She held up her fingers, ticking off a list. "No fingerprints on the trash bags found in either woman. Nothing to trace on any of the items found in the cave. The bloody print on Jacquelyn Zabel's driver's license belongs to Anna. We don't know her last name. We don't know where she lived or worked or if she has family." Faith had run out of fingers.

"The abductor obviously has a method. He's patient.

He excavates the cave, gets it ready for his captives. Like you said, he probably watches the women before he abducts them. He's done this before. Who knows how many times."

"Yeah, but his victims haven't lived to talk about it, or we'd have something come up in the FBI database."

Will's desk phone rang, and Faith picked it up. "Mitchell." She listened for a few beats, then took her notepad out of her purse. She wrote in neat block letters, but Will was incapable of deciphering the words. "Can you follow up on that?" She waited. "Great. Call me on my cell."

She hung up the phone. "That was Leo. The prints came back from Pauline McGhee's SUV. Her real name is Pauline Agnes Seward. She had a missing persons report filed in Ann Arbor, Michigan, back in '89. She was seventeen. According to the report, her parents said there was some kind of argument that set things off. She was off the straight and narrow—doing drugs, sleeping around. Her prints were on file because of a shoplifting rap she pleaded *nolo* on. The locals made a cursory search, put her in the database, but this is the first hit they've had in twenty years."

"That jibes with what Morgan said. Pauline told him she ran away from home when she was seventeen. What about the brother?"

"Nothing came up. Leo's going to do a deeper background search." Faith put the pad back in her pocketbook. "He's trying to track down the parents. Hopefully they're still in Michigan."

"Seward doesn't sound like a common name."

"It's not," she agreed. "Something would've come up

in the computer if the brother was involved in a serious crime."

"Do we have an age range? A name?"

"Leo said he'd get back to us as soon as he found something."

Will sat back in his chair, leaned his head against the wall. "Pauline still isn't part of our case. We don't have a pattern to match her with."

"She looks like our other victims. No one likes her. She's not close to anyone."

"She might be close to her brother," Will said. "Leo says Pauline had Felix through a sperm donor, right? Maybe the brother is the donor?"

Faith made a noise of disgust. "God, Will."

Her tone made him feel guilty for suggesting such a thing, but the fact was their job was all about thinking of the worst things that could happen. "Why else would Pauline warn her son that his uncle is a bad man she needed to protect him from?"

Faith was reluctant to answer. Finally, she said, "Sexual abuse."

"I could be way off," he admitted. "Her brother could be a thief or an embezzler or a drug addict. He could be a con."

"If a Seward had a record in Michigan, Leo would have already pulled him up on the computer search."

"Maybe the brother's been lucky."

Faith shook her head. "Pauline was scared of him, didn't want her son around him. That points to violence, or fear of violence."

"Like you said, if the brother was threatening or stalking her, there'd be a report somewhere."

"Not necessarily. He's still her brother. People don't

run to the police when it's a family matter. You know that."

Will wasn't so sure, but she had a point about Leo's computer search. "What would make you warn Jeremy away from your brother?"

She gave it some thought. "I can't think of anything Zeke could do that would make me tell Jeremy not to talk to him."

"What if he hit you?"

She opened her mouth to answer, then seemed to change her mind. "It's not about whether I would put up with it—it's about what Pauline would do." Faith was quiet, thinking. "Families are complicated. People put up with a lot of shit because of blood."

"Blackmail?" Will knew he was grasping at straws, but he continued, "Maybe the brother knew something bad about Pauline's past? There has to be a reason she changed her name at seventeen. Fast-forward to now. Pauline has a lucrative job. She's good on her mortgage. She drives a nice car. She'd probably be willing to pay a lot of money to keep it that way."

Will shot down his own idea. "On the other hand, if the brother is blackmailing her, he needs her to keep working. There's no reason to take her."

"It's not like she's being held for ransom. Nobody cares that she's gone."

Will shook his head. Another dead end.

Faith said, "Okay, maybe Pauline's not involved in our case. Maybe she's got some kind of weird *Flowers in the Attic* thing going on with her brother. What do we do now? Just sit around and wait for a third—or fourth—woman to be taken?"

Will didn't know how to answer that. Fortunately, he didn't have to.

Faith looked at her watch. "Let's go talk to the Coldfields."

THERE WERE CHILDREN at the Fred Street Women's Shelter—something Will hadn't anticipated, though of course it made sense that homeless women would also have homeless children. A small area at the front of the shelter was cordoned off for their play. Their ages were varied, but he assumed they were all under the age of six, because the older kids would be in school this time of day. All the children were dressed in mismatched, faded clothes and playing with toys that had seen better days: Barbie dolls with short haircuts, Tonka toys with missing wheels. Will supposed he should have felt sad for them, because watching them play was much like a scene from his own childhood, but the exception here was that these kids had at least one parent who was looking out for them, one connection to the normal world.

"Good Lord," Faith mumbled, digging into her purse. There was a jar for donations on the counter by the front entrance, and she shoved in a couple of tens. "Who's watching these kids?"

Will looked down the hall. The walls were decorated with paper Easter cutouts and some of the children's drawings. He saw a closed door with the symbol for a women's restroom. "She's probably in the toilet."

"Anyone could snatch them."

Will didn't think many people wanted these children. That was part of the problem.

"Ring bell for service," Faith said, he supposed reading from the sign below the bell, which even a monkey could have figured out.

Will reached over and rang the bell.

She said, "They do computer training here."

"What?"

Faith picked up one of the brochures on the counter. Will saw pictures of smiling women and children on the front, a couple of corporate logos that named the big-money sponsors along the bottom. "Computer training, counseling, meals." Her eyes went back and forth as she skimmed the text. "Medical counseling with a Christian focus." She dropped the pamphlet back in with the others. "I guess that means they tell you you're going to hell if you have an abortion. Good advice for women who've already got one mouth they can't afford to feed." She tapped the bell again, this time hard enough to make it spin off the counter.

Will picked up the bell from the floor. When he stood, he found a large Hispanic woman behind the counter, an infant in her arms. She spoke in a distinctive Texas drawl, her words directed toward Faith. "If you're here to arrest someone, we ask that you don't do it in front of the children."

"We're here to talk to Judith Coldfield," Faith replied, keeping her voice low, mindful that the kids were not only watching but had guessed her occupation just like the woman.

"Walk around the side of the building to the store-front. Judith's working retail today." She didn't wait for a thank-you. Instead, she turned around with the child and went back down the hallway.

Faith pushed open the door, heading out into the street again. "These places annoy the hell out of me."

Will thought a homeless shelter was a strange thing to hate, even for Faith. "Why is that?"

"Just help them. Don't make them pray about it."

"Some people find solace in prayer."

"What if they don't? Then they're not worthy of being helped? You may be homeless and starving to death, but you can't have a free meal or a safe place to sleep unless you agree that abortion is an abomination and that other people have the right to tell you what to do with your body?"

Will wasn't sure how to answer her, so he just followed her around the side of the brick building, watching her angrily hitch her purse up on her shoulder. She was still mumbling when they rounded the corner to the storefront. There was a large sign out front that probably had the name of the shelter on it. The economy was bad for everybody these days, but especially for charities who depended on people feeling flush enough to help their fellow man. Many of the local shelters took in donations that they sold in order to help pay for basic operations. Window lettering advertised various items inside the store. Faith read them off as they walked to the entrance.

" 'Housewares, linens, clothes, donations welcome, free pickup for larger items.' "

Will opened the door, willing her to shut up.

" 'Open every day but Sunday.' 'No dogs allowed.' "

"I got it," he told her, glancing around the store. Blenders were lined up on a shelf, toasters and small microwaves underneath. There were some clothes on racks, mostly the kind of styles that were very popular during the eighties. Canned soups and various pantry staples were stored away from the sun streaming in through the windows. Will's stomach grumbled, and he remembered sorting cans of food that came into the orphanage over the holidays. Nobody ever gave the good stuff. It was usually Spam and pickled beets, just the sort of thing every kid wanted for Christmas dinner.

Faith had found another sign. " 'All donations are tax deductible. Proceeds go directly to help homeless women and children. God blesses those who bless others.' "

He realized that his jaw was aching from clenching his teeth so hard. Luckily, he didn't have to dwell on the pain for long. A man popped up from behind the counter like Mr. Drucker from *Green Acres*. "How y'all doin'?"

Faith's hand flew to her chest. "Who the hell are you?"

The man blushed so hard that Will could almost feel the heat coming off his face. "Sorry, ma'am." He wiped his hand on the front of his T-shirt. Black finger marks showed where he had done this many times before. "Tom Coldfield. I'm helping my mom with . . ." He indicated the floor behind the counter. Will saw he was working on a push-style lawnmower. The engine was partially disassembled. It looked like he was trying to put on a new fan belt, which hardly explained why the carburetor was on the floor.

Will told him, "There's a nut on the—"

Faith interrupted. "I'm Special Agent Faith Mitchell. This is my partner, Will Trent. We're here to meet with Judith and Henry Coldfield. I assume you're related?"

"My folks," the man explained, a prominent pair of buckteeth sticking out as he smiled at Faith. "They're in the back. Dad's kind of unhappy about missing his golf game." He seemed to realize how inconsequential this seemed to them. "Sorry, I know what happened to that woman was awful. It's just that—well—they told that other detective everything that happened."

Faith kept up her sweet side. "I'm sure they won't mind telling us again."

Tom Coldfield seemed to disagree, but he motioned for them to follow him to the back room anyway. Will let Faith go ahead of him, and they all had to pick their way around boxes and various piles of items that had been donated to the shelter. Will guessed Tom Coldfield had been athletic at one point in his life, but his early thirties had beaten that out of him, giving a round spread to his waist and a stoop to his shoulders. There was a bald spot on the crown of his head, almost like a tonsure that a Franciscan monk would sport. Without even asking, Will guessed that Tom Coldfield had a couple of kids. He looked like a textbook soccer dad. He probably drove a minivan and played online fantasy football.

Tom said, "Sorry about the mess. We're short volunteers."

Faith asked, "Do you work here?"

"Oh, no. I'd go crazy if I did." He gave a chuckle at what must have been Faith's surprised reaction. "I'm an air traffic controller. My mom guilts me into helping out when they're shorthanded."

"Were you in the military?"

"Air Force—six years. How'd you guess?"

Faith shrugged. "Easiest way to get training." Then, probably to build a rapport with the man, she added, "My brother's in the Air Force, stationed in Germany."

Tom moved a box out of their way. "Ramstein?"

"Landstuhl. He's a surgeon."

"That's a bad mess over there. Your brother's doing the Lord's work."

Faith was in cop mode now, her personal opinions set aside. "He certainly is."

Tom stopped in front of a closed door and knocked. Will looked down the hallway, seeing the other end of the shelter, the counter they'd stood in front of while they waited for the woman to come out of the bathroom. Faith noticed this, too, and she rolled her eyes at Will as Tom opened the door.

"Mom, this is Detective Trent and—I'm sorry, is it Mitchell?"

"Yes," Faith confirmed.

Tom introduced his parents, though this was certainly a formality as the room contained only two people. Judith was sitting behind a desk, a ledger opened in front of her. Henry was in a chair by the window. He had a newspaper in his hands, and he shook the paper, creasing it carefully before he gave Will and Faith his attention. Tom hadn't been lying when he'd said his father was annoyed about missing his golf game. Henry Coldfield looked like a parody of a grumpy old man.

"Should I get some more chairs?" Tom offered. He didn't wait for a response, disappearing before anyone could answer. The office was regular-size, which was to say it was big enough for four people to occupy without knocking elbows. Still, Will stood in the doorway while Faith took the only other vacant chair in the room. Normally, they figured out ahead of time who would do the talking, but they were going into this interview cold. When Will looked to Faith for guidance, she only shrugged. The family was hard to read. They would have to figure this out as they went along. The first step in an interview was to make the witness feel comfortable. People didn't tend to open up and start being helpful until you made them realize that you weren't the enemy. Since she was sitting closest to them, Faith started.

"Mr. and Mrs. Coldfield, thank you for meeting with us. I know you already spoke to Detective Galloway, but what you went through the other night was very traumatic. Sometimes it takes a few days before you remember everything."

"We've never really had anything like this happen to us before," Judith Coldfield said, and Will wondered if she thought people routinely rammed their cars into women who had been raped and tortured in an underground cavern.

Henry seemed to realize this as well. "Judith."

"Oh, dear." Judith put her hand to her mouth, covering the embarrassed smile on her face. Will saw where Tom had gotten his buckteeth as well as his easy blush. The woman explained, "I meant to say, we've never talked to the police before." She patted her husband's hand. "Henry got a speeding ticket once, but once was enough. When was that, dear?"

"Summer of '83," Henry answered, the set to his jaw indicating he still hadn't gotten over the experience. He looked at Will as he spoke, as if only a man would understand. "Seven miles over the limit."

Will tried to think of something that sounded commiserating, but his mind drew a blank. He asked Judith, "You're from up North?"

"Is it that obvious?" She laughed, putting her hand to her mouth again, covering her smile. She was painfully self-conscious about her protruding teeth. "Pennsylvania."

"Is that where you lived before you retired?"

"Oh, no," Judith said. "Henry's job moved us around a bit. Mostly in the Northwest. We lived in Oregon, Washington State, California—but we didn't like that, did we?" Henry made a grumpy sound. "We were in Oklahoma, but not for long. Have you ever been? It's so flat there."

Faith cut to the chase. "How about Michigan?"

Judith shook her head, but Henry supplied, "I saw a football game in Michigan back in '71. Michigan and Ohio State. Ten to seven. Nearly froze to death."

Faith lighted on the opportunity to draw him out. "You're a football fan?"

"Can't stand it." His frown seemed to indicate he was still unhappy about the situation, though most people would kill to see a rivalry game.

"Henry was a salesman," Judith supplied. "He traveled around quite a bit even before that. His father was in the Army for thirty years."

Faith took over, trying to find a way to open up the man. "My grandfather was Army."

Judith jumped in again. "Henry had a college deferment for the war." Will guessed she meant Vietnam. "We had friends who served, of course, and Tom was in the Air Force, which we're really proud of. Isn't that right, Tom?"

Will hadn't realized Tom was back. The Coldfields' son smiled an apology. "Sorry, no more chairs. The kids are using them to build a fort."

"Where were you stationed?" Faith asked him.

"I was at Keesler both tours," he answered. "I started

out my training, then worked my way up to the Three-thirty-fourth's master sergeant in charge of tower class fundamentals. They were talking about sending me to Altus when I put in for discharge."

"I was going to ask you why you left the Air Force, then I remembered Keesler's in Mississippi."

The blush came back in full force, and Tom gave an embarrassed laugh. "Yes, ma'am."

Faith turned her attention to Henry, probably guessing that they wouldn't get much from Judith without Henry's blessing. "Ever leave stateside?"

"Always stayed in the U.S."

"You have an Army accent," Faith noted, which Will gathered meant he had no accent at all.

Henry's reticence seemed to slowly melt away under Faith's attention. "You go where they tell you to go."

"That's exactly what my brother said when he shipped overseas." Faith leaned forward. "If you want the truth, I think he likes moving around all the time, never putting down roots."

Henry started to open up some more. "Married?"

"Nope."

"Lady in every port?"

"Lord, I hope not." Faith laughed. "As far as my mother's concerned, it was the Air Force or the priesthood."

Henry chuckled. "Most mothers feel that way about their sons." He squeezed his wife's hand, and Judith beamed proudly at Tom.

Faith turned her attention to the son. "You said you're an air traffic controller?"

"Yes, ma'am," he answered, though Faith was probably younger than Tom.

Tom told them, "I work out of Charlie Brown." He meant the general aviation airport just west of Atlanta. "Been there about ten years. It's a nice gig. Sometimes we handle Dobbins traffic overnight." Dobbins was an Air Force base just outside the city. "I bet your brother's flown out of there before."

"I bet he has," Faith agreed, keeping eye contact with the man just long enough to make him feel flattered. "You live out in Conyers now?"

"Yes, ma'am." Tom smiled openly, his buckteeth jutting out like tusks on an elephant. He was more relaxed now, talkative. "I moved to Atlanta when I left Keesler." He nodded toward his mother. "I was real happy when my parents decided to move down here."

"They're on Clairmont Road, right?"

Tom nodded, still smiling. "Close enough to visit without having to pack a suitcase."

Judith didn't seem to like the easy rapport that was developing between the two. She quickly inserted herself back into the conversation. "Tom's wife loves her flower garden." She started to rummage around in her purse. "Mark, his son, is obsessed with aviation. Every day, he looks more and more like his father."

"Mom, they don't need to see—"

He was too late. Judith pulled out a photograph and handed it to Faith, who made the proper appreciative noises before passing it to Will.

He kept his expression neutral as he looked at the family photo. The Coldfield genes were certainly strong. The girl and boy in the picture were carbon copies of their father. Making matters worse, Tom had not found himself an attractive wife to dilute the Coldfield gene pool. She had stringy-looking blonde hair and a resigned set to her mouth that seemed to indicate this was as good as it would ever get.

"Darla," Judith supplied, naming the wife. "They've been married for almost ten years. Isn't that right, Tom?"

He shrugged in that embarrassed way children shrug at their parents.

"Very nice," Will said, handing the picture back to Judith.

Judith asked Faith, "Do you have children?"

"A son." Faith didn't offer any more information. Instead she asked Judith, "Is Tom an only child?"

"That's right." Judith smiled again, covering her mouth. "Henry and I didn't think we'd be able to . . ." Her voice trailed off, and she just stared at Tom with obvious pride. "He was a miracle."

Again Tom shrugged, obviously embarrassed.

Faith subtly shifted the topic onto the reason they were all here. "And you were visiting Tom and his family the day of the accident?"

Judith nodded. "He wanted to do something nice for our fortieth anniversary. Didn't you, Tom?" Her voice took on a distant quality. "Such a horrible thing to happen. I don't think another anniversary will go by without remembering . . ."

Tom spoke. "I don't understand how this could happen. How could that woman—" He shook his head. "It makes no sense. Who the hell would do something like that?"

"Tom," Judith shushed. "Language."

Faith gave Will a glance that indicated she was using every ounce of willpower in her body not to roll her eyes. She recovered quickly, directing her words toward the elderly couple. "I know you've already told Detective Galloway everything, but let's start fresh from the beginning. You were driving down the road, you saw the woman, and then . . . ?"

"Well," Judith began. "At first I thought it might be a deer. We've seen deer on the side of the road many times. Henry always goes slow if it's dark in case one darts out."

"They see the lights and it just freezes them," Henry explained, as if a deer caught in headlights was an obscure phenomenon.

"It wasn't dark," Judith continued. "It was dusk, I suppose. And I saw this thing in the road. I opened my mouth to tell Henry, but it was too late. We had already hit it. *Her.*" She took out a tissue from her purse and pressed it to her eyes. "Those nice men tried to help her, but I don't think—surely, after all that . . ."

Henry took his wife's hand again. "Has she . . . is the woman . . . ?"

"She's still in the hospital," Faith provided. "They're not sure if she'll ever regain consciousness."

"My Lord," Judith breathed, almost a prayer. "I hope she doesn't."

"Mother—" Tom's voice rose in surprise.

"I know that sounds mean, but I hope she never knows."

The family went quiet. Tom looked at his father. Henry's throat worked, and Will could tell the man was starting to get overwhelmed by his memories. "Thought I was having a heart attack," he managed around a harsh laugh.

Judith lowered her voice, confiding as if her husband were not right beside her, "Henry has heart issues."

"Nothing bad," he countered. "Stupid air bag hit me square in the chest. Safety device, they call it. Damn thing almost killed me."

Faith asked, "Mr. Coldfield, did you see the woman on the road?"

Henry nodded. "It's what Judith said. It was too late to stop. I wasn't speeding. I was going the posted limit. I saw something—thought it was a deer, like she said. Jammed my foot on the brake. She just appeared out of nowhere. Right out of nowhere. I still didn't think it was a woman until we got out of the car and saw her there. Awful. Just awful."

"Have you always worn glasses?" Will broached the subject carefully.

"I'm an amateur pilot. Get my eyes checked twice a year." He took off the glasses, his feathers ruffled but his tone steady. "I may be old, but I'm flight ready. No cataracts, corrected to twenty-twenty."

Will decided he might as well get it all out of the way. "And your heart?"

Judith intervened. "It's nothing really. Just something to keep an eye on, make sure he's not straining himself too much."

Henry took over, still indignant. "Nothing that concerns the doctors. I take some horse pills. I don't do any heavy lifting. I'm fine."

Faith tried to soothe him, changing the subject. "An Army brat flying airplanes?"

Henry seemed to be debating whether or not to let the topic of his health go. Finally, he answered, "My dad got me lessons when I was a kid. We were stationed up in Nowhere, Alaska. He thought it was a good way to keep me out of trouble."

Faith smiled, helping him relax again. "Good flying weather?"

"If you were lucky." He laughed, wistful. "Had to be careful landing—cold wind would whip that plane around like a flyswatter. Some days, I'd just close my eyes and hope I touched down on the field and not in the ice."

"Cold field," Faith pointed out, making a play on his name.

"Right," Henry said, as if he'd heard the pun many times. He put his glasses back on, all business. "Listen, I'm not one to tell other people how to go about their business, but why aren't you asking us about that other car?"

"What other car?" Faith echoed. "The one that stopped to help?"

"No, the other one we saw streaking down the road, opposite. It must have been about two minutes before we hit that girl."

Judith filled their stunned silence. "Surely you know this already. We told the other policeman all about it."

CHAPTER ELEVEN

T HE DRIVE TO THE ROCKDALE COUNTY POLICE STA-
tion was a blur that Faith filled with every expletive she
could think of.

"I knew that jackass was lying to me," she said, cursing Max Galloway and the entire Rockdale police force.
"You should've seen that smug way he looked at me
when he left the hospital." She slammed her palm into
the steering wheel, wishing she were slamming it into
Galloway's Adam's apple. "Do they think this is some
kind of game? Didn't they see what was done to that
woman? For the love of God."

Beside her, Will remained silent. As usual, she had no
idea what was going through his mind. He'd been quiet
the entire trip, and did not speak until she pulled into
the visitors' parking lot in front of the Rockdale
County police station.

He asked, "Are you finished being mad?"

"Hell, no, I'm not finished. They lied to us. They
haven't even faxed us the damn crime-scene report.
How the hell can we work a case when they're holding
back information that could—"

"Think about why they did it," Will countered.
"One woman is dead, the other's just as good as, and
they're still hiding evidence from us. They don't care
about the people involved, Faith. All they care about is

their egos, and showing us up. They're leaking information to the press, they're refusing to cooperate. You think us going in there with guns blazing is going to get us what we want?"

Faith opened her mouth to answer, but Will was already getting out of the car. He walked around to the driver's side and opened her door like they were on a date.

He told her, "Trust me on this one thing, Faith. You can't push a string."

She waved his hand away. "I'm not going to eat shit from Max Galloway."

"I'll eat it," he assured her, holding out his hand like she needed help getting out of the car.

Faith grabbed her purse from the back seat. She followed him up the sidewalk, thinking it was no wonder everyone who met Will Trent took him for a certified public accountant. She could not fathom the man's meagerness of ego. In the year she had worked with him, the strongest emotion she'd seen Will display was irritation, usually at her. He could be moody or wistful and God knew he could beat himself up about a lot of things, but she'd never seen him truly angry. He'd once been alone in a room with a suspect who had just hours before tried to put a bullet in his head, and the only feeling Will had shown was empathy.

The uniformed patrolman behind the front counter obviously recognized Will. His lip went up into a sneer. "Trent."

"Detective Fierro," Will replied, though the man was obviously no longer a detective. His sizable stomach pressed against the buttons of his patrol uniform like the filling oozing out of a jelly doughnut. Considering what Fierro had said to Amanda about greasing Lyle Peterson's pole, Faith was surprised the man wasn't using a wheelchair.

Fierro said, "I should've put that board back over your head and left you in that cave."

"I'm really glad you didn't." Will indicated Faith. "This is my partner, Special Agent Mitchell. We need to speak with Detective Max Galloway."

"About what?"

Faith was over the niceties. She opened her mouth to blast him, but Will cut her off with a look.

He said, "Maybe we could talk to Chief Peterson if Detective Galloway isn't available."

Faith added, "Or we could talk to your buddy Sam Lawson at the *Atlanta Beacon* and tell him those stories you've been feeding him are just your way of covering your fat ass for all the mistakes you've made in this case."

"You are some kind of bitch, lady."

"I haven't even started," Faith told him. "Get Galloway out here right now before we put our boss on this. She already took your shield. What do you think she's going to take next? My guess is your little—"

"Faith," Will said, more a warning than a word.

Fierro picked up the phone, punched in an extension. "Max, you got a couple'a cocksuckers wanna talk to you." He dropped the phone back into the cradle. "Down the hall, take your first right, first room on the left."

Faith led the way because Will would not know how to. The station was the usual 1960s government building with plenty of glass block and very poor ventilation. The walls were lined with commendations, photographs of police officers at city barbecues and fundraisers. As instructed, she took a right and stopped in front of the first door on the left.

Faith read the sign on the door. "Asshole," she breathed. He'd sent them to an interrogation room.

Will leaned across and opened the door. She saw him register the table bolted to the floor, the bars running along the sides so that suspects could be cuffed down while they were interviewed. All he said was, "Ours is more homey."

There were two chairs, one on either side of the table. Faith threw her purse on the one with its back to the two-way mirror, crossing her arms, not wanting to be sitting when Galloway entered the room. "This is bullshit. We should get Amanda involved in this. She wouldn't put up with this goat roping."

Will leaned against the wall, tucked his hands into his pockets. "If we get Amanda in on this, then they've got absolutely nothing to lose. Let them save a little face by jerking us around. What does it matter, if we get the information we need?"

She glanced at the two-way mirror, wondering if there was a peanut gallery. "I'm filing a formal report when this is over. Obstruction of justice, impeding an active case, lying to a police officer. They bumped that fat fuck Fierro back to uniform. Galloway's gonna be lucky if he gets to be county dogcatcher."

Down the hall, she heard a door open, then click closed. Seconds later, Galloway stood in the doorway, looking every bit the ignorant hick he had the night before.

"I heard you wanted to talk to me."

Faith told him, "We just talked to the Coldfields."

Galloway nodded at Will, who returned the gesture, his back still against the wall.

Faith demanded, "Is there a reason you didn't tell me about the other car last night?"

"I thought I had."

"Bullshit." Faith didn't know which was making her angrier, the fact that he was playing at this like it was some kind of game or that she felt compelled to use the same tone she used when she was about to put Jeremy on restriction.

Galloway held up his hands, smiling at Will. "Your partner always this hysterical? Maybe it's her time of month."

Faith felt her fists clench. He was about to see hysterical in the worst way.

"Listen," Will interrupted, stepping between the two of them. "Just tell us about the car, and anything else you know. We're not going to make trouble for you. We don't want to have to get this information the hard way." Will walked over to the chair and picked up Faith's purse before sitting down. He kept the bag in his lap, which made him look ridiculous, a man standing outside the changing room while his wife tried on clothes.

He indicated that Galloway should sit across from him, saying, "We've got one victim in the hospital who's probably in an irreversible coma. Jacquelyn Zabel, the woman from the tree, her autopsy didn't give us any leads. There's another woman missing now. She was taken from the parking lot of a grocery store. Her child was left in the front seat. Felix—six years old. He's in custody now, staying with strangers. He just wants his mom back."

Galloway was unmoved.

Will continued, "They didn't give you that detective shield for your good looks. There were roadblocks last night. You knew about the second car the Coldfields saw. You were stopping people." He changed tactics. "We didn't go to your boss on this. We didn't get our boss to come down like a hammer. We don't have the luxury of time here. Felix's mom is missing. She could be in another cave, strapped to another bed, with another spot underneath for the next victim. You want that on your head?"

Finally, Galloway heaved a heavy sigh and sat down. He leaned up in the chair, pulling his notebook out of his back pocket, groaning like it caused him physical pain.

Galloway said, "They told you it was white, probably a sedan?"

"Yes," Will answered. "Henry Coldfield didn't know the model. He said it was an older car."

Galloway nodded. He handed Will his notebook. Will looked down, flipped through the pages like he was taking the information on board, then handed it to Faith. She saw a list of three names with a Tennessee address and phone number. She took her purse back from Will so she could copy the information.

The detective said, "Two women—sisters—and their father. They were on their way back from Florida, going home to Tennessee. Their car broke down on the side of the road about six miles from where the Buick hit our first victim. They saw a white sedan coming. One of the women tried to flag it down. It slowed but didn't stop."

"Could she see the driver?"

"Black, baseball cap, loud music thumping. She said she was kind of glad he didn't stop."

"Did they see a license plate?"

"Just three letters, alpha, foxtrot, charlie, which pulled up about three hundred thousand cars, sixteen thousand of them are white, half of them are registered in the immediate area."

Faith wrote down the corresponding letters, A-F-C, thinking the license plate was a bust unless they just happened to stumble on the matching car. She flipped through Galloway's notes, trying to find what else he was hiding.

Will said, "I'd like to talk to all three of them."

"Too late," Galloway said. "They went back to Tennessee this morning. The father's an old guy, not doing too well. Sounded like they were taking him home to die. You could call them, maybe drive up there. I'm telling you, though, we got everything out of them that we could."

Will asked, "Was there anything else at the scene?"

"Just what you read in the reports."

"We haven't gotten the reports yet."

Galloway seemed almost contrite. "Sorry. The girl should've faxed them to you first thing. They're probably buried on her desk somewhere."

"We can get them before we leave," Will offered. "Can you just run it down for me?"

"It's what you'd expect. When the cruiser showed up, the guy who stopped, the paramedic, was working on the victim. Judith Coldfield was freaking out about her husband, worried he was having a heart attack. The ambulance came and took the victim away. The old man was better by then, so he waited for the second ambulance. That came a few minutes later. Our guys called in the detectives, started marking out the scene. The usual stuff. I'm being honest here. Nothing came up."

"We'd like to talk to the cop who was first on the scene, get his impressions."

"He's fishing in Montana with his father-in-law right now." Galloway shrugged. "I'm not giving y'all the runaround here. The guy's had this vacation planned for a while."

Faith had found a familiar name in Galloway's notes. "What's this about Jake Berman?" For Will's benefit, she explained, "Rick Sigler and Jake Berman were the two men who stopped to help Anna."

"Anna?" Galloway asked.

"That's the name she gave at the hospital," Will told him. "Rick Sigler was the off-duty EMT, right?"

"Right," Galloway confirmed. "Their story about the movie seemed kind of sketchy to me."

Faith made a noise of disgust, wondering how many dead ends this guy had to hit before he passed out from sheer stupidity.

"Anyway," Galloway said, making a point of ignoring Faith. "I ran them both through the computer. Sigler's clean, but Berman's got a record."

Faith felt her stomach drop. She'd spent two hours on the computer this morning and it had never occurred to her to check the men for a criminal history.

"Solicitation for lewd acts." Galloway smiled at Faith's stunned reaction. "Guy's married with two kids. Got picked up for screwing another guy in a toilet stall at the Mall of Georgia six months ago. Some teenage kid walked in and found them heel to toe. Goddamn pervert. My wife shops at that mall."

"Have you talked to Berman?" Will asked.

"He gave me a bogus number." Galloway shot Faith another scathing look. "The address on his driver's license is out of date, too, and nothing came up on a cross-match."

She saw a hole in his story and pounced. "How do you know he has a wife and two kids?"

"It's in the arrest report. He had them with him at the mall. They were waiting for him to come out of the bathroom." Galloway's lips twisted in disgust. "You want my advice, he's the one you should be looking at."

"The women were raped," Faith said, tossing back his notebook. "Gay men don't go after women. It's sort of what makes them gay."

"This bad guy strike you as the type of person who likes women?"

Faith didn't answer him, mostly because he had a point.

Will asked, "What about Rick Sigler?"

Galloway took his time folding his notebook closed, sticking it into his pocket. "He came back clean. Been working as a paramedic for sixteen years. Guy went to Heritage High School right down the road from here." His mouth twisted in disgust. "Played on the football team, if you can believe that."

Will took his time getting to his last question. "What else are you holding back?"

Galloway looked him right in the eye. "That's all I got, kemo sabe."

Faith didn't believe him, but Will seemed satisfied. He actually reached out and shook the man's hand. "Thank you for your time, Detective."

FAITH TURNED ON the lights as she walked into her kitchen, dropping her purse on the counter, sinking into the very same chair she'd started her day in. Her head was aching, her neck so tense that it hurt to turn her head. She picked up the phone to check her voicemail. Jeremy's message was short and unusually sweet. *"Hi, Mom, just calling to see how you're doing. I love you."* Faith frowned, guessing he'd either made a bad grade on his chem test or needed money.

She dialed his number, but hung up the phone before the call went through. Faith was bone tired, so exhausted that her vision was blurring, and she wanted nothing more than a hot bath and a glass of wine, neither of which was recommended for her current state. She did not need to make matters worse by yelling at her son.

Her laptop was still on the table, but Faith didn't check her email. Amanda had told her to report to her office by the end of the day to talk about the fact that Faith had passed out in the parking lot at the courthouse. Faith glanced at the clock on the kitchen stove. It was well past the end of the business day, almost ten o'clock. Amanda was probably at home draining the blood from the insects that had gotten caught in her web.

Faith wondered if her day could get any worse, then decided it was a mathematical improbability, considering the time. She had spent the last five hours with Will, getting in and out of her car, ringing doorbells, talking to whatever man, woman or child answered the door— if they answered the door at all—looking for Jake Berman. All told, there were twenty-three Jake

Bermans scattered around the metropolitan area. Faith and Will had talked to six of them, ruled out twelve, and been unable to find the other five, who were either not at home, not at work, or not answering the door.

If finding the man was easier, maybe Faith wouldn't have been so worried about him. Witnesses lied to the police all the time. They gave wrong names, wrong phone numbers, wrong details. It was so common that Faith seldom got annoyed when it happened. Jake Berman was another story, though. Everyone left a paper trail. You could pull up old cell phone records or past addresses and pretty soon, you were staring your witness in the face, pretending like you hadn't wasted half a day tracking him down.

Jake Berman didn't have a paper trail. He hadn't even filed a tax return last year. At least, he hadn't filed one in the name of Jake Berman—which in turn raised the specter of Pauline McGhee's brother. Maybe Berman had changed his name just like Pauline Seward. Maybe Faith had sat across the table from their killer in the Grady Hospital cafeteria the first night this case had started.

Or maybe Jake Berman was a tax dodger who never used credit cards or cell phones and Pauline McGhee had walked away from her life because sometimes that's what women did—they just walked away.

Faith was beginning to understand how that option had its benefits.

In between knocking on doors, Will had telephoned Beulah, Edna and Wallace O'Connor of Tennessee. Max Galloway had not been lying about the elderly father. The man was in a home, and Faith gathered from Will's part of the conversation that his mind was none too sharp. The sisters were talkative, and obviously tried to be helpful, but there was nothing more they could offer on the white sedan they'd seen barreling down the road just miles from the crime scene other than to say there was mud on the bumper.

Finding Rick Sigler, the focus of Jake Berman's Route 316 assignation, had been only slightly more productive. Faith had made the call, and the man had sounded as if he was going to have a heart attack the second she'd identified herself. Rick was in his ambulance, taking a patient to the hospital, scheduled for two more pickups. Faith and Will were going to meet him at eight the following morning when he got off work.

Faith stared at her laptop. She knew that she should put this in a report so that Amanda had the information, though her boss seemed quite capable of finding out things on her own. Still, Faith went through the motions. She slid her computer across the table, opened it and hit the space bar to wake it up.

Instead of going into her email program, she launched the browser. Faith's hands hovered over the keys, then her fingers started to move of their own accord: SARA LINTON GRANT COUNTY GEORGIA.

Firefox shot back almost three thousand hits. Faith clicked on the first link, which took her to a page on pediatric medicine that required a username and password to access Sara's paper on ventricular septal defects in malnourished infants. The second link was on something equally as riveting, and Faith scrolled down to the bottom to find an article about a shooting at a Buckhead bar where Sara had been the attending on call at Grady.

Faith realized she was being stupid about this. A general search was fine, but even the newspaper articles would tell only half the story. In an officer-involved death, the GBI was always called in. Faith could access actual case files through the agency's internal database. She opened the program and did a general search. Again Sara's name was all over the place, case after case where she had testified in her capacity as a coroner. Faith narrowed the scope of the search, taking out expert testimony.

This time, only two matches came up. The first was a sexual assault case that was over twenty years old. As with most browsers, there was a short description of the contents underneath the link, a few lines of text that gave you an idea of what the case was about. Faith scanned the description, moving the mouse to the link without actually clicking. Will's words came back to her, his valiant speech about Sara Linton's privacy.

Maybe he was half right.

Faith clicked the second link, opening up the file on Jeffrey Tolliver. This was a cop killing. The reports were lengthy, detailed, the kind of narrative you wrote when you wanted to make sure that every single word held up when you were cross-examined in court. Faith read about the man's background, his years of service to the law. There were hyperlinks connecting the cases he had worked, some of which Faith was familiar with from the news, some she knew about from shoptalk around the squad room.

She scrolled through page after page, reading about Tolliver's life, gleaning the character of the man from the respectful way people described him. Faith didn't stop until she got to the crime-scene photos. Tolliver had been killed by a crude pipe bomb. Sara had been standing right there, seen it all happen, watched him die.

Faith braced herself, opening up the autopsy files. The pictures were shocking, the damage horrifying. Somehow, photographs from the scene had gotten mixed in: Sara with her hands out so the camera could document the blood spray. Sara's face, caught in close-up, dark blood smearing her mouth, eyes looking as flat and lifeless as her husband's photos from the morgue.

All the files listed the case as still open. No resolution was listed. No arrest. No conviction. Strange, in a cop killing. What had Amanda said about Coastal?

Faith opened up a new browser window. The GBI was responsible for investigating all deaths that occurred on state property. She did a search for deaths at Coastal State Prison in the last four years. There were sixteen in all. Three were homicides—a skinny white supremacist who was beaten to death in the rec room and two African-Americans who were stabbed almost two hundred times between them with the sharpened end of a plastic toothbrush. Faith skimmed the other thirteen: eight suicides, five natural causes. She thought about Amanda's words to Sara Linton: *We take care of our own.*

Prison guards called it "paroling an inmate to Jesus." The death would have to be quiet, unspectacular and wholly believable. A cop would know how to cover his tracks. Faith guessed one of the overdoses or suicides was Tolliver's killer—a sad, pitiful death, but justice nonetheless. She felt a lightness in her chest, a relief that the man had been punished, a cop's widow spared a lengthy trial.

Faith closed the files, clicking through them one by one until they were all gone, then opened up Firefox again. She entered Jeffrey Tolliver's name behind Sara Linton's. Articles came up from the local paper. The

Grant Observer wasn't exactly in line for a Pulitzer. The front page carried the daily lunch menu for the elementary school and the biggest stories seemed to revolve around the exploits of the high school football team.

Armed with the correct dates, it didn't take Faith long to find the stories on Tolliver's murder. They dominated the paper for weeks. She was surprised to see how handsome he was. There was a picture of him with Sara at some kind of formal affair. He was in a tux. She was in a slinky black dress. She looked radiant beside him, a totally different person. Oddly, it was this picture that made Faith feel bad about her clandestine investigation into Sara Linton's life. The doctor looked so damn blissful in the photograph, like every single thing in her life was complete. Faith looked at the date. The photo had been taken two weeks before Tolliver's death.

On this last revelation, Faith closed down the computer, feeling sad and slightly disgusted with herself. Will was right at least about this—she should not have looked.

As penance for her sins, Faith took out her monitoring device. Her blood sugar was on the high side, and she had to think for a second about what she needed to do. Another needle, another shot. She checked her bag. There were only three insulin pens left and she had not made an appointment with Delia Wallace as she had promised.

Faith pulled up her skirt, exposing her bare thigh. She could still see the needle mark where she had jabbed herself in the bathroom around lunchtime. A small bruise ringed the injection site, and Faith guessed she should try her luck on the other leg this time. Her hand didn't shake as much as it usually did, and it only took to the count of twenty-six for her to sink the needle into her thigh. She sat back in her chair, waiting to feel better. At least a full minute passed, and Faith felt worse.

Tomorrow, she thought. She would make an appointment with Delia Wallace first thing in the morning.

She pushed down her skirt as she stood. The kitchen was a mess, dishes stacked in the sink, trash overflowing. Faith was not naturally a tidy person, but her kitchen was generally spotless. She had been called out to too many homicide scenes where women were found sprawled on the floor of their filthy kitchens. The sight always triggered a snap judgment in Faith, as if the woman deserved to be beaten to death by her boyfriend, shot and killed by a stranger, because she had left dirty dishes in her sink.

She wondered what Will thought when he came onto a crime scene. She had been around countless dead bodies with the man, but his face was always inscrutable. Will's first job in law enforcement had been with the GBI. He had never been in uniform, never been called out on a suspicious smell and found an old woman dead on her couch, or worked patrol, stopping speeders, not knowing if it was going to be a stupid teenager behind the wheel or a gangbanger who would put a gun in his face, pull the trigger, rather than have the points on his license.

He was just so damn *passive.* Faith didn't understand it. Despite the way Will carried himself, he was a big man. He ran every day, rain or shine. He worked out with weights. He had apparently dug a pond in his backyard. There was so much muscle under those suits he wore that his body could have been carved from rock. And yet, there he was this afternoon, sitting with Faith's purse in his lap while he begged Max Galloway for information. If Faith had been in Will's shoes, she would've backed the idiot against the wall and squeezed his testicles until he sang out every detail he knew in high soprano.

But she wasn't Will, and Will wasn't going to do that. He was just going to shake Galloway's hand and thank him for the professional courtesy like some gigantic, half-witted patsy.

She searched the cabinet under the sink for dishwashing powder, only to find an empty box. She left it in the cabinet and went to the fridge to make a note on the grocery list. Faith had written the first three letters of the word before she realized that the item was already on the list. Twice.

"Damn," she whispered, putting her hand to her stomach. How was she going to take care of a child when she could not even take care of herself? She loved Jeremy, adored everything about him, but Faith had been waiting eighteen years for her life to start, and now that it was here, she was looking at another eighteen-year wait. She would be over fifty by then, eligible for movie discounts through AARP.

Did she want this? Could she actually do it? Faith couldn't ask her mother to help again. Evelyn loved Jeremy, and she had never complained about taking care of her grandson—not when Faith was away at the police academy, or when she had to work double shifts just to make ends meet—but there was no way that Faith could expect her mother to help out like that again.

But then, who else was there?

Certainly not the baby's father. Victor Martinez was tall, dark, handsome . . . and completely incapable of taking care of himself. He was a dean at Georgia Tech, in charge of nearly twenty thousand students, but he could not keep a clean pair of socks in his drawer to save his life. They had dated for six months before he moved into Faith's house, which had seemed romantic and impetuous until reality set in. Within a week, Faith was doing Victor's laundry, picking up his dry cleaning, fixing his meals, cleaning up his messes. It was like raising Jeremy again, except at least with her son she could punish him for being lazy. The last straw had come when she had just finished cleaning the sink and Victor had dropped a knife covered in peanut butter on the draining board. If Faith had been wearing her gun, she would have shot him.

He moved out the next morning.

Even with all that, Faith couldn't help but feel herself softening toward Victor as she gathered up the drawstring on the trash. That was one good difference between her son and her ex-lover: Victor never had to be told six times to take out the trash. It was one of the chores Faith most hated, and—ridiculously—she felt tears well in her eyes as she thought about having to lift the bag and heft it down the stairs, outside, to the garbage can.

There was a knock at the door: three sharp raps followed by the doorbell chime.

Faith wiped her eyes as she walked down the hall, her cheeks so wet that she had to use her sleeve. She still had her gun on her hip, so she didn't bother to check the peephole.

"This is a switch," Sam Lawson told her. "Women usually cry when I leave, not when I show up."

"What do you want, Sam? It's late."

"You gonna invite me in?" He wiggled his eyebrows. "You know you wanna."

Faith was too tired to argue, so she turned around, letting him follow her back to the kitchen. Sam Lawson was an itch she had really needed to scratch for a few years, but now she couldn't remember why she had bothered. He drank too much. He was married. He didn't like kids. He was convenient and he knew how to make an exit, which, as far as Faith was concerned, meant he left shortly after he had served his purpose.

Okay, now she remembered why she had bothered.

Sam took a glob of gum out of his mouth and dropped it into the trash. "I'm glad I saw you today. I need to tell you something."

Faith braced herself for bad news. "Okay."

"I'm sober now. Almost a year."

"You're here to make amends?"

He laughed. "Hell, Faith. You're about the only person in my life I didn't screw over."

"Only because I kicked you to the curb before you could." Faith pulled the string on the trash, tying it tight.

"Bag's gonna tear."

The plastic ripped just as he said the words.

"Shit," she muttered.

"You want me to—"

"I've got it."

Sam leaned against the counter. "I love watching a woman do manual labor."

She shot him a withering look.

He flashed another smile. "I heard you cracked some heads at Rockdale today."

Faith said a silent curse in her head, remembering

that Max Galloway had yet to give them the initial crime-scene reports. She had been so furious that she hadn't thought to follow up on it, and she would be damned if she'd take the man's word for it that everything had been fairly routine.

"Faith?"

She fed him the standard line. "The Rockdale police are cooperating fully with our investigation."

"It's the sister you need to worry about. You seen the news? Joelyn Zabel's all over the place saying your partner's the reason her sister died."

That rankled more than she wanted to let on. "Check the autopsy summary."

"I saw it already," he said. Faith guessed Amanda had shared the report with a few key people in order to spread the news as quickly as possible. "Jacquelyn Zabel killed herself."

"Did you tell that to the sister?" Faith asked.

"She's not interested in the truth."

Faith gave him a pointed look. "Not many people are."

He shrugged. "She got what she wanted from me. She's moved on to network television."

"The *Atlanta Beacon*'s not big enough for her, huh?"

"Why are you being so hard on me?"

"I don't like your job."

"I'm not crazy about yours, either." He went to the sink cabinet and took out the box of trash bags. "Slide a new one over the old one."

Faith took a bag, holding the white plastic in her hands, trying not to think about what Pete had found during the autopsy.

Sam was oblivious as he put back the box. "What's that guy's story, anyway? Trent?"

"All inquiries should go through the public relations office."

Sam had never been one to take no for an answer. "Francis tried to feed me something about Trent getting circle-jerked by Galloway today. Made it out like he was some kinda Keystone Kop."

Faith stopped worrying about the trash. "Who's Francis?"

"Fierro."

Faith took childish pleasure in the girlish name. "And you printed every word the asshole said without bothering to run it by someone who could tell you the truth."

Sam leaned against the counter. "Cut me some slack, babe. I'm just doing my job."

"They let you make excuses in AA?"

"I didn't run the Kidney Killer stuff."

"That's only because it was proved wrong before you went to press."

He laughed. "You never let me bullshit you." He watched her wrestle the old bag into a new one. "Jesus, I've missed you."

Faith gave him another sharp glance, but she felt herself react to his words despite her best intentions. Sam had been her life raft a few years ago—just available enough to be there when she really needed him, but not so much that she felt smothered.

He said, "I didn't print anything about your partner."

"Thank you."

"What's going on with Rockdale anyway? They're really out to get you."

"They care more about screwing us over than find-ing out who abducted those women." Faith didn't give herself time to consider that she was echoing Will's sen-timents. "Sam, it's bad. I saw one of them. This killer—whoever he is . . ." She realized almost too late to whom she was talking.

"Off the record," he said.

"Nothing's ever off the record."

"Of course it is."

Faith knew he was right. She had told Sam secrets in the past that had never been repeated. Secrets about cases. Secrets about her mother, a good cop who had been forced off the job because some of her detectives had been caught skimming off drug busts. Sam had never printed anything Faith had told him, and she should trust him now. Only she couldn't. It wasn't just her anymore. Will was involved. She might hate her partner right now for being a pussy, but she would kill herself before she exposed him to any more scrutiny.

Sam asked, "What's going on with you, babe?"

Faith looked down at the torn trash bag, knowing he'd read everything in her face if she looked up. She re-membered the day she'd found out her mother was being forced off the job. Evelyn hadn't wanted comfort. She had wanted to be alone. Faith had felt the same way until Sam showed up. He had talked his way into her house the same way he had tonight. Feeling his arms around her had sent Faith over the edge, and she had sobbed like a child as he held her.

"Babe?"

She snapped open another new trash bag. "I'm tired, I'm cranky and you don't seem to understand that I'm not going to give you a story."

"I don't want a story." His tone had changed. She looked up at him, surprised to see the smile playing on his lips. "You look . . ."

Faith's mind filled with suggestions: *puffy, sweaty, morbidly obese*.

"Beautiful," he said, which surprised them both. Sam had never been one for compliments, and Faith certainly wasn't used to getting them.

He pushed away from the counter, moving closer. "There's something about you that's different." He touched her arm, and the rough texture of his palm sent heat rushing through her body. "You just look so . . ." He was close now, staring at her lips like he wanted to kiss them.

"Oh," Faith said, then, "No, Sam." She backed away from him. She'd experienced this the first time she was pregnant—men hitting on her, telling her she was beautiful even when her stomach was so huge she couldn't bend over to tie her own shoes. It must be hormones or pheromones or something. At fourteen, it had been skeevy, at thirty-three it was just annoying. "I'm pregnant."

The words hung between them like a lead balloon. Faith realized this was the first time she had said them aloud.

Sam tried to make a joke out of it. "Wow, I didn't even have to take off my pants."

"I'm serious." She said it again. "I'm pregnant."

"Is it . . ." He seemed at a loss for words. "The father?"

She thought about Victor, his dirty socks in her laundry basket. "He doesn't know."

"You should tell him. He has a right."

"Since when are you the arbiter of relationship morality?"

"Since I found out my wife had an abortion without telling me." He leaned closer, put his hands on her arms again. "Gretchen didn't think I could handle it." He shrugged, keeping his hands on Faith's arms. "She was probably right, but still."

Faith bit her tongue. Of course Gretchen was right. She would've been better off asking a dingo to help raise her baby. She asked, "Did this happen when you were seeing me?"

"After." He looked down, watching his hand stroke her arm, his fingers tracing the neck of her blouse. "I hadn't hit bottom yet."

"You weren't exactly in a position to make an informed decision."

"We're still trying to work things out."

"Is that why you're here?"

He pressed his mouth to hers. She could feel the rough prickle of his beard, taste the cinnamon gum he'd been chewing. He lifted her onto the counter, his tongue finding hers. It wasn't unpleasant, and when his hands slid up her thighs, lifting her skirt, Faith didn't stop him. She helped him, actually, and in retrospect, she probably shouldn't have, because it ended things a lot sooner than they needed to.

"I'm sorry." Sam shook his head, slightly out of breath. "I didn't mean to— I just—"

Faith didn't care. Even if her mind had blocked out Sam from her conscious thoughts over the years, her body seemed to remember every part of him. It felt so damn good to have his arms around her again, to feel the closeness of somebody who knew about her family and her job and her past—even if that particular body wasn't of much use to her at the moment. She kissed his mouth very gently and with no other meaning than to feel connected again. "It's okay."

Sam pulled back. He was too embarrassed to see that it didn't matter.

"Sammy—"

"I haven't gotten the hang of things being sober."

"It's okay," she repeated, trying to kiss him again.

He stepped back even farther, looking somewhere over her shoulder instead of in her eyes. "You want me to . . ." He made a halfhearted gesture toward her lap.

Faith let out a heavy sigh. Why were the men in her life such a constant disappointment? God knew she didn't have high standards.

He looked at his watch. "Gretchen's probably waiting up for me. Been working late a lot."

Faith gave up, leaning her head against the cabinet behind her. She might as well try to salvage something out of this. "Do you mind taking out the trash on your way out?"

CHAPTER TWELVE

GODDAMN IT," PAULINE WHISPERED, THEN WONdered why she wasn't screaming it at the top of her lungs. "Goddamn it!" she yelled, her voice catching in her throat. She rattled the handcuffs around her wrists, jerking at them even though she knew the gesture was useless. She was like a goddamn prisoner at a jail, her hands cuffed, strapped tight to a leather belt so that, even if she contorted herself into a ball, her fingertips barely grazed her chin. Her feet were chained, the thick links clanking against each other with every step she took. She had done enough damn yoga to be able to bend her feet up to her head, but what good was that? What the hell kind of help was the inversion plow pose when your fucking life was at stake?

The blindfold made it worse, though she had managed to move it up a little by rubbing her face against the rough concrete blocks lining one of the walls. The scarf was tight. Millimeter by millimeter, the blindfold was forced up, shaving away some of the skin on her cheek in the process. There was no difference above or below the strip of material, but Pauline felt like she had accomplished something, might be prepared when that door opened and she saw a sliver of light under the blindfold.

For now, it was darkness. That was all she saw. No windows, no lights, no way of judging the movement of time. If she thought about it, thought that she could not see, did not know if she was being watched or video-taped or worse, she would lose her mind. Hell, she was half losing her mind already. She was soaking wet, sweat pouring from her skin. Rivulets tickled her nose as they slid down her scalp. It was maddening, made all the more worse by the fucking darkness.

Felix liked the dark. He liked it when she got in bed with him and held him and told him stories. He liked being under the covers, blankets over his head. Maybe she had coddled him too much when he was a baby. She'd never let him out of her sight. She was scared that someone would take him away from her, someone would realize that she really shouldn't be a mother, that she didn't have it in her to love a child like a child should be loved. But she did. She loved her boy. She loved him so much that the thought of him was the only thing that was keeping her from twisting herself into a ball, wrap-ping the chains around her neck and killing herself.

"Help!" she screamed, knowing it was useless. If they were afraid of Pauline being heard, they would have gagged her.

She had paced out the room hours ago, approximat-ing the size at twenty feet by sixteen. Cinderblock walls on one side, sheetrock on the others, with a metal door that was bolted from the outside. Vinyl mattress pad in the corner. A slop bucket with a lid. The concrete was cold against her bare feet. There was a hum in the next room, a hot-water heater, something mechanical. She was in a basement. She was underground, which made her feel as if her skin would crawl right off her body. She hated being underground. She didn't even park in the damn garage at work, she hated it so much.

She stopped pacing, closed her eyes.

No one parked in her space. It was right by the door. Sometimes she'd go out for some air, stand at the entrance to the garage to make sure the space was empty. She could read the sign from the street: PAULINE McGHEE. Christ, the battle with the sign company to get that "c" in lowercase. It had cost someone their job, which was just as well, since apparently they couldn't do it right.

If someone was parked in her space, she would call the attendant and have the asshole towed. Porsche, Bentley, Mercedes—Pauline didn't care. She had earned that fucking space. Even if she wasn't going to use it, she would be damned if someone else would.

"Let me out of here!" she screamed, jerking the chains, trying to wrench off the belt. It was thick, the sort of thing her brother wore back in the seventies. Two rows of riveted holes going the circumference, two prongs in the buckle. The metal felt like a wad of wax, and she knew the prongs had been soldered down. She couldn't remember when it had happened, but she knew what a fucking soldered belt felt like.

"Help me!" she screamed. "Help me!"

Nothing. No help. No response. The belt was biting into her skin, raking across her hip bones. If she wasn't so fucking fat, she could just slide out of the thing.

Water, she thought. When had she last had water? You could live without food for weeks, sometimes months, but water was different. You could go three, maybe four days before it hit you—the cramps, the cravings. The awful headaches. Were they going to give her water? Or were they going to let her waste away, then do whatever they wanted to her while she lay there, helpless as a child?

Child.

No. She would not think about Felix. Morgan would take him. He would never let anything bad happen to her baby. Morgan was a bastard and a liar, but he would take care of Felix, because underneath it all, he was not a bad person. Pauline knew what a bad person looked like, and it was not Morgan Hollister.

She heard footsteps behind her, outside the door. Pauline stopped, holding her breath so she could hear. Stairs—someone was coming down the stairs. Even in the dark, she could see the walls closing in around her. Which was worse: being alone down here, or being trapped with someone else?

Because she knew what was coming. Knew it just as certain as she knew the details of her own life. There was never just one. He always wanted two: dark hair, dark eyes, dark hearts that he could shatter. He had kept them apart for as long as he could stand it, but now he'd want them together. Caged, like two animals. Fighting it out. Like animals.

The first domino would soon fall, then the rest would follow one after the other. A woman alone, two women alone, and then . . .

She heard a chattering, "No-no-no-no," and realized the words were coming from her own mouth. She backed up, pressing herself into the wall, her knees shaking so hard that she would've fallen to the floor but for the rough cinderblock bracing her. The handcuffs rattled as her hands trembled.

"No," she whispered, just one word, shaking herself out of it. She was a survivor. She had not lived the last twenty years of her life so that she would die in some fucking underground hole.

The door opened. She saw a flash of light under the blindfold.

He said, "Here's your friend."

She heard something drop to the floor—a dank exhalation of air, the rattling of chains, then stillness. Then there was a second, quieter sound; a solid thud that echoed in the large room.

The door closed. The light was gone. There was a whistling sound, labored breathing. Groping, Pauline found the body. Long hair, blindfold, thin face, small breasts, hands cuffed in front of her. The whistling was coming from the woman's broken nose.

No time to worry about that. Pauline checked the woman's pockets, tried to find something that could get her out of here. Nothing. Nothing except another person who was going to want food and water.

"Fuck." Pauline sat back on her heels, fighting the urge to scream. Her foot struck something hard, and she reached around, remembering the second thud.

She traced her hands along the thin cardboard box, guessing it was about six inches square. It had some heft—maybe a couple of pounds. There was a perforation line along one side, and she pressed her fingers against it, breaking open the seal. Her fingers found something slick inside.

"No . . ." she breathed.

Not again.

She closed her eyes, felt tears weep from under the blindfold. Felix, her job, her Lexus, her life—all of it slipped away as she felt the slick plastic trash bags between her fingers.

DAY THREE

CHAPTER THIRTEEN

WILL HAD FORCED HIMSELF TO GET UP AT HIS USUAL time of five o'clock. His run had been sluggish, his shower far from bracing. He was standing over the kitchen sink, his breakfast cereal soggy in the bowl, when Betty nudged his ankle to stir him from his stupor.

He found Betty's leash by the door and stooped down to clip it onto her collar. She licked his hand, and despite himself, he petted her little head. Everything about the Chihuahua was an embarrassment. She was the kind of dog a young starlet would carry in a leather satchel, hardly Will's speed. Making it worse, she was roughly six inches off the ground, and the only leash at the pet store that was long enough for him to comfortably hold came in hot pink. The fact that it matched her rhinestone collar was something many attractive women had pointed out to him in the park—right before they'd tried to set up Will with their brothers.

Betty had been an inheritance of sorts, abandoned by Will's next-door neighbor a couple of years ago. Angie had hated the dog on sight, and chastised Will for what they both knew was the truth: A man who was raised in an orphanage was not going to drop off a dog at the pound, no matter how ridiculous he felt when they were out in public.

There were more shameful aspects about his life with the dog that even Angie did not know about. Will worked odd hours, and sometimes when a case was breaking, he barely had time to go home and change his shirt. He had dug the pond in the backyard for Betty, thinking that watching the fish swim would be a nice way for her to pass the time. She had barked at the fish for a couple of days, but then she'd gone back to sitting on the couch, whiling away the hours until Will came home.

He half suspected the animal was playing him, that she jumped on the couch when she heard his key in the lock, pretending that she'd been waiting there all day when in fact she had been running in and out of the dog door, romping it up with the koi in the backyard, listening to his music.

Will patted his pockets, making sure he had his phone and wallet, then clipped his paddle holster onto his belt. He left the house, locking the door behind him. Betty's tail was pointed in the air, swishing back and forth like crazy, as he walked her toward the park. He checked the time on his cell phone. He was supposed to meet Faith at the coffee shop across from the park in half an hour. When cases were in full swing, he usually had her pick him up there instead of home. If Faith ever noticed that the coffee shop was right beside a dog day care center called Sir Barks-A-Lot, she'd been kind enough not to mention it.

They crossed the street against the light, Will slowing his pace so he didn't run over the dog, much as he had done with Amanda the day before. He did not know which was worrying him more—the case, in which they had very little to go on, or the fact that Faith was obviously mad at him. God knew Faith had been mad before, but this particular anger had a tinge of disappointment to it.

He felt her pushing him, even though she wouldn't say the words. The problem was that she was a different cop than Will was. He had long known that his less aggressive way of approaching the Job was at odds with her own, but rather than being a point of contention, it was a contrast that had worked for them both. Now he wasn't so sure. Faith wanted him to be one of those kinds of cops that Will despised—someone who goes in with his fists swinging and worries about the consequences later. Will hated those cops, had worked more than a few cases where he'd gotten them kicked off the force. You couldn't say you were one of the good guys if you did the same thing the bad guys did. Faith had to know this. She'd grown up in a cop's family. Then again, her mother had been forced out of the job for improper conduct, so maybe Faith did know it and just didn't care.

Will couldn't accept that reasoning. Faith was not just a solid cop; she was a good person. She still insisted her mother was innocent. She still believed that there was a distinct line between good and bad, right and wrong. Will couldn't just tell her that his way was best—she would have to see it for herself.

He had never walked a beat like Faith, but he had walked into plenty of small communities and learned the hard way that you don't piss off the locals. By law, the GBI was called in by the bosses, not the detectives and patrolmen on the street. They were invariably still working their cases, still thinking they could crack them on their own and highly resentful of any outside interference. Chances were, you would need something from them later on, and if you left them in the gutter, took away all chances of them saving face, they would actively work to sabotage you, damn the consequences.

Case in point was Rockdale County. Amanda had made an enemy of Lyle Peterson, the chief of police, while she was working another case with him. Now that they needed cooperation from the local force, Rockdale was balking in the form of Max Galloway, who was straddling the line between being a jerk and being grossly negligent.

What Faith needed to realize was that the cops weren't always selfless in their actions. They had egos. They had territories. They were like animals marking their spots: If you encroached on their space, they didn't care about the bodies stacking up. It was just a game to some of them, one they had to win no matter who was hurt in the process.

As if she could read his mind, Betty stopped near the entrance of Piedmont Park to do her business. Will waited, then took care of the mess, dropping the bag into one of the trashcans as they cut through the park. Joggers were out in force, some with dogs, some alone. They were all bundled up to fight the cold in the air, though Will could tell from the way the sun was burning off the fog that it would be warm enough by noon so that his collar would start to rub against his neck.

The case was twenty-four hours old and he and Faith had a full day—talk to Rick Sigler, the paramedic who had been on the scene when Anna was hit by the car; track down Jake Berman, Sigler's hookup; then interview Joelyn Zabel, Jacquelyn Zabel's awful sister. Will knew he shouldn't make snap judgments, but he'd seen the woman all over the television news last night, both local and national. Apparently, Joelyn liked to talk. Even more apparently, she liked to blame. Will was grateful he had been at the autopsy yesterday, had had the burden of Jacquelyn Zabel's death removed from his long list of burdens, or the sister's words would have cut into him like a thousand knives.

He wanted to search Pauline McGhee's house, but Leo Donnelly would probably protest. There had to be a way around that, and if there was any one thing Will wanted to do today, it was find a way to bring Leo on board. Rather than sleep, Will had thought about Pauline McGhee most of last night. Every time he closed his eyes, he mixed up the cave and McGhee, so that she was on that wooden bed, tied down like an animal, while Will stood helplessly by. His gut was telling him that something was going on with McGhee. She had run away once before, twenty years ago, but she had roots now. Felix was a good kid. His mother would not leave him.

Will chuckled to himself. He of all people should know that mothers left their sons all the time.

"Come on," he said, tugging Betty's leash, pulling her away from a pigeon that was almost as big as she was.

He tucked his hand into his pocket to warm it, his mind staying focused on the case. Will wasn't stupid enough to take full credit for the majority of the arrests he made. The fact was that people who committed crimes tended to be stupid. Most killers made mistakes, because they usually were acting on the spur of the moment. A fight broke out, a gun was handy, tempers flared and the only thing to figure out when it was all over was whether or not the prosecution was going to go for second- or first-degree murder.

Stranger abductions were different, though. They were harder to solve, especially when there was more than one victim. Serial killers, by definition, were good at their jobs. They knew they were going to murder. They knew who they were going to kill and exactly how they were going to do it. They had practiced their trade over and over again, perfecting their skills. They knew how to evade detection, to hide evidence or simply leave nothing at all. Finding them tended to be a matter of dumb luck on the part of law enforcement or complacency in the killer.

Ted Bundy had been captured during a routine traffic stop. Twice. BTK—who signed his letters taunting the cops with those initials, indicating he liked to bind, torture and kill his victims—was tripped up by a computer disc he accidentally gave his pastor. Richard Ramirez was beaten by a vigilante whose car he tried to steal. All captured by happenstance, all with several murders under their belts before they were stopped. In most serial cases, years passed, and the only thing the police could do was wait for more bodies to show up and pray that happenstance brought the killers to justice.

Will thought about what they had on their guy: a white sedan speeding down the road, a torture chamber in the middle of nowhere, elderly witnesses who could offer nothing usable. Jake Berman could be a lead, but they might never find him. Rick Sigler was squeaky clean except for being a couple of months behind on his mortgage, hardly shocking considering how bad the economy was. The Coldfields were, on paper, exemplars of an average retired couple. Pauline McGhee had a brother she was worried about, but then she might be worried about him for reasons that had nothing to do with their case. She might not have anything to do with their case at all.

The physical evidence was equally as thin. The trash bags found in the victims were of the sort you would find in any grocery or convenience store. The items in the cave, from the marine battery to the torture devices, were completely untraceable. There were plenty of fingerprints and fluids to enter into the computer, but nothing was coming back as a match. Sexual predators were sneaky, inventive. Almost eighty percent of the crimes solved by DNA evidence were actually burglaries, not assaults. Glass was broken, kitchen knives were mishandled, ChapStick was dropped—all inevitably leading back to the burglar, who generally already had a long record. But, with stranger rape, where the victim had no previous contact with the assailant, it was looking for a needle in a haystack.

Betty had stopped so she could sniff around some tall grass by the lake. Will glanced up, seeing a runner coming toward them. She was wearing long black tights and a neon green jacket. Her hair was pulled up under a matching ball cap. Two greyhounds jogged beside her, heads up, tails straight. They were beautiful animals, sleek, long-legged, muscled. Just like their owner.

"Crap," Will muttered, scooping up Betty in his hand, holding her behind his back.

Sara Linton stopped a few feet away, the dogs heeling beside her like trained commandos. The only thing Will had ever been able to teach Betty to do was eat.

"Hi," Sara said, her voice going up in surprise. When he didn't respond, she asked, "Will?"

"Hi." He could feel Betty licking his palm.

Sara studied him. "Is that a Chihuahua behind your back?"

"No, I'm just happy to see you."

Sara gave him a confused smile, and he reluctantly showed her Betty.

Noises were made, some cooing, and Will waited for the usual question.

"Is she your wife's?"

"Yes," he lied. "Do you live around here?"

"The Milk Lofts off North Avenue."

She lived less than two blocks from his house. "You don't seem like a loft person."

The confused look returned. "What do I seem like?"

Will had never been particularly skilled at the art of conversation, and he certainly didn't know how to artic-ulate what Sara Linton seemed like to him—at least not without making a fool of himself.

He shrugged, setting Betty down on the ground. Sara's dogs stirred, and she clicked her tongue once, sending them back to attention. Will told her, "I'd bet-ter go. I'm meeting Faith at the coffee place across the park."

"Mind if I walk with you?" She didn't wait for an an-swer. The dogs stood and Will picked up Betty, know-ing she would only slow them down. Sara was tall, nearly shoulder-to-shoulder with him. He tried to do some calculations without staring. Angie could almost put her chin on his shoulder if she rose up on her tiptoes. Sara would've had to make very little effort to do the same. Her mouth could have reached his ear if she wanted it to.

"So." She took off her hat, tightened her ponytail. "I've been thinking about the trash bags."

Will glanced her way. "What about them?"

"It's a powerful message."

Will hadn't thought of them as a message—more like a horror. "He thinks they're trash."

"And what he does to them—takes away their senses."

Will glanced at her again.

"See no evil, hear no evil, speak no evil."

He nodded, wondering why he hadn't thought about it that way.

She continued, "I've been wondering if there's some kind of religious angle to this. Actually, something Faith said that first night got me thinking about it. God took Adam's rib to make Eve."

"Vesalius," Will mumbled.

Sara laughed in surprise. "I haven't heard that name since my first year in medical school."

Will shrugged, saying a silent prayer of thanks that he'd managed to catch the History Channel's *Great Men of Science* week. Andreas Vesalius was an anatomist who, among other things, proved that men and women have the same number of ribs. The Vatican almost put him in prison for his discovery.

Sara continued, "Also, there's the number eleven." She paused, as if she expected him to answer. "Eleven trash bags, eleventh rib. There must be a connection."

Will stopped walking. "What?"

"The women. They each had eleven trash bags inside them. The rib that was taken from Anna was the eleventh rib."

"You think the killer is hung up on the number eleven?"

Sara continued walking and Will followed. "If you

consider how compulsive behaviors manifest themselves, like substance abuse, eating disorders, checking behaviors—where someone feels compelled to check things, like the lock on the door or the stove or the iron—then it makes sense that a serial killer, someone who is compelled to kill, would have a specific pattern he likes to follow, or in this case a specific number that means something to him. It's why the FBI keeps their database, so you can cross-reference methods and look for patterns. Maybe you could look for something significant surrounding the number eleven."

"I don't even know if it's set up to search that way. I mean, it's all about *things*—knives, razors, what they do, generally not how many times they do it unless it's pretty blatant."

"You should check the Bible. If there's a religious significance to the number eleven, then maybe you'll be able to figure out the killer's motivation." She shrugged as if she was finished, but added, "Easter's this Sunday. That could be part of the pattern, too."

"Eleven apostles," he said.

She gave him that strange look again. "You're right. Judas betrayed Christ. There were only eleven apostles left. There was a twelfth to replace him—Didymus? I can't remember. I bet my mother would know." She shrugged again. "Of course, it could all be a waste of your time."

Will had always been a firm believer that coincidences were generally clues. "It's something to look into."

"What about Felix's mother?"

"She's just a missing person for now."

"Did you find the brother?"

"'The Atlanta police are looking for him." Will didn't want to give away any more than that. Sara worked at Grady, where cops were in and out of the emergency room all day with suspects and witnesses. He added, "We're not even sure she's connected to our case."

"I hope for Felix's sake she's not. I can't imagine what it's like for him being abandoned, stuck in some awful state home."

"Those places aren't so bad," Will defended. Before he realized what he was saying, he told her, "I grew up in state care."

She was as surprised as he was, though obviously for different reasons. "How old were you?"

"A kid," he answered, wishing he could take back his words, but unable to stop adding more. "Infant. Five months."

"And you weren't adopted?"

He shook his head. This was getting complicated and—worse—embarrassing.

"My husband and I . . ." She stared ahead, lost in thought. "We were going to adopt. We'd been on the list for a while and . . ." She shrugged. "When he was killed, it all . . . it was just too much."

Will didn't know if he was supposed to feel sympathetic, but all he could think about was how many times as a kid he'd gone to a meet-and-greet picnic or barbecue, thinking he'd be going home with his new parents, only to end up back in his room at the children's home.

He felt inordinately grateful to hear the high-pitched horn from Faith's Mini, which she'd illegally parked in front of the coffee shop. She got out of the car, leaving the engine running.

"Amanda wants us back at the station." Faith lifted

her chin toward Sara in greeting. "Joelyn Zabel moved up her interview. She's fitting us in between *Good Morning America* and CNN. We'll have to run Betty back home afterward."

Will had forgotten about the dog in his hand. She had her snout tucked into the space between the buttons on his vest.

"I'll take her," Sara offered.

"I couldn't—"

"I'm home all day doing laundry," Sara countered. "She'll be fine. Just come by after work and get her."

"That's really—"

Faith was more impatient than usual. "Just give her the dog, Will." She stomped off back to her car, and Will shot Sara a look of apology.

"The Milk Lofts?" he asked, as if he had forgotten.

Sara took Betty in her hands. He could feel how cold her fingers were as they brushed against his skin. "Betty?" she asked. He nodded, and she told him, "Don't worry if you're late. I don't have any plans."

"Thank you."

She smiled, hefting Betty like she was a glass of wine being offered in a toast.

Will walked across the street and got into Faith's car, glad that no one else had been in the passenger's seat since the last time he'd ridden with Faith so he didn't look like a monkey bending himself into the cramped space.

Faith cut straight to the chase as she pulled away from the curb. "What were you doing with Sara Linton?"

"I just ran into her." Will wondered why he felt so defensive, which quickly led to him wondering why Faith was being so hostile. He guessed she was still angry with him about his interaction with Max Galloway the day before, and he didn't know what to do about the situation other than try to distract her. "Sara had an interesting question, or theory, about our case."

Faith merged into traffic. "I'm dying to hear it."

Will could tell she wasn't, but he ran down Sara's theory for her anyway, highlighting the number eleven, the other points she had raised. "Easter's this Sunday," he said. "This could have something to do with the Bible."

To her credit, Faith seemed to be considering it. "I don't know," she finally said. "We could get a Bible back at the station, maybe do a computer search for the number eleven. I'm sure there are a lot of religious nutballs out there with web pages."

"Where in the Bible does it say something about a rib being taken from Adam to make Eve?"

"Genesis."

"That's the old stuff, right? Not the new books."

"Old Testament. It's the first book in the Bible. It's where it all begins." Faith gave him the same sideways glance Sara had. "I know you can't read the Bible, but didn't you go to church?"

"I *can* read the Bible," Will shot back. Still, he preferred Faith's nosiness to her fury, so he kept talking. "Remember where I grew up. Separation of church and state."

"Oh, I didn't think about that."

Probably because it was an enormous lie. The children's home couldn't sanction religious activities, but there were volunteers from just about every local church who sent vans to pick up the children every week and cart them off to Sunday School. Will had gone once, realized that it really was a school, where you were expected to read your lessons, then never went back.

Faith pressed, "You've never been to church? Really?"

Will shut his mouth, thinking he had foolishly opened the wrong door.

Faith slowed the car as they pulled up to a light. She mumbled to herself, "I don't think I've ever met anyone who's never been to church."

"Can we change the subject?"

"It's just strange."

Will stared blankly out the window, thinking he had been called strange at one point or another by every person he had ever met. The light changed, and the Mini rolled ahead. City Hall East was a five-minute drive from the park. This morning, it seemed to be taking hours.

Faith said, "Even if Sara's right, she's doing it again, trying to talk her way onto this case."

"She's a coroner. At least, she used to be. She helped Anna at the hospital. It's normal for her to want to know what's going on."

"This is a murder investigation, not Big Brother," Faith countered. "Does she know where you live?"

Will hadn't considered the possibility, but he wasn't as paranoid as Faith. "I don't see how."

"Maybe she followed you."

Will laughed, then stopped when he realized she was being serious. "She lives right down the street. She was just running in the park with her dogs."

"It's just all very convenient."

He shook his head, exasperated. He wasn't going to let Faith use Sara Linton as a stand-in for her problems with him. "We've gotta get past this, Faith. I know you're ticked at me about yesterday, but going into this interview, we've got to be working as a team."

She accelerated as the light changed. "We *are* a team."

For a team, they didn't talk much the rest of the short trip. It wasn't until they were at City Hall East, riding up on the elevator, that Faith finally spoke.

"Your tie is crooked."

Will's hand went to the knot. Sara Linton probably thought he was a slob. "Better?"

Faith was scrolling through her BlackBerry, even though there was no signal in the elevator. She glanced up and gave him a quick nod before turning her attention back to the device.

He was trying to think of something to say when the doors opened. Amanda was waiting outside the elevator, checking her email just like Faith, except on an iPhone. Will felt like an idiot to be empty-handed, the same way he'd felt when Sara Linton had shown up with her big, impressive dogs and he'd scooped Betty into his palm like a ball of yarn.

Amanda used her finger to scroll through emails, her voice taking on a distracted quality as she led them down the hall toward her office. "Catch me up."

Faith ran down the list of things they didn't know, which were innumerable, and the things they did know, which were practically nonexistent. All the while, Amanda read her emails, walking and pretending to listen to Faith tell her what Amanda had surely already read in their report.

Will wasn't a fan of multitasking, mostly because it was more like half-tasking. It was humanly impossible to give two different things your complete attention. As if to prove this, Amanda looked up from her screen, asking, "What?"

Faith repeated, "Linton thinks there might be a biblical angle."

Amanda stopped walking. She held the iPhone at her side, giving them her full attention. "Why?"

"Eleventh rib, eleven trash bags, Easter at the end of the week."

Amanda used her iPhone again, talking as she punched the touch screen. "We've got Legal in for Joelyn Zabel. She's brought her lawyer, so I asked for three of ours. We've got to play this as if the world is listening because I'm sure whatever we say to her will be spun back out to the public at large." She looked at them both meaningfully. "I will do most of the talking. You ask your questions, but don't extemporize."

"We're not going to get anything out of Zabel," Will said. "Just with the lawyers, we've already got four people in the room. Add us and that's seven, with her at the center of it all, knowing she's going to have the cameras rolling as soon as she leaves the building. We need to take this down a notch."

Amanda looked back at her iPhone. "And your brilliant idea for doing this is . . . ?"

Will couldn't think of one. All he could say was, "Maybe we could talk to her after her television interviews, catch her at her hotel without all the press and attention."

Amanda did not do him the courtesy of looking up. "Maybe I'll win the lottery. Maybe you'll get a promotion. Do you see where these maybes are taking us?"

Frustration and lack of sleep caught up with him. "Then why are we here? Why aren't you taking Zabel and letting us get on with doing something more useful than giving her source material for her book deal?"

Amanda finally looked up from her iPhone. She handed the device to Will. "I'm at a loss, Agent Trent. Why don't you read this for me and let me know what you think?"

He felt his vision go sharp, and there was an odd, high-pitched ringing in his ears. The iPhone hung in the air like a well-baited hook. There were words on the screen. That much he could tell. Will tasted blood from biting the edge of his tongue. He reached to take the device, but Faith snatched it from Amanda before he could.

Her voice was terse as she read, " 'Eleven generally represents judgment or betrayal in the Bible. . . . There were eleven commandments originally, but the Catholics combined the first two and the Protestants combined the last two in order to make it an even ten.' " She scrolled down. " 'The Philistines gave Delilah eleven hundred pieces of silver to bring down Samson. Jesus told eleven parables on the way to his death in Jerusalem.' " She paused again, scrolling. " 'The Catholic Church accepts eleven books as canonical in the Apocrypha.' "

Faith handed back the device to Amanda. "We could do this all day. Flight 11 on 9/11 hit one of the Twin Towers, which themselves looked like the number 11. Apollo 11 made the first moon landing. World War I ended on eleven-eleven. You should get an eleventh circle in hell for what you just did to Will."

Amanda smiled, tucking the iPhone into her pocket, continuing down the hall. "Remember the rules, children."

Will didn't know if she meant the rules that put her in charge or the ones she'd given them about interviewing Joelyn Zabel. There was no time to reflect, however, because Amanda walked through the anteroom to her office and opened the door. She made introductions all around as she went behind her desk and took a seat. Her office was, of course, larger than any other in the building, closer to the size of the conference room on Will and Faith's floor.

Joelyn Zabel and a man who could only be her lawyer were in the visitors' seats opposite Amanda. There were two chairs beside Amanda's desk, one each for Faith and Will, he supposed. The state lawyers were on a couch in the back of the room, three in a row, their black suits and muted silk ties giving them away. Joelyn Zabel's lawyer was dressed in a blue the color of a shark, which seemed more than fitting, considering his smile reminded Will of the aquatic carnivore.

"Thank you for coming in," Faith said, shaking the woman's hand, then taking a seat.

Joelyn Zabel looked like a chubbier version of her sister. Not that she was fat, but she had a healthy curve to her hips whereas Jacquelyn had been boyishly thin. Will caught the scent of cigarette smoke as he shook her hand.

He said, "I'm so sorry about your loss."

"Trent," she noted. "You're the one who found her."

Will tried to keep eye contact, to not convey the gut-level guilt he still felt for not reaching the woman's sister in time. All he could think to do was repeat himself. "I'm so sorry about your loss."

"Yeah," she snapped. "I got that."

Will sat down beside Faith, and Amanda clapped her

hands together like a kindergarten teacher getting the class's attention. She rested her hand on top of a manila folder, which Will guessed contained the abridged autopsy summary. Pete had been instructed to leave off the information about the trash bags. Considering the Rockdale County force's cozy relationship with the press, they were running thin on guilty knowledge to pin down any future suspect.

Amanda began, "Ms. Zabel, I take it you've had time to go over the report?"

The lawyer spoke. "I'll need a copy of that for my files, Mandy."

Amanda smiled an even sharkier smile than the lawyer had. "Of course, Chuck."

"Great, so y'all know each other." Joelyn crossed her arms, her shoulders bunching around her neck. "You want to explain to me what the hell you're doing to find my sister's killer?"

Amanda's smile did not falter. "We're doing everything we can to—"

"You find a suspect yet? I mean, shit, this guy's a fucking *animal*."

Amanda didn't answer, which Faith took as her cue to begin. "We agree with you. Whoever did this is an animal. That's why we need to talk to you about your sister. We need to know about her life. Who her friends were. What her habits were."

Joelyn's eyes flashed down a minute, guilty. "I didn't have much contact with her. We were both pretty busy. She lived in Florida."

Faith tried to soften things up. "She lived on the Bay, right? Must've been nice down there. Good reason to sneak in a vacation with a family visit."

"Well, yeah, it would've been, but the bitch never invited me."

Her lawyer reached out, touching her arm as a gentle reminder. Will had watched Joelyn Zabel on every major channel, sobbing anew over the tragic death of her sister for each new reporter. He'd not seen one tear drop from her eyes, though she made all the motions of someone who was crying—sniffling, wiping her eyes, rocking back and forth. She wasn't even doing that now. Apparently, she needed a camera rolling to feel her pain. Even more apparent, the lawyer wasn't going to let her play anything other than the grieving family member.

Joelyn sniffed, still with no tears. "I loved my sister very much. My mother just moved into a nursing home. She's got maybe six months left, and this happens to her daughter. The loss of a child is devastating."

Faith tried to ease into more questions. "Do you have children?"

"Four." She seemed proud.

"Jacquelyn didn't have—"

"Fuck no. Three abortions before she was thirty. She was terrified of getting fat. Can you believe that? Her sole reason for flushing them down the toilet is her fucking weight. And then she gets in the shadow of forty, and suddenly she wants to be a mother."

Faith hid her surprise well. "Was she trying to conceive?"

"Did you not hear me about the abortions? You can look that up. I'm not lying about that."

Will always assumed that when people insisted they weren't lying about a particular thing, that meant they were lying about something else. Finding out the what else would be the key to Joelyn Zabel. She didn't strike him as a particularly caring person, and she would want to make sure her ten minutes of fame stretched out as long as possible.

Faith asked, "Was Jackie looking for a surrogate?"

Joelyn seemed to realize how important her words were. She suddenly had everyone's rapt attention. She took her time answering. "Adoption."

"Private? Public?"

"Who the fuck knows? She had a lot of money. She was used to buying what she wanted." She was gripping the arms of her chair, and Will could see this was a subject she liked talking about. "That's the real tragedy here—not being able to see her adopt some reject retard who ends up stealing from her or going schizophrenic on her ass."

Will could feel Faith stiffen beside him. He took over the questioning. "When was the last time you talked to your sister?"

"About a month ago. She was waxing on about motherhood, like she understands the first thing about it. Talking about adopting some kid from China or Russia or something. You know, some of those kids turn out to be killers. They're abused, just sick in the head. They're never right."

"We see that a lot." Will shook his head sadly, like this was a common tragedy. "Was she making any progress? Do you know what agency she was working with?"

She turned reticent when pressed for details. "Jackie wasn't into sharing. She was always phobic about her privacy." She jerked her head toward the state lawyers, who were doing their best to blend in with the upholstery. "I know those tools sitting on the couch aren't going to let you apologize, but you could at least ac-knowledge that you fucked up."

Amanda jumped back in. "Ms. Zabel, the autopsy shows—"

Joelyn gave a belligerent half-shrug. "All it shows is what I already know: You dumbasses were standing around doing *nothing* while my sister died."

"Perhaps you didn't read the report carefully enough, Ms. Zabel." Amanda's voice was gentle sounding, the soothing sort of tone she'd used earlier in the hall before humiliating Will. "Your sister took her own life."

"Only because y'all weren't doing a damn thing to help her."

"You realize that she was blind and deaf?" Amanda asked.

Will could tell from the way that Zabel's eyes shifted to the lawyer that she had not, in fact, realized this.

Amanda removed another folder from the top drawer of her desk. She thumbed through it, and he could see color photos of Jacquelyn Zabel in the tree, in the morgue. Will found this particularly cruel, even for Amanda. No matter how horrible Joelyn Zabel was, she had still lost her sister in the worst way. He saw Faith shift in her seat and knew she was thinking the same thing.

Amanda took her time searching for the right page, which seemed to be buried among the worst of the pho-tographs. Finally, she found the passage relating to the external examination of the body. "Second paragraph," she said.

Joelyn hesitated before sitting on the edge of her seat. She was trying to get a better look at the photos the way some people slow down to look at a particularly terrible car accident. Finally, she sat back with the report. Will watched her eyes move back and forth as she read, but then they suddenly stopped tracking, and he knew that she wasn't seeing anything at all.

Her throat worked as she swallowed. She stood up, mumbling "Excuse me" as she bolted from the room.

The air seemed to leave with her. Faith stared straight ahead. Amanda took her time stacking the photos into a neat pile.

The lawyer said, "Not nice, Mandy."

"Them's the breaks, Chuck."

Will stood. "I'm going to stretch my legs."

He left the room before anyone could respond. Caroline, Amanda's secretary, was at her desk. Will lifted his chin, and she whispered, "In the bathroom."

Will walked down the hall, hands in his pockets. He stopped in front of the women's-room door, pressing it open with his foot. He leaned in. Joelyn Zabel stood in front of the mirror. She had a lighted cigarette in her hand, and she startled when she saw Will.

"You can't be in here," she snapped, holding up her fist like she expected some kind of fight.

"No smoking is allowed in the building." Will walked into the room and put his back against the closed door, keeping his hands in his pockets.

"What are you doing in here?"

"I wanted to make sure you were okay."

She took a hard hit off the cigarette. "By barging into the ladies' room? This is off-limits, okay? It's not allowed."

Will glanced around. He had never been in a women's restroom before. There was a comfortable-looking couch with flowers in a vase on the table beside it. The air had the scent of perfume, the paper dispensers were stocked and there was no water splashed around the basin so that you got the front of your pants wet when you washed your hands. It was no wonder women spent so much time in this place.

"Hello?" Joelyn asked. "Crazy man? Get out of the ladies' room."

"What aren't you telling me?"

"I told you everything I know."

He shook his head. "Cameras aren't rolling in here. No lawyers, no audience. Tell me what you're not telling me."

"Fuck off."

He felt the door being gently pressed against his back, then close just as quickly. He said, "You didn't like your sister."

"No shit, Sherlock." Her hand shook as she took another hit of smoke into her lungs.

"What did she do to you?"

"She was a bitch."

The same could be said for Joelyn, but Will kept that to himself. "Was there any specific way this manifested itself toward you, or is that just a general statement?"

She stared at him. "What the hell does that mean?"

"It means that I don't care what you're going to do after you leave here. Sue the state. Don't sue the state. Sue me personally. I don't care. Whoever killed your sister probably has someone else—some woman who's being tortured and raped right now as we speak—and your keeping something from me is just as good as saying that what's happening to this other woman is okay."

"Don't put that on me."

"Then tell me what you're hiding."

"I'm not hiding anything." She turned from the mirror, wiping under her eyes with her fingers so she wouldn't smudge her makeup. "It's Jackie who was hiding things."

Will kept silent.

"She was always secretive, always acting like she was better than me."

He nodded, like he got it.

"She got all the attention, all the boyfriends." She shook her head, turning to face Will. She leaned against the counter, hand beside the sink. "My weight went up and down when I was a kid. Jackie used to tease me about being beached whenever we'd go to lay out."

"You've obviously outgrown that problem."

She shook off the compliment, disbelieving. "Everything always came so easy to her. Money, men, success. People liked her."

"Not really," Will disagreed. "None of her neighbors seem too shaken up that she's missing. They didn't even notice until the cops knocked on their doors. I got the feeling they were relieved she's gone."

"I don't believe you."

"Your mother's neighbor, Candy, doesn't seem too broken up about it, either."

She was obviously unconvinced. "No, Jackie said Candy was like a toy poodle nipping at her heels, always wanting to hang out with her."

"That's not true," Will said. "Candy wasn't very fond of her. I'd even say she was less fond of your sister than you are."

She finished the cigarette, then went into one of the stalls to flush it down the toilet. Will could see her processing this new information about her sister, liking it.

Joelyn went back to the sink, leaned against the counter again. "She was always a liar. Lied about little things, things that didn't even matter."

"Like what?"

"Like, that she was going to the store when she was going to the library. Like that she was dating one guy when she was really dating another one."

"Seems kind of devious."

"She was. That's a perfect word for her—'devious.' She drove our mother nuts."

"Did she get into much trouble?"

Joelyn snorted a laugh. "Jackie was always the teacher's pet, always sucking up to the right people. She had them all fooled."

"Not all of them," Will pointed out. "You said she drove your mother nuts. Your mom must've known what was going on."

"She did. Spent all kinds of money trying to get Jackie help. It ruined my fucking childhood. Everything was always about *Jackie*—how *she* was feeling, what *she* was out doing, whether *she* was happy. Nobody worried whether or not *I* was happy."

"Tell me about this adoption thing. What agency was she talking to?"

Joelyn looked down, guilt flashing in her eyes.

Will kept his tone neutral. "This is why I'm asking: If Jackie was trying to adopt a child, we're going to have to go to Florida and find the agency. If there's an overseas connection, we might have to go to Russia or China to see if their operations are legitimate. If Jackie was trying to contract with a surrogate at home, we'll have to talk to every woman who might have spoken to her. We'll have to dig into every agency down there until we find something, anything, that connects to your sister, because she met a very bad person who tortured and raped her for at least a week, and if we can find out how your sister met her abductor, then maybe we can find out who that man is." He let her consider his words for a few seconds. "Will we find a connection through an adoption agency, Joelyn?"

She looked down at her hands, not answering. Will counted the tiles on the wall behind her head. He was at thirty-six when she finally spoke. "I just said that—the stuff about getting a kid. Jackie was talking about it, but she wasn't going to do it. She liked the idea of being a mother, but she knew she would never be able to pull it off."

"Are you sure about that?"

"It's like when people are around well-trained dogs, you know? They want a dog, but they want *that* dog, not a new one they'd have to work with and train on their own."

"Did she like your kids?"

Joelyn cleared her throat. "She never met them."

Will gave the woman some time. "She was picked up on a DUI before she died."

Joelyn was surprised. "Really?"

"Was she much of a drinker?"

She shook her head vehemently. "Jackie didn't like being out of control."

"The neighbor, Candy, says they smoked some grass together."

Her lips parted in surprise. She shook her head again. "I don't buy it. Jackie never did shit like that. She liked it when other people drank too much, got out of hand, but she never did it herself. You're talking about a woman who's weighed the same weight since she was sixteen years old. Her ass was so tight it squeaked when she walked." She thought about it some more, shook her head again. "No, not Jackie."

"Why was she cleaning out your mother's house? Why not pay someone else to do the dirty work?"

"She didn't trust anybody else. She always had the right way to do things, and whoever you were, you were always doing it wrong."

That, at least, jibed with what Candy said. Everything else was a completely different picture, which made sense considering that Joelyn was not particularly close to her sister. He asked, "Does the number eleven mean anything to you?"

She furrowed her brow. "Not a damn thing."

"What about the words 'I will not deny myself'?"

She shook her head again. "But it's funny . . . As rich as she was, Jackie denied herself all the time."

"Denied herself what?"

"Food. Alcohol. Fun." She gave a rueful laugh. "Friends. Family. Love." Her eyes filled with tears—the first real tears Will had seen her cry. He pushed away from the door and left, finding Faith waiting in the hallway for him.

"Anything?" she asked.

"She lied about the adoption thing. At least she said she did."

"We can check it out with Candy." Faith took out her phone and flipped it open. She talked to Will as she dialed. "We were supposed to meet Rick Sigler at the hospital ten minutes ago. I called him to postpone, but he didn't pick up."

"What about his friend, Jake Berman?"

"I put some uniforms on it first thing. They're supposed to call if they find him."

"You think it's odd that we can't track him down?"

"Not yet, but talk to me at the end of the day if we still can't find him." She put the phone to her ear, and Will listened as she left a message for Candy Smith to return her call. Faith closed the phone and gripped it in her hand. Will felt dread well up inside him, wondering what she was going to say next—something about Amanda, a diatribe against Sara Linton, or Will himself. Thankfully, it was about the case.

She said, "I think Pauline McGhee is part of this."

"Why?"

"It's just gut. I can't explain it, but it's too coincidental."

"McGhee is still Leo's case. We've got no jurisdiction over it, no reason to ask him for a piece of it." Still, Will had to ask, "You think you can nuance him?"

She shook her head. "I don't want to make trouble for Leo."

"He's supposed to call you, right? When he tracks down Pauline's parents in Michigan?"

"That's what he said he'd do."

They stood at the elevator, both quiet.

Will said, "I think we need to go to Pauline's work."

"I think you're right."

CHAPTER FOURTEEN

FAITH PACED THE LOBBY OF XAC HOMAGE, THE ridiculously named design firm that employed Pauline McGhee. The offices took up the thirtieth floor of Symphony Tower, an architecturally awkward skyscraper that loomed over the corner of Peachtree and Fourteenth Street like a large speculum. Faith shuddered at the image, thinking about what she had read in Jacquelyn Zabel's autopsy report.

In keeping with the pretentiousness of their name, Xac Homage's window-lined lobby was furnished with low-to-the-floor couches that were impossible to sit in without either clenching every muscle in your ass or just falling back into a slouch that you would need help getting out of. Faith would've gone for the slouch if she hadn't been wearing a skirt that was prone to riding up even when she wasn't sitting like a gangster's whore in a rap video.

She was hungry but didn't know what to eat. She was running out of insulin and she still wasn't sure she was calculating the dosages correctly. She hadn't made an appointment with the doctor Sara had recommended. Her feet were swollen and her back was killing her and she wanted to beat her head against the wall because she could not stop thinking about Sam Lawson no matter how hard she tried.

And she had a sneaking suspicion from the way Will kept giving her sidelong glances that she was acting like a raving lunatic.

"God," Faith mumbled, pressing her forehead into the clean glass that lined the lobby. Why did she keep making so many mistakes? She wasn't a stupid person. Or maybe she was. Maybe all these years she had been fooling herself, and she was, in fact, one of the stupidest people on earth.

She looked down at the cars inching along Peachtree Street, ants scurrying across the black asphalt. Last month at her dentist's office, Faith had read a magazine article that posited that women were genetically wired to become clingy with the men they had sex with for at least three weeks after the event because that's how long it took for the body to figure out whether or not it was pregnant. She had laughed at the time, because Faith had never felt clingy with men. At least not after Jeremy's father, who had literally left the state after Faith had told him she was pregnant.

And yet, here she was checking her phone and her email every ten minutes, wanting to talk to Sam, wanting to see how he was doing and find out whether or not he was mad at her—as if what had happened was her fault. As if he had been such a magnificent lover that she couldn't get enough of him. She was already pregnant; it couldn't be her genetic wiring that was causing her to act like a silly schoolgirl. Or maybe it was. Maybe she was just a victim of her own hormones.

Or maybe she shouldn't be getting her science from *Ladies' Home Journal*.

Faith turned her head, watching Will in the elevator alcove. He was on his cell phone, holding it with both hands so it wouldn't fall apart. She couldn't be mad at him anymore. He had been good with Joelyn Zabel. She had to admit that. His approach to the job was different than hers, and sometimes that worked for them and sometimes that worked against them. Faith shook her head. She couldn't dwell on these differences right now—not when her entire life was on the edge of a gigantic cliff, and the ground would not stop shaking.

Will finished his call and walked toward her. He glanced at the empty desk where the secretary had been. The woman had left to get Morgan Hollister at least ten minutes ago. Faith had images of the pair of them furiously shredding files, though it was more likely that the woman, a bottle blonde who seemed to have trouble processing even the smallest request, had simply forgotten about them and was on her cell phone in the bathroom.

Faith asked, "Who were you talking to?"

"Amanda," he told her, taking a couple of candies out of the bowl on the coffee table. "She called to apologize."

Faith laughed at the joke, and he joined her.

Will took some more candy, offering the bowl to Faith. She shook her head, and he continued, "She's doing another press conference this afternoon. Joelyn Zabel's dropping her lawsuit against the city."

"What prompted that?"

"Her lawyer realized they didn't have a case. Don't worry, she's going to be on the cover of some magazine next week, and the week after she's going to be threatening to sue us again because we haven't found her sister's killer."

It was the first time either of them had voiced their

real fear in all of this: that the killer was good enough to get away with his crimes.

Will indicated the closed door behind the desk. "You think we should just go back?"

"Give it another minute." She tried to wipe away her forehead print on the window, making the smear worse. The momentum of the tension between them had somehow shifted in the ride over, so that Will was no longer worried about Faith being mad at him. It was now Faith's turn to be worried that *she'd* upset *him*.

She asked, "Are we okay?"

"Sure we're okay."

She didn't believe him, but there was no way around someone who kept insisting there wasn't a problem, because all they would do is keep insisting until you felt like you were making the whole thing up.

She said, "Well, at least we know that bitchiness runs in the Zabel family."

"Joelyn's all right."

"It's hard to be the good sibling."

"What do you mean?"

"I mean, if you're the good kid in the family, making good grades, staying out of trouble, et cetera, and your sister's always screwing up and getting all the attention, you start to feel left out, like no matter how good you are, it doesn't matter because all your parents can focus on is your crappy sibling."

She must have sounded bitter, because Will asked, "I thought your brother was a good guy?"

"He is," Faith told him. "I was the bad one who got all the attention." She chuckled. "I remember one time, he asked my parents if they would just give him up for adoption."

Will gave a half-smile. "Everyone wants to be adopted."

She remembered Joelyn Zabel's awful words about her sister's quest for a child. "What Joelyn said—"

He interrupted her. "Why did her lawyer keep calling Amanda 'Mandy'?"

"It's short for Amanda."

He nodded thoughtfully, and Faith wondered if nicknames were another one of his tics. It would make sense. You would have to know how a name was spelled before you could shorten it.

"Did you know that sixteen percent of all known serial killers were adopted?"

Faith wrinkled her brow. "That can't be right."

"Joel Rifkin, Kenneth Bianchi, David Berkowitz. Ted Bundy was adopted by his stepfather."

"How is it that you're suddenly an expert on serial killers?"

"History Channel," he told her. "Trust me, it comes in handy."

"When do you find time to watch so much television?"

"It's not like I've got a busy social life."

Faith looked back out the window, thinking about Will with Sara Linton this morning. From reading the report on Jeffrey Tolliver, Faith gathered he was exactly the kind of cop Will was not: physical, take-charge, willing to do whatever it took to get a case solved. Not that Will wasn't driven, too, but he was more likely to stare a confession out of a suspect instead of beating it out of him. Faith knew instinctively that Will was not Sara Linton's type, which was why she had felt so sorry for him this morning, watching how awkward he was with the woman.

He must have been thinking about this morning, too, because he said, "I don't know her apartment number."

"Sara?"

"She's in the Milk Lofts over on Berkshire."

"There's bound to be a building di—" Faith stopped herself. "I can write out her last name for you so you can compare it to the directory. There can't be that many tenants."

He shrugged, obviously daunted.

"We could look it up online."

"She's probably not listed."

The door opened and the bottle-blonde secretary was back. Behind her was an extremely tall, extremely tanned and extremely good-looking man in the most beautiful suit Faith had ever seen.

"Morgan Hollister," he offered, extending a hand as he walked across the room. "I'm so sorry I left you out here so long. I was on a conference call with a client in New York. This thing with Pauline has put a real spanner in the works, as they say."

Faith wasn't sure who said that sort of thing, but she forgave him as she shook his hand. He was at once the most attractive and most gay man she had met in a while. Considering they were in Atlanta, the gay capital of the South, this was saying quite a lot.

"I'm Agent Trent, this is Agent Mitchell," Will said, somehow ignoring the predatory way Morgan Hollister stared at him.

"You work out?" Morgan asked.

"Free weights, mostly. A little bench work."

Morgan slapped him on the arm. "Solid."

"I appreciate your letting us look through Pauline's things," Will said, although Morgan had made no such offer. "I know the Atlanta police have already been here. I hope it's not too inconvenient."

"Of course not." Morgan put his hand on Will's shoulder as he led him toward the door. "We're really torn up about Paulie. She was a great girl."

"We've heard she could be a bit difficult to work with."

Morgan gave a chuckle, which Faith understood as code for "typical woman." She was glad to hear that sexism was just as rampant in the gay community.

Will asked, "Does the name Jacquelyn Zabel mean anything to you?"

Morgan shook his head. "I work with all the clients. I'm pretty sure I'd remember it, but I can check the computer." He put on a sad face. "Poor Paulie. This came as such a shock to all of us."

"We found temporary placement for Felix," Will told the man.

"Felix?" He seemed confused, then said, "Oh, right, the little guy. I'm sure he'll be okay. He's a trouper."

Morgan led them down a long hallway. Cubicles were on their right, windows looking out onto the interstate behind them. Material swatches and schematics littered the desktops. Faith glanced at a set of blueprints spread out on a conference table, feeling slightly wistful.

As a child, she had wanted to be an architect, a dream that was derailed promptly at the age of fourteen when she was kicked out of school for being pregnant. It was different now, of course, but back then, pregnant teenagers were expected to drop off the face of the earth, their names never mentioned again unless it was in reference to the boy who had knocked them up, and then they were only referred to as "that slut who nearly ruined his life by getting pregnant."

Morgan stopped in front of a closed office door. Pauline McGhee's name was on the outside. He took out a key.

Will asked, "You always keep it locked?"

"Paulie did. One of her things."

"She have a lot of *things*?"

"She had a way she liked to do stuff." Morgan shrugged. "I gave her a free hand. She was good with paperwork, good at keeping subcontractors in line." His smile dropped. "Of course, there was a problem there at the end. She messed up a very important order. Cost the firm a lot of money. Not sure she'd still be here if something hadn't happened."

If Will was wondering why Morgan was talking about Pauline as if she was dead, he didn't press it. Instead, he held out his hand for the key. "We'll lock up when we're finished."

Morgan hesitated. He had obviously assumed he would be there while they searched the office.

Will said, "I'll bring it back to you when we're finished, all right?" He slapped Morgan on the arm. "Thanks, man." Will turned his back to him and went inside the office. Faith followed, pulling the door shut behind her.

She had to ask, "That doesn't bother you?"

"Morgan?" He shrugged. "He knows I'm not interested."

"But, still—"

"There were a lot of gay kids at the children's home.

Most of them were a hell of a lot nicer than the straight ones."

She couldn't imagine any parent giving up their child for any reason, especially that one. "That's awful."

Will obviously didn't want to have a conversation about it. He looked around the office, saying, "I'd call this austere."

Faith had to agree. Pauline's office appeared as if it had never been occupied. There was not a scrap of paper on the desktop. The in and out trays were empty. The design books on the shelves were all arranged in alphabetical order, spines straightened. The magazines stood crisply at attention in colored boxes. Even the computer monitor seemed to be at a precise forty-five-degree angle on the corner of the desk. The only thing of sentimental value on display was a snapshot of Felix on a swing set.

" 'He's a little trouper,' " Will said, mocking Morgan's words about Pauline's son. "I called the social worker last night. Felix isn't handling it very well."

"What's he doing?"

"Crying a lot. He won't eat."

Faith stared at the photograph, the unchecked joy in the young boy's eyes as he beamed at his mother. She remembered Jeremy at that age. He'd been so sweet she'd wanted to eat him up like a piece of candy. Faith had just graduated from the police academy and moved into a cheap apartment off Monroe Drive; the first time either she or Jeremy had lived away from Faith's mother. Their lives had become intertwined in a way she had never known was possible. He was so much a part of her that she could barely stand to drop him off at day care. At night, Jeremy would color pictures while she filled out her daily reports at the kitchen table. He would sing songs to her in his squeaky little voice while she fixed him supper and made lunches for the next day. Sometimes, he would crawl into bed and curl up under her arm like a kitten. She had never felt so important or needed—not before and certainly not since.

"Faith?" Will had said something she'd missed.

She put the photograph back on Pauline's desk before she started bawling like a baby. "Yeah?"

"I said, what do you want to bet Jacquelyn Zabel's house in Florida was neat like this?"

Faith cleared her throat, trying to shift her focus. "The room she was using in her mother's house was extremely orderly. I thought it was something she did because the rest of the house was so messy—you know, calm in the storm. Maybe it's because she's a neat freak."

"Type A personality." Will walked around the desk, opening drawers. Faith looked at what he'd found—a row of colored pencils side by side in a plastic tray. Extra Post-it notes in a squared stack. He opened the next drawer and found a large binder, which he pulled out and put on the desk. He thumbed through the pages, and Faith saw room sketches, swatches, clippings of furniture photos.

Faith booted up the computer while he looked through the other drawers. She was pretty sure they would find nothing here, but, oddly, it felt as if what they were doing was helping the case. She was clicking with Will again, feeling more like his partner and less like an adversary. That had to be a good thing.

"Look at this." Will had opened the bottom drawer on the left side. It was a mess—the equivalent of a kitchen junk drawer. Papers were wadded up, and at the bottom were several empty bags of potato chips.

Faith said, "At least we know she's human."

"It's weird," he said. "Everything's so neat except this one drawer."

Faith picked up a balled piece of paper and smoothed it against the desk. There was a list on it, items checked off as they had probably been completed: grocery store; get lamp fixed for Powell living room; contact Jordan about couch swatches. She took out another balled piece of paper, finding much the same.

Will asked, "Maybe she wadded them up once she finished doing what she needed to do?"

Faith squinted at the list, blurring her eyes, trying to see it the way Will would. He was so damn good at fooling people into thinking he could read that sometimes Faith forgot he even had a problem.

Will searched the bookcase, taking down a magazine box from one of the middle shelves. "What's this?" He pulled down another box, then another. Faith could see the dial of a safe.

Will tried the handle, but there was no luck. He ran his fingers along the seam. "It's concreted into the wall."

"You want to go ask your buddy Morgan for the combination?"

"I'd bet some serious money he doesn't know it."

Faith didn't take the bet. Like Jacquelyn Zabel, Pauline McGhee seemed to enjoy keeping secrets.

Will said, "Check the computer first, then I'll go look for him."

Faith looked at the monitor. There was a box asking for a password.

Will saw it, too. "Try 'Felix.' "

She did, and miraculously, it worked. She made a mental note to change her password from "Jeremy" at home as she clicked open the email program. Faith skimmed the messages as Will went back to the bookshelves. She found the usual correspondence from people working in an office, but nothing personal that would point to a friend or confidant. Faith sat back in the chair and opened the browser, hoping to find an email service in the history. There was no Gmail or Yahoo, but she discovered several websites.

Randomly, she clicked on one, and a YouTube page came up. She checked the sound as the video loaded. A guitar squeaked through the speakers on the bottom of a monitor, and the words, *"I am happy,"* came up, then, *"I am smiling."*

Will stood behind her. She read the words as they faded into the black. *"I am feeling. I am living. I am dying."*

The guitar turned angrier with each word, and a photograph came up of a young girl in a cheerleading outfit. The shorts were low on her hips, the top barely enough to cover her breasts. She was so thin that Faith could count her ribs.

"Jesus," she mumbled. Another picture faded in, this one of an African-American girl. She was balled up on a bed, her back to the camera. Her skin was stretched, her vertebrae and ribs pronounced enough to show each individual piece of bone pressing against the thin flesh. Her shoulder blade stuck out like a knife.

"Is this some kind of relief site?" Will asked. "Money for AIDS?"

Faith shook her head as the next picture came up—a model standing in front of a cityscape, her legs and arms as thin as sticks. Another girl came up; a woman actually. Her clavicle jutted out with painful sharpness. The skin across her shoulders looked like wet paper covering the sinew underneath.

Faith clicked on the browser history button. She pulled up another video. There was different music, but the same sort of intro. She read aloud, *"Eat to live. Don't live to eat."* The words faded into a photo of a girl who was so painfully thin that she was hard to look at. Faith opened another page, then another. *"The only freedom left is the freedom to starve yourself,"* she read. *"Thin is beautiful. Fat is ugly."* She looked at the top of the screen, the video category. "Thinspo. I've never heard of it."

"I don't understand. These girls look like they're starving, but they've got TVs in their rooms, they're wearing nice clothes."

Faith clicked on another link. "Thinspiration," she said. "Good Lord, I can't believe this. They're emaciated."

"Is there a newsgroup or something?"

Faith looked back at the history. She skimmed the list, finding more videos, but nothing that looked like a chat room. She scrolled to the next page and hit pay dirt. "Atlanta-Pro-Anna-dot-com," she read. "It's a pro-anorexia site." Faith clicked on the link, but all that came up was another screen asking for a password. She tried "Felix" again, but it didn't work. She read the fine print. "It's asking for a six-digit password and Felix is only five letters." She typed in variations on his name, saying them aloud for Will's benefit. "Zero-Felix, one-Felix, Felix-zero . . ."

Will asked, "How many letters is 'thinspiration'?"

"Too many," she said. " 'Thinspo' is seven." She tried this, to no avail.

Will asked, "What's her screen name?"

Faith read the name in the box above the password. "A-T-L thin." She realized spelling wouldn't help him. "It's shorthand for 'Atlanta thin.'" She entered in the screen name. "No dice. Oh." Faith mentally kicked herself. "Felix's birthday." She opened up the calendar program and did a search for "birthday." Only two hits came up, one for Pauline and one for her son. "One-two-eight-oh-two." The screen stayed stagnant. "Nope, didn't work."

He nodded, absently scratching his arm. "Safes have six-digit combinations, right?"

"Couldn't hurt to try it." Faith waited, but Will did not move. "One-two-oh-eight-oh-two," she repeated, knowing he was perfectly capable of processing numbers. Still he didn't move, and finally she felt something in her brain click. "Oh. I'm sorry."

"Don't apologize. It's my fault."

"It's mine." She stood up and went to the safe, spinning the dial to the right, locking onto the twelve, then going left two turns and dialing in eight. It wasn't the numbers Will couldn't manage. It was the left and right.

Faith dialed in the last number, and was slightly disappointed it had been so easy when she heard the instant *thunk* of the last tumbler falling into place. She opened the safe and saw a spiral-bound notebook, the sort of thing every schoolkid had, and a single piece of laser paper. She skimmed the page. It was a printed-out email dealing with measuring an elevator so a couch could fit in it, something Faith had never considered had to be done, even though the first refrigerator she'd bought had been too big to fit through the kitchen door. "Work stuff," she told Will, taking out the notebook.

She flipped open the cover to the first page. The hair on the back of her neck went up, and Faith suppressed a shudder as she realized what she was seeing. Neat cursive lined the page, over and over again, the same line. Faith flipped to the next page, then the next. The words had been traced so hard in places that the pen ripped the paper. She was not one to believe in the supernatural, but the anger she felt coming out of the notebook was palpable.

"It's the same, right?" Will had probably recognized the spacing of the lines, the same short sentence repeatedly written, covering the notebook like a sadistic form of art.

I will not deny myself . . . I will not deny myself . . . I will not deny myself . . .

"The same," Faith confirmed. "This connects Pauline to the cave, to Jackie Zabel and Anna."

"It's in pen," Will said. "The pages in the cave were in pencil."

"It's the same sentence, though. *I will not deny myself.* Pauline wrote this on her own, not because she had to. No one made her do it. As far as we know, she was never in that cave." Faith thumbed through the pages, making sure it was the same to the end of the notebook. "Jackie Zabel was thin. Not like the girls in the videos, but very thin."

"Joelyn Zabel said her sister weighed the same weight when she died as she did in high school."

"You think she had an eating disorder?"

"I think she had a lot of the same attributes that Pauline has—likes to be in control, likes to keep secrets." He added, "Pete thought Jackie was malnourished, but maybe she was starving herself already."

"What about Anna? Is she thin?"

"Same thing. You could see her . . ." He put his hand to his collarbone. "We thought it was part of the torture—starving them. But, those girls in the videos, they do that on purpose, right? These videos are like pornography for anorexics."

Faith nodded, feeling a rush as she made the next connection. "Maybe they all met on the Internet." She went back to the password box overlaying the Pro-Anna chat room and entered Felix's birthday in every combination she could think of—leaving out the zeros, adding them back in, doing the full date, reversing the numbers. "It could be that Pauline was assigned a password she couldn't change."

"Or maybe what's in that chat room is more valuable to her than what's on the rest of the computer and in the safe."

"This is a connection, Will. If all the women had eating disorders, then we finally have something that links them all."

"And a chat room we can't get into, and family that isn't being exactly helpful."

"What about Pauline McGhee's brother? She told Felix that he was a bad man." She turned away from the computer, giving Will her full attention. "Maybe we should go back to Felix and see if he remembers anything else."

Will seemed dubious. "He's only six years old, Faith. He's bereft about losing his mom. I don't think we can get anything else out of him."

They both jumped when the phone on the desk rang. Faith reached for it without thinking, saying, "Pauline McGhee's office."

"Hello." Morgan Hollister sounded none too pleased.

Faith asked, "Did you find Jacquelyn Zabel in your books?"

" 'Fraid not, Detective, but—funny thing—I've got a call for you on line two."

Faith shrugged at Will as she pressed the lighted button. "Faith Mitchell."

Leo Donnelly went straight into a tirade. "Didn't occur to you to check with me before barging in on my case?"

Faith's mouth filled with apologies, but Leo didn't give her time to get them out.

"I got a call from my boss who got a call from your butt-boy Hollister asking why the state was pawing through McGhee's office when we'd already been through everything this morning." He was breathing hard. "My *boss,* Faith. He's wanting to know why I can't do my job on this thing. You know how that makes me look?"

"It's connected," Faith said. "We found a connection between Pauline McGhee and our other victims."

"I'm real fucking happy for you, Mitchell. Meanwhile, my balls are in a vise because you couldn't take two seconds to stop and give me a heads-up."

"Leo, I'm so sorry—"

"Save it," he snapped. "I should hold this back from you, but I'm not that kind of guy."

"Hold what back?"

"We've got another missing person."

Faith felt her heart do a double beat. "Another missing woman?" she repeated, for Will's benefit. "Does she match our profile?"

"Midthirties, dark hair, brown eyes. She works at some fancy bank in Buckhead where you gotta be filthy rich just to walk in the door. No friends. Everybody says she's a major bitch."

Faith nodded at Will. Another victim, another clock ticking down. "What's her name? Where does she live?"

"Olivia Tanner." He shot out the name and address so fast that she had to ask him to repeat it. "She's in Virginia Highland."

Faith scribbled the street address on the back of her hand.

He said, "You owe me for this."

"Leo, I'm so sorry I—"

He didn't let her finish. "If I were you, Mitchell, I'd watch myself. Except for the successful part, you're looking a hell of a lot like that profile lately."

She heard a soft *click,* which in some ways was worse than him slamming down the receiver in her ear.

OLIVIA TANNER LIVED in one of those deceptively small-looking Midtown bungalows that from the street appeared to be around a thousand square feet but ended up having six bedrooms and five and a half baths, with a price tag running slightly north of a million dollars. After being in Pauline McGhee's office, seeing the missing woman's psyche laid bare, Faith looked at Olivia Tanner's house differently than she would have otherwise. The flower garden was beautiful, but all the plants were lined up in uniform rows. The outside of the house was crisply painted, the gutters in a graceful line along the eaves. Based on Faith's knowledge of the neighborhood, the bungalow was probably thirty years older than her own lowly ranch house, but comparatively speaking, it looked brand-new.

"All right," Will said into his cell phone. "Thank you for talking to me." He ended the call, telling Faith, "Joelyn Zabel says that her sister struggled with anorexia and bulimia when she was in high school. She's not sure what was going on recently, but it's a pretty fair bet that Jackie hadn't given it up."

Faith let the information settle in her brain. "Okay," she finally said.

"That's it. That's the connection."

"Where does it get us?" she asked, turning off the ignition. "Tech can't break into Jackie Zabel's Mac. It might take weeks for them to find the password on Pauline McGhee's computer, and we don't even know if the anorexia chat room is where she met the other women or if it was just something she cruised during her lunch hour. Not that she ate lunch." She looked back up at Olivia Tanner's house. "What do you want to bet we don't find a damn thing here, either?"

"You're focusing on Felix when you need to be thinking about Pauline," he said softly.

Faith wanted to tell him he was wrong, but it was true. All she could think about was Felix in some foster home, crying his eyes out. She needed to concentrate on the victims, the fact that Jacquelyn Zabel and Anna were precursors to Pauline McGhee and Olivia Tanner. How long could the two women endure the torture, the degradation? Every minute that passed was another minute they would suffer.

Every minute that passed was another minute Felix was without his mother.

Will told her, "The way we help Felix is to help Pauline."

Faith breathed a heavy sigh. "It's really starting to annoy me that you know me so well."

"Please," he muttered. "You are an enigma wrapped in a sticky bun." He opened the car door and got out. She watched him walk toward the house with a determined stride.

Faith got out of the car and followed him, noting, "No garage, no BMW." After her awful phone call with Leo, she had followed up with the desk sergeant who took the initial report on Olivia Tanner's disappearance. The woman drove a blue BMW 325, hardly distinctive in this neighborhood. Tanner was single, worked as a vice president at a local bank, had no children, and her only living relative was her brother.

Will tried the front door. Locked. "What's keeping the brother?"

Faith checked her watch. "His plane landed an hour ago. If traffic's bad . . ." She let her voice trail off. Traffic was always bad in Atlanta, especially around the airport.

He leaned down, checking under the welcome mat for a key. When that didn't work, he ran his hand along the top of the doorsill and checked the flowerpots, coming up empty. "You think we should just go in?"

Faith suppressed a comment about his eagerness to commit breaking and entering. She had worked with him long enough to know that frustration could act like adrenaline to Will, while it acted like Valium to Faith. "Let's give him another few minutes."

"We should go ahead and call a locksmith in case the brother doesn't have a key."

"Let's just take this slow, all right?"

"You're talking to me the way you talk to witnesses."

"We don't even know if Olivia Tanner is one of our victims. She could end up being bottle blonde and vibrant with tons of friends and a dog."

"The bank said she hasn't missed a day of work since she started there."

"She could've fallen down the stairs. Decided to skip town. Run away with a stranger she met in a bar."

Will didn't answer. He cupped his hands and peered into the front windows, trying to see inside. The uniformed patrolman who had taken the missing persons report yesterday would have already done this, but Faith let him waste his time as they waited for Michael Tanner, Olivia's brother, to show up.

Despite his anger, Leo had done them a solid by handing over the call. Procedure would have dictated a detective be assigned to the case. Depending on what the detective had on his books, it might have taken as long as twenty-four hours for Michael Tanner to talk to someone who could do more than fill out a report. From there, it might've taken another day before the GBI was alerted to a match on their profile. Leo had bought them two precious days on a case that desperately needed help. And they had kicked him in the teeth in the way of thanks.

Faith felt her BlackBerry start to vibrate. She checked the mail, saying a silent thank-you to Caroline, Amanda's assistant. "I've got Jake Berman's arrest report from the Mall of Georgia incident."

"What's it say?"

Faith watched the flashing file transfer icon. "It'll take a few minutes to download."

He walked around the house, checking each window. Faith followed him, keeping her BlackBerry in front of her like a divining rod. Finally, the first page of the report loaded, and she read from the narrative title. " *'Pursuant to complaints made by patrons of the Mall of Georgia . . .'* " Faith scrolled down, looking for the relevant parts. " *'Suspect then made the typical hand gesture indicating he was interested in sexual intercourse. I responded by nodding my head twice, at which point he directed me back toward the stalls at the rear of the men's room.'* " She skimmed down some more. " *'Suspect's wife and two sons, approximately age one and three, were waiting outside.'* "

"Is the wife's name listed?"

"No."

Will walked up the steps of the deck that lined the back of Olivia Tanner's house. Atlanta was in the piedmont of the Appalachians, which meant it was riddled with hills and valleys. Olivia Tanner's bungalow was at the base of a steep slope, giving her backyard neighbors a clear view of her house.

"Maybe they saw something?" Will suggested.

Faith looked at the neighbor's house. It was huge, the sort of McMansion you usually only saw in the suburbs. The top two stories had large decks and the basement had a terraced seating area with a brick fireplace. All the shutters and blinds on the back of the house were closed except for a pair of curtains that were pulled back on one of the basement doors.

"Looks empty," she said.

"Probably a foreclosure." Will tried Olivia Tanner's back door. It was locked. "Olivia has been missing since at least yesterday. If she's one of our victims, that means she was either taken right before or right after Pauline."

He checked the windows. "Are we thinking Jake Berman might be Pauline McGhee's brother?"

"It's possible," Faith conceded. "Pauline warned Felix that her brother was dangerous. She didn't want him around her kid."

"She must have been scared of him for a reason. Maybe he's violent. Maybe the brother is the reason Pauline moved away and changed her name. She cut all ties at a very young age. She must have been terrified of him."

Faith listed it out. "Jake Berman was at the scene of the crime. He's disappeared. He wasn't very cooperative as a witness. He hasn't left a paper trail except for the one arrest for indecent exposure."

"If Berman is an alias Pauline's brother is using, then it's pretty established. He was arrested and went through the system with the name intact."

"If he changed it twenty years ago when Pauline ran away from home, that's a lifetime as far as public records are concerned. They were still playing catch-up, trying to enter info and old cases into computers. A lot of those files never made the transition, especially in small towns. Look at how hard it's been for Leo to track down Pauline's parents, and they filed a missing persons report."

"How old is Berman?"

Faith scrolled back to the front of the report. "Thirty-seven."

Will stopped. "Pauline is thirty-seven. Could they be twins?"

Faith rifled around in her purse and found the black-and-white copy of Pauline McGhee's driver's license. She tried to recall Jake Berman's face, but then remembered she was holding his file in her other hand. The BlackBerry was still loading. She held it up above her head, hoping the signal would get stronger.

"Let's go back to the front of the house," Will suggested. They went around the other side, Will checking the windows, making sure nothing looked suspicious. By the time they reached the front porch, the file had finally downloaded.

Jake Berman had a full beard in his arrest photo—the sort of unkempt kind that suburban dads sported when they were trying to look subversive. Faith showed Will the picture. "He was clean-shaven when I talked to him," she said.

"Felix said the man who took his mother had a mustache."

"He couldn't have grown one that quickly."

"We can get a sketch of what Jake would look like without facial hair, with a mustache, whatever."

"It's Amanda's call whether or not we put that out on the wire." Releasing a sketch could make Jake Berman panic and go even deeper into hiding. If he was their bad guy, it could also serve to tip him off. He might decide to kill any witnesses and leave the state—or worse, the country. Hartsfield International Airport offered over twenty-five hundred flights in and out of the city every day.

Will said, "He's got dark hair and dark eyes like Pauline."

"So do you."

Will shrugged, admitting, "He doesn't look like her twin. Maybe her brother."

Faith was being stupid again. She checked the birthdays. "Berman had a birthday after he was arrested. He was born eighteen months before Pauline. Irish twins."

"Was he wearing a suit when he was arrested?"

She scrolled through the file. "Jeans and a sweater. Same as when I talked to him at Grady."

"Does the report list his occupation?"

Faith checked. "Unemployed." She read the other details, shaking her head. "This is such a sloppy report. I can't believe a lieutenant passed this on."

"I've done those stings before. You get ten, maybe fifteen guys a day. Most of them plead it down or just pay the fine and hope it goes away. You're not going to be going to court, because the last thing they want to do is face their accuser."

"What's the 'typical hand gesture' they use to ask for sex?" Faith asked, curious.

Will did something absolutely obscene with his fingers, and she wished she hadn't asked.

He insisted, "There has to be a reason Jake Berman is hiding."

"What are our options? He's either a deadbeat, he's Pauline's brother or he's our bad guy. Or all three."

"Or none," Will pointed out. "Either way, we've got to talk to him."

"Amanda's got the whole team looking for him. They're doing all the derivations on his name they can think of—Jake Seward, Jack Seward. They're trying McGhee, Jackson, Jakeson. The computer will run the permutations."

"What's his middle name?"

"Henry. So, we've got Hank, Harry, Hoss . . ."

"How can he have an arrest record and we still can't find him?"

"He's not using credit cards. He doesn't have a cell phone bill or a mortgage. None of his last known addresses have given up anything useful. We don't know who his employer is or where he's worked in the past."

"Maybe it's all in his wife's name—the name we don't have."

"If my husband got caught getting his willy winked at the mall while I was standing outside with our kids . . ." Faith didn't bother to finish the sentence. "It would help if the lawyer who handled his public indecency case wasn't a total prick." The man was refusing to divulge any of his client's information and insisted he had no way to get in touch with Jake Berman. Amanda was filing warrants to look into the files, but warrants like that took time—something they were running out of.

A blue Ford Escape pulled up in front of the house. The man who got out of the car looked like the textbook example of anxiety, from his wrinkled brow to the way he was wringing his hands in front of his slightly paunched belly. He was average looking, balding, with stooped shoulders. Faith would have pegged his occupation as one that required him to sit in front of a computer for more than eight hours a day.

"Are you the police officers I spoke with?" the man asked brusquely. Then, perhaps realizing how abrupt he had been, he tried again. "I'm sorry, I'm Michael Tanner, Olivia's brother. Are you the police?"

"Yes, sir." Faith pulled out her ID. She introduced herself and Will. "Do you have a key to your sister's house?"

Michael seemed worried and embarrassed at the same time, as if this could all just be a misunderstanding. "I'm not sure we should be doing this. Olivia likes her personal space."

Faith caught Will's eye. Another woman who was good at putting up boundaries.

Will offered, "We can call a locksmith if we need to. It's important we see inside the house in case anything happened. Olivia might've fallen, or—"

"I've got a key." Michael fished into his pocket and pulled out a single key on a springy band. "She mailed it to me three months ago. I don't know why. She just wanted me to have it. I guess because she knew I wouldn't use it. Maybe I *shouldn't* use it."

Will said, "You wouldn't have flown all the way from Houston unless you thought that something was wrong."

Michael's face went white, and Faith caught a glimpse of what the last few hours of his life must have been like—driving to the airport, getting on the plane, renting a car, all the while thinking that he was being foolish, that his sister was fine. All the while knowing in the back of his brain that the exact opposite was probably true.

Michael handed Will the key. "The policeman I spoke with yesterday said he sent a patrolman to knock on the door." He paused, as if he needed them to confirm this had happened. "I was worried they weren't taking me seriously. I know Olivia is a grown woman, but she's a creature of habit. She doesn't depart from her routine."

Will unlocked the door and went inside the house. Faith kept the brother on the porch. She asked him, "What's her routine?"

He closed his eyes for a moment as if to collect his

thoughts. "She works at the private bank in Buckhead, has for almost twenty years. She goes in six days a week—every day but Monday, when she does her shopping and other chores: cleaners, library, grocery store. She's in the bank by eight, out by eight most nights unless there's some kind of event. Her job is community relations. If there's a party or a fundraiser or something the bank is sponsoring, she has to be there. Otherwise, she's always at home."

"Did the bank call you?"

He put his hand to his throat, rubbing a bright red scar. Faith guessed he'd had a tracheotomy or some type of throat surgery.

He said, "The bank didn't have my phone number. I called them when I didn't hear from Olivia yesterday morning. I called them when I landed. They have no idea where she is. She's never missed work before."

"Do you have a recent picture of your sister?"

"No." He seemed to realize why she wanted the photograph. "I'm sorry. Olivia hated to be photographed. Always."

"That's okay," Faith assured him. "We'll pull it from her driver's license if we need to."

Will came down the stairs. He shook his head, and Faith led the man into the house. She tried to make small talk, telling Michael, "This is a beautiful home."

"I've never seen it before," he confessed. He was looking around like Faith, probably thinking the same thing she was: The place was like a museum.

The front hall went all the way back to the kitchen, which gleamed with white marble countertops and white cabinets. The stairs were carpeted in a white runner, and the living room was equally Spartan; everything from the walls to the furniture to the rug on the floor was a pristine white. Even the art on the wall consisted of white canvases in white frames.

Michael shivered. "It's so cold in here."

Faith knew he didn't mean the temperature.

She led both men into the living room. There was a couch and two chairs, but she didn't know whether to sit or stand. Finally, she sat on the couch, the cushion so hard that she barely made a dent. Will took the chair beside her and Michael sat at the other end of the couch.

She said, "Let's take it from the beginning, Mr. Tanner."

"Doctor," he said, then frowned. "Sorry. It doesn't matter. Please call me Michael."

"All right, Michael." Faith kept her voice calm, soothing, sensing he was close to panic. She started with an easy question. "You're a doctor?"

"A radiologist."

"You work at a hospital?"

"The Methodist Breast Center." He blinked his eyes, and she realized he was trying not to cry.

Faith got to the point. "What made you call the police yesterday?"

"Olivia calls me every day now. She didn't do that before. We weren't close for many years, then she went off to college and we drifted even further apart." He gave them a weak smile. "I got cancer two years ago. Thyroid." He touched his hand to the scar on his neck again. "I just felt an emptiness?" He said this as a question, and Faith nodded as if she understood. "I wanted to be with my family. I wanted to have Olivia back in my life. I knew it would be on her terms, but I was willing to make that sacrifice."

"What terms did she impose?"

"I could never call her. She always was the one to call me."

Faith wasn't sure what to say to that. Will asked, "Was there a particular pattern to the calls?"

Michael started nodding his head, like he was glad someone finally understood why he was so worried. "Yes. She's called me every single day for the last eighteen months. Sometimes she doesn't say much, but she always calls at the same time every morning no matter what."

Will asked, "Why doesn't she say much?"

Michael looked down at his hands. "It's hard for her. She went through some things when we were growing up. She's not someone who thinks of the word 'family' and smiles." He rubbed his scar again, and Faith felt a profound sadness coming off him. "She doesn't smile much about anything, actually."

Will glanced at Faith to confirm it was okay for him to take over. She gave him a slight nod. Obviously, Michael Tanner was more comfortable talking to Will. Her job now was to just blend in with the background.

Will asked, "Your sister wasn't a happy person?"

Michael slowly shook his head, his sadness filling the room.

Will was silent for a moment, giving the man some space. "Who abused her?"

Faith was shocked by the question, but the tears that fell from Michael's eyes told her that Will was spot-on. "Our father. Quite the cliché these days."

"When?"

"Our mother died when Olivia was eight. I guess it started shortly after that. It went on for a few months, until Olivia ended up at the doctor. She was damaged. The doctor reported it, but my father just . . ." Tears came in earnest now. "My father said she had hurt herself on purpose. That she had put something down . . . there . . . to injure herself. To draw attention to herself because she missed our mother." He angrily wiped his tears away. "My father was a judge. He knew everyone on the police force, and they thought they knew him. He said that Olivia was lying, so everyone assumed she was a liar—especially me. For years, I just didn't believe her."

"What changed your mind?"

He gave a humorless laugh. "Logic. It didn't make sense that she would . . . that she would be the way she is unless something horrible had happened."

Will kept staring straight into the man's eyes. "Did your father ever hurt you?"

"No." He had answered too quickly. "Not anything sexual, I mean. He punished me sometimes. Took out the belt. He could be a brutal man, but I thought that's what fathers did. It was normal. The best way to avoid a beating was to be a good son, so I was a good son."

Again Will took his time getting to the next question. "How did Olivia punish herself for what happened?"

Michael struggled with his emotions, trying to contain them but failing miserably. He finally pressed his thumb and forefinger into his eyes, sobbing. Will just sat there, motionless. Faith followed his lead. She knew instinctively that the worst thing she could do right now was comfort Michael Tanner.

He used the backs of his hands to wipe his tears. At last, he said, "Olivia was bulimic. I think she might still be anorexic, but she swore to me the purging was under control."

Faith realized she had been holding her breath. Olivia Tanner had an eating disorder, just like Pauline McGhee and Jackie Zabel.

Will asked, "When did it start?"

"Ten, eleven. I don't remember. I'm three years younger. All I can recall is that it was horrible. She just . . . She just started to waste away."

Will only nodded, letting the man speak.

"Olivia was always obsessed with her looks. She was so pretty, but she never accepted . . ." Michael paused. "I guess Dad made it worse. He was always pinching her, teasing her, telling her she needed to get rid of her baby fat. She wasn't fat. She was a normal girl. She was beautiful. *Was* beautiful. Do you know what happens when you starve yourself like that?"

Michael was looking at Faith now, and she shook her head.

"She got pressure sores on her back. Big, gaping wounds where her bones rubbed holes in her skin. She couldn't ever sit down, couldn't get comfortable. She was cold all the time, couldn't feel her hands and feet. Some days she didn't even have the energy to walk to the bathroom. She would just defecate on herself." He stopped as the memories obviously flooded back. "She slept ten, twelve hours a day. She lost her hair. She would go into these uncontrollable shaking fits. Her heart would race. Her skin was just . . . it was disgusting. Flaky, dry scales would just fleck off her body. And she thought it was all worth it. She thought it made her beautiful."

"Was she ever hospitalized?"

He laughed, as if they couldn't begin to understand how horrible the situation had been. "She was in and out of Houston General all the time. They would put her on a feeding tube. She would gain enough weight so that they would let her leave the hospital, then she'd go back to purging herself again as soon as she got out. Her kidneys shut down twice. There was a lot of concern about the damage she was doing to her heart. I was so angry with her then. I didn't understand why she was doing something, willingly doing something so awful to herself. It just seemed . . . Why would you starve yourself? Why would you put yourself through . . ." He looked around the room, the cold place his sister had created for herself. "Control. She just wanted to control one thing, and I guess that one thing was what went into her mouth."

Faith asked, "Was she better? I mean, recently."

He nodded and shrugged at the same time. "She got better when she got away from my father. Went off to college, got a business degree. She moved here to Atlanta. I think the distance helped her."

"Was she in therapy?"

"No."

"How about a support group? Or maybe an online chat room?"

He shook his head, certain. "Olivia didn't think she needed help. She thought she had it all under control."

"Did she have any friends, or—"

"No. She had no one."

"Is your father still alive?"

"He died about ten years ago. It was very peaceful. Everyone was so pleased that he just passed in his sleep."

"Is Olivia a religious person? She doesn't go to church or—"

"She would burn down the Vatican if she could get past the guards."

Will asked, "Do the names Jacquelyn Zabel, Pauline McGhee or Anna mean anything to you?"

He shook his head.

"Have you or your sister ever been to Michigan?"

He gave them a puzzled look. "Never. I mean, I haven't. Olivia has lived in Atlanta all her adult life, but she might have taken a trip there I wasn't aware of."

Will tried, "How about the words, 'I will not deny myself.' Does that mean anything to you?"

"No. But it's the exact opposite of what Olivia does in her life. She denies herself everything."

"How about 'thinspo,' or 'thinspiration'?"

Again, he shook his head. "No."

Faith took over. "What about kids? Did Olivia have children? Or want children?"

"It would have been physically impossible," the man answered. "Her body . . . the damage she did to herself. There was no way she could carry a child."

"She could adopt."

"Olivia hated children." His voice was so low that Faith could barely hear him. "She knew what could happen to them."

Will asked the question that was on Faith's mind. "Do you think she was doing it again—starving herself?"

"No," Michael said. "Not like before, at least. That's why she called me every morning, six sharp, to let me know she was okay. Sometimes I'd pick up the phone and she'd talk to me; other times, she'd just say, 'I'm okay,' and hang up the phone. I think it was a lifeline for her. I hope it was."

Faith said, "But she didn't call you yesterday. Is it possible that she was mad at you?"

"No." He wiped his eyes again. "She never got mad at me. She worried about me. She worried about me all the time."

Will only nodded, so Faith asked, "Why did she worry?"

"Because she was . . ." Michael stopped, clearing his throat a couple of times.

Will said, "She was protecting him from their dad."

Michael kept nodding, and the room got quiet again. He seemed to be working up his courage. "Do you think—" He stopped himself. "Olivia would never change her routine."

Will stared him straight in the eye. "I can be kind or I can be honest, Dr. Tanner. There are only three possibilities here. One is that your sister wandered off. People do that. You wouldn't believe how often it happens. The other is, she's been in an accident or she's hurt—"

"I called the hospitals."

"The Atlanta police did, too. They checked all their reports and everyone's accounted for."

Michael nodded, probably because he already knew this. "What's the third possibility?" he asked softly.

"Someone has taken her," Will answered. "Someone who means to do her harm."

Michael's throat worked. He stared down at his hands for a good long while before finally nodding. "Thank you for your honesty, Detective."

Will stood up. He asked, "Do you mind if we look around the house, check through your sister's things?"

Again the man nodded, and Will told Faith, "I'll check upstairs. You take down here."

He didn't give her time to discuss the plan, and Faith decided not to argue with him, even though Olivia Tanner probably kept her home computer upstairs.

She left Michael Tanner in the living room and wandered into the kitchen. Light poured in from the windows, making everything seem even more white. The kitchen was beautiful, but just as sterile as the rest of the house. The countertops were completely bare except for the thinnest television Faith had ever seen. Even the cords for the cable and plug were hidden, snaking down a thin hole in the lightly veined marble.

The walk-in pantry had very little food. What was there was stacked neatly in line, boxes face-out to show the brands, cans all turned in the same direction. There were six economy-size bottles of aspirin still in their packaging. The brand was different from the one Faith had found in Jackie Zabel's bedroom, but she found it odd that both women took so much aspirin.

Yet another detail that did not make sense.

Faith made some phone calls as she searched the kitchen cabinets. As quietly as she could, she requested a background check on Michael Tanner, just to clear him from the picture. Her next call was a request to borrow some patrolmen from the Atlanta police to canvass the neighborhood. She'd put a phone dump on Olivia Tanner's home phone so they could see who she had been talking to, but the woman's cell phone was probably registered to the bank. If they were really lucky, there was a BlackBerry somewhere so they could read her email. Maybe Olivia had someone in her life that her brother didn't know about. Faith shook her head, knowing this was a long shot. The house was a show-place, but it didn't feel lived in. There were no parties here, no weekend get-togethers. Certainly, no man was living here.

What had Olivia Tanner's life been like? Faith had worked missing persons cases before. The key to finding out what happened to the women—they were all usu-ally women—was to try to put yourself in their shoes. What were their likes and dislikes? Who were their friends? What was so awful about their boyfriend/husband/lover that made them want to pick up and leave?

With Olivia, there were no clues, no emotional an-chors to pounce on. The woman lived in a lifeless house without a comfortable chair to sink into at the end of the day. All her plates and bowls were unscratched, unchipped and looked unused. Even the coffee cups were sparkling at the bottom. How could Faith relate to a woman who lived in a perfectly kept white box?

Faith returned to the kitchen cabinets, again finding nothing out of place. Even what she would've consid-ered the junk drawer was neat—screwdrivers in a plastic case, hammer resting on a ball of twine. Faith ran her finger along the inside seam of the cabinet, finding no grit or dirt. There was something to be said for a woman who dusted her kitchen cabinets inside and out.

Faith opened the bottom drawer and found an over-sized envelope like the kind used for mailing photo-graphs. She opened the top and found a stack of glossy pages that had been neatly cut from magazines. All of them showed models in various stages of undress, no matter whether they were selling perfume or gold watches. These weren't the usual women you found in sweater sets and pearls as they cheerily dusted their houses and cleaned up after adorable children. These models were meant to convey sex, wantonness and, above all, thinness.

Faith had seen some of these bone-thin models before. She skimmed the pages of *Cosmo* and *Vogue* and *Elle* just like every other person who ever waited in line at the grocery store, but seeing these anorexic women now, knowing that Olivia Tanner had chosen these pictures not because she wanted to remember to buy a new eye shadow or lip gloss, but because she considered the airbrushed skeletons an attainable goal, made Faith feel sick to her stomach.

She thought again about Michael Tanner's words, the torture his sister had put herself through in order to be thin. She couldn't figure out why Will was so certain the woman had been trying to protect her brother. It seemed unlikely that a man who raped his daughter would go after his son, but Faith had been a cop too long to believe criminals followed a logical pattern. Despite her own teenage pregnancy, the Mitchell family was fairly normal. There were no abusive alcoholics or sex-crazed uncles. In matters of severe childhood dysfunction, she always deferred to Will.

He had never outright confirmed anything, but she guessed that he had suffered a great deal of abuse as a child. His upper lip had obviously been busted open and not allowed to heal properly. The faint scar running down the side of his jaw and going into his collar looked old, the type of thing you got as a kid and lived with for the rest of your life. She had worked with Will during the hottest months of the summer and never seen him roll up his shirtsleeves or even loosen his tie. His question about how Olivia Tanner punished herself was especially revealing. Faith often thought that Angie Polaski was a punishment that Will continually brought down on himself.

She heard footsteps on the stairs. Will entered the kitchen, shaking his head. "I hit the redial on the upstairs phone. I got the brother's answering machine in Houston."

There was a book in his hand. "What's that?"

He handed her the slim novel, which had a library band on the spine. The jacket showed a naked woman sitting on her haunches. She was wearing high heels, but the pose was more artistic than kinky, sending the distinct message that this was literature, not trash. So, not the type of book Faith would ever read. She skimmed the back copy and told Will, "It's about a woman who's a diabetic meth addict and her abusive father."

"A love story." He guessed the title. *"Exposé?"*

He was close enough. Faith had figured out that he generally read the first three letters of a word and guessed the rest. More often than not, he was right, but odd words threw him off.

She put the book facedown on the counter. "Did you find a computer?"

"No computer. No diary. No calendar." He opened drawers, finding the television remote. He turned on the set, tilting the screen toward him. "This is the only TV in the house."

"There isn't one in the bedroom?"

"No." Will flipped through the channels, finding the usual digital offerings. "She doesn't have cable. There's not a DSL modem on the junction box in the basement."

"So, she doesn't have high-speed Internet," Faith surmised. "Maybe she uses dial-up. She could have a laptop at work."

"Or someone could've taken it."

"Or she just keeps her work at the office. Her brother says she's on the job from sunup till sundown."

He turned off the television. "Did you find anything down here?"

"Aspirin," Faith said, indicating the bottles in the pantry. "What did you mean about Olivia protecting Michael?"

"It's what we were talking about at Pauline's. Did your parents have much time for your brother when you got into trouble?"

Faith shook her head, realizing what he had said made perfect sense. Olivia had drawn all the negative attention away from her brother so that he could have some semblance of a life. No wonder the man was racked with guilt. He was a survivor.

Will was looking out the back window, up at the seemingly vacant house behind Olivia's. "Those curtains on the door are bothering me."

Faith joined him by the window. He was right. All the blinds were closed on the back windows except for the curtains that hung open on the basement doors.

Faith raised her voice. "Dr. Tanner, we're going to step outside a minute. We'll be right back."

"All right," the man returned.

His voice still sounded shaky, so Faith added, "We haven't found anything yet. We're still just looking."

She waited. There was no response.

Will held open the back door and they both walked onto the deck.

He said, "Her clothes are all size two. Is that normal?"

"I wish," Faith mumbled, then realized what she had said. "It's thin, but it's not horrible."

She scanned Olivia Tanner's backyard again. Like most in-town lots, it was barely more than a quarter of an acre, fences delineating the property lines and telephone poles springing up every two hundred feet. Faith followed Will down the deck stairs. Olivia's yard was cordoned off by an expensive-looking cedar fence. The boards were flat, the supports on the outside. She asked, "Does this look new to you?"

He shook his head. "It's been pressure-washed. Fresh cedar is more red than that."

They reached the back of the property and stopped. There were marks on the cedar planks. Deep scratches running up the center. Will leaned down, saying, "It looks like someone did this with their feet, probably trying to get over."

Faith glanced up at Olivia Tanner's backyard neighbor again. "It looks vacant to me. You think it's a foreclosure?"

"Only one way to find out." Will went to a different section of the fence and started to lift himself up and over before realizing that Faith was with him. "Do you want to wait for me here? Or we could walk around."

"Do I look that pathetic to you?" She grabbed the top of the fence. They had done this sort of thing at the police academy, but that was years ago, and she hadn't been in a skirt. Faith pretended not to notice when Will gave her an assist from behind, just as she hoped he would pretend not to notice that she was wearing her powder blue granny underwear.

Somehow, she managed to scramble to the other side. Will made sure she was clear, then bolted the fence like a ten-year-old Chinese gymnast.

"Show-off," she mumbled, making her way up the steep hill toward the empty house. The basement was a wall of windows onto the backyard with French doors at either end. As she got closer, she could see that one of the doors was open. The wind picked up, and a piece of white curtain flapped outside in the breeze.

"This can't be this easy," Will said, obviously thinking what Faith was thinking: *Was their suspect hiding inside? Was this where he was keeping his victims?*

Will walked toward the house with a determined gait.

She asked, "Should I call for backup?"

Will didn't seem concerned. He pushed open the door with his elbow and poked his head inside.

"Ever hear of probable cause?"

"Do you hear that noise?" he asked, even though they both knew that he hadn't heard a thing. Legally, they couldn't go into a private home without a search warrant or threat of imminent danger.

Faith turned around, looking back at Olivia Tanner's house. The woman obviously did not believe in window coverings. From Faith's vantage point, she could see clear through to the kitchen and what must have been Olivia's bedroom. "We should call for a warrant."

Will was already inside. Faith cursed him under her breath as she took her gun out of her purse. She went into the basement, stepping carefully onto the white Berber carpet. The basement was finished, probably a media room at one time. There was a pool table and a wet bar. Wires stuck out of the wall where a home theater system had been. Will was nowhere to be seen. "Idiot," she mumbled, taking another step inside, pressing back the door until it was flat against the wall. She listened, her ears straining so hard that she felt a phantom pain from the effort.

"Will?" she whispered. There was no answer, and Faith ventured farther, her heart pounding in her chest. She leaned over the wet bar, looking behind the counter and seeing an empty box and a soda can on its side. There was a closet behind her, the door partially open. Faith used the muzzle of her gun to open it wide.

"It's empty," Will said, rounding a corner and scaring the shit out of her.

"What the hell are you doing?" Faith snapped. "He could've been in here."

Will didn't seem fazed. "We need to find out who has access to this house. Realtors. Contractors. Anyone interested in buying the house." He took a pair of latex gloves out of his pocket and checked the lock on the French door. "There's tool marks here. Someone picked the lock." He walked over to the windows, which were covered in cheap plastic blinds. One of the blades was bent back. Will twisted open the plastic wand, letting natural light flood in. He squatted down and studied the floor.

Faith put her gun back into her purse. Her heart was still beating like a snare drum. "Will, you scared the crap out of me. Don't walk into a house like that without me with you."

"You can't have it both ways."

"What does that mean?" she demanded, though she figured it out before the question left her mouth. He was trying to be more aggressive to please her.

"Look." He motioned her over. "Footprints."

Faith could see a reddish outline of a pair of shoes on the flat surface of the carpet. One of the great things about living in Georgia was the red clay that stuck to every surface, whether it was wet or dry. She glanced out the window, past the broken blade on the blinds. Olivia's house was on full display.

Will said, "You were right. He's been watching them. He follows them, learns their routines, knows who they are." He walked behind the wet bar, opening and closing cabinet doors. "Someone used this Coke can as an ashtray."

"Movers, probably."

He opened the refrigerator. She heard glass rattling. "Doc Peterson's Root Beer." He had probably recognized the logo.

"We should get out of here before we contaminate the scene any more than we already have."

Thankfully, Will seemed to agree. He followed Faith outside, pulling the door back to where they'd found it.

She said, "This feels different."

"How so?"

"I don't know," she admitted. "We didn't find anything at Jackie's mother's house or Pauline's work. Leo searched her house. There was nothing there. Our guy doesn't leave clues, so why do we have a pair of shoe prints? Why was the door left open?"

"He lost his first two victims. Anna and Jackie escaped. Maybe Olivia Tanner was in the pipeline. Maybe he had to move her ahead to replace them."

"Who would know this house was vacant?"

"Anybody who was paying attention."

Faith looked back at Olivia's house and saw Michael

Tanner standing on the back porch. The thought of wrangling her ass over that fence again was not a welcome one.

Will said, "I'll go. You walk around."

She shook her head, walking back down the yard with a determined gait. The fence would be easier from this side, since the supports were facing out. There was a long two-by-four down the middle that served as a step, and Faith was able to lift herself over with less assistance than before. Will did another swoop, vaulting over with one hand.

Michael Tanner stood at the back door of his sister's house, hands clasped together as he watched them approach. "Is something wrong?"

"Nothing we can share with you right now," Faith told him. "I'm going to need you to—"

Her foot slipped out from under her as she stepped on the bottom stair. A comical noise close to a *woof* came out of her mouth, but there was nothing funny about the way Faith felt. Her vision went crazy for a few seconds, her head spinning. Without thinking, her hand went to her stomach and all she could think about was what was growing inside.

"You okay?" Will asked. He was kneeling beside her, his hand cupping the back of her head.

Michael Tanner was on her other side. "Just breathe very slowly until you catch your breath." His hands went down her spine, and she was about to slap him away before she remembered he was a doctor. "Slow breaths. In and out."

Faith tried to do as he said. She had been panting for no apparent reason.

Will asked, "Are you okay?"

She nodded, thinking maybe she was. "Just knocked the breath out of me," she managed. "Help me up."

Will's hands went under her arms, and she realized how strong he was as he easily lifted her to standing. "You've got to stop falling down like this."

"I'm such an idiot." She still had her hand on her stomach. Faith made herself move it away. She stood there, silent, listening for something inside her body, trying to feel a twinge or a spasm that might indicate something was wrong. She felt nothing, heard nothing. But was she okay?

"What's this?" Will asked, pulling something out of her hair. He held up a piece of confetti between his thumb and forefinger.

Faith ran her fingers through her hair, looked behind her. She saw tiny pieces of confetti in the grass.

"Dammit," Will cursed. "I saw one of these on Felix's book bag. It's not confetti. These are from a Taser."

CHAPTER FIFTEEN

S ARA HAD NO IDEA WHY SHE WAS AT GRADY ON HER day off. She'd only gotten through half her laundry, the kitchen was barely functional and the bathroom was in such a sorry state that she felt a rush of shame every time she thought about it.

Yet, here she was, back at the hospital, climbing the stairs up to the sixteenth floor so that no one would see her as she made her way to the ICU.

She felt responsible for not doing a more thorough examination on Anna when the woman was first brought into the emergency room. X-rays, MRIs, ultrasounds, body scans. Almost every surgeon in the hospital had laid hands on the woman and they had all missed the eleven trash bags. The CDC had even been called in to culture the infection and had come up empty-handed. Anna had been tortured, cut, torn—damaged in countless ways that would not heal because the plastic was inside of her. When Sara removed the bags, the stench had filled the room. The woman was starting to rot from the inside. It was a wonder she hadn't gone into toxic shock.

Logically, Sara knew this was not her fault, but in her gut, she felt that she had done something wrong. All morning as she folded clothes and scrubbed dishes, her mind wandered back to two nights ago when Anna was brought in. Sara saw herself fashioning an alternate reality where she was able to do more than hand the woman off to the next doctor. She had to remind herself that even unbending the woman to do X-rays had caused her excruciating pain. Sara's job had been to stabilize the woman for surgery, not do a full gynecological exam.

And yet she still felt guilty.

Sara stopped at the sixth-floor landing, slightly winded. She was probably the most fit she had ever been in her life, but the treadmill and elliptical machine at her gym were hardly good preparation for real life. Back in January, she had vowed that she would run outside at least once a week. The gym near her building, with its televisions and treadmills and temperature-controlled atmosphere, negated one of the key benefits of running: time alone with yourself. Of course, it was easy to say you wanted time alone with yourself and quite another thing to actually do it. January had passed into February, and now they were already in April, yet this morning was the first time Sara had taken an outside run since she'd made the promise.

She grabbed the railing and heaved herself up the next flight. By the tenth floor, her thighs were burning. By the sixteenth, she had to stop and bend over to catch her breath so the ICU nurses didn't think a madwoman was in their midst.

She tucked her hand in her pocket for some Chap-Stick, then stopped herself. A flash of panic filled her chest as she checked her other pockets. The letter was not there. She had been carrying it forever, a talisman that she touched every time she thought about Jeffrey. It always brought a reminder of the hateful woman who had written it, the person who had been responsible for his murder, and now it was gone.

Sara's mind raced as she tried to remember where she had left it. Had she washed it with the rest of the laundry? Her heart leapt into her throat at the thought. She scanned her memory, finally recalling that she'd put the letter down on the kitchen counter yesterday when she'd gotten home from Jacquelyn Zabel's autopsy.

Her mouth opened, a sharp huff of air coming out. The letter was at home. She'd moved it this morning to the mantel, which seemed an odd place to put it. Jeffrey's wedding ring was there, the urn with some of his ashes beside it. The two things should not be together. What had she been thinking?

The door opened and a nurse came out with a pack of cigarettes in her hand. Sara recognized Jill Marino, the ICU nurse who had been taking care of Anna the morning before.

Jill asked, "Isn't today your day off?"

Sara shrugged. "Can't get enough of this place. How is she?"

"Infection's responding to antibiotics. Good catch on that. If you hadn't taken out those bags, she'd be dead by now."

Sara nodded off the compliment, thinking if she'd seen them in the first place, Anna would have had much more of a fighting chance.

"They took out the breathing tube around five." Jill held open the door for Sara to pass through. "Brain scan results came back. Everything looked good except for the damage to the optic nerve. That's permanent. Ears are fine, so at least she can still hear. Everything else is fine. No reason she's not waking up." She seemed to realize the woman had plenty of reasons not to wake up, and added, "Well, you know what I mean."

"Are you off?"

Jill guiltily indicated the cigarettes. "Up to the roof to ruin the fresh air."

"Should I waste my breath and tell you those things will kill you?"

"Working here will kill me first," the nurse countered, and with that, she began a slow trudge up the stairs.

Two cops still guarded Anna's room. Not the same as the day before, but they still both tipped their hats to Sara. One even pulled back the curtain for her. She smiled her thanks as she went into the room. There was a beautiful arrangement of flowers on the table by the wall. Sara checked them and found no card.

She sat in the chair and wondered about the flowers. Probably someone had checked out of the hospital and given the flowers to the nurses to distribute as they saw fit. They looked fresh, though, as if they'd just been plucked this morning from someone's backyard garden. Maybe Faith had sent them. Sara quickly dismissed the thought. Faith Mitchell didn't strike her as particularly sentimental. Nor was she very smart — at least not about her health. Sara had called Delia Wallace's office that morning. Faith had yet to make an appointment. She would be running out of insulin soon. She'd either have to risk another fainting spell or come back to Sara.

She leaned her arms on Anna's bed, staring at the woman's face. Without the tube down her throat, it was easier to see what she had looked like before all of this had happened. The bruises on her face were starting to heal, which meant they looked worse than the day before. Her skin was a healthier shade now, but it was swollen from all the fluids they were giving her. The malnourishment was so pronounced that it would take several weeks before her bones receded under a healthy layer of flesh.

Sara took the woman's hand, feeling her skin. It was still dry. She found a bottle of lotion in a zippered bag by the flowers. It was the usual kit they gave out at the hospital, filled with the things some administrative committee thought patients might need—slip-proof socks, lip balm, and lotion that smelled faintly of antiseptic.

Sara squirted some into her palm and rubbed her hands together to warm the lotion before taking Anna's frail hand in her own. She could feel each bone of the finger, the knuckles like marbles. Anna's skin was so dry that the lotion disappeared almost as soon as Sara put it on, and she was squirting more into her palms when Anna stirred.

"Anna?" Sara touched the side of the woman's face with a firm, reassuring pressure.

Her head moved just slightly. People in comas did not just magically wake up. It was a process, usually a drawn-out one. One day, they might open their eyes. They might speak without making sense, picking up on some conversation started long ago.

"Anna?" Sara repeated, trying to keep her voice calm. "I need you to wake up now."

Her head moved again, a distinct tilt toward Sara.

Sara made her voice firm. "I know it's hard, sweetie, but I need you to wake up." Anna's eyes slit open, and Sara stood, putting herself directly in her line of vision even though she knew that the woman could not see her. "Wake up, Anna. You're safe now. No one is going to hurt you."

Her mouth moved, the lips so dry and chapped that the skin broke.

"I'm here," Sara said. "I can hear you, sweetie. Try to wake up for me."

Anna's breath quickened in fear. What had happened was starting to dawn on the woman—the agony she had endured, the fact that she could not see.

"You're in the hospital. I know you can't see, but you can hear me. You're safe. Two police officers are right outside your door. No one is going to hurt you."

Anna's hand trembled as it reached up, fingers brushing against Sara's arm. Sara grabbed her hand, held on to it as firmly as she could without causing more pain. "You're safe now," Sara promised her. "No one else is going to hurt you."

Suddenly, Anna's grip tightened, squeezing Sara's hand so tightly that it brought a sharp, shooting pain as the bones crunched together.

The woman was fully alert, wide-awake. "Where is my son?"

CHAPTER SIXTEEN

WHEN YOU PULLED THE TRIGGER ON A TASER, TWO hooked probes were propelled by an inert nitrogen gas, shooting them out at about 160 feet per second. In civilian units, fifteen feet of insulated, conductive wire facilitated fifty thousand volts being delivered to whomever the probes latched onto. The electrical pulses interrupted sensory and motor function as well as the central nervous system. Will had been shot with a Taser during a training session. He still could not remember the time frame immediately before or after the charge hit him, only that Amanda had been the one to pull the trigger and she had been sporting an incredibly pleased grin when he had finally been able to stand up.

Like bullets in a gun, the Taser devices required cartridges that were preloaded with the wires and probes. Because the Constitutional framers were unable to predict the existence of such a device, there was no inalienable right attached to owning a Taser. Some bright thinker had managed to insert one codicil into their manufacture: All Taser cartridges had to be loaded with AFIDS, or Anti-Felon Identification Dots, which scattered out by the hundreds each time a cartridge was fired. At first glance, these small dots looked like confetti. The design was on purpose; the tiny pieces were so vast in number that it was impossible for a perpetrator to pick them all up to cover his trail. The beauty was that, under magnification, the confetti revealed a serial number that identified which cartridge they came from. Because Taser International wanted to keep the legal community on their side, they had enacted their own tracing program. All you had to do was call them up with the serial number from one of the dots and they would give you the name and address of the person who had purchased the cartridge.

Faith was on hold for less than three minutes when the company came back with a name.

"Shit," she whispered, then, realizing she was still on the phone, she added, "No. Thank you. That's all I need." She closed her cell phone as she reached down to crank the key in the Mini's ignition. "The Taser cartridge was purchased by Pauline Seward. The address listed is the vacant house behind Olivia Tanner's place."

"How were the cartridges paid for?"

"With an American Express gift card. No name on the card. It's untraceable." She gave him a meaningful glance. "The cartridges were purchased two months ago, which means he's been watching Olivia Tanner for at least that long. And since he used Pauline's name, we have to assume that he was planning on taking her, too."

"The vacant house is owned by the bank—not the one where Olivia works." Will had called the number on the Realtor's sign in the front yard while Faith was dealing with Taser. "It's been empty almost a year. No one's looked at it in six months."

Faith turned, backing out of the driveway. Will raised his hand at Michael Tanner, who was sitting in his Ford Escape, hands gripping the wheel.

Will said, "I didn't recognize the Taser dots on Felix's book bag."

"Why would you? It was confetti on a kid's satchel. You need a magnifying glass to read the serial numbers." She added, "If you want to blame someone, blame the Atlanta police for not picking up on it at the scene. Their forensic guys were there. They must have vacuumed the carpets in the car. They just haven't processed it yet because a missing woman isn't a priority."

"The address for the cartridge would have led us to the house behind Olivia Tanner's."

"Olivia Tanner was already missing when you saw Felix's book bag." She repeated, "The Atlanta police processed the scene. They're the ones who screwed up." Faith's phone rang. She checked the caller ID and decided not to answer it. She laid it out for him. "Besides, knowing the Taser dots on Felix's bag are from the same lot as the dots we found in Olivia Tanner's backyard hasn't exactly given us a huge break. All it tells us is that our bad guy has been planning this for a while and that he's good at covering his tracks. We knew that when we got up this morning."

Will thought they knew a lot more than that. They had a link now that tied the women together. "We've got Pauline connected to the other victims—'I will not deny myself' ties her to Anna and Jackie, and the Taser dots tie her to Olivia." He thought about it for a few seconds, wondering what else he was missing.

Faith was on the same page. "Let's go through this from the beginning. What do we have?"

"Pauline and Olivia were both taken yesterday. Both women were shot with the same Taser cartridge."

"Pauline, Jackie and Olivia all had eating disorders. We're assuming Anna does, too, right?"

Will shrugged. It wasn't a big leap, but it was an unknown. "Yeah, let's assume."

"None of the women had friends who would miss them. Jackie had the neighbor, Candy, but Candy wasn't exactly a confidante. All three are attractive, thin, with dark hair, dark eyes. All three worked in well-paid jobs."

"All of them lived in Atlanta except for Jackie," Will said, throwing out a flag. "So, how did Jackie get targeted? She'd only been in Atlanta a week, tops, just to clean out her mother's house."

"She must have come up before then to help move her mother to the nursing home in Florida," Faith guessed. "And we're forgetting the chat room. They could've all met there."

"Olivia didn't have a computer at home."

"She could've had a laptop that was stolen."

Will scratched his arm, thinking about that first night in the cave, all the maddening non-clues they had followed up on since, all the brick walls they kept hitting. "This feels like it all starts with Pauline."

"She was the fourth victim." Faith considered the situation. "He could've been saving the best for last."

"Pauline wasn't taken from her home like we assume the other women were. She was taken in broad daylight. Her kid was in the car. She was missed at work because she had an important meeting. The other women weren't missed by anyone except for Olivia, and there was no way to know that Olivia made that phone call every day to her brother unless our bad guy tapped her phone, which he obviously didn't."

"What about Pauline's brother?" Faith asked. "I keep coming back to the fact that she was scared enough about him to mention him to her son. We can't find a record of him anywhere. He could have changed his name like Pauline did when she was seventeen."

Will listed all the men who had come up during the investigation. "Henry Coldfield is too old and has a heart problem. Rick Sigler has lived in Georgia all his life. Jake Berman—who knows?"

Faith tapped her fingers on the steering wheel, deep in thought. Finally she came up with, "Tom Coldfield."

"He's around your age. He would've been barely pubescent when Pauline ran away."

"You're right," she conceded. "Besides, the Air Force psych evaluation would have flagged him up big-time."

"Michael Tanner," Will suggested. "He's the right age."

"I've got a background check running on him. They would've called if something hit."

"Morgan Hollister."

"They're running him, too," Faith said. "He didn't seem really cut up about Pauline being gone."

"Felix said that the man who took his mother was dressed in a suit like Morgan from work."

"Surely, Felix would've recognized Morgan?"

"In a fake mustache?" Will shook his head. "I don't know. Let's keep Morgan on the list. We can talk to him at the end of the day if nothing else has come up."

"He's old enough to be her brother, but why would she work with him if he was?"

"People do stupid things when they're being abused," Will reminded her. "We need to check with Leo and see what he's come up with. He was working the Michigan police, trying to track down Pauline's parents. She ran away from home. Who did she run away from?"

"The brother," Faith said, bringing them back full circle. Her phone rang again. She let it go into voicemail before opening it and dialing in a number. "I'll see where Leo is. He's probably out in the field."

Will offered, "I'll call Amanda and tell her we need to formally take over the Pauline McGhee case." He opened his phone just as the stutter of a ring came out. Since the phone had been broken, it had been doing unusual things. Will pressed his ear to the device, saying, "Hello?"

"Hey." Her voice was cool, casual, like warm honey in his ear. His mind flashed on the image of the mole on her calf, the way he could feel it under his palm when he ran his hand up her leg. "You there?"

Will glanced at Faith, feeling a cold sweat break out over his body. "Yeah."

"Long time."

He glanced at Faith again. "Yeah," he repeated. About eight months had passed since he had come home from work to find Angie's toothbrush missing from the cup in the bathroom.

She asked, "What're you up to?"

Will swallowed, trying to generate some spit. "Working a case."

"That's good. I figured you were busy."

Faith had finished her call. She was looking at the road ahead, but if she had been a cat, her ear would've been cocked in his direction.

He told Angie, "I guess this is about your friend?"

"Lola's got some good intel."

"That's not really my side of the job," he told her. The GBI didn't start cases. They finished them.

"Some pimp's turned a penthouse into a drug pad. They've got all kinds of shit lying around like candy. Talk to Amanda about it. She'll look good on the six o'clock news standing in front of all that dope."

Will tried to concentrate on what she was saying. There was just the whir of the Mini's engine and Faith's ever-listening ear.

"You there, baby?"

He said, "Not interested."

"Just pass it on for me. It's the penthouse in an apartment building called Twenty-one Beeston Place. The name is the same as the address. Twenty-one Beeston."

"I can't help you with that."

"Repeat it back to me so I know you'll remember it."

Will's hands were sweating so much that he worried the phone might slip from his grasp. "Twenty-one Beeston Place."

"I'll owe you one."

He couldn't resist. "You owe me a million." But it was too late. She had already hung up the phone. Will kept it to his ear, then said, "All right. Bye," like he was having a normal conversation with a normal person. To make matters worse, the phone slipped as he tried to close it, the string finally ripping out from under the duct tape. Wires he had never seen before jutted out of the back of the phone.

He heard Faith's mouth open, the smacking of her lips. He told her, "Leave it be."

She closed her mouth, kept her hands tight on the wheel as she made a turn against the light. "I called central dispatch. Leo's on North Avenue. Double homicide."

The car sped up as Faith blew through a light. Will loosened his tie, thinking it was warm in the car. His arms were starting to itch again. He felt light-headed.

"I'll try to get Amanda to—"

"Angie was calling in a tip." The words flooded out before he could stop them. His mind raced to think of a way to get out of saying more, but his mouth hadn't gotten the memo to shut up. "Some Buckhead penthouse has been turned into a drug den."

"Oh" was all Faith offered.

"She's got this girl she used to know back when she worked vice. A prostitute. Lola. She wants out of jail. She's willing to flip on the dealers."

"Is it a good tip?"

Will could only shrug. "Probably."

"Are you going to help her?"

He shrugged again.

"Angie's an ex-cop. Doesn't she know somebody in narcotics?"

Will let her figure it out. Angie wasn't exactly good at leaving bridges unburned. She tended to light them with glee, then throw gasoline on the flames.

Faith obviously reached the same conclusion. She offered, "I can make some calls for you. No one will know you're involved."

He tried to swallow, but his mouth was still too dry. He hated that Angie had this effect on him. He hated it even more that Faith was getting a front-row seat to his misery. He asked, "What did Leo say?"

"He's not answering his phone, probably because he knows it's me calling." As if on cue, her phone rang again. Faith checked the ID and again didn't answer it. Will figured he didn't have a right to ask her what that was about, considering he'd put a moratorium on discussions of his own phone calls.

He cleared his throat a few times so he could speak without sounding like a pubescent boy. "A Taser gun means distance. He would've used a stun gun on them if he was able to get close enough."

Faith returned to their original conversation. "What else have we got?" she asked. "We're waiting for DNA results from Jacquelyn Zabel. We're waiting to hear back from the tech department on Zabel's laptop and the computer from Pauline's office. We're waiting to hear back on any forensic evidence from the vacant house behind Olivia's."

Will heard a distinct buzzing, and Faith pulled out her BlackBerry. She drove with one hand as she read the screen. "Phone dump on Olivia Tanner's line." She scrolled through. "One number every morning around seven o'clock to Houston, Texas."

"Seven our time is six Houston time," Will said. "That's the only number she called?"

Faith nodded. "Going back for months. She probably used her cell for most of her calls." She tucked the BlackBerry back in her pocket. "Amanda's working on a warrant for the bank. They were nice enough to cross-reference their accounts for our missing women's names—no matches—but they're not going to give us access to Olivia's computer, phone or email without a fight. Something about federal banking law. We have to get into that chat room."

"I have to think if she was using an online group, she'd have access at home."

"Her brother says she's at work all the time."

"Maybe they all met in person. Like AA or a knitting group."

"It's hardly something you can pin up on the community bulletin board. 'Like starving yourself to death? Come join us!' "

"How else would they all meet?"

"Jackie is a Realtor, Olivia is a banker who doesn't write mortgages, Pauline is an interior designer and Anna does whatever she does—probably something equally as lucrative." She gave a heavy sigh. "It has to be the chat room, Will. How else would they all know each other?"

"Why do they have to know each other?" he countered. "The only person they have to know is the abductor. Who would have contact with women working in all those different fields?"

"Janitor, cable guy, trash man, exterminator . . ."

"Amanda's had information processing going through all those things. If there was a connection, it would be evident by now."

"Forgive me for not holding out hope. They've had two days and they can't even find Jake Berman." She cut the wheel, turning onto North Avenue. Two Atlanta police cruisers blocked the scene. They could see Leo in the distance, his hands waving wildly as he screamed at some poor kid in uniform.

Faith's phone rang again. She dropped it into her pocket as she got out of the car. "I'm not on Leo's favorite list right now. Maybe you should do the talking."

Will agreed that was best, especially considering the fact that Leo already looked a couple of notches beyond furious. He was still yelling at the cop when they approached him. Every other word was "fuck" and his face was so red Will wondered if he might be having a heart attack.

Overhead, a police helicopter hovered, what the locals called a ghetto bird. The chopper was so close to the ground that Will could feel his eardrums pulsing. Leo waited for it to move on before demanding, "What the fuck are you doing here?"

Will said, "That missing persons case you gave us— Olivia Tanner. There were Taser dots at the scene that trace back to a cartridge purchased by Pauline Seward."

Leo muttered another "fuck."

"We also found some evidence at Pauline McGhee's office that connects her back to the cave."

Leo's curiosity got the better of him. "You think Pauline's your doer?"

Will hadn't even considered the thought. "No, we think she's been taken by the same man who took the other women. We need to know as much as we can—"

"Not much to tell," he interrupted. "I talked to Michigan this morning. I was sitting on it, since your partner's such a ray of fucking sunshine lately."

Faith opened her mouth but Will held out his hand to stop her. "What did you find out?"

Leo said, "I talked to an old-timer they got on the desk. Name's Dick Winters. Been on the job thirty years and they got him straddling the phones. You believe that shit?"

"Did he remember Pauline?"

"Yeah, he remembered her. She was a good-looking kid. Sounded like the old guy had a boner for her."

Will could not possibly care less right now about

some skuzzy old cop bird dogging a teenager. "What happened?"

"He picked her up a couple of times for shoplifting, drinking too much and gettin' loud about it. He never ran her in—just took her back home, told her to straighten up. She was underage, but when she hit seventeen, it was harder to sweep it under the rug. Some store owner got a bee up his ass and pressed charges for the shoplifting. The old cop visits the family to help them out, sees something ain't right. He tucks his dick back in his pants, realizes it's time for him to do his job. The girl's got problems at school, problems at home. She tells the cop that she's being abused."

"Was social services called in?"

"Yeah, but little Pauline disappeared before they could talk to her."

"Did the cop remember the names? The parents? Anything?"

Leo shook his head. "Nothing. Just Pauline Seward." He snapped his fingers. "He did say there was a brother kind of touched in the head, if you know what I mean. Just a strange little fucker."

"Strange how?"

"Weird. You know how it is. You get a vibe."

Will had to ask again, "But the cop doesn't remember his name?"

"All the records are sealed because she was a juvenile. Throw in family court, and that's another obstacle," Leo said. "You're gonna need a warrant in Michigan to get them open. This was twenty years ago. There was some kind of fire in records ten years back, the old guy says. Might not even be a file to look up."

"Exactly twenty years?" Faith asked.

Leo gave her a sideways look. "Twenty years come Easter."

Will wanted to get this straight. "Pauline McGhee, or Seward, went missing twenty years from this Sunday, Easter Sunday?"

"No," Leo said. "Easter was in March twenty years ago."

Faith asked, "Did you look it up?"

He shrugged. "It's always the Sunday following the first full moon that occurs after the spring equinox."

Will took a minute to realize he was speaking English. It was like a cat barking. "Are you sure?"

"Do you really think I'm that stupid?" he asked. "Shit, don't answer that. The old guy was sure of it. Pauline bunked on March twenty-sixth. Easter Sunday."

Will tried to do the math, but Faith beat him to it. "Two weeks ago. That could fit around the time Sara said Anna was probably abducted." Her phone rang again. "Jesus," she hissed, checking the caller ID. She flipped open the phone. "What do you want?"

Faith's expression changed from extreme annoyance to shock, then disbelief. "Oh, my God." Her hand went to her chest.

Will could only think of Jeremy, Faith's son.

"What's the address?" Her mouth dropped open in surprise. "Beeston Place."

Will said, "That's where Angie—"

"We'll be right there." Faith closed her phone. "That was Sara. Anna woke up. She's talking."

"What did she say about Beeston Place?"

"That's where she lives—they live. Anna has a six-month-old baby, Will. The last time she saw him was at her penthouse at Twenty-one Beeston Place."

WILL HAD JUMPED behind the wheel, slamming back the seat, taking off before Faith had even shut her door. He'd raked the gears, pushing the Mini into every turn, bouncing across metal plates covering road construction. On Piedmont, he'd bumped across the median, using the oncoming lane to swerve around traffic at the light. Faith had sat quietly beside him, holding on to the handle over the door, but he could see her teeth gritted with each bump and turn.

Faith said, "Tell me again what she said."

Will didn't want to think about Angie right now, didn't want to consider that she might know there was a kid involved, a baby whose mother had been stolen, a child who had been left alone in a penthouse apartment that had been turned into a crack den.

"Drugs," he told Faith. "That's all she said—they were using it as a drug pad."

She was silent as he downshifted, making a wide turn onto Peachtree Street. Traffic was light for this time of day, which meant that there was a line of cars backed up a quarter of a mile. Will used the oncoming lane again, finally jumping onto the narrow shoulder to avoid a dump truck. Faith's hands slammed palm-down on the dashboard as he banked into a turn, sliding to a stop in front of Beeston Place Apartments.

The car rocked as Will got out. He ran to the entrance. He could hear the sirens of distant cruisers, an ambulance. The doorman was behind a tall counter reading a newspaper. He was plump, his uniform too small for his large gut.

Will pulled out his ID and flashed it in the man's face. "I need to get into the penthouse."

The doorman gave one of the surliest smiles in Will's recent memory. "You do, do you?" He spoke with an accent, Russian or Ukrainian.

Faith joined them, out of breath. She squinted at his nametag. "Mr. Simkov, this is important. We think a child might be in jeopardy."

He gave a helpless shrug. "No one gets in unless they're on the list, and since you're not on the—"

Will felt something inside of him break. Before he knew what was happening, his hand shot out, grabbing Simkov by the back of his neck and slamming his head into the marble countertop.

"Will!" Faith gasped, her voice going up in surprise.

"Give me the key," Will demanded, pressing harder against the man's skull.

"Pocket," Simkov managed, his mouth pressed so hard against the counter that his teeth scraped the surface.

Will jerked him closer, checked his front pockets and found a ring of keys. He tossed them to Faith, then walked into the open elevator car, fists clenched at his sides.

Faith pressed the button for the penthouse. "Christ," she whispered. "You've proven your point, all right? You can be a tough guy. Now back off it."

"He watches the door." Will was so furious he could barely form the words. "He knows everything going on in this building. He's got the keys to every apartment, including Anna's."

She seemed to get that he wasn't putting on a show. "All right. You're right. Let's just take things down a notch, okay? We don't know what we're going to find up there."

Will could feel the tendons in his arms vibrating. The elevator doors opened onto the penthouse floor. He stalked into the hall and waited for Faith to find the correctly labeled key to open the door. She found it, and he put his hand over hers, taking over.

Will didn't go gently. He took out his gun and slammed the door open.

"Ugh," Faith gagged, holding her hand to her nose.

Will smelled it, too—that sickly sweet mixture of burning plastic and cotton candy.

"Crack," she said, waving her hand in front of her face.

"Look." He pointed to the foyer just inside the door. Curled pieces of confetti had dried in a yellow liquid on the floor. Taser dots.

There was a long hallway in front of him, two doors on one side, both closed. Ahead, he could see the living room. Couches were overturned, their stuffing torn out. Trash was everywhere. A large man lay facedown in the hall, his arms splayed, head turned to the wall. His shirtsleeve was rolled up. A tourniquet was tied around his biceps. A syringe was jutting out of his arm.

Will pointed his Glock in front of him as he went down the hall. Faith took out her own weapon, but he signaled for her to wait. Will could already smell the body decaying, but he checked for a pulse just in case. There was a gun by the man's foot, a Smith & Wesson revolver with a custom gold grip that made it look like the kind of thing you used to find in the toy section of a dime store. Will kicked the gun away, even though the man was never going to reach for it.

Will motioned in Faith, then went back to the first closed door in the hallway. He waited until she was ready, then threw open the door. It was a closet, all the coats piled onto the floor in a heap. Will kicked the pile with his foot, checking under the coats before going to the next closed door. He waited for Faith again, then kicked open the door.

They both gagged at the stench. The toilet was overflowing. Feces were smeared on the dark onyx walls. A dark brown liquid had puddled in the sink. Will felt his skin crawl. The smell of the room reminded him of the cave where Anna and Jackie had been kept.

He pulled the door closed and indicated that Faith should follow him down the hall toward the main room. They had to step over broken glass, needles, condoms. A white T-shirt was wadded into a ball, blood smeared on the outside. A sneaker was upended beside it, the laces still tied.

The kitchen was off the living room. Will checked behind the island, making sure no one was there, while Faith picked her way around upended furniture and more broken glass.

She said, "Clear."

"Me too." Will opened the cabinet under the sink, looking for the trashcan. The bag was white, just like the ones they had found inside the women. The can was empty, the only clean thing in the whole apartment.

"Coke," Faith guessed, indicating a couple of white bricks on the coffee table. Pipes were scattered around. Needles, rolled-up bills, razor blades. "What a mess. I can't believe people were living in this."

Will was never surprised by the depths to which a junkie would stoop, or by the destruction that followed them. He had seen nice suburban houses turned into dilapidated meth dens over the course of a few days. "Where'd everybody go?"

She shrugged. "A dead body wouldn't scare them enough to leave this much coke behind." She glanced back at the dead man. "Maybe he's supposed to be security."

They searched the rest of the place together. Three bedrooms, one of them a nursery decorated in shades of blue, and two more bathrooms. All of the toilets and sinks were backed up. The sheets were balled up on the beds, the mattresses were overturned. Clothes were ripped out of the closets. All the televisions were gone. There was a keyboard and mouse on the desk in one of the spare rooms, but no computer. Obviously, whoever had taken over the place had stripped it bare.

Will holstered his gun as he stood at the end of the hallway. Two paramedics and a uniformed patrolman were waiting at the front door. He motioned them in.

"Dead as a doornail," one of the paramedics pronounced, doing only a cursory check for vitals on the junkie by the coat closet.

The cop said, "My partner's talking to the doorman." He used a measured tone, directing his words toward Will. "Looks like he fell. Hit his eye."

Faith shoved her gun into its holster. "Those floors are pretty slippery downstairs."

The cop nodded his complicity. "Looked slippery."

Will returned to the nursery. He rifled through the baby clothes on tiny hangers in the closet. He went back to the crib and lifted the mattress.

"Be careful," Faith warned. "There could be needles."

"He doesn't take the kids," he said, more to himself than Faith. "He takes the women, but he leaves the kids."

"Pauline wasn't abducted from her house."

"Pauline is different." He reminded her, "Olivia was taken in her backyard. Anna was taken at her front door. You saw the Taser dots. I bet Jackie Zabel was taken at her mother's house."

"Maybe a friend has Anna's baby."

Will stopped searching, surprised by the desperation in Faith's tone. "Anna doesn't have friends. None of these women have friends. That's why he takes them."

"It's been at least a week, Will." Faith's voice shook. "Look around you. This place is a mess."

"You want to turn the apartment over to crime scene?" he asked, leaving the rest of the question unspoken: *You want someone else to find the body?*

Faith tried another tack. "Sara said that Anna told her that her last name is Lindsey. She's a corporate lawyer. We can call her office and see—"

Gently, Will lifted the plastic liner of the diaper pail beside the changing table. The diapers were old, certainly not the source of the more pungent smells in the apartment.

"Will—"

He went to the attached bathroom and checked the trash there. "I want to talk to the doorman."

"Why don't you let—"

Will left the room before she had finished. He walked into the living room again, checking under the couches, pulling the stuffing out of some of the chairs to see if anything—anyone—was hidden inside.

The cop was testing the coke, pleased with what he found. "This is a righteous bust. I need to call this in."

"Give me a minute," Will told him.

One of the paramedics asked, "You want us to stick around?"

Faith said "No" just as Will said "Yes."

He made himself clear. "Don't go anywhere."

Faith asked the man, "Do you know an EMT named Rick Sigler?"

"Rick? Yeah," the guy said, like he was surprised she'd asked.

Will blocked out their conversation. He went back to the front powder room, breathing through his mouth so the shit and piss wouldn't make him throw up. He closed the door, then went back to the front entrance, the confetti dots. He stooped down to study them. He was pretty sure they were in dried urine.

Will stood, going out into the hall and looking back in at the apartment. Anna's penthouse took up the entire top floor of the building. There were no other units, no neighbors. No one who could hear her scream or see her attacker.

The killer would've stood outside her door where Will stood now. He glanced down the hall, thinking the man might've come up the stairs—or maybe down. There was a fire exit. He could've been on the roof. Or maybe the worthless doorman would've let him in through the front entrance, even pressed the button for him on the elevator. There was a peephole in Anna's penthouse door. She would've checked it first. All of these women were cautious. Who would she let in? A delivery person. Maintenance. Maybe the doorman.

Faith was coming toward him. Her face was unreadable, but he knew her well enough to know what she was thinking: *It's time to go.*

Will looked down the hall again. There was another door halfway down on the wall opposite the apartment.

Faith said, "Will—" but he was already heading for the closed door. He opened it. There was a small metal door inside for the trash chute. Boxes were piled in a stack, recyclables. There was a basket for glass, one for cans. A baby rested in the bin for plastics. His eyes were closed to a slit, his lips slightly parted. His skin was white, waxy.

Faith came up behind Will. She grabbed his arm. Will could not move. The world had stopped spinning. He held on to the doorknob so his knees would not give out on him. A noise came from Faith's mouth that sounded like a low keening.

The baby turned his head toward the sound, his eyes slowly opening.

"Oh, my God," Faith breathed. She pushed Will out of the way, dropping to her knees as she reached for the child. "Get help! Will, get help!"

Will felt the world return to normal. "Out here!" he called to the paramedics. "Bring your kit!"

Faith held the baby close as she checked for cuts and bruises. "Little lamb," she whispered. "You're okay. I've got you now. You're okay."

Will watched her with the child, the way she smoothed back his hair and pressed her lips to his forehead. The baby's eyes were barely open, his lips white. Will wanted to say something, but his words kept getting caught in his throat. He felt hot and cold at the same time, like he might start sobbing right there in front of the world.

"I've got you, sweetheart," Faith murmured, her voice choked with anguish. Tears streamed down her face. Will had never seen her being a mother, at least not with an infant. It broke his heart to see this gentle side of Faith, the part of her that cared so deeply about another human being that her hands shook as she held the child close to her chest.

She whispered, "He's not crying. Why is he not crying?"

Will finally managed to speak. "He knows no one will come." He leaned down, cupping his hand around the boy's head as it rested on Faith's shoulder, trying not to think about the hours the child had spent alone up here, crying himself out, waiting for someone to come.

The paramedic gasped in surprise. He called to his partner as he took the baby from Faith. The diaper was full. The boy's belly was distended; his head lolled to the side.

"He's dehydrated." The medic checked his pupils for a reaction, lifting his chapped lips to check his gums. "Malnourished."

Will asked, "Is he going to be okay?"

The man shook his head. "I don't know. He's bad off."

"How long—" Faith's voice caught. "How long has he been in here?"

"I don't know," the man repeated. "A day. Maybe two."

"Two days?" Will asked, sure he was wrong. "The mom's been gone at least a week, maybe more."

"More than a week and he'd be dead." Gently, the medic turned the child over. "He's got sores from lying in one place for too long." He cursed under his breath. "I don't know how long it takes for this to happen, but someone's been giving him water, at least. You can't survive without it."

Faith said, "Maybe the prostitute . . ."

She didn't finish, but Will knew what she was saying. Lola had probably been keeping an eye on Anna's baby after Anna had been abducted. Then she'd gotten locked up and the kid was left alone. "If Lola was taking care of him," Will said, "she would need to get in and out of the building."

The elevator doors slid open. Will saw a second cop standing with Simkov, the doorman. There was a darkening bruise underneath his eye and his eyebrow was split where it had been slammed against the hard marble counter.

"That one." The doorman pointed triumphantly at Will. "He's the one who jumped me."

Will's fists tightened. His jaw was so clenched he thought his teeth might break. "Did you know this baby was up here?"

The doorman's sneer was back. "What do I know about a baby? Maybe the night guy was—" He stopped, looking into the open door of the penthouse. "Jesus, Mary and Joseph," he mumbled, then said something in his foreign tongue. "What did they do up here?"

"Who?" Will asked. "Who was up here?"

"Is that man dead?" Simkov asked, still staring into the trashed penthouse. "Holy Christ, look at this place. The smell!" He tried to go into the apartment, but the cop jerked him back.

Will gave the doorman another chance, carefully enunciating each word of his question. "Did you know this baby was up here?"

Simkov shrugged, his shoulders going up high to his ears. "What the fuck do I know what goes on up here with the rich people? I make eight dollars an hour and you want me to keep up with their lives?"

"There's a baby," Will said, so furious that he could barely speak. "A little baby who was dying."

"So there's a baby. What the fuck do I care?"

Rage came in a black, blinding intensity, so that it wasn't until Will was on top of the man, his fist slamming back and forth like a jackhammer, that Will realized what he was doing. And he didn't stop himself. He didn't want to stop. He was thinking about that baby lying in his own shit, the killer shoving him into the trash room so he'd starve to death, the prostitute wanting to trade information about him to get her own ass out of the sling and Angie . . . there was Angie on top of this steaming pile of excrement, pulling Will's strings like she always did, fucking with his head so that he felt like he belonged in the trash heap with all the rest of them.

"Will!" Faith screamed. She was reaching her hands out in front of her the way you do when you're talking to a crazy person. Will felt a deep pain in his shoulders as both cops pinned his arms behind his back. He was panting like a rabid dog. Sweat dripped down his face.

"All right," Faith said, her hands still out as she came closer. "Let's calm down. Just calm down." She put her hands on Will, something he realized she had never done before. Her palms were on his face, forcing him to look at her instead of Simkov, who was writhing on the floor. "Look at me," she ordered, her voice low, like her words were something only they could hear. "Will, look at me."

He forced himself to meet her gaze. Her eyes were intensely blue, wide open in panic. "It's all right," Faith told him. "The baby's gonna be all right. Okay? All right?"

Will nodded, feeling the cops loosen their grip on his arms. Faith was still standing in front of him, still had her hands on his face.

"You're all right," she told him, talking to him in the same tone she had used with the baby. "You're going to be fine."

Will took a step back so that Faith would have to let him go. He could tell she was almost as terrified as the doorman. Will was scared, too—scared that he still wanted to beat the man, that if the cops hadn't been there, if it had just been him and Simkov alone, Will would have beaten him to death with his bare hands.

Faith kept her gaze locked with Will's just a moment longer. Then she turned her attention to the bloodied pulp on the floor. "Get up, asshole."

Simkov groaned, curling into a ball. "I can't move."

"Shut up." She jerked Simkov's arm.

"My nose!" he yelled, so dizzy that the only thing that kept him up was his shoulder slamming into the wall. "He broke my nose!"

"You're fine." Faith glanced up and down the hall. She was looking for security cameras.

Will did the same, relieved to find none.

"Police brutality!" the man screamed. "You saw it. You're all my witnesses."

One of the cops behind Will said, "You fell, buddy. Don't you remember?"

"I didn't fall," the man insisted. Blood was pooling out of his nose, squeezing through his fingers like water from a sponge.

The other paramedic was starting an IV on the baby. He didn't look up, but said, "Better be careful where you walk next time."

And just like that, Will was the kind of cop he had never wanted to be.

CHAPTER SEVENTEEN

FAITH'S HANDS WERE STILL SHAKING AS SHE STOOD IN front of Anna Lindsey's ICU room. The two cops who had been on guard outside the woman's door were chatting with the nurses behind the desk, but they kept glancing up, as if they knew what had happened outside Anna Lindsey's penthouse apartment and weren't quite sure what to think about it. For his part, Will stood across from her, hands in his pockets, eyes staring blankly down the hallway. She wondered if he was in shock. Hell, she wondered if *she* was in shock.

In both her personal and her private life, Faith had been the focus of a lot of angry men, but she had never witnessed anything like the violence Will had shown. There had been a moment in that hallway outside the Beeston Place penthouse when Faith had been afraid that Will would kill the doorman. It was his face that had shocked her—cold, merciless, driven toward nothing but keeping his fist slamming into the other man's face. Like everyone else's mother in the world, Faith's had always told her to be careful what she wished for. Faith had wished that Will would be a little more aggressive. Now she would give anything to have him back the way he was before.

"They won't say anything," Faith told him. "The cops, the paramedics."

"It doesn't matter."

"You found that baby," she reminded him. "Who knows how long it would've taken before somebody—"

"Stop."

There was a loud *ding* as the elevator doors opened. Amanda hit the ground at a trot. She scanned the hall, taking in who was around, probably trying to neutralize witnesses. Faith braced herself for crushing recriminations, lightning-fast suspensions, maybe the loss of their badges. Instead, Amanda asked them, "Are you both all right?"

Faith nodded. Will just stared at the floor.

"Glad to see you finally grow a pair," Amanda told Will. "You're suspended without pay for the rest of the week, but don't think for a goddamn minute that means you're going to stop working your ass off for me."

Will's voice sounded thick in his throat. "Yes, ma'am."

Amanda strode toward the stairwell. They followed, and Faith noticed her boss had none of her usual grace, none of her control. She seemed just as shocked as they were.

"Shut the door."

Faith saw that her hands were still shaking as she pulled it closed.

"Charlie's processing Anna Lindsey's apartment," Amanda told them, her voice echoing up the stairs. She adjusted her tone. "He'll call if he finds anything. Obviously, the doorman is off-limits to you." She meant Will. "Forensics should be back tomorrow morning, but don't get your hopes up, considering the state of the apartment. Tech hasn't been able to break into the computers the women were using. They're running all the password programs they have. It could take weeks or months to crack it. The anorexia website is hosted through a shell company in Friesland, wherever the hell that is. It's overseas. They won't give us registration information, but tech was able to pull up the stats for the site on the web. They get around two hundred unique users a month. That's all we know."

Will didn't speak, so Faith asked, "What about the vacant house behind Olivia Tanner's?"

"The shoe prints are for a men's size eleven Nike sold in twelve hundred outlets across the country. We found some cigarette butts in the Coke can behind the bar. We'll try to pull DNA, but there's no telling who they belong to."

Faith asked, "What about Jake Berman?"

"What the hell do you think?" Amanda took a breath as if to calm herself. "We've released a sketch and his booking photo through the state network. I'm sure the press will pick up on it, but we've asked them to hold off at least twenty-four hours."

Faith's mind was jumbled with questions, but nothing would come out. She had been standing in Olivia Tanner's kitchen less than an hour ago and she could not for the life of her remember one detail about the house.

Will finally spoke. His voice sounded as defeated as he looked. "You should fire me."

"You're not getting off that easy."

"I'm not kidding, Amanda. You should fire me."

"I'm not kidding either, you ignorant jackass." Amanda tucked her hands into her hips, looking more like the usual, annoyed Amanda that Faith was familiar with. "Anna Lindsey's baby is safe because of you. I think that's a win for the team."

He scratched at his arm. Faith could see that the skin on his knuckles was broken and bleeding. She was reminded of that moment in the hallway when she had her hands on his face, the way she had willed him to be okay because Faith didn't know how she could handle being in the world if Will Trent stopped being the man she had shared her life with almost every day for the past year.

Amanda caught Faith's eye. "Give us a minute."

Faith pushed the door open and walked back into the hall. There was a low hum of activity in the ICU, but nothing like downstairs in the emergency room. The cops were back at their station in front of Anna's door, and their eyes followed Faith as she passed.

One of the nurses told her, "They're in exam three."

Faith didn't know why she was being given this information, but she went to exam three anyway. She found Sara Linton inside. The doctor was standing by a plastic bassinet. She was holding the baby in her arms—Anna's baby.

"He's bouncing back," Sara told Faith. "It'll take a couple of days, but he'll be fine. Mostly, I think being back with his mom again will help them both."

Faith couldn't be a human being right now, so she made herself be a cop. "Did Anna say anything else?"

"Not much. She's in a lot of pain. They upped the morphine now that she's awake."

Faith ran her hand down the baby's back, feeling the soft give of his skin, the tiny bones of his spine. "How long do you think he was left alone?"

"The EMT was right. I'd say two days, tops. Otherwise, we'd be in a very different situation." Sara moved the baby to her other shoulder. "Someone was giving him water. He's dehydrated, but not as bad as some I've seen."

"What are you doing here?" Faith asked. The question came out without any forethought. She heard it sound in her ears, and thought it was a good one—good enough to repeat. "Why are you here? Why were you with Anna in the first place?"

Sara gently returned the baby to the bassinet. "She's my patient. I was checking on her." She tucked a blanket around the infant. "Just like I checked on you this morning. Delia Wallace's office said you haven't called."

"I've been a little busy rescuing babies off of trash piles."

"Faith, I'm not the enemy here." Sara's tone took on the annoying tenor of someone trying to be reasonable. "This isn't just about you anymore. You have a child inside of you—another life you're responsible for."

"That's *my* decision."

"Your decision clock is running out. Don't let your body make it for you, because if it's between the diabetes and the baby, the diabetes will always win out."

Faith took a deep breath, but that didn't do anything to help matters. She let loose. "You know, you may be trying to force yourself onto my case, but I'll be damned if I'll let you force yourself into my private life."

"Excuse me?" Sara had the gall to sound surprised.

"You're not a coroner anymore, Sara. You're not married to a police chief. He's dead. You saw him blown to pieces with your own two eyes. You're not going to get him back by hanging out at the morgue and shoving your way onto an investigation."

Sara stood there with her mouth open, seemingly incapable of responding.

Shockingly, Faith burst into tears. "Oh, my God, I'm so sorry! That was so awful." She put her hand to her mouth. "I can't believe I said—"

Sara shook her head, looking down at the floor.

"I'm so sorry. God, I'm sorry. Please forgive me."

Sara took her time speaking. "I guess Amanda caught you up on the details."

"I looked it up on the computer. I didn't—"

"Agent Trent read it, too?"

"No." Faith made her voice firm. "No. He said it was none of his business, and he's right. It's none of my business, either. I shouldn't have looked. I'm sorry. I am just an awful, awful person, Sara. I can't believe I said that to you."

Sara bent down to the baby, put her hand to his face. "It's okay."

Faith floundered for something to say, rattling off all the horrible things she could think about herself. "Look, I lied to you about my weight. I've gained fifteen pounds, not ten. I eat Pop-Tarts for breakfast, sometimes for dinner but usually with a Diet Coke. I never exercise. Ever. The only time I run is when I'm trying to make it to the bathroom before the commercial's over, and honest to God, since I got TiVo, I don't even do that anymore."

Sara was still silent.

"I'm so sorry."

She kept fiddling with the blanket, tucking it in tighter, making sure the baby was in a tight little cocoon.

"I'm sorry," Faith repeated, feeling so awful she thought she might throw up.

Sara kept her thoughts to herself. Faith was trying to

figure out how to gracefully leave the room when the doctor said, "I knew it was fifteen pounds."

Faith felt some of the tension start to dissipate. She knew better than to ruin it by opening her mouth.

Sara said, "No one ever talks to me about him. I mean, in the beginning, of course, but now no one even says his name. It's like they don't want to upset me, like saying his name might send me back to . . ." She shook her head. "Jeffrey. I can't remember the last time I said that out loud. His name is—was—Jeffrey."

"It's a nice name."

Sara nodded. Her throat worked as she swallowed.

"I saw pictures," Faith admitted. "He was good-looking."

A smile curved Sara's lips. "He was."

"And a good cop. You could tell by the way they wrote the reports."

"He was a good man."

Faith floundered, trying to think of something else to say.

Sara beat her to it, asking, "What about you?"

"Me?"

"The father."

In her mortification, Faith had forgotten about Victor. She put her hand to her stomach. "You mean my baby's daddy?"

Sara allowed a smile.

"He was looking for a mother, not a girlfriend."

"Well, that was never Jeffrey's problem. He was very good at taking care of himself." Her eyes took on a far-away look. "He was the best thing that ever happened to me."

"Sara—"

She went through the desk drawers and found a glucose monitor. "Let's test your blood sugar."

This time, Faith was too contrite to protest. She held out her hand, waited for the lancet to pierce her skin.

Sara talked as she went through the procedure. "I'm not trying to get back my husband. Believe me, if it was as simple as walking onto a case, I would sign up at the police academy tomorrow."

Faith winced as the needle pierced her skin.

"I want to feel useful again," Sara said, her voice taking on a confessional tone. "I want to feel like I'm doing more to help people than prescribing ointments for rashes that would probably go away on their own and patching up thugs so they can go back on the street and shoot each other again."

Faith hadn't considered that Sara's motivations might be so altruistic. She supposed it reflected badly on herself that she always assumed everyone approached life with selfish intentions. She told Sara, "Your husband sounded . . . perfect."

Sara laughed as she filled the test strip. "He left his jockstrap hanging on the bathroom doorknob, he slept around the first time we were married—which I found out for myself when I came home from work early one day—and he had an illegitimate son he never knew about until he was forty." She read the machine, then showed it to Faith. "What do you think? Juice or insulin?"

"Insulin." She confessed, "I ran out at lunch."

"I gathered." Sara picked up the phone and called one of the nurses. "You need to get this under control."

"This case is—"

"This case is ongoing, just like all the other cases

you've worked and all the ones you'll work in the future. I'm sure Agent Trent can spare you for a couple of hours while you get this squared away."

Faith wasn't sure Agent Trent could spare anything at the moment.

Sara checked on the baby again. "His name is Balthazar," she said.

"Here I was thinking we had saved him."

She was kind enough to laugh, but her words were serious. "I'm board certified in pediatric medicine, Faith. I graduated at the top of my class at Emory University and I've devoted nearly two decades of my life to helping people, whether they're living or dead. You can question my personal motivations all you like, but don't question my medical abilities."

"You're right." Faith felt even more contrite. "I'm sorry. It's been a really hard day."

"It doesn't help when your blood sugar is out of whack." There was a rap on the door, and Sara walked over, taking a handful of insulin pens from the nurse. She shut the door and told Faith, "You have to take this seriously."

"I know I do."

"Postponing dealing with it isn't going to work. Take two hours out of your day to see Delia so that you can get yourself right and focus on your work."

"I will."

"Mood swings, sudden tempers—these are all symptoms of your disease."

Faith felt like her mother had just scolded her, but maybe that's exactly what she needed right now. "Thank you."

Sara put her hands on the bassinet. "I'll leave you to it."

"Wait," Faith said. "You deal with young girls, right?"

Sara shrugged. "I used to a lot more when I had my private practice. Why?"

"What do you know about thinspo?"

"Not a lot," the doctor admitted. "I know it's a word for pro-anorexia propaganda, usually on the Internet."

"Three of our victims have a connection to it."

"Anna's still very thin," Sara observed. "Her liver and kidney functions are off, but I thought that was because of what she'd been through, not anything she'd done to herself."

"Could she be anorexic?"

"It's possible. I really didn't consider the disorder because of her age. Anorexia is generally a teenage issue." Sara recalled, "Pete flagged up something similar during Jacquelyn Zabel's autopsy. She was very thin, but then again, she was starved and denied water for at least two weeks. I just assumed she had started out slightly underweight. Her frame was small." She leaned down to Balthazar and stroked the side of his cheek. "Anna couldn't have had a baby if she was starving herself. Not without serious complications."

"Maybe she got it under control long enough to have him," Faith guessed. "I'm never quite sure which is which—is anorexia where they throw up?"

"That's bulimia. Anorexia denotes starvation. Sometimes anorexics use laxatives, but they don't purge. There's growing evidence about genetic determinism—chromosomal blips that predispose them to the disorder.

Usually, there's some kind of environmental trigger that sets it off."

"Like child abuse?"

"Could be. Sometimes it's bullying. Sometimes it's body dysmorphia. Some people blame magazines and movie stars, but it's far more complicated than just one thing. Boys are starting to get it more, too. It's extremely difficult to treat because of the psychological component."

Faith thought about their victims. "Is there a certain type of personality that's drawn to it?"

Sara considered the question before replying. "I can only tell you that the handful of patients I dealt with who suffered from the disease got extreme pleasure from starving themselves. It takes a huge amount of willpower to fight the body's physiological imperative for food. They might feel like everything else in their life is out of whack, and the only thing they can manipulate is whether or not they put food in their mouths. There's also a physical response to starvation—lightheadedness, euphoria, sometimes hallucinations. It can duplicate the same type of high you get from opiates, and the feeling can be incredibly addictive."

Faith tried to remember how many times she'd made jokes about wishing she had the willpower to be anorexic for a week.

Sara added, "The biggest problem with treatment is that it's much more socially acceptable for a woman to be too thin than it is for a woman to be overweight."

"I have yet to meet a woman who is happy with her weight."

Sara gave a rueful laugh. "My sister is, actually."

"Is she some kind of saint?"

Faith had been joking, but Sara surprised her, answering, "Close. She's a missionary. She married a preacher a few years ago. They're helping AIDS babies in Africa."

"Good God, I hate her and I've never even met her."

"Trust me, she has her faults," Sara confided. "You said three victims. Does that mean another woman has been taken?"

Faith realized that Olivia Tanner's status hadn't yet hit the news. "Yes. Keep that under wraps if you can."

"Of course."

"Two of them seemed to take a lot of aspirin. The new one we found out about today had six jumbo bottles in her house. Jacquelyn Zabel had a large bottle by her bed."

Sara nodded, like something was starting to make sense. "It's an emetic in high doses. That would explain why Zabel's stomach was so ulcerated." She added, "And it would explain why she was still bleeding when Will found her. You should tell him that. He was upset about not getting there in time."

Will had a hell of a lot more than that to be upset about right now. Still, Faith remembered, "He needs your apartment number."

"Why?" Sara answered her own question. "Oh, his wife's dog."

"Right," Faith said, thinking the lie was the least she could do for Will.

"Twelve. It's on the directory." She put her hands back on the edge of the bassinet. "I should take this boy to his mother."

Faith held open the door and Sara rolled out the bassinet. The hum of the hallway buzzed in her ears until Faith shut the door. She sat on the stool by the counter and lifted her skirt, looking for a spot that wasn't already black and blue from the needles. The diabetes pamphlet had said to move the injection sites around, so Faith checked her stomach, where she found a pristine roll of white fat that she pinched between her thumb and forefinger.

She held the insulin pen a few inches from her belly but didn't inject herself. Somewhere behind all those Pop-Tarts was a tiny baby with tiny hands and feet and a mouth and eyes—breathing every breath she took, peeing every ten minutes when she ran to the bathroom. Sara's words had brought things home for Faith, but holding Balthazar Lindsey had awakened something in Faith that she had never felt in her life. As much as she had loved Jeremy, his birth was hardly a celebration. Fifteen was not an appropriate age for baby showers, and even the nurses at the hospital had looked at her with pity.

This time would be different, though. Faith was old enough so that it was acceptable for her to be a mother. She could walk through the mall with her baby on her hip without worrying people would assume she was her own child's older sister. She could take him to the pediatrician and sign all his forms without getting her mother to cosign. She could tell his teachers to go screw themselves during PTA meetings without worrying about being sent to the principal's office herself. Hell, she could drive now.

She could do it right this time. She could be a good mother from start to finish. Well, maybe not *start*. Faith catalogued all the things she had done to her baby just this week: ignored him, denied his existence, passed out in a garage, contemplated abortion, exposed him to whatever Sam Lawson was carrying, fallen off a porch step and risked both their lives trying to stop Will from pounding a Yugoslavian doorman's head into the fine looped carpet lining the penthouse hallway at Beeston Place.

And here they were now, mother and child in the Grady ICU, and she was about to poke a needle somewhere near his head.

The door opened.

"What the hell are you doing?" Amanda demanded. She figured it out for herself quickly enough. "Oh, for the love of God. When were you going to tell me about this?"

Faith rolled her shirt back down, thinking it was a little late for modesty. "Right after I told you I'm pregnant."

Amanda tried to slam the door but the hydraulic hinge wouldn't let her. "Goddamn it, Faith. You're never going to get ahead with a baby."

Her hackles rose. "I got this far with one."

"You were a kid in uniform making sixteen thousand dollars a year. You're thirty-three now."

Faith tried, "I guess this means you won't be throwing me a baby shower."

Her look would have cut glass. "Does your mother know?"

"I thought I'd let her enjoy her vacation."

Amanda slapped her palm to her forehead, which would've been comical if not for the fact that she held Faith's life in her hands. "A dyslexic half-wit with a temper problem and a fertile, fat diabetic who lacks a rudimentary understanding of birth control." She jabbed her finger in Faith's face. "I hope you like that pairing, young lady, because you're going to be stuck with Will Trent forever now."

Faith tried to ignore the "fat" part, which, honestly, hurt the most. "I can think of worse things than being partnered with Will Trent for the rest of my life."

"You'd just better be damned glad the security cameras didn't catch his little tantrum."

"Will's a good cop, Amanda. He wouldn't still be working for you if you didn't believe that."

"Well—" She cut herself off. "Maybe when he's not putting his abandonment issues on full display."

"Is he all right?"

"He'll live," Amanda replied, not sounding too convinced. "I sent him to track down that prostitute. Lola."

"She's not in jail?"

"There was a pretty big score in the apartment—heroin, meth, coke. Angie Polaski managed to get Lola kicked for being an informant." Amanda shrugged. She couldn't always control the Atlanta police department.

"Do you think it's a good idea to have Will looking for Lola, considering how angry he was about that baby being left alone?"

The old Amanda was back—the one who couldn't be questioned. "We've got two missing women and a serial killer who knows what to do with them. There has to be some movement on this case before it gets away from us. The clock is ticking, Faith. He could be watching his next victim right now."

"I was supposed to meet with Rick Sigler today—the paramedic who worked on Anna."

"I sent someone around to Sigler's house an hour ago. His wife was there with him. He adamantly denied knowing anyone named Jake Berman. He barely admitted he was on the road that night."

Faith could not think of a worse way to question the man. "He's gay. The wife doesn't know."

"They never do," Amanda countered. "At any rate, he wasn't interested in talking, and we don't have enough right now to drag him down to the station."

"I'm not sure he's a suspect."

"Everyone is a suspect as far as I'm concerned. I read the autopsy report. I've seen what was done to Anna. Our bad guy likes to experiment. He's going to keep doing this until we stop him."

Faith had been running on adrenaline for the past few hours, and she felt it spark up again at Amanda's words. "Do you want me to watch Sigler?"

"I've got Leo Donnelly parked outside his house right now. Something tells me you don't want to be trapped in a car with him all night."

"No, ma'am," Faith answered, and not just because Leo was a chain smoker. He would probably blame Faith for putting him on Amanda's shit list. He would be right.

"Someone needs to go to Michigan to find the files on Pauline Seward's family. The warrant's being expedited, but apparently nothing past fifteen years is on the computers. We need to find someone from her past and we need to find them fast—the parents, hopefully the brother, if it's not our mysterious Mr. Berman. For obvious reasons, I can't send Will to read through the files."

Faith put the insulin pen down on the counter. "I'll do it."

"Do you have this diabetes thing under control?"

Faith's expression must've been answer enough. "I'll send one of my agents who can actually do their job." She waved her hand, dismissing any objections Faith might have. "Let's just move on from that until it bites us in the ass again, shall we?"

"I'm sorry about this." Faith had apologized more in the last fifteen minutes than she had in her entire life.

Amanda shook her head, indicating she wasn't willing to discuss the stupidity of the situation. "The doorman's asked for a lawyer. We're scheduled to talk to them first thing in the morning."

"You arrested him?"

"Detained. He's obviously foreign-born. The Patriot Act gives us twenty-four hours to hold him while we check his immigration status. Hopefully, we can turn his apartment upside down and find something more concrete to hammer him with."

Faith wasn't one to argue with the true course of justice.

Amanda asked, "What about Anna's neighbors?"

"It's a quiet building. The apartment below the penthouse has been vacant for months. They could've set off an atom bomb up there and no one would've known."

"The dead guy?"

"Drug dealer. Heroin overdose."

"Anna's employer didn't miss her?"

Faith told her what little she'd managed to find out. "She works for a law firm—Bandle and Brinks."

"Good Christ, this just keeps getting worse. Do you know about the firm?" Amanda didn't give Faith time to answer. "They specialize in bringing lawsuits against municipalities—bad policing, bad social services, anything they can catch you on, they pounce and sue your budget to hell and back. They've sued the state and won more times than I can count."

"They weren't open to questioning. They won't turn over any of her files without a warrant."

"In other words, they're being lawyers." Amanda paced the room. "You and I will talk with Anna now, then we'll go back over to her building and turn it upside down before that law firm of hers realizes what we're doing."

"When's the interview with the doorman?"

"Eight sharp tomorrow morning. You think you can fit that into your busy schedule?"

"Yes, ma'am."

Amanda looked like a parent as she shook her head at Faith again; frustrated, mildly disgusted. "I don't suppose the father's in the picture this time, either."

"I'm a little too old to be trying something new."

"Congratulations," she said, opening the door. It would've been nice except for the "idiot" she muttered as she walked into the hall.

Faith hadn't realized she had been holding her breath until Amanda left the room. Her lips parted in a heavy sigh, and for the first time since this whole diabetes thing started, she jabbed the needle into her skin on the first try. It didn't hurt as much, or maybe she was in such shock that she couldn't feel anything.

She stared at the wall in front of her, trying to get her head back into the investigation. Faith closed her eyes, visualizing the autopsy photos of Jacquelyn Zabel, the cave where Jacquelyn and Anna Lindsey had been kept. Faith catalogued the horrible things that must have happened to the women—the torture, the pain. She put her hand to her stomach again. Was the child that was growing inside of her a girl? What sort of world was Faith bringing her into—a place where young girls were molested by their fathers, where magazines told them they would never be perfect enough, where sadists could take you away from your life, your own child, in the blink of an eye and thrust you into a living hell for the rest of your life?

A shudder racked her body. She stood and left the room.

The cops in front of Anna's door stepped aside. Faith crossed her arms over her chest, feeling a sudden coldness as she entered. Anna was lying in bed, Balthazar in the crook of her bony arm. Her shoulder was pronounced, the bone hard against the skin, the same as the girls Faith had seen in the videos on Pauline McGhee's computer.

"Agent Mitchell has just entered the room," Amanda told the woman. "She's been trying to find out who did this to you."

The whites of Anna's eyes were clouded, as if she had cataracts. She stared unseeingly toward the door. Faith knew there was no etiquette for this kind of situation. She had handled rape and abuse cases before, but nothing like this. She had to think the skills translated. You didn't make small talk. You didn't ask them how they were doing, because the answer was obvious.

Faith said, "I know this is a difficult time. We just have a few questions for you."

Amanda told Faith, "Ms. Lindsey was just telling me she finished a big case and took off work for a few weeks to spend time with her child."

Faith asked, "Did anyone else know you were taking time off?"

"I left a note with the doorman. People at work knew—my secretary, my partners. I don't talk to the people in my building."

Faith felt like a large wall had been erected around Anna Lindsey. There was something so cold about the woman that establishing a connection seemed impossible. She stuck to the questions they needed answered. "Can you tell us what happened when you were taken?"

Anna licked her dry lips, closed her eyes. When she spoke, her voice was little more than a whisper. "I was in my apartment getting Balthazar ready for a walk in the park. That's the last thing I remember."

Faith knew there could be some memory loss with Taser attacks. "What did you see when you woke up?"

"Nothing. I never saw anything again after that."

"Any sounds or sensations you can recall?"

"No."

"Did you recognize your attacker?"

Anna shook her head. "No. I can't remember anything."

Faith let a few seconds pass, trying to get hold of her frustration. "I'm going to give you a list of names. I need you to tell me if any of them sound familiar."

Anna nodded, her hand sliding across the sheets to find her son's mouth. He suckled her finger, tiny gulping noises coming from his throat.

"Pauline McGhee."

Anna shook her head.

"Olivia Tanner."

Again she shook her head.

"Jacquelyn, or Jackie, Zabel."

She shook her head.

Faith had saved Jackie for last. The two women had

been in the cave together. This was the only thing they knew for certain. "We found your fingerprint on Jackie Zabel's driver's license."

Anna's dry lips parted again. "No," she said firmly. "I don't know her."

Amanda glanced Faith's way, eyebrows raised. Was this traumatic amnesia? Or something else?

Faith asked, "What about something called thinspo?"

Anna stiffened. "No," she said, more quickly this time, her voice louder.

Faith gave it another few seconds, letting the woman think. "We found some notebooks where you were kept. They had the same words over and over again—'I will not deny myself.' Does that mean anything to you?"

She shook her head again.

Faith worked to keep the pleading out of her voice. "Can you tell us anything about your attacker? Did you smell something, like oil or gas on him? Cologne? Did you feel any facial hair or any physical—"

"No," Anna whispered, pressing her fingers along her child's body, finding his hand and taking it in hers. "I can't tell you anything. I don't remember any details. Nothing."

Faith opened her mouth to speak, but Amanda beat her to the punch, saying, "You're safe here, Ms. Lindsey. We've had two armed guards outside your door since you were brought in. No one can hurt you anymore."

Anna turned her head toward her baby, making shushing sounds to soothe him. "I am not afraid of anything."

Faith was taken aback at how certain the woman

sounded. Maybe if you survived what Anna had been through, you believed you could endure anything.

Amanda said, "We think he has two more women right now. That he's doing the same thing to them that he's done to you." She tried again, "One of the women has a child, Ms. Lindsey. His name is Felix. He's six years old and he wants to be with his mother. I'm sure wherever she is, she's thinking of him right now, wanting to hold him again."

"I hope she's strong," Anna mumbled. Then, louder, she told them, "As I have said many times now, I don't remember anything. I don't know who did it, or where they took me or why they did it. I just know that it's over now, and I'm putting it behind me."

Faith could feel Amanda's frustration matching her own.

Anna said, "I need to rest now."

"We can wait," Faith told her. "Maybe come back in a few hours."

"No." The woman's expression turned hard. "I know my legal obligations. I'll sign a statement, or make my mark, or whatever it is blind people do, but if you want to talk to me again, you can make an appointment with my secretary when I'm back at work."

Faith tried, "But, Anna—"

She turned her head toward the baby. Anna's blindness had blocked them from her vision, but her actions seemed to block them from her mind.

CHAPTER EIGHTEEN

SARA HAD FINALLY MANAGED TO CLEAN HER APART-
ment. She could not think of the last time it had looked
this good—maybe when she had first seen it with her
real estate agent before she had even moved in. The Milk
Lofts had once been a dairy, serviced by the vast farm-
land that used to cover the eastern part of the city. There
were six floors in the building, two apartments on each
floor separated by a long hallway with large windows at
either end. The main living area of Sara's place was what
was called an open plan, the kitchen looking onto the
enormous living room. Floor-to-ceiling windows that
were a bitch to keep clean lined an entire wall, giving
her a nice view of downtown when the shades were
open. There were three bedrooms in the back, each with
its own bathroom. Sara, of course, slept in the master,
but no one had ever slept in the guest room. The third
room she used as an office and for storage.

She had never thought of herself as a loft person, but
when Sara had moved to Atlanta, she had wanted her
new life to be as different from her old as was humanly
possible. Instead of choosing a cute bungalow on one of
the city's old, tree-lined streets, she had opted for a space
that was little more than an empty box. Atlanta's real estate market was just hitting rock bottom, and Sara had a
ridiculous amount of money to spend. Everything was

new when she'd moved in, but she had renovated the entire place from top to bottom anyway. The price of the kitchen alone would have fed a family of three for a year. Add in the palatial bathrooms and it was downright embarrassing that Sara had been so free with her checkbook.

In her previous life, she had always been careful with her money, never splurging on anything except a new BMW every four years. After Jeffrey's death, there had been his life insurance policy, his pension, his own savings and the proceeds from the sale of his house. Sara had left all of it in the bank, feeling like spending his money would be admitting he was gone. She had even considered refusing the tax exemption she got from the state for being a widow of a slain police officer, but her accountant had balked and it wasn't worth the fight.

Subsequently, the money she sent to Sylacauga, Alabama, every month to help Jeffrey's mother came out of her own pocket while Jeffrey's money compounded meager interest at the local bank. Sara often thought about giving it to his son, but that would have been too complicated. Jeffrey's son had never been told that Jeffrey was his real father. She couldn't ruin the boy's life and then hand over a sum that amounted to a small fortune to a kid who was still in college.

So, Jeffrey's money sat there in the bank, just like the letter sat on Sara's mantel. She stood by the fireplace, fingering the edge of the envelope, wondering why she hadn't put it back into her purse or jammed it into her pocket again. Instead, during her rabid fit of cleaning, she had only picked it up to dust under the envelope as she made her way down the mantel.

Sara saw Jeffrey's wedding ring on the opposite end.

She still wore her wedding ring—a matching white-gold band—but his college ring, a hunk of gold with the Auburn University insignia carved into the top, was more important to her. The blue stone was scratched and it was too big for her finger, so she wore it on a long chain around her neck the way a soldier wears his dog tags. She didn't wear it for anyone to see. It was always tucked into her shirt, close to her heart, so she could feel it at all times.

Still, she took Jeffrey's wedding band and kissed it before putting it back on the mantel. Over the last few days, her mind had somehow put Jeffrey in a different place. It was as if she was going through mourning again, but this time, at a remove. Instead of waking up feeling devastated, as she had for the last three and a half years, she felt enormously sad. Sad to turn over in bed and not have him there. Sad that she would never see him smile again. Sad that she would never hold him or feel him inside of her again. But not utterly devastated. Not like every move or thought was an effort. Not like she wanted to die. Not like there was no light at the end of all of this.

There was something else, too. Faith Mitchell had been so horrible today, and Sara had survived. She hadn't broken down or fallen to pieces. She had not come undone. She had kept herself together. The funny thing was, in some ways Sara felt closer to Jeffrey because of it. She felt stronger, more like the woman he had fallen in love with than the woman who had fallen apart without him. She closed her eyes, and she could almost feel his breath on the back of her neck, his lips brushing so softly that a tingle went down her spine. She imagined his hand wrapping around her waist, and was surprised when she put her hand there to feel nothing but her own hot skin.

The buzzer rang and the dogs stirred along with Sara. She shushed them as she walked to the intercom and buzzed in the pizza delivery guy. Betty, Will Trent's dog, had been adopted quickly by Billy and Bob, her two greyhounds. When she was cleaning earlier, all three dogs had settled onto the couch in a pile, glancing up occasionally when Sara walked into the room, sometimes giving her a sharp look if she made too much noise. Even the vacuum cleaner had not dislodged them.

Sara opened the door to wait for Armando, who delivered pizza to her apartment at least twice a week. The fact that they were on a first-name basis was something she pretended was normal, and she routinely overtipped the deliveryman so that he wouldn't make a big deal about seeing her more than he saw his own children.

"Doin' all right?" he asked as pizza and money changed hands.

"Doing great," she told him, but her mind was back in the apartment, on what she was doing before the buzzer had sounded. It had been so long since she'd been able to remember what it felt like to be with Jeffrey. She wanted to dwell on it, to crawl into bed and let her mind wander back to that sweet place.

"Have a good one, Sara." Armando turned to leave, then stopped. "Hey, there's some strange guy hanging around downstairs."

She lived in the middle of a large city, so this was hardly unusual. "Regular strange or call-the-cops strange?"

"I think he *is* a cop. Doesn't look it, but I saw his badge."

"Thanks," she said. He gave her a nod as he headed toward the elevator. Sara put the pizza box on the kitchen counter and walked to the far side of the living room. She pushed open the window and leaned out. Sure enough, six stories down, she spotted a speck looking suspiciously like Will Trent.

"Hey!" she called. He didn't respond, and she watched him for a moment as he paced back and forth, wondering if he'd heard her. She tried again, raising her voice like a soccer mom at a NASCAR race. *"Hey!"*

Will finally looked up, and she told him, "Sixth floor."

She watched him go into the building, passing Armando on the way out, who tossed Sara a wave and said something about seeing her soon. Sara shut the window, praying Will had not heard the exchange, or at least had the decency to pretend. She checked the apartment, making sure nothing was too horrendously out of place. There were two couches in the middle of the living room, one packed with dogs, the other with pillows. Sara fluffed these up, tossing them back onto the couch in what she hoped was an artful arrangement.

Thanks to two hours of elbow grease, the kitchen was sparkling clean, even the copper backsplash behind the stove, which was gorgeous until you realized it took two different kinds of cleaners. She passed the flat-screen television on the wall and stopped cold. She'd forgotten to dust the screen. Sara tugged down the sleeve of her shirt over her hand and did the best she could.

By the time she opened her door, Will was getting off the elevator. Sara had only met the man a few times, but he looked awful, like he hadn't slept in weeks. She saw his left hand, noticed the skin on his knuckles was split apart in a way that might suggest his fist had smashed repeatedly into someone's mouth.

Occasionally, Jeffrey had come home with the same kinds of cuts. Sara always asked about them, and he always lied. For her part, she made herself believe the lies because she wasn't comfortable with the idea of his walking outside the law. She wanted to believe that her husband was a good man in every way. Part of her wanted to think that Will Trent was a good man, too, so she was prepared to believe whatever story he came up with when she asked, "Is your hand all right?"

"I hit someone. The doorman at Anna's building."

Sara was caught off guard by his honesty. She took a second to form a response. "Why?"

Again, he seemed to give her the truth. "I just snapped."

"Are you in trouble with your boss?"

"Not really."

She realized she was keeping him in the hall and stepped aside so he could come in. "That baby is lucky you found him. I don't know that he could've gone another day."

"That's a convenient excuse." He looked around the room, absently scratching his arm. "I've never hit a suspect before. I've scared them into thinking I might, but I've never actually done it."

"My mother always told me there's a fine line between never and always." He looked confused, and Sara explained, "Once you do something bad, it's easier to do it again the next time, then the next time, and before you know it, you're doing it all the time and it doesn't bother your conscience."

He stared at her for what felt like a full minute.

She shrugged. "It's up to you. If you don't like crossing that line, then don't do it again. Don't ever make it easy."

There was a mixture of surprise in his face, then something like relief. Instead of acknowledging what had just happened, he told her, "I hope Betty wasn't too much trouble."

"She was fine. She's not yippy at all."

"Yeah," he agreed. "I didn't intend to dump her on you like that."

"It was no problem," Sara assured him, though she had to admit that Faith Mitchell was right about Sara's motivations this morning. Sara had offered to watch the dog because she wanted details about the case. She wanted to contribute something to the investigation. She wanted to be useful again.

Will was just standing there in the middle of the room, his three-piece suit wrinkled, the vest loose around his stomach as if he'd lost weight recently. She had never seen anyone look so lost in her life.

She told him, "Have a seat."

He seemed undecided, but finally took the couch across from the dogs. He didn't sit the way men usually sit—legs apart, arms spread along the back of the couch. He was a big guy, but he appeared to work very hard not to take up a lot of space.

Sara asked, "Have you had supper?"

He shook his head and she put the pizza box on the coffee table. The dogs were very interested in this development, so Sara sat on the couch with them in order to keep them in line. She waited for Will to take a slice, but he just sat there opposite, hands resting on his knees.

He asked, "Is that your husband's ring?"

Startled, she turned to the ring, which was flat on the polished mahogany. The letter was on the other end of the mantel, and Sara had a flash of concern that Will would figure out what was inside.

"Sorry," he apologized. "I shouldn't pry."

"It's his," she told him, realizing that she'd been pressing her thumb into the matching ring on her finger, spinning it around in a nervous habit.

"What about . . ." He touched his hand to his chest.

Sara mimicked the movement, feeling exposed as she found Jeffrey's college ring beneath her thin shirt. "Something else," she answered, not going into detail.

He nodded, still looking around the room. "I was found in a kitchen trashcan." His words were abrupt, surprising. He explained, "At least that's what my file says."

Sara didn't know how to respond, especially when he laughed, as if he'd made an off-color joke at a church social.

"Sorry. I don't know why I said that." He pulled a piece of pizza out of the box, catching the dripping cheese in his hand.

"It's all right," she told him, putting her hand on Bob's head as the greyhound's snout slid toward the coffee table. She couldn't even comprehend what Will was saying. He might as well have told her he had been born on the moon.

She asked, "How old were you?"

He waited until he'd swallowed, then told her, "Five months." He took another bite of pizza and she watched his jaw work as he chewed. Sara's mind conjured up an image of Will Trent at five months old. He would've just started trying to sit up on his own and recognizing sounds.

He took another bite and chewed thoughtfully. "My mother put me there."

"In the trashcan?"

He nodded. "Someone broke into the house—a man. She knew he was going to kill her, and probably me, too. She hid me in the trashcan under the sink, and he didn't find me. I guess I must've known to be quiet." He gave a crooked half-grin. "I was in Anna's apartment today, and I looked in every trashcan. All the time, I was thinking about what you said this morning, about how the killer put the trash bags inside of the women to send a message, because he wanted to tell the world that they were trash, meaningless."

"Obviously, your mother was trying to protect you. She wasn't sending a message."

"Yeah," he said. "I know."

"Did they . . ." Her mind wasn't working well enough to ask questions.

"Did they catch the guy who killed her?" Will asked, finishing her sentence. He glanced around the room again. "Did they catch the person who killed your husband?"

He had asked a question, but he wasn't looking for an answer. He was making the point that it didn't matter, something Sara had felt from the moment she'd been told the man who'd orchestrated Jeffrey's death was dead. She said, "Every cop who knows, that's all they care about. Did they catch the guy."

"Eye for an eye." He pointed to the pizza. "Mind if I—"

He had finished half the pie. "Go ahead."

"It's been a long day."

Sara laughed at the understatement. He laughed, too.

She pointed to his hand. "Do you want me to take care of that?"

He glanced at the wounds as if he'd just realized something was wrong. "What can you do?"

"You've waited too long for stitches." She stood up to get her first aid kit from the kitchen. "I can clean it. You need to start some antibiotics so it doesn't get infected."

"What about rabies?"

"Rabies?" She tied up her hair with a band she found in the kitchen drawer, then hooked her reading glasses on her shirt collar. "The human mouth is pretty dirty, but it's very rare—"

"I mean from rats," Will said. "There were some rats in the cave where Anna and Jackie were kept." He scratched his right arm again, and she realized now why he had been doing it. "You can get rabies from rats, right?"

Sara froze, her hand reaching up to take a stainless steel bowl from the cabinet. "Did they bite you?"

"No, they ran up my arms."

"*Rats* ran up your arms?"

"Just two. Maybe three."

"Two or three *rats* ran up your arms?"

"It's really calming the way you keep repeating everything I say, but in a louder voice."

She laughed at the comment, but still asked, "Were they acting erratic? Did they try to attack you?"

"Not really. They just wanted to get out. I think they were as scared of me as I was of them." He shrugged. "Well, one of them stayed down. He was eyeballing me, you know, kind of watching what I was doing. He never came near me, though."

She put on her reading glasses and sat beside him. "Roll up your sleeves."

He took off his jacket and rolled up the shirtsleeve on his left arm, though he had been scratching his right. Sara didn't argue. She looked at the scratches on his forearm. They weren't even deep enough to bleed. He was probably remembering it a lot worse than it actually was. "I think you'll be fine."

"You're sure? Maybe that's why I went a little crazy today."

She could tell he was only half kidding. "Tell Faith to call me if you start foaming at the mouth."

"Don't be surprised if you hear from her tomorrow."

She rested the stainless steel bowl in her lap, then put his left hand in the bowl. "This might sting," she warned, pouring peroxide over the open wounds. Will didn't flinch, and she took his lack of reaction as an opportunity to do a more thorough job.

She tried to take his mind off what she was doing, and, frankly, her own curiosity was raised. "What about your father?"

"There were extenuating circumstances," was all he offered. "Don't worry. Orphanages aren't as bad as Dickens would lead you to believe." He changed the subject, asking, "Do you come from a big family?"

"Just me and my younger sister."

"Pete said your dad's a plumber."

"He is. My sister worked in the business with him for a while, but now she's a missionary."

"That's nice. You both take care of people."

Sara tried to think of another question, something to

say that would make him open up, but nothing would come to mind. She had no idea how to talk to someone who didn't have a family. What stories of sibling tyranny or parental angst could you share?

Will seemed equally at a loss for words, or maybe he was just choosing to be silent. Either way, he didn't speak until she was doing her best to cover the broken skin by crisscrossing several Band-Aids over his knuckles.

He said, "You're a good doctor."

"You should see me with splinters."

He looked at his hand. Flexed his fingers.

She said, "You're left-handed."

He asked, "Is that a bad thing?"

"I hope not." She held up her left hand, which she'd been using to clean his wounds. "My mother says it means you're smarter than everybody else." She started cleaning up the mess. "Speaking of my mother, I called her about the question you had—the apostle who replaced Judas? His name was Matthias." She laughed, joking, "I'm pretty sure if you meet anyone by that name, you've probably found your killer."

He laughed, too. "I'll put out an APB."

"Last seen wearing a robe and sandals."

He shook his head, still smiling. "Don't make light of it. That's the best lead I've heard all day."

"Anna's not talking?"

"I haven't talked to Faith since . . ." He waved his injured hand. "She would've called if anything came up."

"She's not what I thought," Sara told him. "Anna. I know this is odd to say, but she's very dispassionate. Unemotional."

"She's been through a lot."

"I know what you mean, but it's beyond that." Sara shook her head. "Or maybe it's my ego. Doctors aren't used to being talked to as if they're servants."

"What did she say to you?"

"When I brought her baby to her—Balthazar—I don't know, it was weird. I wasn't expecting a medal by any means, but I thought she would at least thank me. She just told me that I could go away."

Will rolled down his shirtsleeve. "None of these women have been particularly likable."

"Faith said there might be an anorexia connection."

"There might be. I don't know a lot about it. Are anorexics generally horrible people?"

"No, of course not. Everyone is different. Faith asked me about the same thing this afternoon. I told her that it takes a very driven personality to starve yourself like that, but it doesn't follow that they're unkind." Sara thought about it. "Your killer probably didn't choose these women because they're anorexic. He chooses them because they're awful people."

"If they're awful people, then he'd have to know them. He'd have to have contact with them."

"Are you finding any connections other than the anorexia?"

"All of them are unmarried. Two of them have kids. One of them hates kids. One of them wanted a kid, but maybe not." He added, "Banker, lawyer, real estate broker and interior designer."

"What kind of lawyer?"

"Corporate attorney."

"Not real estate closings?"

He shook his head. "The banker didn't work mortgages, either. She was in charge of community relations—

doing fundraisers, making sure the president of the bank had his picture in the paper beside kids with cancer. That sort of thing."

"They're not in a support group?"

"There's a chat room, but we can't get into it without a password." He rubbed his eyes with his hands. "It just goes in circles."

"You look tired. Maybe a good night's sleep will help you figure it out."

"Yeah, I should go." But he didn't. He just sat there looking at her.

Sara felt the noise drain from the room, and the air got stuffy, almost hard to breathe. She was acutely aware of the pressure against her skin from the gold band around her fourth finger, and she realized that her thigh was brushing his.

Will was the first to break the spell, turning, reaching for his jacket off the back of the couch. "I really should go," he told her, standing up to put on his jacket. "I need to find a prostitute."

She was certain she had heard wrong. "I'm sorry?"

He chuckled. "A witness named Lola. She was the one who was taking care of the baby and she tipped us off about Anna's apartment. I've been looking for her all afternoon. I think now that it's nighttime, she's probably emerged from her lair."

Sara stayed on the couch, thinking it was probably best to keep some distance between them so Will didn't get the wrong message. "I'll wrap up some pizza for you."

"That's okay." He went to the other couch and extracted Betty from the dog pile. He tucked her close to his chest. "Thanks for the conversation." He paused.

"About what I said . . ." He paused again. "Maybe best just to forget about it, okay?"

Her mind reeled with something to say that wasn't flip or—worse—an invitation. "Of course. No problem."

He smiled at her again, then let himself out of her apartment.

Sara sat back on the couch, hissing out a breath of air, wondering what the hell had just happened. She traced back through their conversation, wondering if she had given Will a sign, an unintentional signal. Or maybe there wasn't anything there. Maybe she was reading too much into the look he gave her as they both sat on the couch. Surely, it didn't help matters that three minutes before Will had arrived, Sara was thinking lewd thoughts about her husband. Still, she went back through it again, trying to figure out what had brought them to that uncomfortable moment, or if, in fact, there had been an uncomfortable moment at all.

It wasn't until she remembered holding his hand over the bowl, cleaning out the wounds on his knuckles, that she realized that Will Trent was no longer wearing his wedding ring.

CHAPTER NINETEEN

WILL WONDERED HOW MANY MEN IN THE WORLD were trolling for prostitutes in their cars right now. Maybe hundreds of thousands, if not millions. He glanced at Betty, thinking he was probably the only one doing it with a Chihuahua in his passenger seat.

At least he hoped so.

Will looked at his hands on the steering wheel, the Band-Aids that covered the broken skin. He couldn't remember the last time he'd gotten into a serious fight. It must have been when he was back at the children's home. There was a bully there who had made his life miserable. Will had taken it and taken it, and then he had snapped, and Tony Campano had ended up with his front teeth broken out like a Halloween pumpkin.

Will flexed his fingers again. Sara had tried to do her best with the Band-Aids, but there was no way to keep them from falling off. Will tried to catalogue the many times he had been to a doctor as a child. There was a scar on his body for just about each visit, and he used the marks to jog his memory, naming the foster parent or group home leader who had been courteous enough to break a bone or burn him or rip open his skin.

He lost count, or maybe he just couldn't keep a thought in his head because all he kept coming back to was the way Sara Linton had looked when he first saw her in the doorway to her apartment. He knew she had long hair, but she'd always kept it up. This time, it was down—soft curls cascading past her shoulders. She was wearing jeans and a long-sleeved cotton shirt that did a very good job of showing everything she had to great advantage. She was in socks, her shoes kicked off by the door. She smelled nice, too—not like perfume, but just clean and warm and beautiful. While she was fixing his hand, it had taken everything in him not to lean down and smell her hair.

Will was reminded of a Peeping Tom he'd caught in Butts County a few years ago. The man had followed women out to the parking lot of the local shopping mall, then offered them money to smell their hair. Will could still remember the news report, the local sheriff's deputy visibly nervous in front of the news camera. The only thing the cop could come up with to tell the reporter was, "He's got a problem. A problem with hair."

Will had a problem with Sara Linton.

He scratched Betty's chin as he waited for a red light to change. The Chihuahua had done a good job of ingratiating herself with Sara's dogs, but Will was not foolish enough to think he had a snowball's chance. No one had to tell him he wasn't the sort of man Sara Linton would go for. For one, she lived in a palace. Will had remodeled his house a few years ago, so he knew the cost of all the nice things he could not afford. Just the appliances in her kitchen had run around fifty thousand dollars, twice the amount he had spent on his whole house.

Two, she was smart. She wasn't obvious about it, but she was a doctor. You didn't go to medical school if you were stupid, or Will would've been a doctor, too. It would take Sara no time at all to figure out he was illiterate, which made him glad that he wasn't going to be spending any more time around her.

Anna was getting better. She would be out of the hospital soon. The baby was fine. There was no reason on earth for Will to ever see Sara Linton again unless he happened to be at Grady Hospital when she was on shift.

He supposed he could hope he got shot. He'd thought Amanda was going to do exactly that when she'd taken him into the stairwell this afternoon. Instead, she had merely said, "I've waited a long time for your short hairs to grow in." Not exactly the words you expect from your superior after you've beaten a man nearly senseless. Everyone was making excuses for him, everyone was covering for him, and Will was the only one who seemed to think that what he had done was wrong.

He pulled away from the light, heading into one of the seedier parts of town. He was running out of places to check for Lola, a revelation which troubled him, and not just because Amanda had told him not to bother coming in to work tomorrow unless he tracked the whore down. Lola had to have known about the baby. She had certainly known about the drugs and what was going on in Anna Lindsey's penthouse apartment. Maybe she had seen something else—something she wasn't willing to trade because it might put her life in danger. Or maybe she was just one of those cold, unfeeling people who didn't care if a child was slowly dying. Word must have gotten around by now that Will was the kind of cop who beat people. Maybe Lola was afraid of him. Hell, there had been a moment in that hallway when Will was afraid of himself.

He had felt numb when he got to Sara's apartment, like his heart wasn't even beating in his chest. He was thinking of all the men who had raised their fists to him when he was a child. All the violence he had seen. All the pain he had endured. And he was just as bad as the rest of them for beating that doorman into the ground.

Part of him had told Sara Linton about the incident because he had wanted to see the disappointment in her eyes, to know with just one look that she would never approve of him. What he got instead was . . . understanding. She acknowledged that he had made a mistake, but she hadn't assumed that it defined his character. What kind of person did that? Not the kind of person Will had ever met. Not the kind of woman Will could ever understand.

Sara was right about how it was easier to do something bad the second time. Will saw it all the time at work: repeat offenders who had gotten away with it once and decided they might as well roll the dice and try it again. Maybe it was human nature to push those boundaries. A third of all DUI offenders ended up being arrested for drunk driving a second time. Over half of all the violent felons captured were already released convicts. Rapists had one of the highest recidivist rates in the prison system.

Will had learned a long time ago that the only thing he could control in any given situation was himself. He wasn't a victim. He wasn't prisoner to his temper. He could choose to be a good person. Sara had said as much. She had made it seem so easy.

And then he had forced that weird moment when they were together on the couch, staring at her like he was an ax murderer.

"Idiot." He rubbed his eyes, wishing he could rub away the memory. There was no use thinking about Sara Linton. In the end, it would lead to nothing.

Will saw a group of women loitering on the sidewalk ahead. They were all dressed in various shades of fantasy: schoolgirls, strippers, a transsexual who looked a lot like the mother from *Leave It to Beaver*. Will rolled down his window and they all did a silent negotiation, deciding who to send over. He drove a Porsche 911 he had rebuilt from the ground up. The car had taken him almost a decade to restore. It seemed to take a decade for the prostitutes to decide who to send.

Finally, one of the schoolgirls sauntered over. She leaned into the car, then backed out just as quickly. "Nuh-uh," she said. "No way. I ain't fuckin' no dog."

Will held out a twenty-dollar bill. "I'm looking for Lola."

Her lip twisted, and she snatched away the cash so quickly Will felt the paper burn his fingertips. "Yeah, that bitch'll fuck your dog. She on Eighteenth. Strolling by the old post office."

"Thank you."

The girl was already sashaying back to her group.

Will rolled up the window and took a U-turn. He saw the girls in his rearview mirror. The schoolgirl had passed the twenty on to her minder, who would in turn pass it on to the pimp. Will knew from Angie that the girls seldom got to keep any cash. The pimps took care of their living quarters, their food, their clothes. All the girls had to do was risk their lives and health every night by tricking whatever john pulled up with the right amount of cash. It was modern slavery, which was ironic, considering most if not all of the pimps were black.

Will turned onto Eighteenth Street and slowed the car to a crawl, coming up on a parked sedan under a streetlight. The driver was behind the wheel, his head back. Will gave it a few minutes and a head popped up from the man's lap. The door opened and the woman tried to get out, but the man reached over and grabbed her by the hair.

"Crap," Will mumbled, jumping out of his car. He locked the door with the remote on his keys as he jogged toward the sedan and yanked open the door.

"What the fuck?" the man yelled, still holding the woman by the hair.

"Hey, baby," Lola said, reaching her hand out to Will. He grabbed it without thinking, and she got out of the car, her wig staying in the man's hand. He cursed and threw it onto the street, pulling away from the curb so fast that the car door slammed shut.

Will told Lola, "We need to talk."

She bent over to get her wig, and courtesy of the streetlight, he saw straight up to her tonsils. "I'm running a business here."

Will tried, "Next time you need help—"

"Angie helped me, not you." She tugged at her skirt. "You watch the news? Cops found enough coke in that penthouse to teach the world to sing. I'm a fucking hero."

"Balthazar's going to be okay. The baby."

"Baltha-what?" She wrinkled her face. "Christ, kid barely had a chance."

"You took care of him. He meant something to you."

"Yeah, well." She put the wig on her head, trying to get it straight. "I got two kids, you know? Had them while I was locked up. Got to spend some time with them before the state took them away." Her arms were bone-thin, and Will was again reminded of the thinspo videos they had found on Pauline's computer. Those girls were starving themselves because they wanted to be thin. Lola was starving because she couldn't afford food.

"Here," he said, tugging the wig straight for her.

"Thanks." She started walking down the street back toward her group. There was the usual mixture of schoolgirls and tramps, but they were older, harder women. The streets usually got tougher the higher the numbers. Pretty soon, Lola and her gang would be on Twenty-first, a street so hopeless that dispatch at the local police station routinely sent out ambulances to pick up women who had died during the night.

He tried, "I could arrest you for obstructing a crime."

She kept walking. "Might be nice in jail. Getting kind of cold out here tonight."

"Did Angie know about the baby?"

She stopped.

"Just tell me, Lola."

Slowly, she turned around. Her eyes searched his, not looking for the right answer, but looking for the answer that he wanted to hear. "No."

"You're lying."

Her face remained emotionless. "He really okay? The baby, I mean."

"He's with his mom now. I think he'll be okay."

She dug around in her purse, finding a pack of

cigarettes and some matches. He waited for her to light up, take a drag. "I was at a party. This guy I know, he said there was this pad in some fancy apartment building. The doorman's easy. Lets people in and out. Mostly, it was high-class stuff. You know, people who needed a nice place for a couple of hours, no questions asked. They come in and party, the maid comes the next day. The rich people who own the different apartments get back from Palm Beach or wherever and have no idea." She picked a stray piece of tobacco off her tongue. "Something happened this time, though. Simkov, the doorman, pissed off somebody in the building. They gave him a two-week notice. He started letting in the lower clientele."

"Like you?"

She lifted her chin.

"What'd he charge?"

"Have to talk to the boys about that. I just show up and fuck."

"What boys?"

She exhaled a long plume of smoke.

Will let it go, knowing not to push her too hard. "Did you know the woman whose apartment you were in?"

"Never met her, never seen her, never heard of her."

"So, you get there, Simkov lets you up, and then what?"

"At first it's nice. Usually, we've been in one of the lower apartments. This was the penthouse. Lots of your better consumers. Good stash. Coke, some H. The crack showed up a couple of days later. Then the meth. Went downhill from there."

Will remembered the trashed state of the apartment. "That happened fast."

"Yeah, well. Drug addicts aren't exactly known for their restraint." She chuckled at a memory. "Couple of fights broke out. Some bitches got into it. Then the trannies went to town and—" She shrugged, like *What do you expect*?

"What about the baby?"

"Kid was in the nursery first time I got there. You got kids?"

He shook his head.

"Smart choice. Angie's not exactly the mothering type."

Will didn't bother to agree with her, because they both knew that was the God's honest truth. He asked, "What did you do when you found the baby?"

"The apartment wasn't a good place for him. I could see what was coming. The wrong kind of people were showing up. Simkov was letting anybody in. I moved the kid down the hall."

"To the trash room."

She grinned. "Ain't nobody worried about throwing away the trash at that party."

"Did you feed him?"

"Yeah," she said. "I fed him what was in the cabinets, changed his diaper. I did that with my own kids, you know? Like I said, they let you keep them for a while before they're turned over. I learned all about feeding and that kind of shit. I took pretty good care of him."

"Why did you leave him?" Will asked. "You were arrested on the street."

"My pimp didn't know about this—I was off the

books, just having a good time. He tracked me down and told me to get back to work, so I did."

"How did you get back upstairs to take care of the baby?"

She jerked her hand up and down. "I tossed off Simkov. He's all right."

"Why didn't you tell me when you called that first night that there was a baby involved?"

"I figured I'd take care of him when I got out," she admitted. "I was doing a good job, right? I mean, I was doing good by him, keeping him fed and changing his little diapers. He's a sweet little boy. You seen him, right? You know he's sweet."

That sweet little boy was dehydrated and hours from dying when Will had seen him. "How did you know Simkov?"

She shrugged. "Otik's a longtime customer, you know?" She gestured toward the street. "Met him here on Millionaire's Row."

"I wouldn't exactly call him a stand-up guy."

"He did me a favor letting me go up there. I made some good cash. I kept the kid safe. What else you want from me?"

"Did Angie know about the baby?"

She coughed, the sound coming from deep in her chest. When she spit onto the sidewalk, Will felt his stomach roll. "You're gonna have to ask her about that."

Lola swung her purse over her shoulder and headed back toward her group.

Will took out his cell phone as he walked toward his car. The thing was on its last legs, but it still managed to make the call.

"Hello?" Faith said.

Will didn't want to talk about what had happened this afternoon, so he didn't give her an opening. "I talked to Lola." He ran down what the prostitute had told him. "Simkov called her in to help her make some extra cash. I'm sure he took his share off the top."

"Maybe that's something we can use," Faith answered. "Amanda wants me to talk to Simkov tomorrow. We'll see if his story matches up."

"What did you find on him?"

"Not much. He lives in the apartment building on the bottom floor. He's supposed to be on the desk from eight until six, but there's been problems with that lately."

"I guess that's why they gave him his two-week notice."

"His criminal report came up clean. His bank account's all right, considering he gets free rent." Faith paused, and he could hear her turning the pages in her notebook. "We found some porn in his apartment, but nothing young or kinky. His phone's clean."

"Sounded to me like he'd let anybody into the building for the right amount of cash. Did Anna Lindsey give you anything?"

She told him about her fruitless conversation with the woman. "I don't know why she won't talk. Maybe she's scared."

"Maybe she thinks if she puts it out of her mind, doesn't talk about it, then it'll go away."

"I suppose that works if you've got the emotional maturity of a six-year-old."

Will tried not to take her words personally.

Faith told him, "We looked at the front-door logs from the apartment building. There was a cable guy and a couple of delivery people. I talked to all of them as well as the building maintenance guy. They're checking out. Clean records, solid alibis."

Will got into his car. "What about neighbors?"

"No one seems to know anything, and these people are too rich to talk to the police."

Will had met the type before. They didn't want to get involved and they didn't want their names in the papers. "Did any of them know Anna?"

"Same as with the others—anyone who knew her didn't like her."

"What about forensics?"

"Should be back in the morning."

"What about the computers?"

"Nothing, and the warrants aren't in for the bank yet, so we don't have access to Olivia Tanner's cell phone, BlackBerry, or her computer at work."

"Our bad guy is smarter at this than we are."

"I know," she admitted. "Everything is starting to feel like a dead end."

There was a lull in the conversation. Will searched for something to fill it, but Faith beat him to the punch.

"So, Amanda and I are going to interview the doorman at eight in the morning, then I've got an appointment I need to go to. It's out in Snellville."

Will couldn't think what anyone would be doing in Snellville.

"I figure it'll take an hour or so. Hopefully, we'll have an ID on Jake Berman by then. We need to talk to Rick Sigler, too. I keep letting him slip through the cracks."

"He's white, early forties."

"Amanda made the same point. She sent someone

around to talk to Sigler earlier today. He was at home with his wife."

Will groaned. "Did he deny even being at the scene?"

"Apparently, he tried to. He wouldn't even acknowledge he was with Jake Berman, which makes it seem more and more like a hookup." Faith sighed. "Amanda's got a tail on Sigler, but his background is clean. No aliases, no multiple addresses, born and raised in Georgia. He's got K-through-twelve school records in Conyers. There's no indication that he's ever been to Michigan, let alone lived there."

"We're only stuck on this brother thing. because Pauline McGhee told her son to watch out for his uncle."

"True, but what else do we have to follow? If we hit any more brick walls, we're both going to start getting concussions."

Will waited a few seconds. "What kind of appointment?"

"It's a personal thing."

"All right."

Neither of them seemed to have anything to say after that. Why was it so easy for Will to spill his guts to Sara Linton, but he could barely manage to have a normal conversation with any other women in his life—especially his partner?

Faith offered, "I'll talk about my thing if you'll talk about yours."

He laughed. "I think we need to start from the beginning. With the case, I mean."

She agreed. "The best way to see if you've missed something is to retrace your steps."

"When you get back from your appointment. We'll

go to the Coldfields', talk to Rick Sigler at his work so he's not freaking out in front of his wife, then go over all the witnesses—anybody who's even remotely connected to this thing. Fellow employees, maintenance men who've been to the house, tech support, anybody they've had contact with."

"Couldn't hurt," she agreed. There was another lull. Again she filled it. "Are you all right?"

Will had pulled up in front of his house. He put the car in park, wishing that a bolt of lightning would just come down from the sky and kill him dead.

Angie's car was blocking the driveway.

"Will?"

"Yeah," he managed. "I'll see you in the morning."

He ended the call and tucked the phone into his pocket. The lights were on in the front room, but Angie hadn't bothered to turn on the porch light. He had cash in his pocket, credit cards. He could stay in a hotel tonight. There had to be a place that wouldn't mind dogs, or maybe he could sneak Betty in under his jacket.

Betty stood and stretched on the seat. The front porch light came on.

Will mumbled under his breath as he scooped up the dog. He got out of his car and locked it, then headed up the driveway. He opened the gate to the backyard and set Betty on the grass, then he stood outside his own house a few minutes, debating, then decided he was being stupid and made himself go in.

Angie was on the couch with her feet curled up under her. Her long dark hair was down the way he liked it, and she was wearing a tight black dress that hugged every curve. Sara had looked beautiful, but Angie looked sexy. Her makeup was dark, her lips a blood red. He wondered if she had made an effort. Probably. She always sensed when Will was pulling away. She was like a shark smelling blood in the water.

She greeted him the same way the prostitute did. "Hey, baby."

"Hey."

Angie stood up from the couch, stretching like a cat as she walked over to him. "Good day?" she asked, putting her arms around his neck. Will turned his head, and she turned it back, kissing him on the lips.

He said, "Don't do that."

She kissed him again because she had never liked being told what to do.

Will kept himself as impassive as he could, and she finally dropped her arms.

"What happened to your hand?"

"I beat someone."

She laughed, like he was joking. "Really?"

"Yeah." He leaned his hand on the back of the couch. One of the Band-Aids was peeling up.

"You beat someone." She was taking him seriously now. "Any witnesses?"

"None that are talking."

"Good for you, baby." She was close to him, right behind him. "I bet Faith wet her pants." Her hand traced down his arm, rested on the back of his wrist. Her tone changed. "Where's your ring?"

"In my pocket." Will had taken it off before he'd gone up to Sara's apartment. At the time, he'd fooled himself into thinking he'd done it because his fingers were swelling and the ring was getting tight.

Angie's hand went to his pants pocket. Will closed his eyes, feeling the day catch up with him. Not just the day, but the last eight months. Angie was the only woman he had ever been with, and his body had been lonely, almost aching for the feel of her.

Her fingers touched him through the thin material of his pocket. His reaction was immediate, and when she breathed into his ear, he gripped the couch so that he could still stand.

She took his ear between her teeth. "You miss me?"

He swallowed, unable to speak as she pressed her breasts, her body, into his back. He leaned his head back and she kissed his neck, but it wasn't Angie he was thinking about when her fingers wrapped around him. It was Sara, her long, thin fingers working on his hand as they both sat on the couch. The way her hair had smelled, because he had let himself bend down just for a moment and inhaled as quietly as he could. She smelled of goodness and mercy and kindness. She smelled of everything that he had ever wanted—everything that he could never have.

"Hey." Angie had stopped. "Where'd you go?"

With effort, Will managed to zip up his pants. He shouldered Angie out of the way as he walked across the room.

She asked, "Is it your time of the month again?"

"Did you know about the baby?"

She cocked her hand on her hip. "What baby?"

"I don't care what the answer is, but I want the truth. I need to know the truth."

"You gonna beat me if I don't tell you?"

"I'm gonna hate you," he answered, and they both knew what he was saying was true. "That baby could've been you or me. Hell, that baby *was* me."

Her tone was sharp, defensive. "Mommy leave him in the trashcan?"

"It was that or whore him out for speed."

She pressed her lips together, but would not look away. "Touché," she finally said, because Diedre Polaski had done just that very thing to her baby girl.

Will repeated his question, the only question that mattered anymore. "Did you know that there was a baby in that penthouse?"

"Lola was taking care of it."

"What?"

"She's not bad. She was making sure it was okay. If she hadn't got popped—"

"Wait a minute." He put out his hands to stop her. "You think that whore was taking care of that baby?"

"He's fine, right? I made some calls to Grady. Mother and son are united again."

"You made some calls?" He couldn't believe what he was hearing. "Jesus Christ, Angie. He's a tiny baby. He would've been dead if we'd waited any longer."

"But you didn't and he's not."

"Angie—"

"People always take care of babies, Will. Who looks out for people like Lola?"

"You're worried about some crack whore when there's a baby in a trash heap starving to death?" He didn't let her answer. "That's it. That's it for me."

"What the hell does that mean?"

"It means I'm finished. It means the string on our yo-yo has broken."

"Fuck you."

"No more back and forth. No more screwing around on me, running out on me in the middle of the night, then running back in a month or a year later pretending like you can lick my wounds all better."

"You make it sound so romantic."

He opened the front door. "I want you out of my house and out of my life." She didn't move, so he walked over to her, started pushing her toward the door.

"What are you doing?" She pushed back, and when he wouldn't budge, she slapped him. "Get the fuck away from me."

He lifted her from behind, and she used her foot to kick the door closed.

"Get out," he said, trying to reach the doorknob even as he held on to her.

Angie had been a beat cop before she'd been a detective, and she knew how to take him down. Her foot kicked out, popping him in the back of the knee, dropping him to the floor. Will held on, pulling her down with him so they were struggling on the floor like a couple of angry dogs.

"Stop it," she screamed, kicking him, punching him, using every part of her body to cause pain.

Will rolled her onto her stomach, pushing her flat against the wood floor. He grabbed both her hands in one of his, squeezing them together so she couldn't fight him. Without even thinking, he reached down and ripped away her underwear. Her nails dug into the back of his hand as he slid his fingers inside her.

"Asshole," she hissed, but she was so wet Will could barely feel his fingers moving in and out. He found the right spot, and she cursed again, pressing her face into the floor. She never came with him. It was part of her power play. She always squeezed every last bit of soul out of Will, but she would never let him do the same to her.

"Stop it," she demanded, but she was moving against his hand, tensing with each stroke. He unzipped his pants and pushed himself inside her. She tried to tighten against him, but he pushed harder, forcing her to open up. She groaned and there was a sweet release as she took him in deeper, then even more. He pulled her up to her knees, fucking her as fast as he could while his fingers worked to bring her to the edge. She started to moan, a deep, guttural sound he had never heard before. Will rammed himself into her, not caring if he left marks up and down her body, not caring if he broke her. When she finally came, she gripped him so hard that it almost hurt to be inside of her. His own release was so savage that he ended up collapsed on top of her, panting, every part of him sore.

Will rolled onto his back. Angie's hair was tangled around her face. Her makeup was smeared. She was breathing as hard as he was.

"Jesus Christ," she mumbled. "Jesus Christ." She tried to reach out and touch his face, but he slapped her hand away.

They lay there like that, both panting on the floor, for what seemed like hours. Will tried to feel remorse, or anger, but all he felt was exhaustion. He was so sick of this, so sick of the way Angie drove him to extremes. He thought again about what Sara had said: *Learn from your mistakes*.

Angie Polaski was looking like the biggest mistake Will had ever made in his miserable life.

"Christ." She was still breathing hard. She rolled over on her side, slid her hand up under his shirt. Her hands were hot, sweaty against his skin. Angie said, "Whoever she is, tell her I said thanks."

He stared up at the ceiling, not trusting himself to look at her.

"I've been screwing you for twenty-three years, baby, and you've never fucked me like that before." Her fingers found the ridge at the bottom of his rib, the place where the skin puckered from a cigarette burn. "What's her name?"

Will still didn't answer.

Angie whispered, "Tell me her name."

Will's throat hurt when he tried to swallow. "Nobody."

She gave a deep, knowing laugh. "Is she a nurse or a cop?" She laughed again. "Hooker?"

Will didn't say anything. He tried to block Sara out of his mind, didn't want her in his thoughts right now because he knew what was coming. Will had scored one point, so Angie had to score ten.

He flinched as Angie found a sensitive nerve on his damaged skin.

She asked, "Is she normal?"

Normal. They had used that word in the children's home to describe people not like them—people with families, people with lives, people whose parents didn't beat them or pimp them out or treat them like trash.

Angie kept tracing the tip of her finger around the burn. "She know about your problem?"

Will tried to swallow again. His throat scratched. He felt sick.

"She know you're stupid?"

He felt trapped under her finger, the way it was pressing into the round scar where the burning cigarette had melted his flesh. Just when he thought he couldn't take it anymore, she stopped, putting her mouth close to his ear, sliding her fingers up the sleeve of his shirt. She found the long scar running up his arm where the razor had opened his flesh.

"I remember the blood," she said. "The way your hand shook, the way the razor blade opened up your skin. Do you remember that?"

He closed his eyes, tears leaking out. Of course he remembered. If he thought about it hard enough, he could still feel the tip of the sharp metal scraping across his bone because he had known that he should send the razor deep—deep enough to open the vein, deep enough to make sure it was done right.

"Remember how I held you?" she asked, and he could feel her arms around him even though she wasn't holding him now. The way she had wrapped her whole body around him like a blanket. "There was so much blood."

It had dripped down her own arms, onto her legs, her feet.

She had held on to him so tight that he couldn't breathe, and he had loved her so much, because he knew she understood why he was doing it, why he had to stop the madness that was going on around him. Every scar on his body, every burn, every break—Angie knew about it the same way she knew everything about herself. Every secret Will had, Angie held somewhere deep inside her. She held on to it with her life.

She *was* his life.

He gulped, his mouth still spitless. "How long?"

She rested her hand on his stomach. She knew she

had him back, knew it was just a matter of snapping her fingers. "How long what, baby?"

"How long do you want me to love you?"

She didn't answer him immediately, and he was about to ask the question again when she said, "Isn't that a country music song?"

He turned to look at her, searching her eyes for some sign of kindness that he had never seen before. "Just tell me how long so I can count the days, so I know when this is finally going to be over."

Angie traced her hand down the side of his face.

"Five years? Ten years?" His throat was closing, like someone had fed him glass. "Just tell me, Angie. How long until I can stop loving you?"

She leaned in, put her mouth to his ear again. "Never."

She pushed herself up from the floor, smoothing down her skirt, finding her shoes and underwear. Will lay there as she opened the door, then left without bothering to look back. He didn't blame her. Angie never looked back. She knew what was behind her, just like she always knew what was ahead.

Will didn't get up when he heard her shoes on the porch stairs or her car starting up in the driveway. He didn't get up when he heard Betty scratching at the dog door, which he'd forgotten to open for her. Will did not move for anything. He lay on the floor all night, until the sun coming in through the windows told him it was time to go back to work.

DAY FOUR

CHAPTER TWENTY

PAULINE WAS HUNGRY, BUT SHE COULD HANDLE THAT. She understood the pains in her stomach and lower intestines, the way the spasms reverberated through her gut as they grasped for any type of nourishment. She knew it well, and she could handle it. The thirst was different, though. There was no way around the thirst. She had never gone without water for this long before. She was desperate, willing to do anything. She'd even peed on the floor and tried to drink it, but it just made her thirst even wilder so that she'd ended up sitting on her knees, baying like a wolf.

No more. She couldn't be in that dark place for long. She couldn't let it get to her again, envelop her so that all she wanted to do was curl into a ball and pine for Felix.

Felix. He was the only reason to get out of here, to fight, to stop the fuckers from taking Pauline away from her baby boy.

She lay on her side, arms pinned to her waist, feet sticking straight out, and lifted her upper body, straining her neck so that she could line herself up right. She held herself like that, muscles tight, sweating, the blindfold rubbing her skin, as she took aim. The chains around her wrists rattled from exertion, and before she could stop herself, she reared back her head and pounded it into the wall.

Pain streaked through her neck. She saw stars—literal stars—swimming through her vision. She fell onto her back, panting, trying not to hyperventilate, willing herself not to pass out.

"What are you doing?" the other woman asked.

The bitch had been lying on her back like a corpse for the last twelve hours, unresponsive, uncaring, and now she was asking questions?

"Shut up," Pauline snarled. She didn't have time for this shit. She rolled over onto her side again, lining up her body with the wall, moving down a few more inches. She held her breath, squeezed her eyes shut and pounded her head into the wall again.

"Fuck!" she screamed, her head exploding with pain. She fell onto her back again. There was blood on her forehead, sliding underneath the blindfold, getting into her eyes. She couldn't blink it away, couldn't wipe it. She felt like a spider was crawling across her eyelids, seeping into her eyeballs.

"No," Pauline said, and she found herself wrapped in a full-on hallucination, spiders crawling across her face, digging into her skin, laying eggs in her eyes. "No!"

She jerked up to sitting, head spinning from the sudden motion. She was panting again, and she bent her head to her knees, touched her chest to her thighs. She had to get hold of herself. She couldn't give in to the thirst. She couldn't let the dementia settle into her brain again so that she lost where she was.

"What are you doing?" the stranger whispered, terrified.

"Leave me alone."

"He'll hear you. He'll come down."

"He's not coming down," Pauline snapped. Then, to

prove it, she screamed, "Come down here, you mother-fucker!" Her throat was so raw that she started coughing from the exertion, but she still screamed, "I'm trying to escape! Come stop me, you limp-dicked mother-fucker!"

They waited and waited. Pauline ticked off the seconds. There were no footsteps on the stairs. No lights turned on. No doors opened.

"How do you know?" the stranger said. "How do you know what he's doing?"

"He's waiting for one of us to break," Pauline told her. "And it's not going to be me."

The woman asked another question, but Pauline ignored her, lining herself up with the wall again. She braced herself to pound her head into the wall again, but she couldn't do it. She couldn't hurt herself again. Not right now. Later. She would rest a few minutes and then do it later.

She rolled onto her back, tears streaming down her face. She didn't open her mouth, because she didn't want the woman to know she was crying. The stranger had heard the sobbing, heard Pauline sliding around in her own piss. That show was over. No more tickets would be sold.

"What's your name?" the stranger asked.

"None of your goddamn business!" Pauline barked. She didn't want to make friends. She wanted to get out of here any way she could, and if that meant walking over the stranger's dead body to freedom, Pauline would do it. "Just shut up."

"Tell me what you're doing and maybe I can help you."

"You can't help me. You got that?" Pauline twisted

to face the stranger, even though they were in total darkness. "Listen up, bitch. Only one person is going to make it out of here alive and it's not going to be you. You understand me? Shit rolls downhill, and I'm not going to be the one smelling like a sewer when this is over with. All right?"

The stranger was silent. Pauline fell onto her back, looking up at darkness, trying to brace herself for the wall again.

The woman's voice was barely a whisper. "You're Atlanta Thin, aren't you?"

Pauline's throat tightened like a noose had been put around it. "What?"

" 'Shit rolls downhill, and I'm not going to be the one smelling like a sewer,' " she repeated. "You say that a lot."

Pauline chewed her lip.

"I'm Mia-Three."

Mia—slang for "bulimia." Pauline recognized the screen name, but still insisted, "I don't know what you're talking about."

Mia asked, "Did you show them that email at work?"

Pauline opened her mouth, just tried to breathe a while. She tried to think of the other things she had told the Pro-Anna Internet group, the desperate thoughts that raced through her mind and somehow ended up being typed onto the keyboard. It was almost like purging, but instead of emptying your stomach, you were emptying your brain. Telling somebody those awful thoughts you had, knowing they had them, too, somehow made it easier to get up every morning.

And now the stranger wasn't a stranger anymore.

Mia repeated, "Did you show them the email?"

Pauline swallowed, even though there was only dust in her throat. She couldn't believe she was tied up like a fucking hog and this woman wanted to talk about work. Work didn't matter anymore. Nothing mattered anymore. The email was from another life, a life where Pauline had a job she wanted to keep, a mortgage, a car payment. They were waiting down here to be raped, tortured, murdered, and this woman was worried about a fucking email?

Mia said, "I didn't get to call Michael, my brother. Maybe he's looking for me."

"He won't find you," Pauline told her. "Not out here."

"Where are we?"

"I don't know," she answered—the truth. "I woke up in the trunk of a car. I was chained. I'm not sure how long I was in there. The trunk opened. I started to scream, then he Tased me again." She closed her eyes. "Then I woke up here."

"I was in my backyard," Mia told her. "I heard something. I thought maybe a cat . . ." She let her words trail off. "I was in a trunk when I came to. I'm not sure how long he kept me in there. It felt like days. I tried to count away the hours, but . . ." She went into a long silence that Pauline didn't know how to interpret. Finally she said, "Do you think that's how he found us—on the chat board?"

"Probably," she lied. Pauline knew how he had found them, and it wasn't that damn chat room. It was Pauline who had led them here—Pauline's big mouth that had gotten them into trouble. She wasn't going to tell Mia what she knew. There would be more questions, and with the questions would come accusations that Pauline knew she wouldn't be able to handle.

Not now. Not when her brain felt like it was stuffed with cotton and the blood dripping down her eyes felt like the tiny, hairy legs of a million spiders.

Pauline gasped for breath, trying to keep herself from freaking out again. She thought about Felix and the way he smelled when she bathed him with the new soap she picked up at Colony Square during her lunch break.

Mia asked, "It's still in the safe, right? They'll find the email in the safe and they'll know you told the upholsterer to measure the elevator."

"Bitch, what does it matter? Do you not understand where we are, what's going to happen to us? So what if they find the email? Some fucking consolation. 'She's dead, but she was right all along.' "

"More than you got in life."

They shared a moment of commiseration. Pauline tried to remember what little she knew about Mia. The woman didn't post much on the board, but when she did, she was pretty on point. Like Pauline and a few other posters, Mia didn't like whiners and she didn't take much bullshit.

"They can't starve us," Mia said. "I can go nineteen days before I start to shut down."

Pauline was impressed. "I can go about the same," she lied. Her max had been twelve, and then they'd put her in the hospital and plumped her up like a Thanksgiving turkey.

Mia said, "Water is the issue."

"Yeah," Pauline agreed. "How long can you—"

"I've never tried to go without water," Mia interrupted, finishing the sentence. "It doesn't have any calories."

"Four days," Pauline told her. "I read somewhere that you can only last about four days."

"We can last longer." It wasn't wishful thinking. If Mia could last nineteen days without eating, she sure as hell could last longer than Pauline without water.

That was the problem. She could outlast Pauline. No one had outlasted Pauline before.

Mia asked the obvious question. "Why hasn't he fucked us?"

Pauline pressed her head to the cool concrete floor, tried to keep the panic from building up inside of her. The fucking wasn't the problem. It was the other stuff—the games, the taunting, the tricks . . . the trash bags.

"He wants us weak," Mia guessed. "He wants to make sure we can't fight back." Mia's chains rattled as she moved. Her voice sounded closer, and Pauline guessed she'd turned onto her side. "What were you doing? Before, I mean. Why were you hitting the wall with your head?"

"If I can punch through the sheetrock, maybe I can get out. It's standard building code that the two-by-fours have to be sixteen inches apart."

Mia's tone filled with awe. "You have a sixteen-inch waist?"

"No, you dumbass. I can turn sideways and slide out."

Mia laughed at her own stupidity, but then she pointed out something that made Pauline feel equally as idiotic. "Why aren't you using your feet?"

They were both quiet, but Pauline felt something

welling up inside her. Her stomach twinged, and she heard laughter in her ears, honest-to-God, all-out laughter, as she thought about how fucking stupid she was.

"Oh, God," Mia sighed. She was laughing, too. "You are such an idiot."

Pauline twisted her body around, trying to spin on her shoulder. She lined up her feet, bracing them together so that the chains wouldn't throw her off, and kicked. The sheetrock caved on the first try.

"Dumbass," she muttered, this time at herself. She slid back around to face the opening, using her teeth to bite off the broken chunks of sheetrock. There was poison in the dust, but she didn't care. She would rather die with her head poking six inches out of this room than be trapped here while she waited for that fucker to come for her.

"Did you get it?" Mia asked. "Did you break—"

"Shut up," Pauline told her, biting into foam padding. He had soundproofed the walls. That was to be expected. No big deal. She just grabbed it with her teeth, taking chunk after chunk out, aching for the feel of fresh air on her face.

"Fuck!" Pauline screamed. She inched around so that her waist was lined up with the hole. She reached out with her fingers, which barely went past the broken sheetrock. She tore out the foam, then her fingers brushed something that felt like a screen. She arched her back, reaching her hands out as far as they would go. Her fingers traced along crisscrossed wire. "Goddamn it!"

"What is it?"

"Chicken wire." He had lined the walls with chicken wire so they couldn't break out.

Pauline angled herself around again and jammed her feet against the wire. The soles of her shoes met solid resistance. Instead of the screen giving, the counterforce moved her several inches across the floor. She inched back to try again, rolling over onto her stomach and placing her sweaty palms to the cement. Pauline reared her feet back and kicked with all her strength. Again she met solid resistance, her body sliding away from the wall.

"Oh, Jesus," she gasped, falling onto her back. The tears came, the tiny spider legs encroaching on her vision. "What am I going to do?"

"Can your hands reach?"

"No," Pauline cried. Hope drained out of her with every breath. Her hands were too tight to the belt. The chicken wire was attached to the back of the two-by-four. There was no way she could reach it.

Pauline's body shook with sobs. She had not seen him in years, but she still knew how his mind worked. The basement was his staging ground, a carefully prepared prison where he would starve them into submission. But this was not the worst of it. There would be a cave somewhere, a dark place in the earth that he had lovingly dug out by hand. The basement would break them. The cave would destroy them. The bastard had thought of everything.

Again.

Mia had managed to inch her way over. Her voice was close, almost on top of Pauline. "Shut up," Mia ordered, pushing Pauline out of the way. "We'll use our mouths."

"What?"

"It's thin metal, right? Chicken wire?"

"Yeah, but—"

"You bend it back and forth and it breaks."

Pauline shook her head. This was crazy.

"All we need is for one piece to give," Mia said, as if the logic was clear. "Just grab it in your mouth and pull back and forth, back and forth. It'll break eventually, then we can kick it. Or we can just break every single piece off with our mouths."

"We can't—"

"Don't tell me can't, you fucking bitch." Mia's foot was chained, but she managed to kick Pauline in the shin.

"Ouch! Jesus—"

"Start counting," Mia ordered, inching toward the hole in the wall. "When you get to two hundred, it'll be your turn."

Pauline wasn't going to do it because she would be damned if she let this bitch tell her what to do. She heard something then—teeth on metal. Grinding, twisting. Two hundred seconds. Their skin would rip open. Their gums would be in shreds. There was no telling if it would even work.

Pauline rolled over, sat up on her knees.

She started counting.

CHAPTER TWENTY-ONE

FAITH HAD NEVER THOUGHT OF HERSELF AS A MORN-
ing person, but she had gotten into the habit of going in
to work early when Jeremy was a child. You couldn't *not*
be a morning person when there was a hungry boy to
feed, dress, scrutinize and send off to the bus stop by
7:13 at the latest. If not for Jeremy, she might have been
one of those late-night people, the sort who rolls into
bed well after midnight, but Faith's usual bedtime ran
closer to ten, even after Jeremy was a teenager and his
waking hours were few and far between.

For his own reasons, Will was always at work early,
too. Faith saw his Porsche parked in its usual space as she
pulled the Mini into the lot under City Hall East. She
put the car in park, then sat there trying to get the
driver's seat back where she could reach the pedals and
the steering wheel at the same time without being im-
paled by one while having to stretch to reach the other.
After several minutes, she finally found the right combination and briefly thought about having the seat bolted
into place. If Will wanted to drive her car again, he'd
have to do it with his knees around his ears.

There was a tap at her window, and Faith looked up,
startled. Sam Lawson stood there, a cup of coffee in his
hand.

Faith opened the car door and wedged herself out,

feeling like she'd put on twenty pounds overnight. Finding something to wear this morning had been a nearly impossible task. She was carrying enough water weight to fill a tank at SeaWorld. Thankfully, her giddiness over Sam Lawson had been a twenty-four-hour virus. She did not relish having a conversation with him now, especially since her mind needed to be focused on the day ahead of her.

"Hey, babe," Sam said, looking her up and down in his usual predatory way.

Faith got her purse out of the back seat. "Long time no see."

He gave a half-shrug that implied he was merely the victim of circumstance. "Here," he said, offering her the coffee. "Decaf."

Faith had tried to drink some coffee this morning. The smell had sent her rushing to the bathroom. "Sorry." She ignored the cup, walking away from him, trying not to get sick again.

Sam tossed the cup into the trashcan as he caught up with her. "Morning sickness?"

Faith glanced around, afraid they'd be heard. "I haven't told anyone but my boss." She tried to remember when you were supposed to tell people. There had to be a certain number of weeks before you were sure it took. Faith must be coming up on that mark. She should start telling people soon. Should she get them all together, invite her mother and Jeremy to dinner, get her brother on speakerphone, or was there a way to send a bulk anonymous email and perhaps jump on a flight to the Caribbean for a few weeks to avoid the fallout?

Sam's fingers snapped in front of her face. "You in there?"

"Barely." Faith reached for the door to the building just as he did. She let him open it for her. "I've got a lot on my mind."

"About last night—"

"It was two nights ago, actually."

He grinned. "Yeah, but I wasn't really thinking about it until last night."

Faith sighed as she pressed the elevator button.

"Come here." He pulled her toward the alcove on the other side of the elevator. There was a vending machine with three rows of sticky buns, which Faith knew without having to look.

Sam stroked her hair behind her ear. Faith pulled back. She wasn't ready for intimacy this early in the morning. She wasn't sure she was ever ready for it. Without thinking, she glanced up to make sure there wasn't a security camera watching them.

He said, "I was an ass the other night. I'm sorry."

She heard the elevator doors open, then close. "It's all right."

"No, it's not." He leaned in to kiss her, but she pulled back again.

"Sam, I'm at work." She didn't add the rest of what she was thinking, which was that she was in the middle of a case where one woman had died, another woman had been tortured and two more were missing. "This isn't the time."

"It's never the time," he said, something he'd often told her years ago when they were seeing each other. "I want to try this again with you."

"What about Gretchen?"

He shrugged. "Hedging my bets."

Faith groaned, pushing him away. She went back to

the elevator and pressed the button. Sam didn't leave, so she told him, "I'm pregnant."

"I remember."

"I don't want to break your heart, but the baby's not yours."

"Doesn't matter."

She turned to face him. "Are you trying to work out some ghosts because your wife had an abortion?"

"I'm trying to get back into your life, Faith. I know it has to be on your terms."

Faith balked at the backhanded compliment. "I seem to recall one of the problems between us, other than you being a drunk, me being a cop and my mother thinking you were the Antichrist, was you didn't like the fact that I had a son."

"I was jealous of the attention you gave him."

At the time, she had accused him of this very thing. To hear him admit to it now left her nearly breathless.

"I've grown up," he said.

The elevator opened. Faith made sure the car was empty, then held the door open with her hand. "I can't have this conversation now. I've got work to do." She got into the elevator and let the doors go.

"Jake Berman lives in Coweta County."

Faith nearly lost her hand stopping the doors. "What?"

He took his notebook out of his pocket and wrote as he talked. "I tracked him down through his church. He's a deacon and a Sunday School teacher. They've got a great website with his picture on it. Lambs and rainbows. Evangelical."

Faith's brain couldn't process the information. "Why did you find him?"

"I wanted to see if I could beat you to the punch."

Faith didn't like where this was going. She tried to neutralize the situation. "Listen, Sam, we don't know that he's a bad guy."

"I guess you've never been in the men's room at the Mall of Georgia."

"Sam—"

"I haven't talked to him," he interrupted. "I just wanted to see if I could track him down when no one else could. I'm tired of Rockdale squeezing my balls. I much prefer it when you do."

Faith let that comment go, too. "Give me the morning to talk to him."

"I told you, I'm not looking for a story." He grinned, showing all his teeth. "It was an exercise in *faith*."

She narrowed her eyes at him.

"I wanted to see if I could do your job." He tore off the piece of paper, giving her a wink. "Pretty easy stuff."

Faith grabbed the address before he changed his mind. He held her gaze as the doors closed, then Faith found herself staring at her reflection on the backs of the doors. She was sweating already, though she supposed in a pinch that could pass for a pregnant glow. Her hair was starting to frizz because, even though it was only April, the temperature was inching up the thermometer.

She looked at the address Sam had given her. There was a heart around the entire thing, which she found annoying and endearing in equal parts. She didn't quite trust that he wasn't looking for a story in Jake Berman. Maybe the *Atlanta Beacon* was doing a down-low exclusive, outing married churchgoers who were trolling glory holes and finding raped and tortured women in the middle of the road.

Could Berman be Pauline's brother? Now that she had an address, Faith wasn't so sure. What were the odds that Jake Berman had hooked up with Rick Sigler, and both men just happened to be on the road at the same time the Coldfields' car hit Anna Lindsey?

The doors opened and Faith walked out onto her floor. None of the hall lights were on, and she flipped the switches as she walked toward Will's office. No light seeped from under his door, but she knocked anyway, knowing from his car that he was in the building.

"Yes?"

She opened the door. He was sitting at his desk with his hands clasped in front of his stomach. The lights were off.

She asked, "Everything okay?"

He didn't answer her question. "What's up?"

Faith shut the door and opened the folding chair. She saw the back of Will's hand, and that some new scratches had been added to the cuts he'd received while beating Simkov's face. She didn't mention this, instead going to the case. "I got Jake Berman's address. He's in Coweta. That's about forty-five minutes from here, right?"

"If the traffic's good." He held out his hand for the address.

She read it off to him. "Nineteen-thirty-five Lester Street."

He still had his hand out. For some reason, all Faith could do was stare at his fingers.

Will snapped, "I'm not a fucking idiot, Faith. I can read an address."

His tone was sharp enough to make the hair on the

back of her neck rise. Will seldom cursed, and she had never heard him say "fuck" before. She asked, "What's wrong?"

"Nothing's wrong. I just need the address. I can't do the interview with Simkov. I'll go find Berman and we'll meet back here after your appointment." He shook his hand. "Now give me the address."

She crossed her arms. She would die before she gave him the piece of paper. "I don't know what the hell is wrong with you, but you need to get your head out of your ass and talk to me about this before we've got a real problem."

"Faith, I've only got two testicles. If you want one, you're going to have to talk to Amanda or Angie."

Angie. With that one word, all the fight seemed to go out of him. Faith sat back in the chair, her arms still crossed, studying him. Will looked out the window, and she could see the faint line of the scar going down the side of his face. She wanted to know how it had happened, how his skin had been gouged from his jaw, but as with everything else, the scar was just another thing they did not talk about.

Faith put the paper on his desk and slid the address across to him.

Will gave it a cursory glance. "There's a heart around it."

"Sam drew it."

Will folded the paper and put it in his vest pocket. "Are you seeing him?"

Faith was loath to use the words "booty call," so she just shrugged. "It's complicated."

He nodded—the same nod they always used when

there was something personal that wasn't going to be discussed.

She was sick of this. What was going to happen in a month when she started showing more? What was going to happen in a year when she collapsed on the job because she had miscalculated her insulin? She could easily see Will making excuses for her weight gain or simply helping her up and telling her she should be careful where she stepped. He was so damn good at pretending the house wasn't on fire even as he ran around looking for water to put it out.

She threw up her hands in surrender. "I'm pregnant."

His eyebrows shot up.

"Victor's the father. I'm also diabetic. That's why I passed out in the garage."

He seemed too shocked to speak.

"I should've told you before. That's what my secret appointment is in Snellville. I'm going to the doctor so she can help me with this diabetes thing."

"Sara can't be your doctor?"

"She referred me to a specialist."

"A specialist means it's serious."

"It's a challenge. The diabetes makes it more difficult. It's manageable, though." She had to add, "At least that's what Sara said."

"Do you need me to go to your appointment with you?"

Faith had a glimpse of Will sitting in the waiting room of Delia Wallace's office with her purse in his lap. "No. Thank you. I need to do this on my own."

"Does Victor—"

"Victor doesn't know. No one knows except you and

Amanda, and I only told her because she caught me shooting up with insulin."

"You have to give yourself shots?"

"Yeah."

She could almost see his mind working, the questions he wanted to ask her but didn't know how to frame.

Faith said, "If you want another partner—"

"Why would I want another partner?"

"Because it's a problem, Will. I don't know how much of a problem, but my blood sugar drops or goes up, and I get emotional, and I either bite your head off or feel like I'm going to burst into tears, and I don't know how I'm going to do my job with this thing."

"You'll work it out," he said, always reasonable. "I worked it out. My problem, I mean."

He was so adaptive. Anything bad that happened, no matter how horrible, he just nodded and moved on. She supposed that was something he'd learned at the orphanage. Or maybe Angie Polaski had drilled it into him. As a survival skill, it was commendable. As the basis of a relationship, it was irritating as hell.

And there was absolutely nothing Faith could do about it.

Will sat up in his chair. He did his usual trick, making a joke to ease the tension. "If I get a vote, I would rather you bite my head off than start crying."

"Back at you."

"I need to apologize." Suddenly, he was serious again. "For what I did to Simkov. I've never laid hands on anyone like that before. Not ever." He looked her directly in the eye. "I promise it won't happen again."

All Faith could say was, "Thank you." Of course she didn't agree with what Will had done, but it was hard to shout out recriminations when he was so obviously already doing a good job of hating himself.

It was Faith's turn to lighten things up. "Let's stay away from good cop/bad cop for a while."

"Yeah, stupid cop/bitchy cop works a lot better for us." He reached into his vest pocket and handed her back Jake Berman's details. "We should call Coweta and have them put eyes on Berman to make sure he's the right guy."

The wheels in Faith's brain took their time moving in a new direction. She looked at Sam's block handwriting, the stupid heart around the address. "I don't know why Sam thinks he can track down the guy in five minutes when our entire data processing division can't find him in two days."

Faith took out her cell phone. She didn't want to bother with the proper channels, so she called Caroline, Amanda's assistant. The woman practically lived in the building, and she picked up the phone on the first ring. Faith relayed Berman's address and asked her to have the Coweta County field agent verify that this was the Jake Berman they had been looking for.

"Do you want him to bring the guy in?" Caroline asked.

Faith thought about it, then decided she didn't want to make the decision on her own. She asked Will, "Do you want them to bring in Berman?"

He shrugged, but answered, "Do we want to tip him off?"

"A cop knocking on his door is a tip-off no matter what."

Will shrugged again. "Tell him to try to verify Berman's identity from a distance. If it's the right guy, then we'll go down there and snatch him up. Give the agent my cell number. We'll go after you finish talking to Simkov."

Faith passed this on to Caroline. She ended the call, and Will turned his computer monitor toward her, saying, "I got this email from Amanda."

Faith slid over the mouse and keyboard. She changed the color settings so her retinas didn't spontaneously combust, then double-clicked on the file. She summarized for Will as she read. "Tech hasn't been able to break into any of the computers. They say the anorexia chat room is impossible to open without a password—it's got some kind of fancy encryption. The warrants for Olivia Tanner's bank should be in this afternoon so we can get into her phone and files." She scrolled down. "Hmm." She read silently, then told Will, "Okay, well, this might be something to take to the doorman. The fire exit door on the penthouse floor had a partial on the handle—right thumb."

Will knew Faith had spent most of yesterday afternoon combing through Anna Lindsey's building. "How are the stairs accessed?"

"Either the lobby or the roof," she said, reading the next passage. "The fire escape ladder that runs down the back of the building had another print that matched the one from the door. They're sending it to the Michigan State Police to run comparables. If Pauline's brother has a record, it should come up. If we can get a name, then we're halfway there."

"We should check for parking tickets in the area. You can't just park anywhere in Buckhead. They're pretty good about catching you."

"Good idea," Faith said, opening up her email account to send out the request. "I'll open it up to parking tickets in or around the area of all the last known locations of our victims."

"Son of Sam was caught by a parking ticket."

Faith tapped the keys. "You've got to stop watching so much television."

"Not much else to do at night."

She glanced at his hands, the new scratches.

He asked, "How did he get Anna Lindsey out of the building? He couldn't have thrown her over his shoulder and taken her down the fire escape ladder."

Faith sent off the email before answering. "The exit door for the stairs was wired. An alarm would have gone off if anyone had opened the door." She asked, "Did he take her down the elevator and into the lobby?"

"That's something to ask Simkov."

"The doorman isn't there twenty-four hours," Faith reminded him. "The killer could've waited for Simkov to clock out, then used the elevator to bring her body down. Simkov was supposed to keep an eye on things after hours, but he was hardly dedicated to his job."

"There wasn't another doorman to relieve him?"

"They've been trying to find someone to fill the position for six months," she told him. "Apparently, it's hard to find someone who wants to sit on their ass behind a desk for eight hours a day—which is why they put up with so much bullshit from Simkov. He was willing to double up his shifts, such as they were."

"What about security tapes?"

"They tape over them every forty-eight hours." She had to add, "Except for the ones from yesterday, which seem to be missing." Amanda had made sure the tape of

Will slamming Simkov's face into the counter had been destroyed.

Will's face flooded with guilt, but still he asked, "Anything in Simkov's apartment?"

"We tossed it upside down. He drives an old Monte Carlo that leaks like a sieve and there aren't any receipts for storage units."

"There's no way he could be Pauline's brother."

"We've been so focused on that that we haven't seen anything else."

"All right, so let's take the brother out of the equation. What about Simkov?"

"He's not smart. I mean, he's not stupid, but our killer is choosing women he wants to conquer. I'm not saying our bad guy is a genius, but he's a hunter. Simkov is a pathetic schmuck who keeps porn under his mattress and takes blowjobs to let whores into empty apartments."

"You've never believed in profiles before."

"You're right, but we're spinning our wheels everywhere else. Let's talk about our guy," Faith said, something Will usually suggested. "Who's our killer?"

"Smart," Will admitted. "He probably works for an overbearing woman, or has overbearing women in his life."

"That's pretty much every man on the planet these days."

"Tell me about it."

Faith smiled, taking his words as a joke. "What kind of job does he have?"

"Something that lets him exist under the radar. He has flexible hours. Watching these women, learning about their habits, takes a lot of time. He's got to have a job that lets him come and go as he pleases."

"Let's ask the same boring, stupid question one more time: What about the women? What do they have in common?"

"The anorexia/bulimia thing."

"The chat room." She shot that one down on her own: "Of course, even the FBI can't find out who the site is registered to. No one has been able to break Pauline's password. How could our guy find it?"

"Maybe he started the site himself in order to troll for victims?"

"How would he find out their true identities? Everyone's tall, thin and blonde on the Internet. And usually twelve and horny."

He was twisting his wedding ring again, staring out the window. Faith couldn't stop looking at the scratches on the back of his hand. In forensic parlance, they would have called the marks defensive wounds. Will had been behind someone who had gouged her fingernails deep into his skin.

She asked, "How did it go with Sara last night?"

Will shrugged. "I just picked up Betty. I think she likes Sara's dogs. She's got two greyhounds."

"I saw them yesterday morning."

"Oh, that's right."

"Sara's nice," Faith told him. "I really like her."

Will nodded.

"You should ask her out."

He laughed, shaking his head at the same time. "I don't think so."

"Because of Angie?"

He stopped twisting the ring. "Women like Sara Linton . . ." She saw a flash of something in his eyes that she couldn't quite read. Faith expected him to shrug it off, but he kept talking. "Faith, there's no part of me that's not damaged." His voice sounded thick in his throat. "I don't mean just the things you can see. There's other stuff. Bad stuff." He shook his head again, a tight gesture, more for his own benefit than Faith's. He finally told her, "Angie knows who I am. Somebody like Sara . . ." Again his voice trailed off. "If you really like Sara Linton, then you don't want her to know me."

All Faith could think to say was his name. "Will."

He gave a forced laugh. "We gotta stop talking about this stuff before one of us starts lactating." He took out his cell phone. "It's almost eight. Amanda will be waiting for you in the interrogation room."

"Are you going to watch?"

"I'm going to make some calls up to Michigan and annoy the crap out of them until they run those fingerprints we found on Anna's fire escape. Why don't you call me when you're out of your doctor's appointment? If Sam found the right Jake Berman, we can go talk to him together."

Faith had forgotten about her doctor's appointment. "If he's the right Jake Berman, then we should scoop him up immediately."

"I'll call you if that's the case. Otherwise, go to your doctor's appointment, then we'll start from scratch like we'd planned."

She listed it off. "The Coldfields, Rick Sigler, Olivia Tanner's brother."

"That should keep us busy."

"You know what's bugging me?" Will shook his head, and she told him, "We haven't gotten the reports from Rockdale County yet." She held up her hands, knowing Rockdale was a sore point. "If we're going to start from the beginning, we need to do just that—get the initial crime-scene report from the first responding cop and go over every detail point by point. I know Galloway said the guy's fishing in Montana, but if his notes are good, then we don't need to talk to him."

"What are you looking for?"

"I don't know. But it bothers me that Galloway hasn't faxed it over."

"He's not exactly on top of things."

"No, but everything he's held back until now has been for a reason. You said it yourself. People don't do stupid things without a logical explanation."

"I'll put a call in to his office and see if the secretary can handle it without getting Galloway involved."

"You should get those scratches on the back of your hand looked at, too."

He glanced down at his hand. "I think you've looked at them plenty."

EXCEPT FOR TALKING to Anna Lindsey in the hospital the day before, Faith had never worked directly with Amanda on a case. The extent of their interaction tended to be with a desk between them, Amanda on one side with her hands steepled in front of her like a disapproving schoolmarm and Faith fidgeting in her chair as she gave her report. Because of this, Faith tended to forget that Amanda had clawed her way up the ranks back during a time when women in uniform were relegated to fetching coffee and typing reports. They weren't even allowed to carry guns, because the brass thought that, given the choice between shooting a bad guy and breaking a nail, the latter would win out.

Amanda had been the first female officer to disabuse them of this theory. She had been at the bank cashing her paycheck when a robber decided to take an early withdrawal. One of the tellers had panicked, and the robber had started to pistol-whip her. Amanda shot him once in the heart, what was called a K-5 for the circle it corresponded to on the shooting range target. She'd told Faith once that she had gotten her nails done afterward.

Otik Simkov, the doorman from Anna Lindsey's building, would have benefited from knowing this story. Or maybe not. The little troll had an air of arrogance about him, despite being stuffed into a too-small Day-Glo orange prison uniform and open-toed sandals that had been worn by a thousand prisoners before him. His face was bruised and battered, but he still held himself upright, shoulders squared. As Faith entered the interrogation room, he gave her the same look of appraisal a farmer might give a cow.

Cal Finney, Simkov's lawyer, made a show of looking at his watch. Faith had seen him on television many times; Finney's commercials had their own annoying jingle. He was as handsome in person as he was on the set. The watch on his arm could've put Jeremy through college.

"Sorry I'm late." Faith directed the apology toward Amanda, knowing she was the only one who mattered. She sat in the chair opposite Finney, catching the look of distaste on Simkov's face as he openly stared at her. This was not a man who had learned to respect women. Maybe Amanda would change that.

"Thank you for speaking with us, Mr. Simkov,"

Amanda began. She was still using her pleasant voice, but Faith had been in enough meetings with her boss to know that Simkov was in trouble. She had her hands resting lightly on a file folder. If experience was anything to go by, she would open the folder at some point, unleashing the gates of hell.

She said, "We just have a few questions to ask you regarding—"

"Screw you, lady," Simkov barked. "Talk to my lawyer."

"Dr. Wagner," Finney said. "I'm sure you're aware that we filed a lawsuit against the city this morning for police brutality." He snapped open his briefcase and pulled out a stack of papers, which he dropped with a *thunk* on the table.

Faith felt her face flush, but Amanda didn't seem fazed. "I understand that, Mr. Finney, but your client is looking at a charge of obstructing justice in a particularly heinous case. Under his watch, one of the tenants in his building was abducted. She was raped and tortured. She barely managed to escape with her life. I'm sure you saw it on the news. Her child was left to die, again under Mr. Simkov's watch. The victim will never regain her vision. You can see why we are somewhat frustrated that your client has been less than forthcoming about what, exactly, was.going on in his building."

"I know nothing," Simkov insisted, his accent so thick Faith expected him at any moment to start talking about capturing Moose and Squirrel. He told the lawyer, "Get me out of here. Why am I a prisoner? I am soon a wealthy man."

Finney ignored his client, asking Amanda, "How long will this take?"

"Not long." Her smile indicated otherwise.

Finney wasn't fooled. "You've got ten minutes. Keep all your questions to the Anna Lindsey case." He advised Simkov, "Your cooperation now will reflect well during your civil suit."

Unsurprisingly, he was swayed by the prospect of money. "Yeah. Okay. What are your questions?"

"Tell me, Mr. Simkov," Amanda continued. "How long have you been in our country?"

Simkov glanced at his lawyer, who nodded that he should answer.

"Twenty-seven years."

"You speak English very well. Would you describe yourself as fluent, or should I get a translator here to make you more comfortable?"

"I am perfect with my English." His chest puffed out. "I read American books and newspapers all the time."

"You are from Czechoslovakia," Amanda said. "Is that correct?"

"I am Czech," he told her, probably because his country no longer existed. "Why do you ask me questions? I am suing you. *You* should be answering *my* questions."

"You have to be a United States citizen in order to sue the government."

Finney piped up, "Mr. Simkov is a legal resident."

"You took my green card," Simkov added. "It was in my wallet. I saw you see it."

"You certainly did." Amanda opened the folder, and Faith felt her heart leap. "Thank you for that. It saved me some time." She slipped on her glasses and read from a page in the folder. " 'Green Cards issued between 1979 and 1989, containing no expiration date, must be replaced within 120 days of this notice. Affected lawful permanent residents must file an Application to Replace Lawful Permanent Residence Card, form I-90, in order to replace their current green card or their permanent lawful resident status will be terminated.' " She put the page down. "Does that sound familiar to you, Mr. Simkov?"

Finney held out his hand. "Let me see that."

Amanda passed him the notice. "Mr. Simkov, I'm afraid Immigration and Naturalization Services has no record of you filing form I-90 to renew your legal status as a resident in this country."

"Bullshit," Simkov countered, but his eyes went nervously to his lawyer.

Amanda passed Finney another sheet of paper. "This is a photocopy of Mr. Simkov's green card. You'll note there's no expiration date. He's in violation of his terms of status. I'm afraid we'll have to turn him over to the INS." She smiled sweetly. "I also got a call from Homeland Security this morning. I had no idea Czech-made weapons were falling into the hands of terrorists. Mr. Simkov, I believe you were a metalworker before you came to America?"

"I was a farrier," he shot back. "I put shoes on horses."

"Still, you have a specialized knowledge of metal tooling."

Finney muttered a curse. "You people are unbelievable. You know that?"

Amanda was leaning back in her chair. "I don't recall from your commercials, Mr. Finney—do you have a subspecialty in immigration law?" She gave a cheery whistle, a pitch-perfect imitation of the jingle on Finney's television commercials.

"You think you're going to get away with a beat-down on a technicality? Look at this man." Finney pointed to his client, and Faith had to concede the lawyer's point. Simkov's nose was twisted to the side where the cartilage had been shattered. His right eye was so swollen the lid wouldn't open more than a slit. Even his ear was damaged; an angry row of stitches bisected the lobe where Will's fist had split the skin in two.

Finney said, "Your officer beat the shit out of him, and you think that's okay?" He didn't expect an answer. "Otik Simkov fled a communist regime and came to this country to start his life all over again from scratch. You think what you're doing to him now is what the Constitution is all about?"

Amanda had an answer for everything. "The Constitution is for innocent people."

Finney snapped his briefcase closed. "I'm calling a press conference."

"I'd be more than happy to tell them how Mr. Simkov made a whore suck him off before he'd let her go up to feed a dying six-month-old baby." She leaned over the table. "Tell me, Mr. Simkov: Did you give her a few extra minutes with the child if she swallowed?"

Finney took a second to regroup. "I'm not denying this man is an asshole, but even assholes have rights."

Amanda gave Simkov an icy smile. "Only if they're United States citizens."

"Unbelievable, Amanda." Finney seemed genuinely disgusted. "This is going to catch up with you one day. You know that, don't you?"

Amanda was having some kind of staring contest with Simkov, blocking out everything else in the room.

Finney turned his attention to Faith. "Are you all right with this, Officer? Are you okay with your partner beating up a witness?"

Faith wasn't at all okay with it, but now was not the time to equivocate. "It's Special Agent, actually. 'Officer' is generally what you call patrolmen."

"This is great. Atlanta's the new Guantánamo Bay." He turned back to Simkov. "Otik, don't let them push you around. You have rights."

Simkov was still staring at Amanda, as if he thought he could break her somehow. His eyes moved back and forth, reading her resistance. Finally, he gave a tight nod. "Okay. I drop my lawsuit. You make this other stuff go away."

Finney didn't want to hear it. "As your lawyer, I am advising you to—"

"You're not his lawyer anymore," Amanda interrupted. "Isn't that right, Mr. Simkov?"

"Correct," he agreed. He crossed his arms, staring straight ahead.

Finney muttered another curse. "This isn't over."

"I think it is," Amanda told him. She picked up the stack of pages detailing the suit against the city.

Finney cursed her again, adding Faith for good measure, then left the room.

Amanda tossed the lawsuit into the trashcan. Faith listened to the noise the pages made as they fluttered through the air. She was glad that Will was not here, because as much as Faith's conscience was bothering her over this, Will's was nearly killing him. Finney was right. Will was getting away with a beat-down thanks to a technicality. If Faith hadn't been in that hallway yesterday, she might be feeling differently right now.

She summoned the image of Balthazar Lindsey lying in the recycling bin a few feet from his mother's penthouse apartment and all that came to mind were excuses for Will's behavior.

"So," Amanda said. "Shall we assume there's honor among criminals, Mr. Simkov?"

Simkov nodded appreciatively. "You are a very hard woman."

Amanda seemed pleased with the assessment, and Faith could see how thrilled she was to be back in an interrogation room again. It probably bored her to death sitting through organizational meetings and looking at budgets and flowcharts all day. No wonder terrorizing Will was her only hobby.

She said, "Tell me about the scam you had going on in the apartments."

He gave an open-handed shrug. "These rich people are always traveling. Sometimes I rent out the space to someone. They go in. They do a little—" He made a screwing gesture with his hands. "Otik gets a little money. The maid's in the next day. Everyone is happy."

Amanda nodded, as if this was a perfectly understandable arrangement. "What happened with Anna Lindsey's place?"

"I figure, why not cash out? That asshole Mr. Regus in 9A, he knew something was up. He don't smoke. He come back from one of his business trips and there was a cigarette burn on his carpet. I saw it—barely there. No big deal. But Regus caused some problems."

"And they fired you."

"Two-week notice, good referral." He shrugged

again. "I already got another job lined up. Bunch of town houses over near the Phipps Plaza. Twenty-four-hour watch. Very classy place. Me and this other guy, we switch out. He takes days. I take the nights."

"When did you first notice Anna Lindsey was missing?"

"Always at seven o'clock, she comes down with the baby. Then one day she's not there. I check my message box where the tenants leave me things, mostly complaints—can't get a window open, can't figure out the television, stuff that's not my job, right? Anyway, there's a note from Ms. Lindsey saying she's on vacation for two weeks. I figure she must have left. Usually, they tell me where they go, but maybe she thinks since I won't be here when she's back, it don't matter."

That jibed with what Anna Lindsey said. Amanda asked, "Is that how she usually communicated with you, through notes?"

He nodded. "She don't like me. Says I'm sloppy." His lip curled in disgust. "Made the building buy me a uniform so I look like a monkey. Made me say 'yes, ma'am' and 'no, ma'am' to her like I'm a child."

That sounded like the kind of thing their victim profile trended toward.

Faith asked, "How did you know she was gone?"

"I don't see her come downstairs. Usually, she go to the gym, she go to the store, she take the baby for walks. Wants help getting the stroller in and out of the elevator." He shrugged. "I think, 'She must be gone.' "

Amanda said, "So you assumed Ms. Lindsey would be gone for two weeks, which coincided nicely with the date your employment would terminate."

"Easy peasy," he agreed.

"Who did you call?"

"This pimp. The dead guy." For the first time, Simkov seemed to lose a bit of his arrogance. "He's not so bad. They call him Freddy. I don't know his real name, but he was always honest with me. Not like some of the others. I tell him two hours, he stay two hours. He pay for the maid. That's it. Some of the other guys, they get a little pushy—try to negotiate, don't leave when they're supposed to. I push back. I don't call them when an apartment's available. Freddy, he film a music video up there once. I watch for it on the TV, but I don't see. Maybe he couldn't find an agent. Music is a hard business."

"The party at Anna Lindsey's got out of hand." Amanda stated the obvious.

"Yeah, out of hand," he agreed. "Freddy's a good guy. I don't go up there to check on them. Every time I'm in the elevator, someone say, 'Oh, Mr. Simkov, could you look at this in my apartment.' 'Could you water my plants?' 'Could you walk my dog?' Not my job, but they trap you like that, what can you say? 'Fuck off'? No, you can't. So I stay at my desk, tell them I can't do anything because my job is to watch the desk, not walk their puppy dogs. Right?"

Amanda said, "That apartment was a mess. It's hard to believe it got that bad in just a week."

He shrugged. "These people. They got no respect for nothing. They shit in the corner like dogs. Me, I'm not surprised. They're all fucking animals, do anything to get the drug in their arm."

"What about the baby?" Amanda asked.

"The whore—Lola. I thought she was going up there to do some business. Freddy was there. Lola got a soft spot for him. I didn't know he was dead. Or that they had trashed Ms. Lindsey's place. Obviously."

"How often was Lola going up there?"

"I don't keep up with it. Couple times a day. I figure she get a bump every now and then." He rubbed his hand under his nose, sniffing—the universal sign for snorting coke. "She not so bad. A good woman brought down by bad circumstance."

Simkov didn't seem to realize he was one of the bad circumstances. Faith asked, "Did you see anything unusual in the building over the last two weeks?"

He barely gave her a glance, asking Amanda, "Why is this girl asking me questions?"

Faith had been snubbed before, but she knew this guy needed to be on a short leash. "You want me to get my partner back in here to talk to you?"

He snorted, as if the thought of another beat-down was inconsequential, but he answered Faith's question. "What do you mean, unusual? It's Buckhead. Unusual is everywhere."

Anna Lindsey's penthouse had probably set her back three million dollars. The woman hardly lived in the ghetto. "Did you see any strangers loitering around?" Faith persisted.

He waved her off. "Strangers everywhere. This is a big city."

Faith thought about their killer. He had to have access to the building in order to Taser Anna and take her away from the apartment. Simkov obviously wasn't going to make this easy, so she tried to bluff him. "You know what I'm talking about, Otik. Don't bullshit me or I'll have my partner go back to work on your ugly face."

He shrugged again, but there was something different about the gesture. Faith waited him out, and he finally said, "I go for a smoke sometimes behind the building."

The fire escape that led to the roof was behind the building. "What did you see?"

"A car," he said. "Silver, four-door."

Faith tried to keep her reaction calm. Both the Coldfields and the family from Tennessee had seen a white sedan speeding away from the accident. It had been dusk. Maybe they had mistaken the silver car for white. "Did you get a license plate number?"

He shook his head. "I saw the ladder to the fire escape was unlatched. I went up to the roof."

"On the ladder?"

"Elevator. I can't climb that ladder. It's twenty-three floors. I got a bad knee."

"What did you see on the roof?"

"There was a soda can there. Someone used it for an ashtray. Lots of butts inside."

"Where was it?"

"On the ledge of the roof, right by the ladder."

"What did you do with it?"

"I kicked it off," he said, giving another one of his shrugs. "Watched it hit the ground. It exploded like—" He put his hands together, then flung them apart. "Pretty spectacular."

Faith had been behind that building, had searched it top to bottom. "We didn't find any cigarette butts or a soda can behind the building."

"That's what I'm saying. Next day, it was all gone. Someone cleaned it up."

"And the silver car?"

"Gone, too."

"You're sure you didn't see any suspicious men hanging around the building?"

He blew out a puff of air. "No, lady. I told you. Just the root beer."

"What root beer?"

"The soda can. It was Doc Peterson's Root Beer."

The same as they'd found in the basement of the house behind Olivia Tanner's.

CHAPTER TWENTY-TWO

As will drove to Jake Berman's house in Coweta County, he debated with himself the level of fury Faith would feel when she found out that he had tricked her. He wasn't sure which would make her angrier: the outright lie he had told her on the phone about Sam finding the wrong Jake Berman or the fact that Will was going down South to talk to the man on his own. There was no way she would've kept her doctor's appointment if Will had told her that the real Jake Berman was alive and well and living on Lester Drive. She would have insisted on coming along, and Will wouldn't have been able to come up with a good excuse for her not to, other than that she was pregnant and diabetic and had enough on her plate without having to put herself at risk by interviewing a witness who could very well be a suspect.

That would have gone over really well with Faith. Like a lead football over the Mississippi.

Will had gotten Caroline, Amanda's assistant, to cross-reference Jake Berman with the address on Lester Drive. With that key piece of information, they had opened up Berman's background fairly easily. The mortgage was in his wife's name, as were all of the credit cards, the cable bill and the utilities. Lydia Berman was a schoolteacher. Jake Berman had drawn his full lot of unemployment and still not found a job. He had declared bankruptcy eighteen months ago. He'd walked away from around half a million dollars in debt. The reason behind his being hard to find might have been as simple as a desire to elude creditors. Considering he'd been arrested a few months ago for public indecency, it made sense that Berman would want to keep a low profile.

Then again, it would also all make sense if Berman was their suspect.

The Porsche wasn't comfortable for long distances, and Will's back was aching by the time he reached Lester Drive. Traffic had been worse than usual, an overturned tractor-trailer jackknifed across the interstate bringing everything to a standstill for almost a full hour. Will hadn't wanted to be alone with his thoughts. He had listened to every station on the dial by the time he crossed into Coweta County.

Will pulled up beside an unmarked Chevy Caprice at the mouth of Lester Drive. A lawnmower was sticking out of the back of the trunk. The man behind the wheel was dressed in overalls, a thick gold chain hanging around his neck. Will recognized Nick Shelton, the regional field agent for District 23.

"How they hangin'?" Nick asked, turning down the bluegrass blaring from the radio. Will had met the agent a few times before. He was so country his neck glowed red, but he was a solid investigator, and he knew how to do his job.

Will asked, "Is Berman still in the house?"

"Unless he sneaked out the back," Nick answered. "Don't worry. He struck me as the lazy type."

"Did you talk to him?"

"Posed as a landscaper looking for work." Nick handed him a business card. "I told him it'd be a hundred bucks a month, and he said he could take care of his own damn lawn, thank you very much." He snorted a laugh. "This from a guy who's still in his pajamas at ten o'clock in the morning."

Will looked at the card, seeing a drawing of a lawn-mower and some flowers. He said, "Nice."

"The fake phone number comes in handy with the ladies." Nick chuckled again. "I got a good look at ol' Jakey while he was lecturing me on competitive pricing. He's definitely your guy."

"Did you get into the house?"

"He wasn't that stupid." Nick asked, "You want me to stick around?"

Will thought about the situation, the fact that if he had given her the chance, Faith would have been right: Don't go into an unknown situation without backup. "If you don't mind. Just hang back here and make sure I don't get my head blown off."

They both laughed a little louder than the words called for, probably because Will wasn't really joking.

He rolled up his window and drove down the road. Just to make things easier, Caroline had called Berman before Will had left the office. She had posed as an operator for the local cable television company. Berman had assured her he would be home to let in the technician who was doing a general upgrade so that their service wouldn't be interrupted. There were a lot of tricks you could use to make sure people were home. The cable ruse was the best. People would go without a lot of things, but they would put their lives on hold for days at a time in order to wait for the cable company to show up.

Will checked the numbers on the mailbox, making

sure they matched the note Sam Lawson had given Faith. Courtesy of MapQuest, which printed large arrows on their directions, and a couple of stops at some convenience stores, Will had managed to navigate his way through the rural town with only a few wrong turns.

Still, he checked the number with the mailbox a third time before getting out of the car. He saw the heart Sam had drawn around the address, and wondered again why a man who was not the father of Faith's child would do such a thing. Will had only met the reporter once, but he didn't like him. Victor was all right. Will had talked to him on the phone a couple of times and sat by him during an incredibly tedious awards ceremony that Amanda had insisted her team attend, mostly because she wanted to make sure someone clapped when her name was called. Victor had wanted to talk about sports, but not football and baseball, which were the only two sports Will paid attention to. Hockey was for Yankees and soccer was for Europeans. He wasn't quite sure how Victor had gotten interested in both, but it made for pretty dull conversation. Whatever Faith had seen in the guy, Will had been glad a few months ago when he started to notice that Victor's car wasn't in Faith's driveway when he went to pick her up for court days.

Of course, Will was not one to judge about relationships. His whole body was still sore from being with Angie last night. It was not a good sore—it was the kind of sore that made you want to crawl up into bed and sleep for a week. Will knew from experience it wouldn't matter, because as soon as he started putting one foot in front of the other, rebuilding some semblance of a life, Angie would return and he'd be back in that same place again. It was the pattern of his life. Nothing was ever going to change it.

The Berman home was a one-story ranch spread out over a large lot. The house looked lived-in, but not in a good way. The grass was overgrown and weeds tangled the flowerbeds. The green Camry in the driveway was filthy. Mud caked the tires and there was a sheen of filth on the car that looked like it had been there for quite a while. There were two baby seats in back and the requisite Cheerios stuck to the windshield. Two yellow, diamond-shaped signs were hanging from the side window, probably reading *Baby on Board*. Will pressed his hand to the hood of the car. The engine was cold. He looked at the time on his phone. It was coming up on ten o'clock. Faith would probably be at her doctor's by now.

Will knocked on the door and waited. He thought about Faith again, how furious she would be, especially if Will was about to come face-to-face with the killer. Though it looked as if he wasn't going to come face-to-face with anyone. No one answered the door. He knocked on the door again. When that didn't work, he stepped back from the house and looked up at the windows. All the shades were open. Some lights were on. Maybe Berman was in the shower. Or maybe he was fully aware that the police were trying to talk to him. Nick's hayseed landscaper act was pretty impressive, but he'd been sitting at the end of the road for about an hour. In a neighborhood this small, phones had probably been ringing off the hook.

Will tried the front door, but it was locked. He walked around the house, peering in the windows. There was a light at the end of the hallway. He was going to the next window when he heard a noise inside like a door slamming shut. Will put his hand to the gun on his belt, feeling all the hair on the back of his neck stand up. Something wasn't right, and Will was keenly aware that Nick Shelton was sitting in his car listening to the radio right now.

There was the unmistakable sound of a window banging shut. Will jogged around to the back of the house in time to see a man darting through the backyard. Jake Berman was wearing pajama pants with no shirt, but he'd managed to put on his sneakers. He glanced over his shoulder as he ran past an elaborate swing set, toward the chain-link fence that separated the property from the neighbor on the opposite side.

"Crap," Will mumbled, bolting after him. Will was a good runner, but Berman was fast—his arms pumping, legs moving in a blur.

"Police!" Will yelled, misjudging the height of the fence so badly that his foot caught. He fell to the ground and scrambled up as quickly as he could. He saw Berman go down a side yard, past another house and toward the street. Will did the same, taking advantage of the angle, shortening the distance as he chased Berman across the road.

There was a screech of wheels as Nick Shelton's Caprice pulled up. Berman dodged the car, slamming his hand on the hood as he made his way toward another backyard.

"Dammit," Will cursed. "Police! Stop!"

Berman kept going, but he was a sprinter, not a marathoner. If Will was good at anything, it was endurance. He caught his second wind as Jake Berman slowed, trying to open the wooden gate to a neighbor's backyard. He glanced over his shoulder, saw Will, then took off again. Berman was too winded, though, and Will could tell from the slow way his legs were moving that the man was about to give up. Still, Will wasn't going to take any chances. When he got close enough, he lunged, bringing Berman down in a heavy tackle that knocked the wind out of both of them.

"Dumbass!" Nick Shelton yelled, kicking Berman in the side.

Considering his run-in with the doorman at Anna's building yesterday, Will would've thought he'd be more gentle in his approach, but his heart was beating so hard in his chest that he felt nauseated. Worse, adrenaline was pumping all kinds of bad thoughts into his head.

Nick kicked Berman again. "Never run from the law, motherfucker."

"I didn't know you were cops—"

"Shut up." Will started to put the cuffs on him, but Berman squirmed, trying to get away. Nick raised his foot again, but Will drove his knee into Berman's back so hard that he could feel the ribs bend. "Stop it."

"I didn't do anything!"

"Is that why you ran?"

"I was going for a run," he screamed. "I always run this time of day."

Nick asked, "In your pj's?"

"Fuck off."

"It's a felony to lie to the police." Will stood, yanking up Berman with him. "Five years in prison. Plenty of men's bathrooms in jail."

Berman's face turned white. Some of his neighbors had congregated. They didn't look happy—or, Will noticed, particularly supportive.

"It's all right," Berman told them. "Just a misunder-standing."

Nick said, "A misunderstanding by this dumbass who thinks he can run away from the police."

Will wasn't worried about appearances. He jerked Berman's hands high, making him bend over as he walked him back across the street.

"My lawyer is going to hear about this."

Nick said, "Be sure to tell him how you ran away like a scared little schoolgirl."

Will pushed Berman into the road. He asked Nick, "Mind calling this in?"

"You want the cavalry?"

"I want a police car screeching up to his house with lights and sirens blaring so everyone in the neighbor-hood knows it's there."

Nick gave him a salute as he trotted off toward his car.

Berman said, "You're making a mistake."

"Your mistake was fleeing the scene of a crime."

"What?" He turned around, a look of genuine sur-prise on his face. "What crime?"

"Route 316."

He still looked confused. "That's what this is about?"

Either the man was delivering an Oscar-worthy performance or he was completely clueless. "You wit-nessed a car accident four days ago on 316. A woman was hit by a car. You talked to my partner."

"I didn't leave that girl alone. The ambulance was there. I told that cop at the hospital everything I saw."

"You gave a false phone number and address."

"I was just—" He glanced around, and Will won-dered if he was going to bolt again. "Get me out of here," Berman pleaded. "Just take me to the police station, okay? Take me to the station, give me my phone call, and we'll work all of this out."

Will turned him around, keeping a hand on his shoulder in case the man decided to try his luck again. Every step, Will could feel his temper getting more and more riled up. Berman was looking more and more like a pathetic, weaselly excuse for a human being. They had wasted the last two days looking for the asshole, and then the idiot had made Will chase him across half the neighborhood.

Berman turned around. "Why don't you take off these cuffs so I can—"

Will spun him back around so hard that he had to catch Berman before he fell flat on his face. The nearest neighbor was standing in her open front doorway, watching them. Like the other women, she didn't look exactly displeased to see the man being led away in handcuffs.

Will asked, "Do they hate you because you're gay? Or because you're sponging off your wife?"

Berman spun around again. "Where the fuck do you get off—"

Will pushed him back around so hard that this time he lost his balance. "It's ten o'clock and you're still in your pajamas." He marched Berman through the tall grass in his yard. "You don't have a lawnmower?"

"We can't afford a gardener."

"Where are your kids?"

"Day care." He tried to turn around again. "What business is this of yours?"

Will shoved him again, forcing him go up the driveway. He hated the guy for so many reasons, not least of which because he had a wife and kids who probably cared about him a great deal and he couldn't even cut the grass or wash the car for them.

Berman demanded, "Where are you taking me? I said take me to the police station."

Will kept quiet, shoving him up the driveway, yanking up his arms whenever he slowed or tried to turn around.

"If I'm under arrest, then you have to take me to jail."

They walked to the back of the house, Berman protesting the entire way. He was a man who was used to being listened to, and it seemed to irk him more to be ignored than to be pushed around, so Will kept silent as he shoved him toward the patio.

Will tried the back door, but it was locked. He looked at Berman, whose smug look seemed to indicate he thought he was getting the upper hand. The window the man had sneaked out had guillotined closed. He slid it back open, the cheap springs clanging.

Berman said, "Don't worry. I'll wait for you."

Will wondered where Nick Shelton was. He was probably in front of the house, thinking he was doing Will a favor by giving him time alone with the suspect.

"Right," Will muttered, loosening one side of the cuffs and clamping Berman to the barbecue grill. He lifted himself up and angled his body through the open window. Will found himself in the kitchen, which was decorated in a goose theme: geese on the wallpaper border, geese on the towels, geese on the carpet under the kitchen table.

He looked back out the window. Berman was there,

smoothing down his pajamas like he was trying them on at Macy's.

Will did a quick check of the house, finding only what he expected: a children's room with bunk beds, a large master and attached bath, a kitchen, a family room and a study with one book on the shelves. Will couldn't read the title, but he recognized Donald Trump's picture on the jacket and assumed it was a get-rich-quick scheme. Obviously, Jake Berman hadn't taken the man's advice. Though, considering Berman had lost his job and declared bankruptcy, maybe he had.

There was no basement, and the garage was empty but for three boxes that seemed to contain the contents of Jake Berman's old office: a stapler, a nice desk set, lots of papers with charts and graphs on them. Will opened the sliding glass door to the patio and found Berman sitting under the grill, his arm dangling over his head.

"You have no right to search my house."

"You were fleeing your residence. That's all the cause I needed."

Berman seemed to buy the explanation, which sounded reasonable even to Will's ears, though he knew it was highly illegal.

Will dragged around a chair from the table set and sat down. The air was still chilly, and the sweat he'd generated from chasing after Berman was drying in the cold.

"This isn't fair," Berman said. "I want your badge number and your name and—"

"You want the real one or you want me to make up something, like you did?"

Berman had the sense not to answer.

"Why did you run, Jake? Where were you going to go in your pajamas?"

"I didn't think that far," he grumbled. "I just don't want to deal with this right now. I've got a lot on my plate."

"You've got two choices here: Either you tell me what happened that night or I take you to jail in your pajamas." To make the threat clear, Will added, "And I don't mean the Coweta Country Club. I'll stroll you straight into the Atlanta Pen, and I won't let you change." He pointed to Berman's chest, which was heaving up and down from panic and anger. The man obviously spent time on his body. He was cut, his abs well defined, his shoulders broad and muscled. "You'll find all those pull-ups at the gym didn't go to waste."

"Is that what this is about? You're some kind of homophobic jerk?"

"I don't care who you're blowing in the toilet." This much was true, though Will kept an edge to his voice to imply the opposite. Everybody had a button, and Berman's was his sexual orientation. At the moment, Will's seemed to be that the cheating prick chained to the Grillmaster 2000 was screwing around on his wife and expecting her to just suck it up and be a good spouse. The *Oprah*-esque irony was not lost on Will.

He said, "The guys down at the pen love it when new meat comes along."

"Fuck you."

"Oh, they will. They'll fuck you in places you didn't know could be fucked."

"Go to hell."

Will let him sulk for a few seconds, trying to get his own emotions under control. He concentrated on how much time they had pissed away looking for this pathetic idiot when they could've been following real clues. Will listed it out for him. "Resisting arrest, lying to the police, wasting police time, obstructing an investigation. You could get ten years for this, Jake, and that's if the judge likes you, which is doubtful considering you've got a record and you present like an arrogant asshole."

Berman seemed to finally realize that he was in trouble. "I've got kids." There was a pleading sound to his voice. "My sons."

"Yeah, I read about them in your arrest report when they picked you up at the Mall of Georgia."

Berman looked down at the concrete patio. "What do you want?"

"I want the truth."

"I don't know what the truth is anymore."

He was obviously feeling sorry for himself again. Will wanted to kick him in the face, but he knew that would accomplish nothing. "You need to understand I'm not your therapist, Jake. I don't care about your crisis of conscience, or that you have kids or that you're cheating on your wife—"

"I love her!" he said, for the first time showing an emotion other than self-pity. "I love my wife."

Will pulled back on the pressure, trying to get his temper under control. He could be mad or he could get information. Only one of them was the reason he was here.

Berman said, "I used to be somebody. I used to have a job. I used to go to work every day." He looked up at the house. "I used to live somewhere nice. I drove a Mercedes."

"You were a builder?" Will asked, though he'd been

told as much when Caroline had found Berman's tax returns.

"High-rises," he said. "The bottom dropped out of the market. I was lucky to walk away with the clothes on my back."

"Is that why you put everything in your wife's name?"

He gave a slow nod. "I was ruined. We moved here from Montgomery a year ago. It was supposed to be a fresh start, but . . ." He shrugged, as if it was pointless to continue.

Will had thought his accent was a little deeper than most. "Is that where you're originally from—Alabama?"

"Met my wife there. Both of us went to Alabama." He meant the state university. "Lydia was an English major. It was more like a hobby until I lost my job. Now she's teaching at school and I'm with the kids all day." He stared out at the play set, the swings stirring in the wind. "I used to travel a lot," he said. "That's how I got it out of my system. I'd travel around, and I'd do what I needed to do, and then I'd come home and be with my wife and go to church, and that's how it worked for almost ten years."

"You were arrested six months ago."

"I told Lydia it was a mistake. All those queers from Atlanta trolling the mall, trying to pick up straight men. The cops were clamping down. They thought I was one because . . . I don't know what I told her. Because I had a nice haircut. She wanted to believe me, so she did."

Will guessed he'd be forgiven for his sympathies leaning more toward the spouse who was being lied to and cheated on. "Tell me what happened on 316."

"We saw the accident, people in the road. I should've been more helpful. The other man—I don't even know his name. He had medical training. He was trying to help the woman who'd been hit by the car. I was just standing there in the street trying to think of a lie to tell my wife. I don't think she'd believe me if it happened again, no matter what I came up with."

"How did you meet him?"

"I was supposed to be at the bar watching a game. I saw him go into the theater. He was a nice-looking guy, alone. I knew why he was there." He gave a heavy sigh. "I followed him into the bathroom. We decided to go somewhere else for more privacy."

Jake Berman was no neophyte, and Will didn't ask him why he had driven forty minutes away from his home in order to watch a game at a bar. Coweta might have been rural, but Will had passed at least three sports bars as he headed off the interstate, and there were even more downtown.

Will warned him, "You have to know that it was dangerous getting into a car with a stranger like that."

"I guess I've been lonely," the man admitted. "I wanted to be with somebody. You know, be myself with somebody. He said we could go in his car, maybe find a place out in the woods to be together for more than a few minutes in the toilet." He gave a harsh laugh. "The smell of urine is not a big aphrodisiac for me, be-lieve it or not." He looked Will in the eye. "Does it make you sick to hear about this?"

"No," Will answered truthfully. He had listened to countless witnesses tell stories of meaningless hookups and mindless sex. It really didn't matter if it was a man or a woman or both. The emotions were similar, and

Will's goal was always the same: get the information he needed to break the case.

Jake obviously knew Will wasn't going to give him much more rope. He said, "We were driving down the road, and the guy I was with—"

"Rick."

"Rick. Right." He looked as if he wished he didn't know the man's name. "Rick was driving. He had his pants unbuttoned." Jake colored again. "He pushed me away. He said there was something on the road ahead. He started to slow down, and I saw what looked like a bad accident." He paused, measuring his words, his culpability. "I told him to keep driving, but he said he was a paramedic, that he couldn't leave the scene of an accident. I guess that's some kind of code or something." He paused again, and Will guessed he was forcing himself to remember what had happened.

Will told him, "Take your time."

Jake nodded, giving it a few seconds. "Rick got out of the car, and I stayed inside. There was this old couple standing in the street. The man was clutching his chest. I kept sitting there in the car, just staring like it was all a movie being played out. The older woman got on the phone—I guess to call an ambulance. It was weird, because she kept her hand to her mouth, like this." He cupped his hand over his mouth the way Judith Cold-field did when she smiled. "It was like she was telling a secret, but there was no one around to hear, so . . ." He shrugged.

"Did you get out of the car?"

"Yeah," he answered. "I finally moved. I could hear the ambulance coming. I went to the old guy. I think his name was Henry?" Will nodded. "Yeah, Henry. He was in bad shape. I think both of them were in shock. Judith's hands were shaking like crazy. The other guy, Rick, he was working on the naked woman. I didn't see much of her. It was hard to see, you know? Hard to look at her, I mean. I remember when their son got there, he just stared at her, like, 'Oh, Jesus.' "

"Wait a minute," Will said. "Judith Coldfield's son was at the scene?"

"Yeah."

Will went back through his interview with the Coldfields, wondering why Tom would leave out such an important detail. There had been plenty of opportunity for the man to speak up, even with his domineering mother in the room. "What time did the son get there?"

"About five minutes before the ambulance."

Will felt ridiculous for repeating everything Berman said, but he had to be clear. "Tom Coldfield got to the scene before the ambulance arrived?"

"He was there before the cops. They didn't even show up until after the ambulances had left. No one was there. It was brutal. We had, like, twenty minutes with that girl just dying in the road, and no one came to help her."

Will felt a piece of the puzzle click into place—not the one they needed for the case, but the one that explained why Max Galloway had been so openly hostile about sharing information. The detective must have known that the ambulance had taken the victim away *before* the police arrived. Faith had been right all along. There was a reason Rockdale wasn't faxing over the initial responder's report, and that reason was because they were covering their asses. Slow police response times were the sort of thing local news stations built their feature stories on. This was the last straw as far as Will was concerned. He would have Galloway's detective shield by the end of the day. There was no telling what other evidence had been hidden or, worse, compromised.

"Hey," Berman said. "You wanna hear this or not?"

Will realized he had been too caught up in his own thoughts. He picked up the narrative. "So, Tom Coldfield showed up," he said. "Then the ambulances came?"

"Just one at first. They put the woman in first, the one who'd been hit by the car. Henry said he would wait because he wanted to go with his wife, and there wasn't room for all of them in one ambulance. There was kind of an argument about it, but Rick said, 'Go, just go,' because he knew the woman was in a bad way. He gave me the keys to his car and got into the ambulance so he could keep working on her."

"How long before the next ambulance arrived?"

"About ten, maybe fifteen minutes later."

Will did the math in his head. Almost forty-five minutes had elapsed in the story, and the police still hadn't shown up. "Then what?"

"They loaded up Henry and Judith. The son followed them, and I was left in the road."

"And the police still weren't there?"

"I heard the sirens right after the last ambulance left. The car was there—the one the Coldfields had been driving. The scene of the crime, right?" He looked back at the play set in the yard, as if he could visualize his children playing in the sun. "I thought about taking Rick's car back to the theater. They wouldn't know me, right? I mean, you wouldn't have any way of identifying me if I hadn't gone to the hospital and given my name."

Will shrugged, but it was true. If not for the fact that

Jake Berman had given them his real name, Will wouldn't be sitting here right now.

Jake continued, "So, I got in the car and headed back toward the theater."

"Toward the police cars?"

"They were coming in the opposite direction."

"What changed your mind?"

He shrugged, and tears came into his eyes. "I was tired of running, I guess. Running away from . . . everything." He put his free hand to his eyes. "Rick told me they were taking her to Grady, so I got on the interstate and went to Grady."

His courage had apparently run out shortly afterward, but Will did not point this out to the man.

Berman asked, "Is the old man okay?"

"He's fine."

"I heard on the news that the woman's all right."

"She's healing," Will told him. "What happened to her will always be with her, though. She won't be able to run away from it."

He wiped his eyes with the back of his hand. "Some kind of lesson for me, right?" His self-pity had returned. "Not that you care, right?"

"You know what I don't like about you?"

"Please enlighten me."

"You're cheating on your wife. I don't care who with—it's cheating. If you want to be with someone else, then be with them, but let your wife go. Let her have a life. Let her have someone who really loves her and understands her and wants to be with her."

The man shook his head sadly. "You don't understand."

Will guessed that Jake Berman was beyond lessons.

He stood from the table and uncuffed him from the grill. "Be careful about getting into cars with strangers."

"I'm finished with that. I mean it. Never again."

He sounded so certain of himself that Will almost believed him.

WILL HAD TO WAIT until he was out of Jake Berman's neighborhood before his phone registered enough bars to make a call. Even then, service was spotty, and he had to pull over onto the side of the road just to get a call to go through. He dialed Faith's cell phone and listened to it ring. Her voicemail picked up, and he ended the call. Will checked the clock. 10:15. She was probably still with her doctor in Snellville.

Tom Coldfield hadn't mentioned that he had been at the crime scene—yet another person who had lied to them. Will was getting pretty sick and tired of people lying. He flipped open his phone and dialed information. They connected him to the tower at Charlie Brown Airport, where yet another operator told Will that Tom was taking a cigarette break. Will was in the process of leaving a message when the operator offered to give him Coldfield's cell phone number. A few minutes later, he was listening to Tom Coldfield yell over the sound of a jet engine.

"I'm glad you called, Agent Trent." His voice was just shy of a shout. "I left a message for your partner earlier, but I haven't heard back."

Will put his finger in his ear, as if that might help drown out the noise of a plane taking off on the other side of town. "Did you remember something?"

"Oh, nothing like that," Tom said. The roar subsided, and his voice went back to normal. "My folks and I were talking last night, wondering how your investigation was going."

There was a deafening rush of jet engine. Will waited it out, thinking this was crazy. "What time do you get off work?"

"About ten minutes, then I've got to pick up the kids from my mom's."

Will figured he would kill two birds with one stone. "Can you meet me at your parents' house?"

Tom waited for more engine noise to pass. "Sure. Shouldn't take me more than forty-five minutes to get there. Is something wrong?"

Will looked at the clock on the dash. "I'll see you in forty-five minutes."

He ended the call before Tom could ask any more questions. Unfortunately, he also ended it before he could get the Coldfields' address. Their retirement community shouldn't be too hard to find. Clairmont Road stretched from one side of DeKalb County to the other, but there was only one area where senior citizens flocked, and that was in the vicinity of the Atlanta Veterans Administration hospital. Will put the car in gear, got back onto the road, and headed toward the interstate.

As Will drove, he debated about whether to call Amanda and tell her that Max Galloway had screwed them over again, but she would ask where Faith was, and Will did not want to remind their boss that Faith was having medical issues. Amanda hated weakness of any kind, and she was relentless where Will's disability was concerned. There was no telling what abuse she would visit on Faith for being diabetic. Will wasn't going to give her more ammunition.

He could, of course, call Caroline, who would in turn feed the information to Amanda. He cradled the phone in his hand, praying it would not come apart as he dialed in the number for Amanda's assistant.

Caroline made much use of her caller ID. "Hi, Will."

"Mind doing me another favor?"

"Sure."

"Judith Coldfield called 9-1-1 and two ambulances got to the scene before the Rockdale police did."

"That ain't right."

"No," Will agreed. It wasn't. The fact that Max Galloway had lied meant that instead of talking to a trained first responder about what he had recorded at the scene, Will was going to have to rely on the Coldfields to reconstruct what they had seen. "I need you to track down the timeline. I'm pretty sure Amanda's going to want to know what took them so long."

Caroline said, "You know Rockdale's where I'll call for the response times."

"Try Judith Coldfield's cell phone records." If Will could catch them in a lie, that would be yet another weapon Amanda could use against them. "Do you have her number?"

"Four-oh-four—"

"Hold on," Will said, thinking it would be useful to have Judith's number. He drove with his fingertips as he took out the digital recorder he kept in his pocket and turned it on. "Go ahead."

Caroline gave him Judith Coldfield's cell number. Will clicked off the recorder and put the phone back to his ear to thank her. He used to have a system for keeping up with witnesses' and suspects' personal information, but Faith had gradually taken over everything to do with paperwork, so that Will was lost without her. With the next case, he would have to correct that. He didn't like the idea of being so dependent on her—especially since she was pregnant. She'd probably be out at least a week when the baby came.

He tried Judith's cell, which only got him as far as her voicemail. He left a message for her, then called Faith again and told her that he was on his way to the Coldfields'. Hopefully, she would call him back and give him their address on Clairmont Road. He didn't want to call Caroline again because she would wonder why an agent didn't have all this written down somewhere. Besides, his cell phone had started making a clicking noise in his ear. He would have to do something to fix it soon. Will gently placed it on the passenger's seat. There was only one string and a quickly degrading piece of duct tape holding it together now.

Will kept the radio low as he headed into the city. Instead of going through the downtown connector, he jumped on I-85. Traffic on the Clairmont exit was backed up more than usual, so he took the long way, skirting around DeKalb Peachtree Airport, driving through neighborhoods that were so culturally diverse even Faith wouldn't be able to read some of the signs out in front of the businesses.

After fighting more traffic, he finally found himself in the right area. He turned into the first gated community across from the VA hospital, knowing the best way to go about this would be the methodical one. The guard at the gate was polite, but the Coldfields weren't on his residents' list. The next place yielded the same negative result, but when Will got to the third compound, the nicest one of them all, he hit pay dirt.

"Henry and Judith." The man at the gate smiled, as if they were old friends. "I think Hank's out on the links, but Judith should be home."

Will waited while the guard made a phone call to get him buzzed in. He looked around the well-kept grounds, feeling a pang of envy. Will didn't have children and he had no family to speak of. His retirement was something that worried him, and he had been saving a nest egg since his first paycheck. He wasn't a risk taker, so he hadn't lost much in the stock market. T-bills and municipal bonds were where most of his hard-earned cash went. He was terrified of ending up some lonely old guy in a sad, state-run nursing home. The Coldfields were living the sort of retirement Will was hoping for—a friendly security guard at the gate, nicely kept gardens, a senior center where you could play cards or shuffleboard.

Of course, knowing how things worked, Angie would get some terrible, wasting disease that lasted just long enough to suck away all his retirement money before she died.

"You're in, young man!" The guard was smiling, his straight white teeth showing beneath a bushy gray mustache. "Go left right out of the gate, then take another left, then right, and you'll be on Taylor Drive. They're 1693."

"Thanks," Will said, understanding only the street name and the numbers. The man had made a hand gesture indicating which way Will should go first, so he went through the gate and turned the car in that direction. After that, it was anyone's guess.

"Crap," Will mumbled, obeying the ten-mile-per-hour speed limit as he circled the large lake in the middle of the property. The houses were one-story cottages that all looked the same: weathered shingles, single-car garages and various assortments of concrete ducks and bunnies spotting the trimmed lawns.

There were old people out walking, and when they waved at him, he waved back, he supposed to convey the impression that he knew where he was going. Which was not the case. He stopped the car in front of an elderly woman who was dressed in a lilac wind suit. She had ski poles in her hands as if she were Nordic skiing.

"Good morning," Will said. "I'm looking for sixteen-ninety-three Taylor Drive."

"Oh, Henry and Judith!" the skier exclaimed. "Are you their son?"

He shook his head. "No, ma'am." He didn't want to alarm anyone, so he said, "I'm just a friend of theirs."

"This is a very nice car, isn't it?"

"Thank you, ma'am."

"I bet I couldn't get myself into there," she said. "Maybe even if I got in, I couldn't get out!"

He laughed with her to be polite, scratching this particular community off the list of places to which he'd want to retire.

She said, "Do you work with Judith at the homeless shelter?"

Will hadn't been questioned so much since he had trained for interrogations at the GBI academy. "Yes, ma'am," he lied.

"Got this at their little thrift store," she said, indicating the wind suit. "Looks brand-new, doesn't it?"

"It's lovely," Will assured her, though the color was nothing like what you would find in nature.

"Tell Judith I've got some more knickknacks I can give her if she wants to send the truck by." She gave a knowing look. "At my age, I find I don't need so many things."

"Yes, ma'am."

"Well." The woman nodded, pleased. "Just go up here to the right." He watched the way her hand curved. "Then Taylor Drive is on the left."

"Thank you." He put the car in gear, but she stopped him.

"You know, it would've been easier next time if, right when you left the gate, you took a left, then an immediate left, then—"

"Thank you," Will repeated, rolling the car along. His brain was going to explode if he talked to another person in this place. He kept the Porsche inching along, hoping he was going in the right direction. His phone rang, and he nearly wept with relief when he saw it was Faith.

Carefully, he opened the broken phone and held it to his ear. "How was your doctor's appointment?"

"Fine," she said. "Listen, I just talked to Tom Coldfield—"

"About meeting him? So did I."

"Jake Berman's going to have to wait."

Will felt his chest tighten. "I already talked to Jake Berman."

She was quiet—too quiet.

"Faith, I'm sorry. I just thought it would be better if I . . ." Will didn't know how to finish the sentence. His grip on his cell phone slipped, bringing a crackling static onto the line. He waited for it to die down, then repeated, "I'm sorry."

She took a painfully long time letting the ax fall. When she finally spoke, her tone was clipped, like her words were getting strangled in her throat. "I don't treat you differently because of your disability."

She was wrong, actually, but he knew this was not the time to point that out. "Berman told me that Tom Coldfield was at the crime scene." She wasn't yelling at him, so he continued, "I guess Judith called him because Henry was having a heart attack. Tom followed them to the hospital in his car. The cops didn't show up until everyone was already gone."

She seemed to be debating between screaming at him and being a cop. As usual, her cop side won out. "That's why Galloway was jerking us around. He was covering Rockdale County's ass." She moved on to the next problem. "And Tom Coldfield didn't tell us he was at the scene."

Will paused for some more static. "I know."

"He's early thirties, closer to my age. Pauline's brother was older, right?"

Will wanted to talk to her about this in person rather than through his cracked phone. "Where are you?"

"I'm right outside the Coldfields'."

"Good," he told her, surprised she had gotten there so fast. "I'm right around the corner. I'll be there in two minutes."

Will ended the call and dropped the phone on the seat beside him. Another wire had slipped out between the clamshells. This one was red, which was not a good sign. He glanced at his rearview mirror. The skier was making her way toward him. She was coming up fast, and Will pushed the car up to fifteen miles per hour so he could get away from her.

The street signs were larger than normal, the letters a crisp white on black, which was a horrible combination for Will. He turned as soon as he could, not bothering to try to read the first letter on the sign. Faith's Mini would stand out like a beacon among the Cadillacs and Buicks the retired folks seemed to favor.

Will got to the end of the street, but there was no Mini. He turned down the next street, and nearly smacked into the skier. She made a motion with her hand, indicating he should roll down the window.

He put on a pleasant smile. "Yes, ma'am?"

"Right there," she said, pointing to the cottage on the corner. This particular model had a lawn jockey outside, its white face freshly painted. Two large cardboard boxes were by the mailbox, each labeled in black marker. "I guess you're not taking those back in this tiny car of yours."

"No, ma'am."

"Judith said her son was going to bring the truck later on today." She glanced up at the sky. "Better not be too late."

"I'm sure it won't be long," Will told the skier. She didn't seem as keen to continue the conversation this time. She tossed him a wave as she continued her walk down the street.

Will looked at the boxes in front of Judith and Henry Coldfield's house, reminded of the trash Jacquelyn Zabel had set outside her mother's place. Though the cardboard boxes and black trash bags Jackie had put on the curb weren't meant to be trash. Charlie Reed had said he'd shooed off a Goodwill truck just before Will and Faith had arrived. Had he meant Goodwill specifically, or was he using the word as a catchall, the way people always called plastic bandages Band-Aids and tissues Kleenexes?

All along, they had been looking for a physical link between the women, one thing that tied them all together. Had Will just stumbled onto it?

The front door to the house opened and Judith came out, walking cautiously as she tried to navigate her way down the two porch stairs with a large box in her hands. Will got out of the car and rushed over, catching the box before she dropped it.

"Thank you," she told him. She was out of breath, her cheeks flushed. "I've been trying to get this stuff out all morning and Henry's been no help whatsoever." She walked toward the curb. "Just put it here by the others. Tom's supposed to be by later to pick them up."

Will set the box down on the ground. "How long have you volunteered at the shelter?"

"Oh . . ." She seemed to think about it as she walked back toward the house. "I don't know. Since we moved here. I guess that's a couple of years now. Goodness, how time flies."

"Faith and I saw a brochure the other day when we were at the shelter. It had a list of corporate sponsors on it."

"They want to get their money's worth. They're not being charitable because it's the right thing to do. It's public relations for them."

"There was a logo for a bank on the one we saw." Even now, he recalled the image of the four-point deer at the bottom of the pamphlet.

"Oh, yes. Buckhead Holdings. They donate the most

money, which, between you and me, isn't nearly enough."

Will felt a bead of sweat roll down his back. Olivia Tanner was the community relations director for Buckhead Holdings. "What about a law firm?" he asked. "Does anyone do pro bono work for the shelter?"

Judith opened the front door. "There are a couple of firms who help out. We're a women's-only shelter, you know. Lots of the women need help filing divorce papers, getting restraining orders. Some of them are in trouble with the law. It's all very sad."

"Bandle and Brinks?" Will asked, giving her the name of Anna Lindsey's law firm.

"Yes," Judith said, smiling. "They help out quite a lot."

"Do you know a woman named Anna Lindsey?"

She shook her head as she went into the house. "Was she staying in the shelter? I'm ashamed to say there are so many that I often don't have the time to speak to them individually."

Will followed her inside, glancing around. The layout was exactly as he would have guessed from the street. There was a large living room that looked onto a screen porch and the lake. The kitchen was on the side of the house that had the garage, and the other side held the bedrooms. All the doors leading off the hallway were closed. The startling thing was that it looked as if an Easter egg had exploded inside the house. Decorations were everywhere. There were bunnies in pastel suits sitting on every available surface. Baskets with plastic eggs lying in silky green grass were scattered along the floor.

Will said, "Easter."

Judith beamed. "It's my second-favorite time of the year."

Will loosened his tie, feeling a sweat come all over him. "Why is that?"

"The Resurrection. The rebirth of our Lord. The cleansing of all our sins. Forgiveness is a powerful, transformative gift. I see that at the shelter every day. Those poor, broken women. They want redemption. They don't realize it's not something that can just be given. Forgiveness has to be earned."

"Do they all earn it?"

"Considering your job, I think you know the answer to that better than I do."

"Some women aren't worthy?"

She stopped smiling. "People like to think that we've moved on from biblical times, but we still live in a society where women are cast out, don't we?"

"Like trash?"

"That's a bit harsh, but we all make our choices."

Will felt more beads of sweat roll down his back. "Have you always loved Easter?"

She straightened a bow tie on one of the rabbits. "I suppose part of it's because Henry's work only gave him off Easter and Christmas. It was always such a special time for us. Don't you love being with family?"

He asked, "Is Henry home?"

"Not at the moment." She turned her watch around on her wrist. "He's always late. He loses track of time so easily. We were supposed to go to the community center after Tom picked up the kids."

"Does Henry work at the shelter?"

"Oh, no." She gave a small laugh as she walked into her kitchen. "Henry's much too busy enjoying his retirement. Tom's good about helping out, though. He complains, but he's a good boy."

Will remembered Tom had been trying to fix a lawnmower when they'd found him at the charity shop. "Does he mostly work in the store?"

"Lord, no, he hates working in the store."

"So, what does he do?"

She picked up a sponge and wiped the counter. "A little bit of everything."

"Like what?"

She stopped wiping. "If a woman needs legal help, he tracks down one of the lawyers, or if one of the kids makes a spill, he grabs a mop." She smiled proudly. "I told you, he's a good boy."

"Sounds like it," Will agreed. "What else does he do?"

"Oh, this and that." She paused, thinking it through. "He coordinates the donations. He's very good on the phone. If it sounds like he's talking to someone who might give a bit more, he'll drive the truck over to pick up their stuff, and nine times out of ten, he comes back with a nice check in addition. I think he likes getting out and talking to people. All he does at the airport is stare at blips on a screen all day. Would you like some iced water? Lemonade?"

"No, thank you," he answered. "What about Jacquelyn Zabel? Have you heard her name before?"

"That strikes a bell, but I'm not sure why. It's a very unusual name."

"How about Pauline McGhee? Or maybe Pauline Seward?"

She smiled, putting her hand over her mouth. "No."

Will forced himself to slow things down. The first rule of interviewing was to be calm, because it was hard to spot whether or not someone else was tense when you were tense yourself. Judith had gone still when he'd asked the last question, so he repeated it. "Pauline McGhee or Pauline Seward?"

She shook her head. "No."

"How often does Tom pick up donations?"

Judith's voice took on a falsely cheerful tone. "You know, I'm not sure. I've got my calendar in here somewhere. I usually mark the dates." She opened one of the kitchen drawers and started to rummage around. She was visibly nervous, and he knew she had opened the drawer to give herself something to do other than look him in the eye. She chattered on, telling Will, "Tom is so good about giving his time. He's very involved in the youth group at his church. The whole family volunteers at the soup kitchen once a month."

Will didn't let her get sidetracked. "Does he go out alone to pick up donations?"

"Unless there's a couch or something large." She closed the drawer and opened another. "I have no idea where my calendar is. All those years I wanted my husband home with me, and now he drives me crazy putting things up where they don't belong."

Will glanced out the front window, wondering what was keeping Faith. "The children are here?"

She opened another drawer. "Napping in the back."

"Tom said he would meet me here. Why didn't he tell us he was at the crime scene where your car hit Anna Lindsey?"

"What?" She looked momentarily confused, but told him, "Well, I called Tom to come see Henry. I thought he was having a heart attack, that Tom would want to be there, that—"

"But Tom didn't tell us he was there," Will repeated. "And neither did you."

"It didn't . . ." She waved her hand, dismissing it. "He wanted to be with his father."

"These women who were abducted were cautious women. They wouldn't open the door to just anybody. It would have to have been someone they trusted. Somebody they knew was coming."

She stopped looking for the calendar. Her face showed her thoughts as clear as a picture: She knew something was horribly wrong.

Will asked, "Where is your son, Mrs. Coldfield?"

Tears welled into her eyes. "Why are you asking all these questions about Tom?"

"He was supposed to meet me here."

Her voice was almost a whisper. "He said he had to go home. I don't understand. . . ."

Will realized something then—something Faith had said on the phone. She'd already talked to Tom Coldfield. The reason she wasn't here yet was because Tom had sent her to the wrong house.

Will made his voice deadly serious. "Mrs. Coldfield, I need to know where Tom is right now."

She put her hand to her mouth, tears spilling from her eyes.

There was a phone on the wall. Will snatched the receiver off the hook. He dialed in Faith's cell phone number, but his finger didn't make it to the last digit. There was a searing pain in his back, the worst muscle spasm he'd ever had in his life. Will put his hand to his shoulder, his fingers feeling for a knot, but all he felt was cold, sharp metal. He looked down to find the bloody tip of what had to be a very large knife sticking out of his chest.

CHAPTER TWENTY-THREE

Faith sat outside thomas coldfield's house, her cell phone to her ear as she listened to Will's cell ring. He'd said he was two minutes away, but it was looking more like ten. The call went to voicemail. Will was probably lost, driving around in circles, looking for her car because he was too pigheaded to ask for help. If she was in a better mood, she'd go out and look for him, but she was scared of what she'd say to her partner if she had him alone.

Every time she thought about Will lying to her, going to talk to Jake Berman behind her back, she had to squeeze the steering wheel to keep from punching a hole into the dashboard of the car. They couldn't go on like this—not with Faith being a liability. If he thought she couldn't handle herself in the field, then there was no reason for them to be together anymore. She could put up with a lot of Will's crazy shit, but she had to have his trust or this would never work out. It wasn't as if Will didn't have his own liabilities. For instance, not knowing the difference between something as freaking simple as left and right.

Faith checked the time again. She would give Will another five minutes before going into the house.

The doctor hadn't given her good news, though Faith had foolishly been expecting it. From the minute she'd made the appointment with Delia Wallace, her health had improved dramatically. She hadn't woken up in a cold sweat this morning. Her blood sugar was high, but not off the chart. Her mind felt sharp, focused. And then Delia Wallace had sent it all crashing down.

Sara had ordered some kind of test at the hospital that showed Faith's blood sugar pattern over the last few weeks. The results had not been good. Faith was going to have to meet with a dietitian. Dr. Wallace had told her she was going to have to plan out every meal, every snack and every single moment of her life until she died—which she might do prematurely anyway, because her blood sugar was fluctuating so wildly that Dr. Wallace had told Faith the best thing she could do was take a couple of weeks off from work and focus on educating herself about the care and maintenance of a diabetic.

She loved when doctors said things like that, as if taking two weeks off from work was something that could be achieved with the snap of a finger. Maybe Faith could go to Hawaii or Fiji. She could call up Oprah Winfrey and ask for the name of her personal chef.

Fortunately, there was some good news with the bad. Faith had seen her baby. Well, not really *seen* it—the child was little more than a speck right now—but she had listened to his heartbeat, watched the ultrasound and seen the gentle up and down of the tiny blob inside her, and even though Delia Wallace had insisted that it wasn't quite time for such things, Faith would have sworn that she saw a tiny little hand.

Faith dialed in Will's cell phone number again. It rang over into voicemail almost immediately. She wondered if his phone had finally given up the ghost. Why he would not get a new one was beyond her. Maybe there was some sort of emotional attachment he had to the thing.

Either way, he was holding her up. She opened the door and got out of the car. Tom Coldfield lived only ten minutes from where his parents had met with their unfortunate accident. His house was in the middle of nowhere, the closest neighbor barely within walking distance. The home itself had that boxlike feel of modern suburban architecture. Faith preferred her own ranch house, with its sloping floorboards and hideous fake paneling in the family room.

Every year when she got her tax rebate, she told herself she was going to have something done to the paneling, and every year Jeremy magically managed to need something around the same time as the check came in. Once, she thought she was going to get away clean, but the little scamp had broken his arm while trying to prove to his friends that he could jump his skateboard off the roof of the house and onto a mattress they had found in the woods.

She put her hand to her stomach. That paneling was going to be up until she died.

Faith fished in her purse for her ID as she walked to the front door. She was wearing heels and one of her nicest dresses, because for some reason this morning it had seemed important to look respectable in front of Delia Wallace—a silly affectation, since Faith had spent their entire time together in a thin paper gown.

She turned around, looking out into the empty street. Still no sign of her partner. She didn't understand what was taking him so long. Tom had told Faith on the phone that he'd already given Will directions to his house. Even taking into account the left/right thing, Will was good at finding his way. He should be here by now. Regardless, he should definitely be answering his phone. Maybe Angie had called again. The way Faith was feeling toward Will right now, she hoped his wife was being every bit her pleasant self.

Faith rang the doorbell and waited much too long for the door to be answered, considering she had been parked in the driveway for nearly a quarter of an hour.

"Hi." The woman who came to the door was thin and angular, but not pretty by any stretch. She gave Faith an awkward, forced smile. Her blonde hair was lank across her forehead, the dark roots growing in. She had that run-down look you get when you have small children.

"I'm Special Agent Faith Mitchell," Faith said, holding up her badge.

"Darla Coldfield." The woman's voice was one of those breathy whispers that implied delicacy. She picked at the collar of the purple blouse she was wearing. Faith could see the edge was worn, threads sticking up where she had picked open the seam.

"Tom said he'd meet me here."

"He should be home any second." The woman seemed to realize she was blocking the doorway. She stepped aside. "Won't you come in?"

Faith walked into the foyer, which was lined with black and white tile. She saw that the tile went all the way through to the back of the house, into the kitchen and family room. Even the dining room and study on either side of the front door were tiled.

Still, she made the perfunctory noise about the woman having a lovely home, her own footsteps echoing in her ears as they made their way to the family room. The furnishings were more masculine than Faith would have guessed. There was a brown leather couch and matching recliner. The rug on the floor was black with not a speck of dirt or fuzz showing. There were no toys, which was odd considering the Coldfields had two children. Maybe they weren't allowed in the room. She wondered where they spent their time. The part of the house she had seen was hot and uncomfortable even though it was cool outside. Faith felt her skin on the edge of breaking into a sweat. Sun was streaming through the windows, yet every light in the place was on.

Darla asked, "Would you like some tea?"

Faith was looking at her watch again, wondering about Will. "Sure."

"Sweet? Unsweet?"

Faith's answer was not as automatic as it should have been. "Unsweet. Have you lived here long?"

"Eight years."

The place looked about as lived-in as a vacant warehouse. "You have two kids?"

"A boy and a girl." She smiled uncertainly. "Do you have a partner?"

The question seemed strange, given the conversation. "I have a son."

She smiled, putting her hand to her mouth. She had probably picked up the gesture from her mother-in-law. "No, I meant someone you work with."

"Yes." Faith looked at the family photos on the mantel. They were taken from the same series as the one Judith Coldfield had shown them at the shelter. "Maybe you could call Tom and see what's keeping him?"

Her smile faltered. "Oh, no. I wouldn't want to bother him."

"It's police business, so I really *do* need you to bother him."

Darla pressed her lips together. Faith couldn't read her expression. She was almost completely blank. "My husband doesn't like to be rushed."

"And I don't like to be kept waiting."

Darla gave her that same weak smile from before. "I'll go get that tea for you."

She started to leave, but Faith asked, "Do you mind if I use your bathroom?"

Darla turned again, her hands clasped in front of her chest. Her face was still blank. "Down the hall, on the right."

"Thank you." Faith followed her directions, her heels clicking like a drum major's on the tile as she walked past a pantry and what must have been the door to the basement. She was getting a creepy feeling off of Darla Coldfield, but she couldn't quite figure out why. Maybe it was Faith's instinctive hatred of women who constantly deferred to their husbands.

Inside the bathroom, she went straight to the sink, where she splashed cold water on her face. The lights were just as intense in the powder room, and Faith flipped down the switches, but nothing happened. She flipped them back up and then back down again. Still the lights stayed on. She looked up. The bulbs were probably a hundred watts each.

Faith blinked her eyes several times, thinking that looking directly into a burning lightbulb was probably not the smartest thing she had ever done. She grabbed the doorknob to the linen closet to keep herself steady as she waited for the feeling to pass. Maybe she would wait in here for Will instead of sitting on the sofa drinking tea with Darla Coldfield, straining to make small talk. The bathroom was nice if sparsely furnished. The room was L-shaped, with a linen closet filling in the void between the top and bottom of the L. Faith guessed the laundry room was on the other side of the wall. She could hear the gentle rumble of a clothes dryer through the partition.

Because Faith was a nosy person, she opened the closet door. There was a slow squeak from the hinges, and she stood there waiting for Darla Coldfield to come in and chastise her for being rude. When this did not happen, Faith looked inside. The space was deeper than she would've guessed, but the shelves were narrow—stacked with towels that were neatly folded and a set of sheets with race cars on them that probably belonged to the children.

Where were the children? Maybe they were outside playing. Faith closed the closet door and looked out the small window. The backyard was empty—not even a swing set or tree house. Maybe the kids were taking naps in preparation for Grandma and Grandpa's visit. Faith had never let Jeremy sleep before her parents came to visit. She'd wanted her mother and father to run him ragged so that he was tired enough to sleep in the next morning.

She groaned out a long sigh as she sat on the toilet beside the sink. She was still feeling light-headed, probably from the heat. Or maybe from her blood sugar. She had been on the high side at the doctor's office.

She put her purse on her lap and dug around for her monitor. There had been a huge display for different blood glucose monitors on the wall in the doctor's office. Most of them were either cheap or free, because the real money came from the specialized strips they all used. Each manufacturer had a different one, so once you chose a monitor, you were locked in forever. Unless you dropped it on the bathroom floor and broke it.

"Shit," Faith mumbled, leaning down to pick up the monitor, which had slipped out of her hand and skittered over by the wall. She heard a faint, sonorous noise coming from the machine.

Faith picked up the monitor, wondering what damage she had done. The readout on the machine was still at zero, waiting for a strip. She shook the device, holding it to her ear and listening for the sound again. She leaned down, trying to duplicate the motion that had caused the monitor to make the noise. The sound repeated, more like the kind of thing you would hear on a playground this time—loud and frenzied.

And not coming from the monitor.

Could it be a cat? Some animal caught in the heating ducts? One Christmas, Jeremy's gerbil had been killed in the dryer, and Faith had sold the machine to a neighbor rather than deal with the carnage. But whatever this thing was, it was alive, and obviously intended to stay that way. She leaned down a third time, hovering near the heating grate at the base of the toilet.

The noise was clearer this time, but still muffled. Faith got down on her knees, pressing her ear to the grate. She thought of all the animals that could make that sort of noise. It sounded almost like words.

Help.

It wasn't an animal. It was a woman calling for help.

Faith's hand went into her purse, pulling out the velvet bag where she kept her Glock when she wasn't wearing it on her hip. Her hands were sweating.

There was a sudden, loud knock on the door: Darla. "Are you okay in there, Agent Mitchell?"

"I'm fine," Faith lied, trying to keep her voice normal. She found her cell phone, tried to ignore that her hands had started shaking. "Is Tom here yet?"

"Yes." The woman went silent. Just that one word hanging in the air.

"Darla?" There was no answer. "Darla, my partner is on the way. He's going to be here any minute." Faith's heart was pounding so hard that her chest hurt. "Darla?"

There was another bang on the door, but this one was sharper. Faith dropped the phone and held the gun with both hands, ready to fire at whoever came into the bathroom. The Glock did not have a conventional safety. The only way it could be fired was if you pulled the trigger all the way back. Faith aimed at the center of the doorway, bracing herself to yank back the trigger as hard as she could.

Nothing. No one came through the door. The knob was not turning. Quickly, she glanced down, looking for her cell phone. It was behind the toilet. She kept her gun trained on the door while she reached down for the phone, snatching it up.

The door stayed closed.

Faith's hands were sweating so badly that her fingers couldn't stay on the buttons. She hissed a curse as she dialed in the number wrong. She was trying again when she heard the closet door squeak open behind her.

She spun around, her gun pointing straight at Darla's chest. Faith took in everything at once—the false door in the closet wall, the washing machine on the other side, the Taser in Darla's hands.

Faith lurched to the side, not bothering to aim as she pulled back on the trigger. The Taser hooks sailed past her, the thin metal wires shimmering in the bright light as the hooks bounced off the wall.

Darla stood there, the spent Taser in her hands. A chunk of sheetrock had been taken out over her left shoulder.

"Don't move," Faith warned, keeping the gun trained on Darla's chest as she fumbled for the doorknob. "I mean it. Don't move."

"I'm sorry," the woman whispered.

"Where's Tom?" When she didn't answer, Faith screamed, "Where the fuck is Tom?"

Darla would only shake her head.

Faith threw open the door, still pointing the gun at Darla as she backed out of the room.

"I'm so sorry," the woman repeated.

Two strong arms wrapped around Faith from behind—a man, his body hard, his strength palpable. It had to be Tom. He lifted her off the floor and, without thinking, Faith pulled the trigger again, firing the Glock into the ceiling. Darla was still standing in the closet, and Faith pulled the trigger with purpose this time, wanting to put a bullet in the woman that could be traced back to her gun. The Glock missed, and Darla ducked away, shutting the false door behind her.

Faith fired again and again as Tom backed her out into the hallway. His hand clamped around Faith's wrist like a vise, the pain so sharp that she was sure her bones had snapped. She held on to the gun as long as she could, but she was no match for his strength. Dropping the weapon, she started kicking with all her might, reaching out to grab anything she could find—the edge of the door, the wall, the knob on the basement door. Every muscle in her body screamed from pain.

"Fight," Tom grunted, his lips so close to Faith's ear that she felt like he was inside of her head. She could feel his body responding to the struggle, the pleasure he was deriving from her fear.

Faith felt a surge of fury tighten her resolve. Anna Lindsey. Jacquelyn Zabel. Pauline McGhee. Olivia Tanner. She would not be another one of his victims. She would not end up at the morgue. She would not abandon her son. She would not lose her baby.

She twisted around and scratched Tom's face, digging her fingernails into his eyes. She used every part of her body—her hands, her feet, her teeth—to fight him. She would not give in. She would kill him with her bare hands if she had to.

"Let me out of here!" someone screamed from the basement. The noise was a surprise. For a split second, Faith stopped struggling. Tom stopped, too. The door shook. "Let me the fuck out!"

Faith came to her senses. She started kicking again, flailing, doing everything she could to free herself. Tom held on, his powerful arms like a clamp around her body. Whoever was behind the basement door was beating it, trying to break it down. Faith opened up her mouth and screamed as loud as she could. "Help! Help me!"

"Do it!" Tom yelled.

Darla stood at the end of the hallway, the reloaded Taser in her hands. Faith saw her Glock at the woman's feet.

"Do it!" Tom demanded, his voice barely audible over the banging behind the door. "Shoot her!"

All Faith could think about was the child inside her, those tiny fingers, that delicate heartbeat pressing up and down against her baby's tissue-thin chest. She went completely limp, relaxing every muscle in her body. Tom hadn't been expecting her to give in, and he stumbled as he took on her full weight. They both dropped to the floor. Faith scrambled across the tile, reaching for the gun, but he yanked her back like a fish on a line.

The door splintered open, shards of wood flying. A woman ran out, half-fell into the hallway, screaming obscenities. Her hands were at her waist, her feet chained, but she moved with almost laser precision as she slammed her body into Tom's.

Faith took advantage of the distraction and grabbed the Glock, twisting around, aiming at the bodies thrashing on the floor.

"Fucker!" Pauline McGhee screeched. She was kneeling on Tom's chest, leaning over him. Her hands were cuffed tight to a belt around her waist, but she had managed to wrap her fingers around his neck. "Die!" she screamed, blood spraying from her torn mouth. Her lips were shredded, her eyes wild. She was forcing all of her weight into Tom's neck.

"Stop," Faith managed, her breath rasping between her lips. She felt a deep, searing pain in her belly, like something had torn. Still, she kept her gun trained at Pauline's chest. There was at least half a magazine left in the Glock; she would use it if she had to. "Get off him," Faith ordered.

Tom bucked, hands clawing at Pauline. Pauline

pressed harder, pivoting on her knees, putting her full weight into his neck.

"Kill him," Darla begged. She was curled into a ball by the bathroom door, the Taser on the floor beside her. "Please . . . kill him."

"Stop," Faith warned Pauline, willing her hand not to shake as she gripped the gun.

"Let her do it," Darla pleaded. "Please, let her do it."

Faith groaned as she staggered to her feet. She put the gun to Pauline's head, made her voice as steady and strong as possible. "Stop right now or I will pull this fucking trigger, so help me God."

Pauline looked up. Their eyes locked, and Faith willed every ounce of resolve into her face, even though all she wanted to do was fall to her knees and pray that the life inside of her was going to continue.

"Let him go right now," Faith demanded.

Pauline took her time obeying the order, as if she hoped that one more second of pressure would do the trick. She sat back on the floor, her hands still clenched. Tom rolled over, coughing so hard that his entire body spasmed from the effort.

"Call an ambulance," Faith said, though no one seemed to be moving. Her mind raced. Her vision kept blurring. She had to call Amanda. She had to find Will. Where was he? Why wasn't he here?

"What's wrong with you?" Pauline asked, giving Faith a nasty look.

Faith's head was spinning. She sagged against the wall, trying not to pass out. She felt something wet between her legs. There was another twinge in her belly, almost like a contraction. "Call an ambulance," she repeated.

"Trash . . ." Tom Coldfield muttered. "You're all nothing but trash."

"Shut up," Pauline hissed.

Tom rasped, " 'Put now this woman out from me . . . and bolt the door after her . . .' "

"Shut up," Pauline repeated through clenched teeth.

A guttural sound came from Tom's throat. He was laughing. " 'O, Absalom, I am risen.' "

Pauline struggled to get to her knees. "You're going straight to hell, you sick bastard."

"Don't," Faith warned, raising the gun again. "Get a phone." She glanced over her shoulder at Darla. "Get my phone out of the bathroom."

Faith snapped her head around as Pauline leaned over Tom.

"Don't," Faith repeated.

Pauline smiled a grotesque jack-o'-lantern sneer down at Tom Coldfield. Instead of wrapping her hands around his throat again, she spit in his face. "Georgia's a death penalty state, motherfucker. Why else do you think I moved here?"

"Wait," Faith said, bewildered. "You know him?"

Raw hatred flashed in the woman's eyes. "Of course I know him, you stupid bitch. He's my brother."

CHAPTER TWENTY-FOUR

WILL LAY ON HIS SIDE ON JUDITH COLDFIELD'S kitchen floor, watching Judith sob into her hands. His nose was itching, which was a funny thing to bother him, considering the fact that he had a kitchen knife sticking out of his back. At least he thought it was a kitchen knife. Every time he tried to turn his head to look, the pain got so bad that he felt himself start to pass out.

He wasn't bleeding badly. The real threat came from the knife moving, shifting away from whatever vessel or artery it was damming and causing the blood to start flowing in earnest. Just thinking about the mechanics of the thing, the metal blade pressing between muscle and sinew, made his head swim. Sweat drenched his body, and he was starting to get chills. Oddly, holding up his neck was the hardest part. The muscles were so tense that his head throbbed with every heartbeat. If he let go for even a second, the pain in his shoulder brought the taste of vomit into his mouth. Will had never realized how many parts of his body were connected to his shoulder.

"He's a good boy," Judith told Will, her voice muffled by her hands. "You don't know how good he is."

"Tell me. Tell me why you think he's good."

The request startled her. She finally looked up at

him, seemed to realize he was in danger of eventually dying. "Are you in pain?"

"I'm hurting pretty badly," he admitted. "I need to call my partner. I need to know if she's okay."

"Tom would never hurt her."

The fact that she felt compelled to make that statement sent an icy dread through Will. Faith was a good cop. She could take care of herself, except the times when she couldn't. She had passed out a few days ago—just dropped to the pavement in the parking garage at the courthouse. What if she passed out again? What if she passed out and when she finally came to, she opened her eyes to see another cave, another torture chamber excavated by Tom Coldfield?

Judith wiped her eyes with the back of her hand. "I don't know what to do. . . ."

Will didn't think she was looking for suggestions. "Pauline Seward left Ann Arbor, Michigan, twenty years ago. She was seventeen years old."

Judith looked away.

He took a calculated guess. "The missing persons report filed on her said that she left home because her brother was abusing her."

"That's not true. Pauline was just . . . she made that up."

"I've read the report," he lied. "I saw what he did to her."

"He didn't do anything," Judith insisted. "Pauline did those things to herself."

"She hurt herself?"

"She hurt herself. She made up stories. From the moment she was born, she was always making trouble."

Will should have guessed. "Pauline's your daughter."

Judith nodded, obviously disgusted by the fact.

"What kind of trouble did she get into?"

"She wouldn't eat," Judith told him. "She starved herself. We took her to doctor after doctor. We spent every dime we had trying to get help for her, and she repaid us by going to the police and telling them awful stories about Tom. Just awful, awful things."

"That he hurt her?"

She hesitated, then gave the slightest of nods. "Tom has always had a sweet nature. Pauline was just too—" She shook her head, unable to find words. "She made things up about him. Awful things. I knew they couldn't be true." Judith kept coming back to the same point. "Even when she was a small child, she told lies. She was always looking for ways to hurt people. To hurt Tom."

"His name isn't really Tom, is it?"

She was looking somewhere over his shoulder, probably at the handle of the knife. "Tom is his middle name. His first is—"

"Matthias?" he guessed. She nodded again, and for just a moment Will let himself think about Sara Linton. She had been joking at the time, but she had also been right. *Find the guy named Matthias and you find your killer.*

"After Judas's betrayal, the apostles had to decide who would help them tell the story of the resurrection of Jesus." She finally met his gaze. "They chose Matthias. He was a holy man. A true disciple to our Lord."

Will blinked to get the sweat out of his eyes. He told Judith, "Every woman who is missing or dead has a connection to your shelter. Jackie donated her mother's things. Olivia Tanner's bank sponsored your community outreach. Anna Lindsey's law firm did pro bono work. Tom must've met them all there."

"You don't know that."

"Then tell me another connection."

Judith's eyes scanned his back and forth, and he could read the desperation in her face. "Pauline," she suggested. "She might be—"

"Pauline is missing, Mrs. Coldfield. She was abducted from a parking lot two days ago. Her six-year-old son was left in the car."

"She has a child?" Judith's mouth opened in shock. "Pauline has a baby?"

"Felix. Your grandson."

She put her hand to her chest. "The doctors said she wouldn't—I don't understand. How could she have a baby? They said she'd never be able to carry—" She kept shaking her head in disbelief.

"Did your daughter have an eating disorder?"

"We tried to get help for her, but in the end . . ." Judith shook her head, as if it was all useless. "Tom teased her about her weight, but all little brothers tease their older sisters. He never meant her any harm. He never meant . . ." She stopped, holding back a strangled sob. There was a crack in her façade as she let herself consider the possibility that her son might be the monster Will had described. Just as quickly, she recovered, shaking her head. "No. I don't believe you. Tom would never hurt anyone."

Will's body started to shiver. He still wasn't losing much blood, but his mind wasn't capable of ignoring the pain for longer than a minute at a time. His head would drop, or he would flick sweat out of his eye, and it would flare up like hellfire. The darkness kept calling to him, the sweet relief of letting go. He let his eyes close for a few seconds, then a few more. Will jerked himself awake, groaning at the searing pain.

Judith said, "You need help. I should get you help." She made no move to do this. The phone started to ring again, and she simply stared at the receiver on the wall.

"Tell me about the cave."

"I don't know anything about that."

"Did your son like to dig holes?"

"My son likes to go to church. He loves his family. He loves helping people."

"Tell me about the number eleven."

"What about it?"

"Tom seems drawn to it. Is it because of his name?"

"He just likes it."

"Judas betrayed Jesus. There were eleven apostles until Matthias came along."

"I know my Bible stories."

"Did Pauline betray you? Were you incomplete until your son came along?"

"This means nothing to me."

"Tom's obsessed with the number eleven," Will told her. "He took Anna Lindsey's eleventh rib. He shoved eleven trash bags up inside her womb."

"Stop!" she shouted. "I don't want to hear any more."

"He electrocuted them. He tortured and raped them."

She screeched, "He was trying to save them!"

The words echoed around the tiny room like a pinball striking metal.

Judith covered her mouth with her hand, horrified.

Will said, "You knew."

"I didn't know anything."

"You must have seen it on the news. Some of the women's names were released. You had to recognize them from your work at the shelter. You saw Anna Lindsey in the road after Henry hit her with the car. You called Tom to take care of her, but there were too many people around."

"No."

"Judith, you know—"

"I know my son," she insisted. "If he was with those women, it was only because he was trying to help them."

"Judith—"

She stood up, and Will could tell she was angry. "I'm not going to listen to you lie about him. I nursed him when he was a baby. I held him—" She cradled her arms. "I held him to my chest and promised him that I would protect him."

"You didn't do that with Pauline, too?"

Her face became emotionless. "If Tom doesn't come, I'm going to have to take care of you myself." She took a knife out of the butcher block. "I don't care if I go to prison for the rest of my life. I will not let you destroy my son."

"You sure you can do that? Stabbing someone in the back isn't the same as stabbing them to their face."

"I'm not going to let you hurt him." She held the knife awkwardly, gripped in both hands. "I won't let you."

"Put the knife down."

"What makes you think you can tell me what to do?"

"My boss is behind you with a gun pointed at your head."

She gasped, the sound catching in her throat when she whirled around and saw Amanda standing on the other side of the window. Without warning, Judith raised the knife and lunged toward Will. The window exploded. Judith fell to the floor in front of him, the knife still gripped in her hand. A perfect circle of blood seeped into the back of her shirt.

He heard a door break open. People ran in, heavy shoes on the floor, orders being barked. Will couldn't take it anymore. He dropped his head and the pain shot through to his core. Amanda's high heels swam into his vision. She knelt down in front of him. Her mouth was moving, but Will couldn't hear what she was saying. He wanted to ask about Faith, about her baby, but it was too easy to surrender to the darkness.

THREE DAYS LATER

CHAPTER TWENTY-FIVE

Pauline mcghee was hard to look at, even as she held her child in her lap. Her mouth had been ripped to shreds by the metal wire she'd chewed through, so she mumbled as she tried to speak, her lips tightly held together. Tiny sutures held the skin in place like something out of *Frankenstein*. And yet, she was hard to feel any sympathy for, perhaps because she kept referring to Faith as "bitch" more than any man ever had.

"Bitch," she said now, "I don't know what I can tell you. I haven't seen my family in twenty years."

Will shifted in his chair beside Faith. His arm was in a sling tight to his chest and he was in visible pain, but he had insisted on coming in for the interview. Faith couldn't blame him for wanting answers. Unfortunately, it was fast becoming obvious that they weren't going to get them from Pauline.

"Tom has lived in sixteen different cities over the last thirty years," Will told her. "We've found cases in twelve of them—women who were abducted and never returned. They were always in pairs. Two women at a time."

"I know what a fucking pair is."

Will opened his mouth to speak, but Faith reached under the table, pressing his knee. Their usual tactics weren't working. Pauline McGhee was a survivor, willing to step over anything or anyone to save her own skin. She had kicked Olivia Tanner into unconsciousness in order to make sure she was the first one to escape the basement. She would have strangled her own brother to death if Faith hadn't stopped her. She wasn't someone who could be reached through empathy.

Faith took a gamble. "Pauline, stop the bullshit. You know you can leave this room at any time. You're staying for a reason."

The injured woman looked down at Felix, stroking his hair. For just an instant, Pauline McGhee seemed almost human. Something about the child transformed her so that Faith suddenly understood the hard outer shell was a defense against the world that only Felix could penetrate. The boy had fallen asleep in her arms as soon as his mother sat down at the conference table. His thumb kept going to his mouth, and Pauline moved it away a few times before giving in. Faith could understand why she wouldn't want to let her son out of sight, but this was hardly the kind of thing you'd want to bring a kid to.

Pauline asked, "Were you really going to shoot me?"

"What?" Faith asked, even though she knew exactly what the woman meant.

"In the hall," she said. "I would've killed him. I wanted to kill him."

"I'm a police officer," Faith answered. "It's my job to protect life."

"*That* life?" Pauline asked, incredulous. "You know what that bastard did." She lifted her chin toward Will. "Listen to your partner. My brother killed at least two dozen women. Do you really think he deserves a trial?" She pressed her lips to the top of Felix's head. "You should've let me kill him. Put him down like a fucking dog."

Faith didn't answer, mostly because there was nothing to say. Tom Coldfield was not talking. He wasn't bragging about his crimes or offering to tell where the bodies were buried in exchange for his life. He was resolved to go to prison, probably death row. All he had asked for was bread and water and his Bible, a book that had so many scribbled notations in the margins that the words were barely legible.

Still, Faith had tossed and turned in bed over the last few nights, reliving those few seconds in the hallway. Sometimes she let Pauline kill her brother. Sometimes she ended up having to shoot the woman. None of the scenarios sat well with her, and she had resigned herself to knowing that these emotions were the type that only time could heal. The process of moving on was helped by the fact that the case was no longer Faith and Will's responsibility. Because Matthias Thomas Coldfield's crimes had crossed state lines, he was the FBI's problem now. Faith was only allowed to interview Pauline because they thought the women shared a bond. They were dead wrong.

Or maybe not.

Pauline asked, "How far along are you?"

"Ten weeks," Faith answered. She had been at the edge of insanity when the paramedics arrived at Tom Coldfield's house. All she could think about was her baby, whether or not it was still safe. Even when the heartbeat had bleated through the fetal monitor, Faith had kept sobbing, begging the EMTs to take her to the hospital. She'd been sure they were all wrong, that something horrible had happened. Oddly, the only person who could convince her otherwise had been Sara Linton.

On the plus side, her whole family knew she was pregnant now, thanks to the Grady nurses referring to Faith as "that hysterical pregnant cop" her entire stay in the ER.

Pauline stroked back Felix's hair. "I got so fat with him. It was disgusting."

"It's hard," Faith admitted. "It's worth it, though."

"I guess." She brushed her torn lips across her son's head. "He's the only thing good about me."

Faith had often said the same thing about Jeremy, but now, facing Pauline McGhee, she saw how lucky she was. Faith had her mother, who loved her despite all Faith's faults. She had Zeke, even though he had moved to Germany to get away from her. She had Will, and for better or worse, she had Amanda. Pauline had no one— just a small boy who desperately needed her.

Pauline said, "When I had Felix, it just made me think about her. Judith. How could she hate me so much?" She looked up at Faith, expecting an answer.

Faith said, "I don't know. I can't imagine how anyone could hate their own child. Any child, for that matter."

"Well, some kids just suck, but your own kid . . ."

Pauline went quiet again for such a long time that Faith wondered if they were back to square one again.

Will spoke. "We need to know why all of this happened, Pauline. I need to know."

She was staring back out the window, her son held close to her heart. She spoke so quietly that Faith had to strain to hear her. "My uncle raped me."

Faith and Will were both silent, giving the woman space.

Pauline confided, "I was three years old, then four, then coming up on five. I finally told my grandmother what was happening. I thought the bitch would save me, but she turned it around like I was some devil child." Her lips twisted into a bitter sneer. "My mother believed them, not me. She chose their side. Like always."

"What happened?"

"We moved away. We always moved when things got bad. Dad put in for a transfer at work, we sold the house and then we started all over again. Different town, different school, same fucking situation."

Will asked, "When did it get bad with Tom?"

"I was fifteen." Pauline shrugged again. "I had this friend, Alexandra McGhee—that's where I got my name when I changed it. We lived in Oregon a couple of years before we moved to Ann Arbor. That's when it really started with Tom—when everything got bad." Her tone had turned to a dull narrative, as if she was giving a secondhand account of something mundane instead of revealing the most horrible moments of her life. "He was obsessed with me. Like, in love with me. He followed me around, and he would smell my clothes and try to touch my hair and . . ."

Faith tried to hide her revulsion, but her stomach clenched at the image the other woman's words conjured.

Pauline said, "Suddenly, Alex stopped coming over. We were best friends. I wanted to know if I'd said something, or done something . . ." Her voice trailed off. "Tom was hurting her. I don't know how. At least, I didn't know how in the beginning. I found out soon enough."

"What happened?"

"She was writing this sentence everywhere, over and over again. On her books, on the soles of her shoes, the back of her hand."

"I will not deny myself," Will guessed.

Pauline nodded. "It was this exercise one of the doctors at the hospital gave me. I was supposed to write the sentence, convince myself not to binge and purge, like writing a fucking sentence a zillion times would make it all go away."

"Did you know Tom was making Alex write the sentence?"

"She looked like me," Pauline admitted. "That's why he liked her so much. She was like a substitution for me—same color hair, same height, about the same weight but she looked fatter than me."

The same qualities that had drawn Tom to all the recent victims: Each woman resembled his sister.

Pauline told them, "I asked him about it—why he was making her write the sentence. I mean, I was pissed, right? And I yelled at him, and he just hit me. Not like a slap, but with his fist. And when I fell down, he started beating me."

Faith asked, "What happened next?"

Pauline stared blankly out the window, as if she was alone in the room. "Alex and I were in the woods. We'd go out there to smoke after school. The day that Tom beat me, I met her out there. At first, she wouldn't say anything, but then she just broke down. She finally told me that Tom had been taking her into the basement of our house and doing things to her. Bad things." She closed her eyes. "Alex took it because Tom said if she didn't, then he would start doing it to me. She was protecting me."

She opened her eyes, staring at Faith with startling intensity. "Alex and I were talking about what to do. I told her it was useless telling my parents, that nothing would happen. So we decided to go to the police. There was this cop I knew. Only, I guess Tom followed us out to the woods. He was always watching us. He had this baby monitor he hid in my room. He'd listen to us and . . ." She shrugged, and Faith could very easily guess what Tom had been doing while he listened to his sister and her friend.

Pauline continued, "Anyway, Tom found us in the woods. He hit me in the back of the head with a rock. I don't know what he did to Alex. I didn't see her for a while. I think he was working on her, trying to break her. That was the hardest part. Was she dead? Was he beating her? Torturing her? Or maybe he'd let her go and she was keeping quiet because she was scared of him." She swallowed. "But it wasn't that."

"What was it?"

"He was keeping her in the basement again. Priming her for the really bad stuff."

"No one heard her down there?"

Pauline shook her head. "Dad was gone, and Mom . . ." She shook her head again. Faith was convinced they would never really know what Judith Coldfield knew about her son's sadistic ways.

Pauline said, "I don't know how long it lasted, but eventually, Alex ended up in the same place as me."

"Where was that?"

"In the ground," she said. "It was dark. We were blindfolded. He put cotton in our ears, but we could still hear each other. We were tied up. Still . . . we knew we were underground. There's a taste, right? Kind of like a wet, dirty taste you get in your mouth. He had dug a cave. It must've taken him weeks. He always liked to plan everything, to control every last detail."

"Was Tom with you all the time after that?"

"Not at first. I guess he was still working on his alibi. He just left us there for a few days—tied up so we couldn't move, couldn't see, could barely hear anything. We screamed at first, but . . ." She shook her head as if she could shake away the memory. "He brought us water, but not food. I guess a week went by. I was okay—I'd gone longer than that without eating. But Alex . . . She broke. She kept crying all the time, begging me to do something to help her. Then Tom would come, and I'd beg him to shut her up, to make it so I didn't have to hear it." She went silent again, lost in her memories. "And then one day, something changed. He started in on us."

"What did he do?"

"At first, he just talked. He was all into biblical stuff—stuff my mom put into his head about him being a replacement for Judas, who betrayed Jesus. She was always saying how I had betrayed her, how she had carried me to be a good kid, but I had turned out rotten, made her family hate her with my lies."

Faith quoted the last sentence she had heard Tom Coldfield utter. " 'O Absalom, I am risen.' "

Pauline shivered, as if the words cut through her. "It's from the Bible. Ammon raped his own sister, and once he was finished with her, he cast her out for being a whore." Her torn lips twisted into an approximation of a smile. "Absalom was Ammon's brother. He killed him for raping their sister." She gave a harsh laugh. "Too bad I didn't have another brother."

"Was Tom always obsessed with religion?"

"Not a regular religion. Not normal. He twisted the Bible to suit whatever he wanted to do. That's why he was keeping me and Alex underground—so that we would have a chance to be reborn like Jesus." She looked up at Faith. "Crazy shit, right? He'd go on and on for hours, telling us how bad we were, talking about how he was going to redeem us. He'd touch me sometimes, but I couldn't see . . ." She shuddered again, her whole body shaking from the movement. Felix stirred, and she soothed him back to sleep.

Faith felt her heart thumping in her chest. She could remember her own struggle with Tom, the feel of his hot breath in her ear when he told her, "Fight."

Will asked, "What did Tom do when he stopped talking to you and Alex?"

"What do you think he did?" she asked sarcastically. "He didn't know what he was doing, but he knew he liked it when he hurt us." She swallowed, her eyes tearing up. "It was our first time—both of us. We were only fifteen. Girls didn't sleep around a lot back then. We weren't angels or anything, but we weren't sluts, either."

"Did he do anything else?"

"He starved us. Not like what he did to the other women, but bad enough."

"The trash bags?"

She gave a single, tight nod. "We were trash to him. Nothing but trash."

Tom had said as much in the hallway. "No one missed you or Alex when Tom had you in the cave?"

"They thought we'd run away. Girls do that, right? They just run away from home, and if the parents are there to say that the girls are bad, that they lie all the

time and can't be trusted, then it's no big deal, right?"
She didn't let them answer. "I bet Tom got a hard-on
lying to the cops, telling them he had no idea where
we'd gone."

"How old was Tom when this happened?"

"Three years younger than me."

"Twelve," Will said.

"No," Pauline corrected. "He hadn't had his birthday
yet. He was only eleven when it happened. He turned
twelve a month later. Mom had a party. The little freak
was out on bail and she threw him a birthday party."

"How did you get out of the cave?"

"He let us go. He said he was going to kill us if we
told anybody, but Alex told her parents anyway, and
they believed her." She snorted a laugh. "Fuck me if
they didn't believe her."

"What happened to Tom?"

"He was arrested. The cops called, and Mom took
him down to the station. They didn't come get him.
They didn't arrest him. They just called us on the phone
and said to bring him in." She paused, collecting herself.
"Tom had a psychiatric evaluation. There was all this
talk about sending him to adult prison, but he was
only a kid, and the shrinks were screaming about how
he needed help. Tom could look younger when he
wanted—much younger than he actually was. Bewildered, like he didn't understand why people were saying
all these bad things about him."

"What did the courts decide to do?"

"He was diagnosed with something. I don't know.
Psychopath, probably."

"We have his Air Force records. Did you know he

served?" Pauline shook her head, and Faith told her, "Six years. He was discharged in lieu of court-martial."

"What does that mean?"

"Reading between the lines, I'd guess that the Air Force didn't want—or know how—to treat his disorder, so they offered him an honorable discharge and he took it." Tom Coldfield's military records were written in the sort of departmental code only a seasoned vet could decipher. As a doctor, Faith's brother, Zeke, had recognized all the clues. The nail in the coffin was the fact that Tom had never been called back up to serve in Iraq, even at the height of the war when enlistment standards had dropped to almost nonexistent.

Will asked, "What happened to Tom in Oregon?"

Pauline answered in a measured tone. "He was supposed to go to the state hospital, but Mom talked to the judge, said we had family back east and could we take him back and put him in a hospital there so he could be close to the people who cared about him. The judge said okay. I guess they were glad to get rid of us. Sort of like with the Air Force, huh? Out of sight, out of mind."

"Did your mother get him treatment?"

"Hell no," she laughed. "My mother did the same fucking thing all over again. She said Alex and I were lying, that we had run away and gotten hurt by a stranger, and we were trying to pin it on Tom because we hated him and we wanted people to feel sorry for us."

Faith felt a sickness in the pit of her stomach, wondering how a mother could be so blind to her child's suffering.

Will asked, "Is that when you changed your names to Coldfield?"

"We changed them to Seward after what happened to Tom. It wasn't easy. There were bank accounts, all sorts of documents to file to make it legal. My dad started asking questions. He wasn't happy, because he actually had to *do* something, you know? Go down to the courthouse, get copies of birth certificates, fill out forms. They were in the middle of changing everything over to Seward when I ran away. I guess when they left Michigan, they changed it back to Coldfield. It's not like Oregon was following up on Tom. As far as they were concerned, his case was closed."

"Did you ever hear from Alex McGhee?"

"She killed herself." Pauline's voice was so cold it sent a chill down Faith's spine. "I guess she couldn't take it. Some women are like that."

Will asked, "You're sure your father didn't know what was going on?"

"He didn't want to know," Pauline answered. But there was no way of confirming this. Henry Coldfield had suffered a massive coronary upon hearing what had happened to his wife and son. He'd died en route to the hospital.

Will kept pressing. "Your father never noticed—"

"He traveled all the time. He was gone for weeks, sometimes as much as a whole month. And even when he was home, he was never really home. He was flying his plane or off hunting or playing golf or just doing whatever the hell he wanted to do." Pauline's tone got angrier with every word. "They had this kind of bargain, you know? She kept the house running, didn't ask him to help with anything, and he got to do whatever he wanted so long as he handed over his paycheck and didn't ask any questions. Nice life, huh?"

"Did your father ever hurt you?"

"No. He was never there to hurt me. We saw him at Christmas and Easter. That was about it."

"Why Easter?"

"I don't know. It was always special to my mother. She would dye eggs and hang up streamers and stuff. She would tell Tom the story of his birth, how he was special, how she had wanted a son so badly, how he'd made her life complete."

"Is that why you chose to run away on Easter?"

"I ran away because Tom was digging another hole in the backyard."

Faith gave her a moment to collect her thoughts. "This was in Ann Arbor?"

Pauline nodded, a faraway look in her eyes. "I didn't recognize him, you know?"

"When he abducted you?"

"It happened so fast. I was so damn happy to see Felix. I thought I'd lost him. And then my brain started to make the connection that it was Tom standing there, but it was too late by then."

"You recognized him?"

"I *felt* him. I can't describe it. I just knew with every part of my body that it was him." She closed her eyes for a few seconds. "When I came to in the basement, I could still feel him. I don't know what he did to me while I was passed out. I don't know what he did."

Faith suppressed a shudder at the thought. "How did he find you?"

"I think he always knew where I was. He's good at tracking people down, watching them, figuring out their habits. I guess I didn't make it too hard, using Alex's name like I did." She gave a humorless laugh. "He called me at work about a year and a half ago. Can you believe that? What are the odds that I'd take a call like that and it would be Tom on the other end?"

"Did you know it was him on the phone?"

"Fuck no. I would've grabbed Felix and run."

"What did he want when he called?"

"I told you. It was a cold call." She shook her head, disbelieving. "He told me about the shelter, that they would take donations and give blank receipts. We've got all these rich clients, and they give away their furniture to charity for the tax write-off. It makes them feel better about ditching a fifty-thousand-dollar living room set and buying an eighty-thousand-dollar one."

Faith couldn't even comprehend the numbers. "So, you decided to refer your clients to the shelter?"

"I was pissed at Goodwill. They give you a time frame, like between ten and noon. Who can wait for that? My clients are millionaires. They can't sit around all morning waiting for some homeless dude to show up. Tom said the shelter would make an exact appointment and be there on time. And they always were. They were friendly and clean, which, trust me, is saying a lot. I told everybody to use them." She realized what she had said. "I told everybody."

"Including the women on your Internet board?"

She kept silent.

Faith told her what they had found out over the last few days. "Anna Lindsey's firm started giving the shelter legal advice six months ago. Olivia Tanner's bank became a major donor last year. Jackie Zabel called the shelter to pick up things from her mother's house. They all heard about the shelter somewhere."

"I didn't . . . I didn't know."

They still hadn't managed to break into the chat room. The site was too sophisticated, and cracking the passwords no longer had a priority for the FBI, since their guy was already sitting in jail. Faith needed the confirmation, though. She had to hear it from Pauline. "You posted about the shelter, didn't you?"

Pauline still did not answer.

"Tell me," Faith said, and for some reason, the request worked.

"Yeah. I posted it."

Faith hadn't realized that she had been holding her breath. She let it out in a slow stream. "How did Tom know they all had eating disorders?"

Pauline looked up. Some of her color seeped back into her cheeks. "How did you know?"

Faith thought about the question. They knew because they had investigated the women's lives, just as methodically as Tom Coldfield had. He'd followed them around, spied on their most intimate moments. And none of them had known he was doing it.

Pauline asked, "Is the other woman all right? The one I was with."

"Yes." Olivia Tanner was well enough to refuse to talk to the police.

"She's a tough bitch."

"So are you." Faith told her, "It might help to talk to her."

"I don't need help."

Faith didn't bother to argue.

Pauline said, "I knew Tom would find me eventually. I kept training myself. Making sure I could go without food. Making sure I could last." She explained, "When it was me and Alex, he would hurt whoever screamed the loudest, whoever broke first. I made sure it wasn't me. That's how I helped myself."

Will asked, "Your father never asked why your mother wanted to change your names and move?"

"She told him it was to give Tom a fresh start—give us all a fresh start." She gave a humorless laugh, directing her words toward Faith. "It's always about the boys, isn't it? Mothers and their sons. Fuck the daughters. It's the sons they really love."

Faith put her hand to her stomach. The gesture had become second nature over the last few days. All along, she had been thinking that the child inside of her was a boy; another Jeremy who would draw pictures and sing to her. Another toddler who would puff out his chest when he told his friends that his mom was a cop. Another young man who was respectful of women. Another adult who knew from his single mother how hard it was to be the fairer sex.

Now Faith prayed that she would have a daughter. Every woman they had met on this case had found a way to hate herself long before Tom Coldfield had gotten hold of her. They all were used to depriving their bodies of everything from nourishment to warmth to something as vital as love. Faith wanted to show her own child a different path. She wanted a girl she could raise who might have a chance of loving herself. She wanted to see that girl grow into a strong woman who knew her value in the world. And she never wanted either of her children to meet someone as bitter and damaged as Pauline McGhee.

Will told Pauline, "Judith's in the hospital. The bullet just missed her heart."

The woman's nostrils flared. Tears came into her

eyes, and Faith wondered if there was still a part of her, no matter how small, that wanted some kind of bond with her mother.

Faith offered, "I can take you to see Judith if you want."

She snorted a laugh, angrily wiping away her tears. "Bitch, don't even. She was never there for me. I'm sure as shit not going to be there for her." She shifted her son on her shoulder. "I need to get him home."

Will tried. "If you could just—"

"Just what?"

He didn't have an answer for her. Pauline stood up and walked to the door, trying to hold Felix as she reached for the knob.

Faith told her, "The FBI will probably be getting in touch with you."

"The FBI can kiss my ass." She managed to get the door open. "And so can you."

Faith watched her walk down the hallway, shifting Felix as she turned toward the elevators. "God," she said softly. "It's hard to feel sorry for her."

"You did the right thing," Will told her.

Faith saw herself in Tom Coldfield's hallway again, her gun pointed at Pauline's head, Tom bucking on the floor. They weren't trained to wing suspects. They were trained to fire a rapid bullet spread straight over the center of the chest.

Unless you were Amanda Wagner. Then you squeezed off a single shot that did enough damage to take them down but not take their life.

Will asked, "If you had to do it again, would you let Pauline kill Tom?"

"I don't know," Faith confessed. "I was operating on autopilot. I just did what I was trained to do."

"Considering what Pauline's been through . . ." Will began, then stopped himself. "She's not very nice."

"She's a cold-blooded bitch."

"I'm surprised I haven't fallen in love with her."

Faith laughed. She had seen Angie at the hospital when they brought Will out of surgery. "How is Mrs. Trent doing?"

"She's making sure my life insurance policies are paid up." He took out his phone. "I told her I'd be back by three."

Faith didn't make a comment about the new phone, or the wary look on his face. She supposed Angie Polaski was back in Will's life now. Faith would just have to get used to her, the same way you tolerated an annoying sister-in-law or the boss's whorishly obnoxious daughter.

He pushed back his chair. "I guess I should go."

"You want me to drive you home?"

"I'll walk."

He only lived a few blocks over, but he'd been in surgery less than seventy-two hours ago. Faith opened her mouth to protest, but Will stopped her.

"You're a good cop, Faith, and I'm glad you're my partner."

There were few things he could have said that would have stunned her more. "Really?"

He leaned down and kissed the top of her head. Before she could respond, he told her, "If you ever see Angie on top of me like that, don't give her a warning, all right? Just pull the trigger."

EPILOGUE

SARA STOOD BACK AS THEY ROLLED HER PATIENT OUT of the trauma room. The man had been in a head-on collision with a motorcyclist who thought red lights were only for cars. The cyclist was dead, but the man had a good chance thanks to the fact that he was wearing his seatbelt. Sara was constantly amazed at the number of people she saw in the Grady ER who believed seatbelts were unnecessary. She had seen almost as many in the morgue during her years as coroner for Grant County.

Mary came into the room to clean up the mess for the next patient. "Good save," she said.

Sara felt herself smiling. Grady saw only the worst of the worst. She didn't hear that often enough.

"How's that hysterical pregnant cop doing? Mitchell?"

"Faith," Sara supplied. "Good, I guess." She hadn't talked to Faith since the woman had been airlifted to the emergency room two weeks ago. Every time Sara thought to pick up the phone to check on her, something stopped her from making the call. For her part, Faith hadn't called, either. She was probably embarrassed that Sara had seen her at such a low moment. For a woman who hadn't been sure whether or not she was going to keep her baby, Faith Mitchell had sobbed like a child when she thought she'd lost it.

Mary asked, "Isn't your shift over?"

Sara glanced at the clock. Her shift had ended twenty minutes ago. "You need help?" She indicated various detritus she'd thrown on the floor minutes earlier as she'd worked to save her patient's life.

"Go on," Mary told her. "You've been here all night."

"So have you," Sara reminded her, but she didn't have to be told twice to leave.

Sara walked down the hall toward the doctors' lounge, stepping aside as gurneys whizzed by. Patients were stacked up like sardines again, and she ducked under the counter at the nurses' station to take a short-cut away from them. CNN was on the television over the desk; she saw that the Tom Coldfield case was still in the news.

As big as the story was, Sara found it remarkable that more people had not come forward to tell their version of events. She hadn't expected Anna Lindsey to exploit herself for money, but the fact that the other two surviving women were equally as tight-lipped was surprising in this age of instant movie deals and television exclusives. Sara had gleaned from the news reports that there was more to the story than GBI was letting on, but she was hard-pressed to find anyone who was willing to share the truth.

She certainly could not be faulted for trying. Faith had been incapable of communicating anything when she'd been brought into the ER, but Will Trent had been kept overnight for observation. The kitchen knife had missed all the major arteries, but his tendons were another story. He was looking at months of physical therapy before he got back his full range of motion. Despite this, Sara had gone into his room the next morning with the blatant intent of pumping him for information. He'd been different with her, and kept pulling up the bedsheet, finally tucking it under his chin in an oddly chaste manner, as if Sara had never seen a man's chest before.

Will's wife had shown up a few minutes later, and Sara had realized instantly that the awkward moment she'd had with Will Trent on her couch was purely a figment of her imagination. Angie Trent was striking and sexy in that dangerous-looking way that drives men to extremes. Standing beside her, Sara had felt slightly less interesting than the hospital wallpaper. She had made her excuses and left as quickly as politeness would allow. Men who liked women like Angie Trent did not like women like Sara.

She was relieved by the revelation, if only slightly disappointed. It had been nice thinking that a man had found her attractive. Not that she would do anything about it. Sara would never be able to give her heart away to another human being the way she had with Jeffrey. It wasn't that she was incapable of love; she was simply incapable of repeating that kind of abandon.

"Hey there." Krakauer was walking out of the lounge as she went in. "You off?"

"Yes," Sara told him, but the doctor was already down the hall, staring straight ahead, trying to ignore the patients who were calling to him.

She went to her locker and spun the dial. She took out her purse and dropped it on the bench behind her. The zipper gaped open. She saw the edge of the letter tucked in between her wallet and her keys.

The Letter. The explanation. The excuse. The plea for absolution. The shifting of blame.

What could the woman who had single-handedly brought about Jeffrey's death possibly have to say?

Sara took out the envelope. She rubbed it between her fingers. There was no one else in the lounge. She was alone with her thoughts. Alone with the diatribe. The ramblings. The juvenile justifications.

What could be said? Lena Adams had worked for Jeffrey. She was one of his detectives on the Grant County police force. He had covered for Lena, bailed her out of trouble and fixed her mistakes for over ten years. In return, she had put his life in jeopardy, gotten him mixed up with the kind of men who killed for sport. Lena had not planted that bomb or even known about it. There was no court of law that would condemn her for her actions, but Sara knew—knew to the core of her being— that Lena was responsible for Jeffrey's death. It was Lena who had gotten him involved with those bloodless mercenaries. It was Lena who had put Jeffrey in the way of the men who murdered him. As usual, Jeffrey had been protecting Lena, and it had gotten him killed.

And for that, Lena was as guilty as the man who had planted the bomb. Even guiltier, as far as Sara was concerned, because Sara knew that Lena's conscience was eased by now. She knew that there were no charges that could be brought, no punishment to bring down on her head. Lena would not be fingerprinted or humiliated as they photographed and strip-searched her. She would not be put into solitary confinement because the inmates wanted to kill the cop who'd just been sentenced to prison. She would not feel the needle in her arm. She would not look out into the viewing area of the death chamber at the state penitentiary and see Sara sitting there, waiting for Lena Adams to finally die for her crimes.

She had gotten away with cold-blooded murder, and she would never be punished for it.

Sara tore off the corner of the envelope and slipped her thumb along the edge, breaking the seal. The letter was on yellow legal paper, one-sided, each of the three pages numbered. The ink was blue, probably from a ballpoint pen.

Jeffrey had favored yellow legal pads. Most cops do. They keep stacks of them on hand, and they always produce a fresh one when a suspect is ready to write a confession. They slide the tablet across the table, uncap a fresh new pen and watch the words flow from pen to paper, the confessor turning from suspect to criminal.

Juries like confessions written on yellow legal paper. It's something familiar to them, less formal than a typed statement, though there was always a typed statement to back it up. Sara wondered if somewhere there was a transcription of the printed capital letters that crossed the pages she now held in her hands. Because, as sure as Sara was standing in the doctors' lounge at Grady Hospital, this was a confession.

Would it make a difference, though? Would Lena's words change anything? Would they bring back Jeffrey? Would they give Sara back her old life—the life where she belonged?

After the last three and a half years, Sara knew better. Nothing would bring that back, not pleading or pills or punishments. No list would ever capture a moment. No memory would ever re-create that state of bliss. There would only be the emptiness, the gaping hole in Sara's life that had once been filled by the only man in the world she could ever possibly love.

In short, no matter what Lena had to say, it would never bring Sara any peace. Maybe knowing this made it easier.

Sara sat down on the bench behind her and read the letter anyway.

ACKNOWLEDGMENTS

FIRST OFF, I WANT TO THANK MY READERS FROM THE bottom of my heart for their continued support. I felt such a sense of purpose while I was writing Sara's story, and I hope y'all think it was worth it.

On the publishing side, the usual suspects are to be thanked: the Kates (M and E, respectively), Victoria Sanders, and everyone at Random House U.S., U.K. and Germany. Special appreciation goes to my friends at the Busy Bee. I wanted to thank you in Dutch, but the only Dutch words I know are the bad ones. *Schijten!*

The Georgia Bureau of Investigation was kind enough to let me go behind the scenes with some of their special agents and technicians. Holy crap at the job y'all do. Director Vernon Keenan, John Bankhead, Jerrie Gass, Assistant Special Agent in Charge Jesse Maddox, Special Agent Wes Horner, Special Agent David Norman and others unnamed here—thank you all for your time and patience, especially when I was asking the crazier questions.

Sara continues to benefit from Dr. David Harper's many years in medicine. Trish Hawkins and Debbie Teague were again instrumental in giving Will obstacles—and helping me figure ways around them. Don Taylor, you are a peach and a true friend.

My daddy made me vegetable soup when I was too

loopy from cold medicine to string two sentences together. D.A. ordered pizza when my fingers were too tired from typing.

Oh—and, yet again, I have taken liberties with roads and landmarks. For instance, Georgia Route 316 in Conyers is not meant to be Highway 316, which runs through Dacula. It's fiction, y'all.

If you enjoyed *Undone,*
you won't want to miss any
of Karin Slaughter's electrifying thrillers.

Read on for an exciting early look at

BROKEN

*Coming from Delacorte Press
in Summer 2010*

CHAPTER ONE

Fortunately, the winter weather meant the body at the bottom of the lake would be well preserved, though the chill on the shore was bone-aching, the sort of thing that made you strain to remember what August had been like. The sun on your face. The sweat running down your back. The way the air conditioner in your car blew out a fog because it could not keep up with the heat. As much as Lena Adams strained to remember, all thoughts of warmth were lost on this rainy November morning.

"Found her," one of the divers called, his voice muffled by the constant *shush* of the pouring rain. Lena held up her hand in a wave, water sliding down the sleeve of the bulky parka she had thrown on when the call had come in at three this morning. The rain wasn't hard, but it was relentless, tapping her back insistently, slapping against the umbrella that rested on her shoulder. Visibility was about thirty feet. Everything beyond that was coated in a hazy fog. She closed her eyes, thinking back to her warm bed, the warmer body that had been wrapped around her.

The shrill ring of a phone at three in the morning was never a good sound, especially when you were a cop. Lena had woken out of a dead sleep, her heart pounding, her hand automatically snatching up the receiver, pressing it to her ear. She was the senior detective on call, so she in turn had to start other phones ringing across south Georgia. Her chief. The coroner. Fire and rescue. The Georgia Bureau of Investigation to let them know that a body had been found on state land. The Georgia Emergency Management Authority, who kept a list of eager civilian volunteers ready to look for dead bodies on a moment's notice.

They were all gathered here at the lake, but the smart people were waiting in their vehicles, heat blasting while a chill wind rocked the chassis like a baby in a cradle. Dan Brock, the proprietor of the local funeral home who did double duty as the town coroner, was asleep in his van, head back against the seat, mouth gaping open. Even the EMTs were safely tucked inside the ambulance. Lena could see their faces peering through the windows in the back doors. Occasionally, a hand would reach out, the ember of a cigarette glowing in the dawn light.

She held an evidence bag in her hand. It contained a letter found under a rock by the shore. The paper had been torn from a larger piece—college ruled, approximately eight and a half inches by six. The words were all caps. Ballpoint pen. One line. No signature. Not the usual spiteful or pitiful farewell, but clear enough: I want it over.

In many ways, suicides were more difficult investigations than homicides. With a murdered person, there was always someone you could blame. There were clues you could follow to the bad guy, a clear pattern you could lay out to explain to the family of the victim exactly why their loved one had been stolen away from them. Or, if not why, then who the bastard was who'd ruined their lives.

With suicides, the victim is the murderer. The person upon whom the blame rests is also the person whose loss is felt most deeply. They are not around to take the reproach for their death, the natural anger anyone feels when there is a loss. What the dead leave instead is a void that all the pain and sorrow in the world can never fill. Mother and father, sisters, brothers, friends and other relatives—all find themselves with no one to punish for their loss.

And people always want to punish someone when a life is unexpectedly taken.

This was why it was the investigator's job to make sure every single inch of the death scene was measured and recorded. Every cigarette butt, every discarded piece of trash or paper had to be catalogued, fingerprinted, and sent to the lab for analysis. The weather was noted in the initial report. The various officers and emergency personnel on scene were recorded in a log. If a crowd was present, photographs were taken. License plates were checked. The suicide victim's life was investigated just as thoroughly as with a homicide: Who were her friends? Who were her lovers? Was there a husband? Boyfriend? Girlfriend? Were there angry neighbors or envious coworkers?

Lena knew only what they had found so far: a pair of women's sneakers, size eight, placed a few feet away from the suicide note. Inside the left shoe was a cheap ring—twelve-carat gold with a lifeless ruby at the center. The right shoe contained a white Swiss Army Watch with fake diamonds for numbers. Underneath this was the folded note.

I want it over.

Not much of a comfort for those left behind.

Suddenly, there was a splash of water as one of the divers surfaced from the lake. His partner came up beside him, then another. In all, there were four divers, and they each struggled against the silt on the lake bottom as they dragged the body out of the cold water and into the cold rain. The dead girl was small, making the effort seem exaggerated, but quickly Lena saw the reason for their struggle. A thick, industrial-looking chain was wrapped around her waist with a bright yellow padlock that hung low, like a belt buckle. Attached to the chain were two heavy cinder blocks.

Sometimes in policing, there were small miracles. The victim had obviously been trying to make sure she couldn't back out. If not for the cinder blocks weighing her down, the current would have probably taken the body into the middle of the lake, making it almost impossible to find her.

Lake Grant was a thirty-two hundred acre man-made body of water that was three hundred feet deep in places. Underneath the surface were abandoned houses, small cottages and shacks where people had once lived before the area was turned into a reservoir. There were stores and churches and a cotton mill that had survived the Civil War only to be shut down during the Depression. All of this had been wiped out by the rushing waters of the Ochawahee River so that Grant could have a reliable source of electricity.

The National Forestry Service owned the best part of the lake, over a thousand acres that wrapped around the water like a cowl. One side touched the residential area where the more fortunate lived and the other held back the Grant Institute of Technology, a small but thriving state university with almost five thousand students enrolled.

Sixty percent of the lake's eighty-mile shoreline was owned by the State Forestry Division. The most popular spot by far was this one, what the locals called Lover's Point. Campers were allowed to stake tents. Teenagers came here to party, often leaving behind empty beer bottles and used condoms. Occasionally, there would be a call about a fire someone had let get out of control and once, a rabid bear had been reported, only to turn out to be an elderly chocolate Labrador who had wondered away from his owners' campsite.

And bodies were occasionally found here, too. Once, a girl had been buried alive. Several men, predictably teenagers, had drowned performing various acts of stupidity. Last summer, a child had broken her neck diving into the shallow waters of a cove.

The police divers paused, letting the water drip off the body before resuming their task. Finally, nods went all around and they dragged the young woman onto the shore. The cinder blocks left a deep furrow in the sandy ground. It was six-thirty in the morning, and the moon seemed to wink at the sun as it began its slow climb over the horizon. The ambulance doors swung open. The EMTs cursed at the bitter cold as they rolled out the gurney. One of them had a pair of bolt cutters hefted over his shoulder. He slammed his hand on the hood of the coroner's van and Dan Brock startled, comically flailing his arms in the air. He gave the EMT a stern look, but stayed where he was. Lena couldn't blame him for not wanting to rush into the rain. The victim wasn't going anywhere except the morgue. There was no need for lights and sirens.

Lena walked closer to the body, carefully folding the evidence bag containing the suicide note into her jacket pocket and taking out a pen and her spiral-bound notebook. Crooking her umbrella between her neck and shoulder, she wrote the time, date, weather, number of EMTs, number of divers, number of cars and cops, what the terrain was like, noted the solemnity of the scene, the absence of spectators — all the details that would need to be typed exactly into the report.

The victim was around Lena's height, five four, but she was built much smaller. Her wrists were delicate, like a bird's. The fingernails were uneven, bitten down to the quick. She had black hair and extremely white skin. She was probably in her early twenties. Her open eyes were clouded like cotton. Her mouth was closed. The lips looked ragged, as if she chewed them out of nervous habit. Or maybe a fish got hungry. Muck from the bottom of the lake covered her head to toe.

Her body was lighter without the drag of the water, and it only took three of the divers to heft her onto the waiting gurney. Water dripped from her clothes— blue jeans, a black fleece shirt, white socks, no sneakers, an unzipped, dark blue warm-up jacket with a Nike logo on the front. The gurney shifted, and her head turned away from Lena.

Lena stopped writing. "Wait a minute," she called, knowing something was wrong. She put her notebook in her pocket as she took a step closer to the body. She had seen a flash of light at the girl's neck— something silver, maybe a necklace. Pondweed draped across the victim's throat and shoulders like a shroud. Lena used the tip of her pen to push away the slippery green tendrils. Something was moving beneath the skin, rippling the flesh the same way the rain rippled the tide.

The divers noticed the undulations, too. They bent down for a better look. The skin fluttered like something out of a horror movie.

One of them asked, "What the—"

"Jesus!" Lena jumped back quickly as a small minnow slithered out from a slit in the girl's neck.

The divers all laughed the way men do when they don't want to admit they've just soiled themselves. For her part, Lena put her hand to her chest, hoping no one noticed that her heart had practically exploded in her chest. Her mouth opened. She took a gulp of air. The minnow was floundering in the mud. One of the men picked it up and tossed it back into the lake. Another made the inevitable joke about something being fishy.

She shot them a hard look before leaning down toward the body. The slit where the fish had come out was about two inches below the ear. She guessed it was an inch wide, tops. The open flesh was puckered from the water, but at one point the injury had been clean, precise—the kind of incision that was left by a very sharp and very long knife.

"Somebody go get Brock," she said.

This wasn't a suicide investigation anymore.

*Enter
the bestselling
world of
Karin Slaughter....*

UNDONE

In the trauma center of Atlanta's busiest hospital, Sara Linton treats the city's poor, wounded, and unlucky — and finds refuge from the tragedy that rocked her life in rural Grant County. Then, in one instant, Sara is thrust into a frantic police investigation, coming face-to-face with a tall, driven detective and his quiet female partner. . . . In *Undone*, three unforgettable characters from Karin Slaughter's *New York Times* bestselling novels *Faithless* and *Fractured* collide for the first time, entering an electrifying race against the clock — and a duel with unspeakable human evil.

"Slaughter has always been a talented writer, but in recent years her work has just gotten better and better. . . . Razorsharp suspense and emotional depth."
—The Daily Beast

FRACTURED

Ansley Park is one of Atlanta's most upscale neighborhoods—but in one gleaming mansion, in a teenager's lavish bedroom, a girl has been savagely murdered. And in the hallway, her mother stands amid shattered glass, having killed her daughter's attacker with her bare hands. Detective Will Trent of the Georgia Bureau of Investigation is one of the first on the scene. Trent soon sees something that the Atlanta cops are missing, something in the trail of blood, in the matrix of forensic evidence, and in the eyes of the stunned mother. When another teenage girl goes missing, Trent knows that this case, which started in the best of homes, is about to cut quick and deep through the ruins of perfect lives broken wide-open: where human demons emerge with a vengeance.

"Karin Slaughter's *Fractured* is a superior crime novel. . . . Denser, more challenging and ultimately more rewarding than most . . . Still in her thirties, Slaughter continues to be angry, fiercely focused, and one of the most talented young crime novelists."
—*The Washington Post*

BEYOND REACH

In a stifling hospital room in a small Georgia town, Detective Lena Adams sits, silent and angry—the only suspect in a horrific murder. Soon, a hundred miles away, Police Chief Jeffrey Tolliver will get the call that his young detective has been arrested. And Jeffrey's wife, pediatrician and medical examiner Sara Linton, has troubles of her own and little patience for Lena or her dramas. Fighting a heartbreaking malpractice suit, Sara cannot guess that within days she herself will be at the center of a bizarre and murderous case. For Lena has fled back to the place where she grew up hard, careening back through the shadows of her past and into a shocking underground world of bigotry and rage. And now only Jeffrey and Sara can free Lena from the web of lies and brutality that has trapped her—as this powerhouse of a novel races toward its shattering climax . . . and a final, unforgettable twist.

"Bone-chilling . . . Slaughter builds the suspense to a perfect crescendo, connecting every loose plot strand in a devastating and unforgettable climax. . . . A timely and unsettling read." —*Publishers Weekly* (starred review)

TRIPTYCH

In the city of Atlanta, young women are dying—at the hands of a killer who signs his work with a single, chilling act of mutilation. Leaving behind enough evidence to fuel a frenzied police hunt, this cunning madman is bringing together dozens of lives, crossing the boundaries of wealth and race. And the people who are chasing him must cross those boundaries too. Among them is Michael Ormewood, a veteran detective whose marriage is hanging by a thread—and whose arrogance and explosive temper are threatening his career. And Angie Polaski, a beautiful vice cop who was once Michael's lover before she became his enemy. But another player has entered the game: a loser ex-con who has stumbled upon the killer's trail in the most coincidental of ways—someone who may be the key to breaking the case wide open. . . .

"Karin Slaughter writes with a razor. . . . *Triptych* elevates her to the top of my list of favorite crime writers." —*The Plain Dealer*

FAITHLESS

New York Times bestseller Karin Slaughter brings back her two most fascinating and complex characters—medical examiner Sara Linton and her ex-husband, police chief Jeffrey Tolliver—in a heart-pounding tale of faith, doubt, and murder. The victim was buried alive in the Georgia woods—then killed in a horrifying fashion. When Sara Linton and Jeffrey Tolliver stumble upon the body, both become consumed with finding out who killed the pretty young woman. For them, a harrowing journey begins, one that will test their own turbulent relationship and draw dozens of life into the case. For as Jeffrey and Sara move further down a trail of shocking surprises and hidden passions, neither is prepared for the most stunning discovery of all: the identity of a killer who is more evil and dangerous than anyone could have guessed.

"The people in *Faithless* are so real and so well-developed that the reader can't help but feel empathy for them, and thus we are drawn even deeper into the ingenious plot. This is the best thing Slaughter has written, both shocking and painful, but also gripping and resonant. *Faithless* launches a major new phase in her career, and it's a delight to behold." —*Chicago Sun-Times*